Praise for SE

National B

D0663758

"A fast-paced intellectual thriller . . . Dr. Gildiner's insights about the desires that motivate us will keep you hooked." —*Chatelaine*

"Hilarious tale. . . . A great read." —*Red Deer Advocate*

"*Seduction* introduces crime fiction to literary mystery. . . . An addictive thriller that combines a crash course on Freudian theory with an old-fashioned detective story . . . *Seduction* is written with the kind of wit and intelligence reminiscent of another page-turner: *The Da Vinci Code*." —*The Hour* (Montreal)

"There are enough twists, turns and identity shifts to keep you guessing. . . . Like a dream, it makes you question what's real and imagined." —*TIME*

"A stylish, suspenseful romp through psychoanalytical academia." —*The Bay Street Bull*

"Book-review clichés come to mind: 'I couldn't put it down,' 'compulsively readable,' etc. . . . Gildiner's riff on the possible truth behind the Anna O. case alone is worth the price of admission. As are the delicious parallels between the lives and thoughts of Darwin and Freud." —*The Gazette* (Montreal)

"A psychologically deep novel that combines two ex-cons, Anna Freud, and ambitious archivist and a zany catalogue of characters." —*Elle* (Canada)

"Very clever . . . definitely a cut above other thrillers." —*NOW* (Toronto)

SEDUC

Vintage Canada

A NOVEL BY

CATHERINE GILDINER

TION

—

To my husband, Michael
And my sons Jamey, David and Sam

—

VINTAGE CANADA EDITION, 2005

Copyright © 2005 Catherine Gildiner

Published in Canada by Vintage Canada, a division of Random House of Canada
Limited, Toronto, in 2005. Originally published in hardcover in Canada by
Alfred A. Knopf Canada, a division of Random House of Canada Limited, Toronto.
Distributed by Random House of Canada Limited, Toronto.

Vintage Canada and colophon are registered trademarks of
Random House of Canada Limited.

Pages 483 to 486 constitute a continuation of the copyright page.

www.randomhouse.ca

Library and Archives Canada Cataloguing in Publication

Gildiner, Catherine Ann
Seduction : a novel / by Catherine Gildiner.

ISBN 13: 978-0-676-97654-0
ISBN 10: 0-676-97654-9

I. Title.

PS8613.I43S34 2005A   C813'.6   C2005-904048-3

Book design by CS Richardson

Printed and bound in the United States of America

2 4 6 8 9 7 5 3 1

—

While locked in my wee carrel at the university library for the better part of the sixties and seventies, I wrote a Ph.D. thesis on the subject of Darwin's influence on Freud. (I've never been one for small projects.) As I whiled away the hours in my windowless cubbyhole, Charles Darwin and Sigmund Freud became increasingly interesting to me both on theoretical and personal levels. Freud wrote over twenty volumes, not including letters, and Darwin wrote far more. Naturally, as I read them, the personalities of the men developed and became more complex and occasionally contradictory. I began to notice inconsistencies, not in the theories, but in the motivations behind them. Ideas were suddenly changed—What *did* make Freud give up his seduction theory? Did he think he was wrong? Were there personal reasons? Or had the theory simply evolved? Darwin wrote about sexuality late in his life, but he'd had all of his evidence for years. Why did he wait? Clearly both men were involved in their own PR—aren't we all?

To keep myself from drowning in Darwin's insect world and Freud's libidinal cathexes, I gave both men personalities and histories as I saw them being revealed between the lines.

The characters of Darwin and Freud that I created during my thesis years remained in my imagination for over twenty-five years, until I felt compelled to portray them in fiction.

I have used many historical details from both their lives, but the story has sprung not from history books but entirely from my own imagination. While remaining true to the spirit of Sigmund Freud, Anna Freud and Charles Darwin, I have freely altered aspects of their life stories to make them fit into the fictional plot. I have not only stretched historical details of their lives, but stretched the lifelines of Anna and Sigmund Freud. Like many fiction writers my imaginary storyline grew out of history, but the characters other than Sigmund Freud, Anna Freud and Charles Darwin were invented for the sole purpose of advancing my fictional storyline and are not intended to be a true depiction of any living person. The machinations within the plot are strictly used as literary devices and are in no way meant to resemble any particular scientific or historical hypothesis.

I'd like to thank Darwin and Freud for lighting up my life for those decades of intense study twenty-five years ago and again for the last decade, while this novel has been incubating. Every day anew I feel some appreciation for what it must have been to be a genius, to swim upstream in a society that loathes your ideas, and to amass a theory that offered a profound, if not perfect, explanation for the motivations of mankind.

Catherine Gildiner
Toronto, August 2004

—

Every normal person, in fact, is only normal on the average. His ego approximates to that of the psychotic in some part or other and to a greater or lesser extent.

— FREUD,
Analysis Terminable and Interminable

CONTENTS

—

PART I

—

PEN PALS

—

CELLULAR ACTIVITY

—

Look into the depths of your own soul and learn first to know yourself, then you will understand why this illness was bound to come upon you and perhaps you will thenceforth avoid falling ill.

—FREUD, *One of the Difficulties of Psychoanalysis*

IT'S REALLY EMBARRASSING to admit, but I forget why I killed my husband.

The vast majority of people do not kill their spouses. I've faced that I'm in an extreme minority. Since I'm locked in here anyway, I decided to try to figure out what I missed that everyone else seems to understand. In a former life I studied Darwin and examined how drives become instincts. It was great for watching birds make their nests and fly south, but it didn't give me any clues as to why I killed my husband, or help me figure out how to conduct myself when, and if, I ever get out of this cinder-block cell. I tried reading religion, but it didn't grab me. Philosophy was interesting, but it only made me wonder if I was here at all.

However in 1974, about eight years ago—I've been in this cooler surrounded by frozen tundra for nine years now—I ran across Freud. I started with volume one of his collected works, because I'm that kind of person, and read all twenty-three. (I'm that kind of person too.) Freud's theory is a turnkey operation. You only have to buy into the unconscious and the rest falls into place. It's like buying the model suite: you may have quibbles with the furnishings, but you have somewhere decent to live.

My greatest interest was early Freud, in all the discoveries he made before he was famous. In his letters he would explain that he'd seen patients all day and was then alone in his small study working through the night. Even when he went to sleep, he had dreams of planing wood—still honing the theory. Freud called this first decade of his most original discoveries, before he had any followers except for one loopy buddy named Wilhelm Fliess, his time of "splendid isolation."

I was also alone, reading Freud day and night in my six-by-nine-foot cell. Maybe it was the similarity of our splendidly isolated circumstances, but I felt Freud was writing to *me*. I even answered his letters in a notebook that I kept hidden in my cell. When I got on a real roll in the middle of the night after ten straight hours, I felt we were co-authors.

They say prison is hell and I suppose it is in most conventional ways, though I look at it as a monastic opportunity where all distraction is mercifully wiped away. Not many people share a cell for nearly a decade with one of the greatest geniuses of all time. Of course, I never said as much to my prison psychiatrist—he would think it was delusional—but I feel doing time with Freud kept me sane.

Fifty percent of female prisoners have a grade nine or lower education; forty percent are illiterate; the majority were unemployed at the time of their crime. Even though Native people make up two percent of the population nationally, they are thirty-eight percent of the Canadian prison population. Two-thirds of female prisoners are single mothers. Eighty percent have histories of sexual or physical abuse. Less than one percent of women in prison are there for violent crimes. On the rare occasions when their crimes are violent, the aggression is almost always toward a spouse who has repeatedly abused them first.

Not one of these statistics applies to me. And I've always been a fan of stats, since numbers pretty well paint the picture.

The only thing I've had in common with my fellow prisoners, as my psychiatrist likes to remind me, is that we've all committed crimes. Somehow I don't find that an icebreaker. Now Freud, on the other hand, was a biologist turned psychologist, like me. In fact he described himself as "Not a man of science, not an observer, not an experimenter, not a thinker . . . I am by temperament nothing but a conquistador—an adventurer, if you want it translated—with all the curiosity, daring, and tenacity characteristic of a man of this sort." These are traits I also have in spades. In terms of curiosity I've studied everything I could get my hands on since I was a kid. If you want to talk about daring, then let me remind you that I killed my husband. If these are the qualities that make a conquistador, then Freud was a great one and I, albeit pathological, am one as well. No wonder I bonded to him.

I was determined to read everything to find out why I was so *unusual.* Depending on what psychological assessment you read on me, you can substitute the word *psychopathic* or *paranoid* for *unusual.* I never got too riled up over those labels because, let's face it, psychiatrists get paid to call you something.

Before prison, I liked science with all the bells and whistles—hypothesis testing, finding physical or numerical results, and measuring the difference. It's called *hard* science when you have something hard or physical to measure. There's a lot of comfort in measuring something you can see. Although Freud was a medical doctor, his greatest love was physiology and the biological research it entailed. When, at the age of forty, he didn't get the academic research appointment he wanted, he qualified as a neurologist and set up a private practice. Back in the days before psychiatry was an official discipline, the psychotics wound up in insane asylums run by doctors who were called Alienists. As far as I can tell, they were fairly alienated from the patients. Their job was to make sure the doors were locked and the lunatics had straw in their cells. The neurotics of the nineteenth century had nowhere to go, and out of desperation wound up dragging their anxiety, hysteria and nervous tics into neurologists' offices. Freud, one of the few neurologists who agreed to investigate hysteria, spent hour after hour seeing patients, mostly women, who had all kinds of symptoms with no apparent physical basis. Wanting to follow the rigours of the scientific tradition, Freud was in a quandary because he needed to study the mind in order to help his patients, but the hard sciences didn't have any methodology for doing so. You can't measure and quantify mental phenomena. Wanting to stick with the sciences, he had to invent his own science or method, which became known as psychoanalysis.

Freud proposed that everyone is born with two drives, very broadly conceived as the sexual and the aggressive. You have to have sex to procreate and you have to be aggressive enough to fight for food and turf and to protect your young. (Anyone who thinks female humans aren't aggressive should try taking their young.) Freud says what interests him is what happens in a civilized society when sex and aggression are curtailed. You can't have sex or kill whenever you want; there are laws against it. If you let your drives run the show, you'll wind up on my side of the bars looking out.

Freud says all of us have this cauldron of sex and aggression boiling away in our unconscious minds. In order not to act on those drives, we have defences—different ways of modifying our drives or watering them down so we don't directly act on them. He proposed several defences. The most common is repression: I am not angry at my husband. Then there is denial: what husband? (That one's fairly primitive but I like it.) Then there is intellectualization: writing about killing a husband. And finally sublimation: I feel like killing my husband, so instead I'll go shopping.

What happens if the defence mechanisms failed? Freud says society stepped in and used religion or just raw *guilt*. If that failed, then they got out the bigger guns and tried *shame* and even *taboo*. (The big taboos are to prevent sex within the family and killing.)

I liked Freud's theory so far because it let me know I wasn't that different from everyone else in substance. I mean, we all had the same drives revving around in our brain and mine was clearly in fourth gear. The problem was, I acted on my aggression and forgot to use a defence.

Freud invented some ingenious ways of measuring the unconscious. He said that under certain circumstances the unconscious leaks out. He proposed looking into dreams, slips of the tongue and symptoms of the mentally ill.

Who hasn't had a sexual or violent dream? Freud learned to analyze these dreams. He could work backwards and find out what unconscious drive or conflict the dream was camouflaging. He called dreams *the royal road to the unconscious*. Too bad I didn't *dream* I killed my husband.

When you look at symptoms of the mentally ill, you can see why Freud saw the unconscious leaking out. Freud assumed that all symptoms had a cause, which means *nothing* is random. He invented a method called free association, a sort of WD-40 for the mind. The patient is advised to let her defences down, not to filter out any thoughts and to say any old thing that pops into her head. The subject of one of his first case studies, the famous Anna O., called this method a "chimney sweep" for the mind.

Probably Freud's most amazing feat is that he managed to analyze himself. It is one thing to be a genius, but it is almost superhuman to be able to push beyond your own defences. It is like playing a tennis game on both sides of the net. Anybody who is defending against some unconscious material usually has a pretty good reason for not wanting to know whatever it is their unconscious is defending against.

It is the job of the defences to protect people's unconscious minds from their concious thoughts. Defences know how to look up unconscious materials in vaults so that the door doesn't fly open, letting dangerous unconscious material run wild. For example, I could never deal with the anger, or whatever it was, that I felt for my husband. I was too busy defending against it.

Lesser mortals than Freud need a psychiatrist, psychologist or psychoanalyst to guide them through their defensive mazes and barriers and dead ends. My ex-cellmate said, "Remember, you only have this guy Freud's word for things." She said if she alone could be in charge of writing her own parole assessment, she could really make it sound good. She was one who, although not a thinker by any stretch of the imagination, always had her ear to the ground. She managed to get her parole on the first go-round, while I'm still up here beating my head against the permafrost, watching the polar bears.

Now here's the rub. I can read Freud on my own since I'm not stupid. However, I need a decent psychiatrist to analyze me. I can tell where I went wrong. It was in the area of defences.

Either they let me down or I let them down. I don't know why, though. For that I need to understand my own personal dynamics, that is, all of the minutiae that contributed to the choices I've made in my tawdry little life. I'm not asking for Freud, for Christ's sake, just not Dr. Gardonne, the dunderhead to whom I've been assigned.

Prison psychiatrists are the bottom feeders of an already suspect profession. No one wants the job of treating psychopaths since they don't get better and the ones in prison have no money, so it is the lazy or incompetent psychiatrists who fall into it. You set your own hours and there is no accountability. If a patient complains about bad care, she is labelled a *disenfranchised psychopath* who is a permanent malcontent. The assumption is that her dissatisfaction is part of her problem.

You get the mildly incompetent who work in city prisons, but you get the dregs of humanity up here north of the treeline. You have to fly in and then travel by dogsled or Tundra Buggy to my prison. There are so few women prisoners in Canada that ours are housed in an old psychiatric facility in a male prison. The sign on the door says *P4W — Prison for Women* so everyone calls it that. About ten years ago the government gave it some Native name that I forget. No one calls it that anyway, not even the Indians.

The Canadian government, desperate to get doctors off the golf course and anywhere near the Arctic Circle, offered cash incentives to lure them toward the pole. Dr. Gardonne must have been equally desperate to come up here one day a week, up past Churchill, Manitoba, to the Northwest Territories on Hudson Bay. I guess that's one way to get isolation pay. Usually the only people who take the jobs are those who couldn't get jobs elsewhere or those who want their income doubled. Greed and incompetence is a bad combination.

When he gets here, he has a pretty leisurely day. He only sees the prisoners who have some social cachet either through their family or by having committed a notorious crime. He leaves the self-mutilated repeat offenders for the social service workers who have recently arrived from other countries and barely speak English. The rest of the week he hovers around angst alley, down south in Toronto, psychoanalyzing rich housewives. There are only two groups that rarely get better: neurotic, rich housewives and psychopaths. No one wants to listen to either.

I've had to be on my toes with this shrink since I first met him. He's not smart, but he's wily. He couldn't analyze himself out of a paper bag; but he knows how to be a street fighter, using analytical tools as brass knuckles. I've really had to be careful not to listen to his interpretations or to believe in him. I know I have an Achilles heel for authoritarian males. My father was the first. I had no intention of going there again.

Sometimes Dr. Gardonne, like all borderline narcissistic personality disorders, throws me off my game and I begin to wonder if I *am* nuts (he prefers the technical term *paranoid*) for not believing in him. In fact, I ward him off as though he were a psychological bat, but sometimes he gets to me and my head swivels like that of the girl in *The Exorcist*.

Within the last month he has come up with something that has, for the first time in nine years, really knocked me off-kilter. Before he went on vacation a few weeks ago, he proposed a Temporary Absence (known as a TA) for me, accompanied by a work plan. It's an unusual leave to receive, and it lasts from about a month to six weeks. You have to have a specific reason why you want to do it and a bigwig has to recommend you. If the TA goes well, you're pretty much a shoo-in for a parole.

Gardonne says he's willing to suggest to the North American Psychoanalytic Association that they hire me to investigate a strange event that has happened in the Freudian community. The director of the Freud academy, Anders Konzak, has, within a year of receiving the most prestigious appointment in the Freudian world, published a paper chastising Freud. Konzak, himself a psychoanalyst, recently went to the media saying that Freud was a phony and a liar, and that psychoanalysis was and still is a fraud. The major newspapers all over the world have headlined his story. He was even on 60 *Minutes*.

Dr. Gardonne is the head of the public relations committee for a psychoanalytic organization that has a general membership twenty thousand strong. (He loves to give details that assure the listener he is not chicken feed.) The psychoanalytic group is concerned that Konzak is publishing inflammatory lies about Freud that are damaging Freud's reputation and that of psycho-analysis in general. What that boils down to is, if the public believes Konzak, then shrinks like Gardonne and his compadres will be out of a job and have to move from their Fifth Avenue apartments. As usual, self-interest is at the heart of his concern.

Presumably Dr. Gardonne wants me to interview Konzak to find out where he's getting his information and why he's having such a sudden change of heart. If Konzak isn't forthcoming, I'd have to dig around and try to figure out his sources and his moti-vation. Konzak and I have exactly the same interest in early Freud, and I'd probably love the job, but I also know that Gardonne has a hidden agenda.

I'm faced with a dilemma. I have been turned down for parole twice. There is only one person whose opinion matters to the parole board—the shrink's. If he says no, I'll be turned down again and have to wait five years to reapply. If I do take this job and something goes awry, I could be thrown back into the slammer for life. Once you are in for murder, no one takes kindly to another offence of *any* kind.

I have no idea what he wants from me on this Freud detective project. Probably I will have to make psychoanalysis smell like a rose or I'll be thrown back here faster than I can say "Freud's your uncle." Actually, I don't mind finding out the truth, which I suspect is neither Konzak's nor Gardonne's, given that Freud had about the same IQ as Gardonne and Konzak put together.

I walked over to my window, where I had a great view of Hudson Bay and the polar bears, to think. In the winter I liked to watch the little cubs romp onshore, getting all excited as their moms swam back with some seals for lunch. Sometimes they had a picnic on an ice floe. Today, with the first signs of the spring breakup, I saw the polar bears lumbering away from the shore of the bay heading inland. They knew it was time for a well deserved hibernation. They'd put in their time, day and night, galumphing across the ice, diving for seals and fish for their young. Instinct told them they needed time off for good behaviour. As they were almost out of sight, I saw one of the cubs trapped out in the bay on a fast moving ice flow looking terrified as it lost sight of its mom who had shambled away without ever looking back. Had she forgotten her cub? Was she too tired to care? Or was it supposed to grow up on its own now? Judging by its terrified little face I'd say it was just getting the drift.

The North is white and harsh, so much so that at certain times it is blinding. There is a kind of peace I've found in the monotony. However, along with the imposed tranquillity, I know I've lost a part of myself every year I've been here. I've made it so far, but the spring thaw seems later and later every year. Who knows what would be left of the essential me in another five years?

The problem is that even in five years, with my luck, Gardonne will still be the one deciding if I get paroled. There is no assurance he'd say yes even then. Gardonne has hinted at my "paranoia," but what he doesn't know is that I have read everything he's ever written in terms of a formal report. My prison job is to "man" the computer. P4W has a giant old computer humming away in the bowels of the building that some programmer is supposed to operate. He has managed to write some simple programs. All I had to do was write another program to override everything he wrote. I had my own punch cards, and I may never have learned the language of intimacy, emotional intelligence or how not to kill your husband, but I do know Basic and Fortran, which is two languages more than the computer technician had mastered. I can go to any terminal in the library and plug in Gardonne's account number and get every assessment he ever wrote. Gardonne has no idea that I know he scuppered my last attempt at parole.

I know he'd say the choice to take this Freudian job is mine. He'd stick to the psychiatric newspeak mantra: *All choices for change are mine.* I, however, know what lies in his hollow heart. I can predict exactly what he'd write about the possibility of parole if I refuse to take his Freudian carrot.

PSYCHOLOGICAL ASSESSMENT DISCHARGE SUMMARY
—

Kate Fitzgerald upon retesting has unfortunately only repeated her previously disappointing test results with no significant statistical difference. She has elevated scores on the MMPI lie detector. She still sees dissociated body parts on the Rorschach and her behaviour can only be described as psychopathic. She is no closer psychologically to understanding why she committed a brutal crime than she was nine years ago. Unfortunately I cannot, in good conscience, recommend her for parole because I believe her to be a danger to herself and others.

Or how about this little ditty, the one he'd write *after* I head his Freud–Konzak dirty tricks campaign:

> Kate Fitzgerald has done a great deal of therapy and has moved toward realizing her conscious and unconscious conflicts. Her schizoid behaviour, which detached the rational from the emotional, has been bridged in our sessions where she has formed a true therapeutic alliance. This optimistic diagnosis has been reinforced through her psychological testing. She has come to terms with her aggressive drives and has learned to incorporate these impulses into a more disciplined intellectual setting.
>
> I would recommend this inmate for a parole in a structured situation of employment where she can utilize her overly intellectualized faculties to help her with ego integration.
>
> Dictated but not read

As I was hoisting myself up to the bars of my tiny window, doing my chin-ups and contemplating the minefield called my future, I heard a sudden bellow of "*man* on block." I lowered myself to meet the gaze of Dalton. He purposefully strode up to my cell dressed in his perma-press uniform with the P4W badge around his neck. He was sporting new Velcro running shoes.

"So where's the man?" I asked.

He nodded his Jerry Lee Lewis–coiffured head, acknowledging he'd heard this before.

"Dalton, where in this day and age do you still find Brylcreem?"

"Make all the fun you want, Miss High and Mighty. At least I don't have prison issue. I actually walk around outside and choose my own hair products."

"Now there's free will," I said.

As my bars slid open and slammed in their socket, he said, "It's time for your appointment with Dr. Gardonne. I heard some dirt through the head honchos at the shift orientation meeting that there are some big changes coming down the pipe for you, girl."

Lumbering down my cellblock, I said over my shoulder, "Dalton, by the time dirt reaches you, it's compost."

"Yeah," he said loud enough to drown out the swearing, fighting and radio sounds, "I betcha the Doc just can't wait to tell you what a paranoid bitch you are and how much worse you're getting." As he dumped me off in the social services wing, he added, "Remember, you heard it from the mouth of me."

2

THE KEEPER OF THE KEYS

—

> He that has eyes to see and ears to hear may convince himself
> that no mortal can keep a secret. If his lips are silent, he chatters
> with his fingertips; betrayal oozes out of him at every pore.
> —FREUD, *Psychical Treatment*

THE WAITING ROOM was crowded with woebegone women
who were past help, especially from social services. I sat reading
a six-year-old *Field & Stream* magazine. We were in this sorry
room for one reason and one reason only—for that happy day
when we'd get a red stamp on our parole forms that said *complied with treatment*. The "treatment options" range from nurse's
assistant to psychiatrist.

In order to understand the hierarchy of psychiatric prison
treatment, you need to imagine an Escher-type drawing of a
cross-section of a tower with many floors connected by trap
doors leading to slides that go only one way: down. Picture a
psychiatric Snakes and Ladders game. The psychiatrist's office is
on the top floor. After the patient states her problem, picture the
psychiatrist saying, "Sorry, you're too fucked up for therapy."

Now imagine the psychiatrist's hand reaching for a lever on his armrest that connects to a trap door underneath the patient's chair. The door opens. Picture a pit below, where patients who are too far gone to reflect or are too wary to play the "insight-oriented game" are dropped down the chute. This is the too-fucked-up-for-therapy pit where the patients are plied with pills. Those who are too far gone for therapy *and* medication fall into yet another, deeper pit, the I'm-too-stupid-to-remember-to-take-my-pill pit, or in psychiatric parlance simply the "resistant patients" pit. In this chasm patients are shot up with a monthly patch of subcutaneous Modicate by a beefy male orderly who quickly replaces the trap door lid.

My daydream was interrupted as Dr. Gardonne's real office door swung open exactly on the hour and he gave me the barely perceptible nod. As I sauntered in, he took off his jacket and hung it on the back of his chair. I studied the family portrait on his desk, which was placed so that it just barely peeked out at the patients. It was Dr. Gardonne's reminder that he was not among the incarcerated. He was the handsome psychiatrist with the family who had done it all right—whose children wore private school blazers and university-bound smiles. I'd had a childhood packed with those family Christmas card scenes. They didn't fool me. I knew how barbed those boughs of holly could be.

He was waiting for me to begin, but in the course of nine years I'd said all I wanted to say and was perfectly happy to sit in silence for the hour. He leaned forward, resting his elbows on his armrests, and placed the fingers of each hand together so they made five little steeples pointing heavenward. Then he waited . . . and waited. I knew he was anxious to hear what I'd decided about the Temporary Absence and the Freud academy proposition. In fact he was so anxious that he'd called me in on time for a change. He was trying to force me into opening the discussion, which would place me in the role of "the needy one" and him in the role of "benevolent despot." This was just another variation on his all-too-familiar theme of demonstrating who wore the pants and who was supposed to have penis envy.

Two can play this game. I decided not to mention the proposition and to let him bring it up, thus forcing him out of the closet of nonchalance. Finally he said, "Kate, how are things going?"

"Whatever."

"It must have been a fairly significant session last time. We talked of your leaving prison, albeit temporarily, and taking a TA. I would be changing roles in your life from psychiatrist to employer. You would be losing me as your therapist after nine years. That is fairly momentous. Would you like to discuss the closure of nine years of important work?"

"*Momentous?* Why is it every week you find some way of insinuating that you are important to me?"

"Oh? And how have I done that?"

"A classic was when you asked me if I was attracted to you. When I said no, you asked me if I was a lesbian. Talk about delusions of grandeur," I said, shaking my head and laughing.

"If that is the case, Kate, then grandiosity seems to be something we share. You have been labelled as"—he paused, glancing down to read aloud from my open file—"'a psychopathic troublemaker who believes herself to be above the system and will have nothing to do with the rhythm of prison life because of her grandiosity.'"

He'd dug up that old progress report from the occupational therapist who was offended when I wouldn't take her Preparing for Festivals cooking class. (I thought one of the perks of prison life was that they cooked Christmas dinner *for* you.) How come he didn't quote the report from the outdoor education intern who said I was born to dogsled—an activity I did enjoy wholeheartedly, and just about the only benefit of being locked up in this northern wasteland? He said I was the best athlete he'd ever seen and that I was great at teamwork. Mind you, that was with dogs, but humans aren't everything.

He looked up, met my eyes and said, "Then of course there was the altercation that has been described in this report as 'vicious' with Veronica Firedancer in the linen department." Responding to the disgust on my face, he added, "I hope I haven't taken anything out of context."

"I've been here nine years and they've finally figured out that I haven't learned stain removal in the laundry. I'm so sorry that I studied Freud and Darwin in my cell for twelve hours a day and worked in the library on the computer and set up the systems that the drone you so handsomely pay couldn't program."

"I expect a Ph.D. in philosophy of science to have a slightly more sophisticated argument than that," Dr. Gardonne offered.

"When I do, you call it intellectualization."

"Kate," he said, letting out an exasperated sigh, "I wish you could help solve your emotional issues instead of defending against them."

"Okay. Let's take the doc, the psychiatrist who never once donated, or even stumbled upon, an insight."

"It is unfortunate that someone for whom you have such a low opinion has such a large influence over your life."

"That's been true since birth."

"Kate, I am the one who has to amass all of this information and make a recommendation for a TA. You don't make things that easy for yourself, or for me, when your file is full of negative reports from the day staff. I can pull for you, but only so far."

This is his lead-up to why I should grab his once-in-a-lifetime job prospect. What he isn't saying is that he will write me a good exit summary if, and only if, I take on this Freudian job.

"Have you thought about the job offer?"

"I've been pretty busy with social engagements and shopping, but it has crossed my mind."

He looked at his watch, letting me know that he was a busy man and needed a decision now. "Kate, I am sorry to rush you with this, but there have been some new developments, which have forced me to expedite the process. The investigation needs to start right away, before Konzak's malfeasance strikes again."

"Of course I'm in. My future will be electrocuted if I don't take it," I said, crossing my legs.

Folding his hands behind his head while leaning back on his swivel chair, he said, "Again, your lack of trust has coloured our relationship. I offered you the job because it's my belief that intellectualization is your most successful defence. Your schizoid behaviour recedes when you are engaged in an intellectual task. I could then justify your TA, pointing out that you are going to do a job that will help you to maintain your most highly developed defence."

"There is a reason that you want me to do this job, and I very much doubt that it's all for my benefit. Save the John Howard speech for your charity boards. Unless you are deviating from your normal leitmotif of self-interest, you have a stake in this as well."

"Kate, it is very common for the prison to set up a job placement for the inmate. We place a third of the women who leave P4W."

"Tell me something I don't know—just once."

Why was he attempting to set this up for me? Christ, was he actually trying to *help* me? I had the horrible sinking feeling that if it was true, then I had done nothing but undermine my therapy for years. However, if I trusted him and he turned out to be the toady I thought he was, then I was dead in the water.

I got out of my chair, walked to his window, rested my arms against the bars and stretched my calves. I was doing a familiar isometric exercise of wanting, yet refusing, to believe. He was probably exasperated with what he interpreted as my lack of gratitude.

"I am willing to tell you whatever you want to know, if that will help you to deal with your fears," he said.

"Great—now it is my fears and not your self-interest."

"Kate, I can admit my self-interest. Can you admit your fears?"

"I wouldn't call this a fear, I would call it a request for information. Have you ever heard of those job interviews where the interviewer says to the applicant, 'Now, Miss Fitzgerald, is there anything you would like to ask me?'"

"Of course you're right," he responded, flipping his arms in the air. "I'll try to clarify whatever you wish."

"Why hire a con on TA? Why not form a subcommittee from the psychological association and investigate?"

"We thought of that. There are psychoanalysts or some academics in cultural studies or philosophy or science who could do the job, but Konzak would probably not speak to them, let alone confide in them. He has already disparaged them to Dvorah Little in her long article on the Freud academy debacle in *Metropolitan Life*." Dr. Gardonne shuffled some papers on his desk and read aloud, quoting Konzak: "'Most psychoanalysts are boring, obsessive depressives who burrow into the brains of their patients and live off their emotions.' He describes their moral character in the following way—I quote from *The Times*: 'Most psychoanalysts are duplicitous opportunists. They know psychoanalysis never helped anyone get better. The psychoanalysts want to fill their offices and the Freudian academics want to get their papers published at least long enough to get tenure or count their superannuation. So why would they ever listen to what I say, or much less agree with me?'"

Looking up from his file, he asked, "Kate, why *would* Konzak confide in them? He would smell a rat right away. We need someone who is out of the system, someone who has no stake in Freud's possible demise." Dr. Gardonne leaned on his desk and looked directly at me. "Konzak knows that you know Freud. Most importantly, he is interested in communicating with you. Those papers that we allowed you to present on guarded day pass, and all of the papers that you submitted to journals from your cell, made an impact over the years."

That was news to me. However, I decided not to let that out.

Gardonne droned on. "In *The Psychoanalytic Monitor*, Konzak described you as one of the most knowledgeable Freudians."

"That sycophantic rag?"

"Kate, we need someone Konzak will talk to and possibly confide in, and who is, in turn, willing to come back to us and tell us what he said."

Genuinely bewildered, I observed, "But you don't trust me or really even like me."

"That is your projection, Kate. I have stood by your bruised psyche for nine years of very difficult therapy, and this is our last session. I have always cared for you and seen you as the victim you were in your family. I know you are warding me off because you can't trust me, it's still too much of a risk. We have had a successful therapy in that we have resolved some of your conflicts and you have trusted me with your dreams."

"You believed those dreams?" Jesus, I hated it when doubt wormed its way in. As long as I had Gardonne pigeonholed, my life ticked along. Granted, it was at a snail's pace, but it wasn't mired in the quicksand of betrayal. I didn't want to go there again.

"Kate—" He hesitated. "You know Freud like the back of your hand. Secondly, you have great powers of deduction. Most importantly, he has to want to confide and talk to someone he likes and will find attractive."

Recasting his plan, I said, "So, Pander, you want me to whore around with Anders Konzak?"

"Kate, you have the need to put things in their most tawdry light. Naturally Konzak would have to find you engaging in order to confide in you."

Engaging?

"He will divulge plenty to feed his ego as a Lothario. I need a steadfast Freudian who knows early Freud, someone Konzak likes and someone who has some loyalty to the committee. I am aware that you are not without flaws, but given the parameters of the job, you are the best candidate. Kate, this is the real world. In terms of self-interest, which is really the interest of the psychoanalytic society at large, I've laid all of my cards on the table. Now may we proceed?"

I had to push ahead or I'd appear to be wallowing in paranoia. Besides, what he said did make some sense. I nodded, indicating I was ready to move on and discuss the job specifics.

Dr. Gardonne leaned back in his chair, and if you hadn't known him for nine years you might have missed the tiny smile that passed over his earnest Mr.-Deeds-goes-to-prison face. He pushed back his chair, stood up and purposefully strode over to his file cabinet. He stood there momentarily, clearly having forgotten the number code for the drawer. I could have told him it was 347, the first three letters of his car licence, but I decided to let him use his key.

He pulled out a spanking clean folder, returned to his chair and said, "Let's get the basics down. What can be done about what Konzak has already said? We need damage control. He has clearly defiled Freud's name and that of psychoanalysis."

"So what? Freud's dead. You can't slander the dead." I stood up and began pacing in front of his desk. As I tightened the prison belt on my one-piece, I said, "Focus on the future. What we have to do is find out what he is going to do next. The only way to control him is to be one step ahead."

"Konzak said he has found evidence that will prove that Freud was a fraud and that psychoanalysis is based on a lie." He read again from a clipping file, quoting Konzak: "'My findings will rock the philosophy of science and make psychoanalysis obsolete.'"

"That's grandiose verbiage. I have read all of the Freud letters. There is nothing in them that would besmirch Freud. I know that last year, according to what Konzak said in the *Metropolitan Life* article, Anna Freud gave him another packet of letters that were previously marked Personal. But she would never give anyone, especially someone she hardly knew, like Konzak, anything that would smear Freud. I don't believe this so-called 'evidence' exists. I guess we'll know soon enough, since he says the letters are soon to be published as the new, unexpurgated edition of the Freud–Fliess correspondence."

"We also need to know whether Konzak is working *for* anyone or if he's working alone. You'll both need to find out where he gets his information."

Smelling the familiar fragrance of a rat, I asked, "Did you say 'both'?" He looked up from writing in point form in his folder as though he didn't quite follow my gist. Betraying only a fraction of the trepidation I felt, I asked, "I'd be working alone, reporting only to you, right?"

"You're half right. You will be answering only to me, yes, but you'll have a partner. An ex-con who lives in Toronto."

Oh Christ, I knew there'd be a catch. "Some nitwit who wrote bad cheques for her boyfriend's car payments, right?" I asked.

"No. He was released fifteen years ago. His name is Jackie Lawton and he is a private investigator." When I didn't ask about him, Gardonne continued, "He had been institutionalized since the age of seven. Violent. In and out for everything from heroin trafficking to grand larceny. Final stint was armed bank robbery, and that put him in for fifteen straight."

In the silence that followed, I heard the forced air go on and then off before the penny finally dropped. He really was giving me a Temporary Absence, but he was simultaneously programming my demise so I'd never get parole. I'd be chain-ganged to an idiot, probably an XYY chromosome (the jails are full of them, tall, violent and low IQ), and together we were supposed to do the job. Yet when I failed, I'd be back in for more years than the Birdman of Alcatraz. My eyes narrowed, giving Dr. Gardonne an idea of where he could stuff his TA.

As I began to push my chair back to leave, Dr. Gardonne, who liked to play with his kill before devouring it, paused and then added, "Despite Jackie's extreme deprivation, he must have been blessed with intelligence and a stalwart constitution. When he got out, he went to university on his own, managed a BA in international affairs and was employed on contract by the CIA until they had a difference of opinion."

"Hey, maybe he was Deep Throat."

"From what I heard, he did amazing work for them, mostly in Europe—accomplished jobs no one else would even try. But it wouldn't be fair if I didn't tell you that he has trouble working with others. He can be very engaging one minute then have sudden, inexplicable bursts of temper the next. He spent more time in solitary than any other male on record."

"Two people who can't work with others—now there's a plan."

"From what I understand, he has done all kinds of personal work in the area of self-actualization and Buddhism and has managed to trim his edges."

"A bank robber with a mantra—can this get any worse?"

Ignoring my tone, a trait he had perfected over the years, Gardonne continued, "Jackie, like you, educated himself in prison. He, however, had no Ph.D. to start with. He taught himself a lot about psychology. Because he spent so much time in solitary, he had no one to talk to about what he assimilated, so some of his interpretations are . . . unorthodox."

"I work alone."

"I'm afraid that won't be possible," Gardonne said as he opened Jackie's prison file. It was held together by industrial-size staples. "A bit of advice on Jackie: don't cross him. He can be ruthless."

"Ruthless—who *needs* ruthless? Why do you need two people to get information from Anders Konzak? He won't shut up."

"First of all we have a devout Freudian who takes one of the most coveted jobs in academia and then suddenly turns against Freud. An intellectual, like you, can handle that." Before continuing, Gardonne laid his hands out flat on his blotter and leaned forward, lowering his voice. "Konzak has recently complained to our association, of which he is still a dues-paying member, that his life has been threatened since he began making anti-Freudian statements."

"And they call me paranoid."

"When your Temporary Absence is granted," he said, holding up some forms, "the investigation will take you to Vienna, where the academy is located, to England, where Freud moved during the war and where, as you know, his daughter Anna still lives and has set up the most extensive archive, New York, the center of psychoanalysis, and finally in Canada, to Toronto, the Canadian Centre for Psychoanalysis and your former stomping grounds, and possibly to Montreal where Anders Konzak had a fifteen-year sojourn as a professor of Russian at McGill University." He closed Jackie's file and said, "You need Jackie because while you were becoming an expert on Freud, he was learning how to manoeuvre his way through all kinds of barbed political situations all over Europe, and particularly in the countries you'll be visiting."

"I can imagine what he did for the CIA."

"It is probably hyperbole that Konzak's life has been threatened, but you need someone who can check out all the angles, and they may not all be theoretical. Let's not equivocate, Kate — you have no experience at detective work." As I sat there looking disgusted, he concluded, sounding very sure of himself, "If something untoward happens, we need someone who has been in that position since childhood and knows in his gut how to react."

My head was spinning. He knows I can't work with someone. Even Dalton figured out I needed a cell alone. I've never been able to work with others, even before I was a murderer. Now they want to hook me up with a bad-tempered con who was probably a hit man for the CIA, to trace a loud-mouthed Freudian buffoon. If I know Gardonne, then he knows me. This is a set-up for failure.

As calmly as I could, I asked, "If I turn this job down, do I still get recommended for parole?"

"Whatever the testing shows and whatever I believe to be the best for society at large will be the basis of my recommendation," Gardonne replied. "Whether you take the job or not has no bearing on the possibility of parole."

I knew what testing meant: whatever the psychiatrist wanted it to mean. There are thousands of ways to interpret an ink blot. Psychiatric testing was the electric chair that left no charred remains.

He leaned toward me, pulling his let's-speak-frankly face. "Kate, I'm not your father offering you something only if you perform for me. This is a way to help you. Despite your attacks over the last nine years, I'm trying to help you get a footing on the outside. I want nothing from you."

I nodded, no longer able to hear him. I closed my eyes and tried to access the directory in my mind that housed the file entitled *Genuine Male Concern* but came up with a formatting error. I'd known him too long to start believing in him now. However, I had learned the hard way—at least, it seemed far harder for me than it did for the rest of the world—who was sitting on the powerful side of the desk. Nine years had definitely taught me that.

Why bother? I said, "I'm in, and I'll have to make the best of this Jack shit guy."

As I stood up to leave, Dr. Gardonne came around from his desk to shake my hand. I don't like touching people, so I scurried to the door, but I was not fast enough.

"Well, Kate . . ." he said with my back to him. God, I hated the part where the guy says how much he enjoyed working with you. I'd rather face a firing squad; at least I'd know where the bullets were coming from. I could see I'd have to be really rude to get him to back off, but I couldn't think of anything to say. Even I had used up my rude quotient.

As the seconds ticked away, he said, "Kate, despite all that has happened in our sessions, and all of the protecting of yourself you felt you had to do in order not to be psychologically vulnerable, I believe we made some progress."

"Sure. After nine years it would be impossible to deny that I've changed and realized *something* about myself. A newt would have learned something about herself in nine years, swimming past her plastic palm tree."

"You may be right, Kate. One thing I have always admired about you is your insight combined with your personal honesty—something that will be needed for the job ahead. I don't want to give myself too much credit."

"People always say that right before they give themselves too much credit."

"One thing I will say is there are few psychiatrists who would have endured your wrath for all of these years and persevered with the therapy."

I was slapped in the face with the truth of his words and actually reeled at the office door as he stood behind me. I hoped he didn't see my tears welling. I was shocked by this surge of emotion. No matter what I thought of him as a person or a psychiatrist, he *had* stuck it out with me for nine years. That's a lot of logged time. And what's bonding if not logged time? I guess it would be stupid to think I wouldn't feel something. Most therapists would have canned me as hopeless years ago. I'm sure I would have.

"Why did you do it?" I asked, still with my back to him as I stood facing the door. If I turned around I'd be faced with shaking hands or, God forbid, a departing embrace.

"I tried not to let my own ego get involved and to realize your abuse toward me was a defence—one you needed."

"Can you say something real and not shrink-wrapped jargon just once in nine years?"

In the silence that blanketed the room, I could almost hear his brain searching for something real to say. Christ, he'd interpreted my question literally when I meant it to be rhetorical.

Maybe my tone had betrayed me. My impoliteness hadn't thrown him off the scent. Maybe I really did want him to say something that somehow referred to the fact that we'd been not only doctor and patient but two, albeit inadequate, humans locked in a room together for nearly a decade. Wouldn't any two creatures of the same species feel something?

I felt suffocated as my neediness filled the room like dry ice. He retreated behind his desk. His eyes burned through my government-issue grey threads, inviting me to turn around, but I wasn't getting into that.

He must have beamed his card at the steel door. I heard the click as it slid open. As I walked through, he said, "Kate, I'll see you again, but not as your psychiatrist. I'll miss you. You've taught me a lot."

The electronic eye in the door frame read my code and closed behind me.

3

—

THE BENDS

—

"I hope you care to be recalled to life?"
And the old answer:
"I can't say."
—DICKENS, *A Tale of Two Cities*

AN HOUR LATER, I was sitting in the office of the discharge officer, who wore one of those blousy Indian dresses that she
imagined camouflaged decades of Dunkin' Donuts drive-thru,
signing my Temporary Absence papers. "Well, Miss Fitzgerald,
you're leaving us," she said in that sappy voice of trained empathy. She handed me a vacuum-sealed bag with the clothes I'd
worn crossing this barbed wire threshold nearly a decade ago.

As I opened the bag and looked at the clothes, the reality that
I'd lost 1971 to 1981 smacked me in the face. I had no idea if the
clothes were stylish any more or not. They probably weren't even
stylish at the time. Although I hadn't watched television or had
visitors, I tried to keep up with the outside through my reading.
I knew about U.S. politics, knew the U.S. bombed out in
Vietnam and crept home with no yellow ribbons to greet them.

I had read the Pentagon Papers, and even my ex-roommate and all her friends who usually read only the horoscopes read all about Watergate and Nixon's resignation. I knew exactly what had happened in computers since I read all those magazines. To me the microprocessor and floppy disk were more exciting than any other news. I mean, this was hotter than the Gutenberg printing press. The first thing I was going to spend my money on was my own personal computer made by Apple. The problem with only reading what interested me was that things like style slipped through the cracks.

I pulled on the skirt and sweater that were in the bag, along with my red, high-topped running shoes. I wasn't used to anything fitted and although the waistband was loose, I felt like a burnt sausage in my straight black skirt.

The discharge officer chattered away while I changed. I guess she assumed that if I hadn't had any privacy for a decade, I wouldn't need it now. "We informed your family of your parole date, but received only this fax." I wondered what she meant by *family* and the word *fax*. By *family* I guess she was referring to my parents. I felt weak and saw spots of dark colour dancing on the strange shiny paper. I hoped the warden's office hadn't sent some cloying request to them.

What the hell was a so-called fax? It sounded like the word *fuck* said with a Buffalo accent. It must be that machine on the desk grunting and excreting this shiny paper. It looked dangerously like a large colon. It looked so obscene I wished it had its own cubicle. I guess it was some kind of instant telegraph.

I unrolled the fax at both ends, like Julius Caesar reading a proclamation:

Please inform Kate Fitzgerald that the tenants vacated her Harbourfront condominium three years ago. Her furniture remains, her clothes are in a locked closet in the spare bedroom and her books and other personal effects are in the basement storage locker of the same building. The maintenance fees have been paid by the trustee of her fund and are up to date. Six years of mortgage payments have been placed in her trustee account. Her key has been left with the chief of security of the building.

    Sincerely,

    Andrea Wing,

    Articling student at Glorie and Glorie

There had been a split second there where I actually fantasized my parents waiting outside for me in their sable Lincoln with the heated seats.

The discharge officer made a tent over my hand with her plump one and practically whispered with a sibilant *s*, "I'm so sorry that no one has seen fit to meet you. Dr. Gardonne says you are to fly south with Denise Wapasha. She has to be flown by air ambulance to Toronto General Hospital's high-risk obstetrical unit."

An hour later, I was standing on a barren slab of ice that served as the takeoff runway. I helped the infirmary staff roll a gurney with a rotund, barely conscious Denise onto the plane. The pilot, ignoring everyone, sat adjusting the knobs of the twelve-seater Learjet.

There was a guard sent along to accompany us. He sat in the back seat of the plane with his ears occluded with bizarre little plugs attached to small wires that were connected to a small radio or personal stereo system. It was a thoroughly strange device, which ostensibly placed him in solitary confinement. (As I was getting out of jail, he was getting in.) These contrivances would never be successful. Had Sony forgotten that human beings are social animals? At least they used to be when I went into jail a decade ago.

When we were airborne, the pilot said, "I don't like doing this on Good Friday, but I get time and a half." Jerking his head toward Denise as the plane banked, he asked, "What's wrong with her, anyway?"

Since the guard couldn't hear him, I lifted the chart off the gurney, scanned it and said, "She is overweight and a diabetic with a multiple pregnancy. She has toxemia, which they can't get under control. They suspect the fetuses of fetal alcohol syndrome since they have small heads on the ultrasound."

"Jesus H. Christ, I'm so sick of this socialist state we live in. The Queen couldn't get better medical care than this irresponsible drunk. Why does she get flown to Toronto to have two babies who are going to be on the country's payroll for their whole life because she decided to drink? And where the hell did she get alcohol in jail? Or pregnant, for land's sake? I don't feel up to this on Good Friday. It's the only time all year I always go to church with the wife."

Glancing over at an ashen Denise, who was fighting for every breath, I said, "I don't think she feels up to it either."

As we passed from Hudson Bay to James Bay, he asked me, "What're you in for?"

"Killing my husband."

That ended further conversation until we landed in Moosonee. I asked if we were refuelling and he said that we were transferring to the Sick Children's Hospital helicopter. While two men were moving Denise, I hopped into my seat and again reread the letter that I'd tapped into from my file, which Dr. Gardonne had written to my supposed sidekick, Jackie Lawton. It was dated last week.

Dear Mr. Lawton,

We have engaged a Freudian expert named Kate Fitzgerald to assist you in your investigation of the director of the Freud academy, Anders Konzak. While you are establishing the veracity of the threats on his life, and whether he is working alone, she will try to ascertain what Anders Konzak has in store for the Freudian community when he releases the unexpurgated Freud–Fliess correspondence. This will give my psychoanalytic organization time to organize our damage control.

You will undoubtedly want to know something about the person with whom you will be working. Kate Fitzgerald is a statistician by undergraduate training, a Ph.D. in the philosophy of science, and an expert on Freud by inclination.

By way of introduction, I know Ms. Fitzgerald personally as she has been incarcerated in the prison of my employ for a violent crime committed nine years ago, and which, of course, I am not at liberty to discuss. She is from a prominent Toronto family, and the case was widely bandied about in the press.

I realize Ms. Fitzgerald may seem an odd choice to work for you on this assignment. I have selected her because I believe her knowledge of Freud is unsurpassed, and even Konzak has acknowledged that. He will undoubtedly be interested in discussing Freud with her as she has already made a mark in that field. Also, she has a fortunate confluence of physical attributes to attract him.

I should warn you that she can be quite abusive at times, and the closer she gets to someone the more marked her aggressive behaviour becomes. When she feels the least bit of emotional conflict or emotional ambiguity, she lashes out in a classically paranoid style.

At the risk of presumption, I suggest you steer clear of even the slightest emotional entanglement. Fortunately, your reputation for professionalism has preceded you. I mention this only because I am responsible for granting her Temporary Absence. I feel she is ready for re-entry into normal society, but her pathology could be activated by emotional involvement, which she is ill equipped to handle. She has the perfect qualifications for the job, both physically and mentally, thus we will simply have to overlook the idiosyncrasies of her personality.

You are both booked at the same hotel in Vienna. I have enclosed a picture of her taken from her trial publicity. If you have any questions or concerns about this partnership, please write to me c/o my St. Clair Ave. private practice, with no return address on the envelope.

Sincerely,
Dr. Willard Gardonne

Thanks for the psychological rape, Gardonne. It should help me create a trusting relationship with someone who is already emotionally maimed. Oh well, it wasn't like anything he wrote is a surprise. It just wasn't exactly what I'd hoped for in terms of a fresh start.

After several hours, we finally landed on the pad on the roof of the Hospital for Sick Children in Toronto. The pilot had wired ahead because Denise's portable vital signs machine was bleeping out warning noises. By the time the helicopter door opened, the emergency team was rushing her out and getting ready to roll her through the underground tunnels to the General Hospital next door.

No one paid any attention to me, so I grabbed my things and walked out the emergency exit and down the empty staircase to the street, where a line of cabs was parked. One pulled up as soon as he saw my suitcase. I told him "the Harbourfront condos" and then was silent, overwhelmed by the feeling that I was making a getaway and they would be after me in a few minutes. I had to keep telling myself that I was free. No one would find me missing at bed count.

As we drove south, I looked out the window and saw the island of ice pansies and the tall ferns on the avenue's divide. The pansy colours of white, yellow, purple, pale orange and maroon with different-colour centres were shivering on this chilly but thankfully sunny day. The ferns were that virgin green to greet the new season, the colour they have before photosynthesis darkens them. Their response to the breeze was a graceful waving of their fronds like ballerinas in *Swan Lake*. How had I walked by them for years and never noticed their beauty?

The cab driver had a barred cage surrounding his entire seat. The customer slipped her payment through a slot. I had seen that in New York, years ago, but never in Canada. I guessed times had changed. Suddenly claustrophobic and short of breath, I felt that I'd had enough of bars and had to get out. I told the driver to pull over at Front Street, paid with my old folded dollar bills and walked the rest of the way.

As I ambled along, the sunset was so bright I had to squint. After having been subjected to a decade of "climate control," the lake breeze slapped my face and dried my eyes. The seagulls were careening ominously toward me. Manic squirrels and marauding dogs were furtively glancing my way. As I cut through the park, the bark on the trees seemed more three-dimensional than I remembered and the Japanese maple was lit from behind, making the maroon stems look like pulsating veins.

The brilliant hues were way too much for me. The rods and cones of my eyes must have atrophied or adjusted to one light and little variation in pigment. The signal lights were flashing like the rides at Coney Island. Flags announcing museum exhibits flapped off telephone poles in my peripheral vision. Hot dog vendors stood under brightly striped umbrellas, and everyone seemed to be wearing iridescent shades of spring. Toronto was just beginning to bud, although a few snow piles remained in the parking lots. Hudson Bay was still in a deep freeze in an all-white landscape — even the bears and the wolves were white. Here, the dogs were multicoloured and some wore scarves. Overwhelmed, I made straight for my condo on Lake Ontario. Evidently my ability to experience sunlight and the texture of nature had lain dormant far too long.

Approaching my condo, I saw a clothing store called Sportables. The name rang a distant bell. I think I used to shop there. Speaking of clothes, what was I going to wear in Vienna? This old skirt and sweater and red, high-top Keds? What clothes did I have in my closet? All I could remember were bell-bottom jeans, a fisherman-knit sweater, Roots shoes, Kodiak boots and flannel shirts. I'd have to stop in here and buy something. I wondered what female detectives wore? The only female detective I could think of was Miss Marple.

Since it was Good Friday, the store was mercifully empty. Maybe I was used to depressed faces in the pen, but the saleswoman coming at me was more frightening than the marauding squirrels. She had gigantic hair and a manner like Anita Bryant. Her smile showed all of her gums. "What a gorgeous day. Spring is finally with us." I nodded, fearful that she might burst with happiness right in front of me. "I'm Brandi, with an *i*. Can I help you?"

"I need some clothes. I've" — I hesitated — "been away, so I need some advice on the styles in Canada."

"Oh, where have you been?"

"Sort of near Greenland—for a decade."

"Cool," she said, walking over to one of the racks. "Well, we'll just get you all set up for the Easter parade right here in Toronto. Power suit or occasional wear?"

"Oh, maybe a power suit that I'll just wear occasionally. I'm a size ten." I attempted to look around and all I saw was Spock wear—garish clothes of an undecipherable fabric that could be worn on the Starship *Enterprise*. Finally I told the truth. "These clothes look strange to me."

I began to feel tired, exhausted, and I had no ability to distinguish any particular object any more. I felt like there were cherry bombs of colour going off in my head. My brain, more specifically my sorting mechanism, was unable to leave behind the last thing I'd looked at. The sights and colours were becoming oddly cumulative since I'd left the landing pad. I needed a rest—a black-and-white rest in a confined space.

Brandi seemed to recognize that my sorting mechanism had checked out, or, as she said, "You look tired. Why don't you go into the dressing room and I'll bring in some suits and coordinates."

I felt more comfortable in the change room as I drew the curtain shut—that is, until I spotted a full-length mirror. I really didn't want to look, but I, like Narcissus, was drawn in. People should look in the mirror every day, not once a decade; it's not good for your self-image. I stood there stripped to my old greying underwear. I looked like a boiled chicken in the last minute before the meat comes off the bone. I had left only a few years out of university and was returning a few years before forty. My honey-blonde hair had faded, as had my skin. The detritus of my life had ground away my youthful glow and left me pale where I'd once been fair. I could hear my mother saying to my brunette sisters when they whined about me being "the pretty one": "Don't worry, blondes peak early."

At that moment Brandi entered with the first suit, which was royal blue with large brushed-gold buttons. When I put it on, I looked like a little girl trying to dress up like Margaret Thatcher. It had shoulder pads that extended the width of the dressing room.

Brandi came back in and said, "Well, first of all you are a size six or a four, so you look lost."

"I guess I've lost weight."

"I guess so! Gee, I wish I'd lost twenty-five pounds and not even noticed."

Looking in the mirror at the huge blue clown suit, I said, "If this is a power suit, then I don't need one. Let's move on to 'occasional wear' that I guess I'll have to wear more than occasionally."

Brandi brought in neon-coloured shirts and oversized sweaters—all made of some hideous fabric. Pointing to a neon-green shirt, she said, "This would be fabulous with a wide belt and black peg pants. I'd finish off with slouch socks and Ugg boots. That would be sensational."

I tried on the tiny black pants with zippers on the side of the legs. I said, "I look like a pencil in mourning."

"Well, you have got to accent them with the neon colours. It's the eighties. It's all about colour—saying you've arrived. We are the women who want to be noticed—no longer wallpaper."

I thought killing my husband had made me more than wallpaper, but now in the eighties I guess I needed neon slouch socks.

"What about jeans?" I asked hopefully. "Do people still wear those?"

Nodding, she dashed out and returned with some mottled jeans that looked worse than the black skirt and sweater I wore out of prison. She said, "These are stonewashed jeans—what everyone wears. We have matching jackets that hug the hips."

On it went. One thing was worse than the next, but I finally left with two gigantic bags of neon idiocy, Ugg boots, socks that slouched and jeans that looked like they'd had acid thrown on them. Thank God I could dip into my trust fund until I got my first Freudian dick paycheque.

I walked into the foyer of my apartment and opened the hall closet to toss in my shoes. There was my life piled in LCBO boxes. The first thing I unpacked was my collection of LeSportsac items. It was a little family of purses—tote bags, key case, wallet, passport case and makeup case—all in the same plain aubergine fabric. (I said I liked complete systems.) I have no idea why this parade of LeSportsacs gave me comfort, but it did.

I entered the living room to find my apartment looked huge and astonishingly luxurious. I guess when you live in a cell, you forget things like windows. I was overlooking the lake and it wasn't frozen—it moved. I had trouble gauging how close I should walk near the window. I gingerly walked into the kitchen feeling like Goldilocks in my own home, and was suddenly struck with something I had clearly forgotten. This was a whole room devoted to food preparation, eating and storage. I had to buy groceries. No one was going to make any meal for me. What a colossal time-waster it would be to make meals three times a day—to say nothing of shopping. No wonder most women don't have time to read Freud. Well, I guess that was why God invented restaurants. Anyway, there would be no point buying food that would spoil while I was in Vienna. Besides, I was honestly too tired to eat or to think of seeing more people. Freedom had become profoundly exhausting.

I walked into my bedroom, and my queen-sized bed looked the size of the Sick Kids' helicopter landing pad. I had only lived here with my husband for three months between arriving from Europe and going up north. I didn't remember buying any of the furniture or drapes, yet I must have. My room decor was excremental. I had no memory of choosing the Marimekko periwinkle giant-polka-dot bedspread, matching drapes and wall hanging. I guess my love of complete systems had overcome me.

I barely crawled out of my clothes before I fell asleep. It was the first night in my living memory that I didn't brush my teeth. As I was nodding off, I thought that I should have known Gardonne would pull some stunt to make me sweat. Giving me only twelve hours of decompression after a decade of incarceration before starting a job was particularly inspired on his part. He must have known I'd be doubled over with the psychological bends by the time I got to Vienna the next day to meet my Neanderthal co-investigator.

The next morning at the airport, brightly clad human specks were fleeing in different directions like crazed ants whose colony had been stepped on. Beleaguered by the cacophony, I ducked into a dark lounge where expense account managers tanked up before their free drinks on the plane. I sank onto a stool at the U-shaped bar that had mirrors on the walls. Was I paranoid, or was everyone looking at me?

Slightly calmed after taking deep breaths, I realized everyone was violating the no-eye-contact rule I'd observed for the last decade. Prison etiquette was based on the lack of privacy of the institution. Since we all lived in barred fishbowls with surveillance cameras, the way people built their own personal space was to *never* make eye contact with anyone else even if they were sitting next to someone and talking. As my eyes adjusted to the dark, I could see a row of gloom-suited men perched across from me like grackles on a telephone wire. Their eyes protruded and scanned me with jerky movements.

I knew by the sweat on my upper lip how badly I needed to pull the eye-contact circuit breaker.

I decided to do a little security check, trying to ground myself. I sat up and looked in the mirror behind the bar, focusing on three men who had swept-up hairdos in various stages of upsweep—a sort of David Bowie do with a Liberace lift. The two women with smoker's cough next to me wore the same type of big-shouldered Spockwear I'd seen in Sportables yesterday. At first I thought they had figures like Betty Boop, but then I realized that big shoulder pads give the illusion of a small waist. I guess Joan Crawford was on to that one. I'd assumed Brandi was out of her gourd; that's why I didn't bring that neon crap I bought the day before. But now I saw I could have looked normal in it. But what's with the big hair?

Having bought into Coco Chanel's "basic black never goes out of style" line, I wore the new peg pants I bought and a black boat-neck cable sweater I had found in my closet in a cleaning bag. I did wear the new suede boots because they were really comfortable. My shoulder-length hair was haphazardly piled on top of my head, and the numerous strands that had escaped clung to my moist neck. Looking in this huge mirror was haunting. Mercifully it was smoked, for I'd had enough of a gander at myself in the dressing room yesterday to last for another decade. Whoever invented tinted mirrors must have been over thirty-five because in this mirror I could still see the vestiges of the woman the papers had described as a "steely-eyed beauty."

My eye caught the guy across from me, who, thank God, assiduously avoided eye contact. He seemed to be concentrating on his cigarette as though it were imperative he fill his lung capacity. He seemed out of place in the airport executive lounge in a white T-shirt and black jeans, but he didn't look like he worked for the baggage department either. You could tell by the way he smoked his cigarette that he'd once cut quite a swath with the ladies. He probably had a liver the size of his ego.

While focusing on the distant mirror, I'd missed the waiter standing in front of me impatiently waiting to take my order.

"Uh . . . water, please," I stammered.

"San Pellegrino okay?"

"Water," I said impatiently, wondering if this guy understood English.

"Would you prefer Apollinaris?"

Is this guy saying water in several languages? I backtracked on the water and opted for an American icon. "Just give me a Coke."

I had piled a dollar's worth of quarters on the counter. As the waiter banged down a Coke with a wedge of lime cut into *Tyrannosaurus rex* teeth, he said "Three dollars and eighty-eight cents."

For a Coke?

As I reached into my twenty-year-old aubergine LeSportsac purse to get some more money, the bartender picked up the quarters and said, "Wow, this is a Centennial quarter. It has the Alex Colville bobcat on it. That makes it last minted in 1967. I collect these. Look, she's got three of them. What are the chances that would happen? Now here is a woman who knows how to hang on to her coin!"

One of the men on the other side of the bar said, "Wow, did you just get off Gilligan's Island?"

God, I'd outed myself on my first day. Maybe I should have worn those shoulder pads.

"Put the Coke on my tab," the T-shirted guy said, letting me off the hook but never glancing my way.

I guess I was supposed to thank him, but I knew why men bought women drinks, especially in airport lounges when they were far from home, so I decided to just pretend I was wearing horse blinkers and slowly drink from my trough till takeoff.

4

—

SEDUCTION IN THE AIR

—

Sexuality poorly repressed unsettles some families;
well repressed, it unsettles the whole world.
—KARL KRAUS, *Die Fackel*

WHILE FEIGNING INTEREST in *En Route* magazine, I sat
buckled into my window seat watching the other passengers as
they entered the business class cabin. The déclassé bodybuilder
turned Pillsbury Doughboy, who'd bought my Coke, with the
Dashiell Hammett pencil moustache—minus the dash—
boarded, keeping his eyes fixed on some distant point. He
stopped abruptly at my row, threw his luggage into the overhead
and flopped down next to me. He unfolded a photocopy picture
of someone on the cover of a newspaper and seemed to be assiduously studying it. He lit a cigarette and put his match in the
tiny ashtray between us.

When I thought I could do so undetected, I glanced over
and saw the cocky face of a twenty-six-year-old looking back at
me in black and white. It was at that moment I realized how
much I'd aged in ten years. There I looked like a willowy

blonde and now I felt like my features were sharper and my cheeks were hollower, like an albino Ichabod Crane in drag. Christ, have I learned anything since that picture was taken at my trial? Am I wiser now, or just broken? Maybe that's what wiser means. Who knows?

I suddenly understood why Mr. Beefy hadn't made eye contact: he was following the same prison rules as me. "So, Jackie, thanks for the Coke," I ventured. It would have been a hell of a lot easier if Gardonne had said we were on the same flight.

He turned and looked at me for the first time. "It's all expense account, Kate—not to worry."

I opened my book, *Ontogeny and Phylogeny*, just as he reached for his, *Care for the Soul*. After about half an hour I could see this guy was either antsy to talk to me or else claustrophobic. What the hell had Gardonne got up his straitjacket, hooking me up with someone who had small yellow teeth that had worn away as though he'd once been a professional hide softener? I mean, really—the guy looked dangerous. I'll have to make the best of it; there may be someone worse waiting in Vienna. He's clearly engrossed, reading up on the housekeeping of his soul. Is he thinking of sweeping all those armed robberies out of the corners? Opting for a ribald approach, I tried, "So, we're actually Freudian dicks."

"I've never met a Freudian who isn't a dick," he replied, never lifting his eyes from the page.

I wasn't even going to go there. Just another repressed dimwit in denial who's never read Freud, or else he's read him and is afraid of his own unconscious and decided to shoot the messenger. For God's sake, now I have to deal with Konzak *and* slack-jawed Jackie. One adequate narcissist and one inadequate.

Finally I guess he decided to break the ice. "Have you ever met this Freudian director guy Konzak?"

"Once, when I gave a paper on Freud about five years ago. It was a casual meeting in the lobby after a conference. A week later I actually got a letter from him praising my work on Freud's theory of defence. I doubt that he'll remember it."

"A six-foot blonde convicted murderer delivering a paper at an academic conference on Freud under armed guard isn't the kind of thing most men would forget," Jackie said while carefully writing notes in a leatherbound notebook.

"Five foot ten," I said.

"What did Konzak's letter say?"

"He pretended he knew me, which was strange since I didn't know him any better than I knew anyone else at the conference. He referred to 'our' dissonance as 'brave' in the face of 'the conservative backlash,' which was also ridiculous because it was simply a paper pointing out errors in another paper. The author wrote a cordial letter thanking me for a fresh perspective."

"Ten days that shook the world."

"Exactly," I replied.

"Was he flirting with you, hoping to strike up a correspondence that would lead to conjugal visits?" he asked while devouring his Nuts 'n Bolts.

A romantic angle had never occurred to me. I wasn't the kind of woman men flirted with, although I wasn't sure I knew exactly what flirtation was. "I don't know. I didn't answer the note, nor did I hear from or see him again."

"How did he get such an important job?" Jackie inquired.

"He's charming, and some people buy into being noticed and flattered."

"According to my research," Jackie said, paging through some notes, "he's the cherished son of a second-generation Polish immigrant—grew up in Rhode Island. His grandfather developed an import-export business with the Russians and the father continued it, making millions by selling pre-revolutionary treasures smuggled out of Russia. He also sold dollars before everyone in Russia was doing it. To top it off, he sold big defence contracts that he gathered through his contacts."

"You mean we were in a cold war with Russia and they were being sold the raw materials for missiles from the U.S.?" I asked.

"Yeah, not from the government, but from U.S. suppliers who are in the business, you know, like steel and aircraft companies. Those contacts and shipping were done through Konzak's trading company. Eventually Russia defaulted on too many payments and Konzak senior got out in the 1970s before everything went to rat shit in Russia. He retired with millions. His wife was from an old, arrived-on-the-*Mayflower* type of American WASP family."

"So Konzak was raised on the Edith Wharton American dream," I said.

"Who's Edith Wharton?"

"A turn-of-the-century American writer who wrote about East Coast, upper-crust life." While he carefully wrote down her name and starred it, I continued, "Why didn't he go into the father's business?"

"The father knew he could never do the job and would only bring the whole house down. So his old man donated a wing to Princeton, and off his son trundled through the Ivy League to emerge as a professor of Russian literature at McGill University in Montreal, where he was eventually tenured for doing slightly more than an amoeba." Jackie looked up from his notebook for the first time. "Amazing, isn't it?" I guess my expression said I had no idea exactly what he found so astonishing, so he added, "I mean, having a father who actually helps you instead of knocking the stuffing out of you."

"I'm not sure he was helping his son, since Konzak doesn't seem to have any idea of his limitations." As I spoke, I looked down at Jackie's arm and noticed a tattoo that read *Try It.* I wondered if that was encouragement or a threat. I continued, "Konzak probably glommed on to psychobabble early in his career. That jargon can get you a long way if you work in the prison system — I don't know what it does in a Russian department. However, I suspect you're pretty close on the professor-Russian-amoeba work front because when he did write anything, it was inflated psychoanalytic studies of the characters in Russian literature. You know the type of thing — 'Raskolnikov as an Obsessive-compulsive.' He was thought by some to be brilliant and by others to be shallow and glitzy. He had an arsenal of psychoanalytic weapons and eventually became a lay analyst himself."

"What's a *lay* analyst?"

"A psychoanalyst who is not a medical doctor."

"I thought an analyst who got laid would be too good to be true," he said.

"Why did he leave academia?" I asked.

"He was bored," Jackie replied. "The seventies were exciting on college campuses and he managed to have lots of success with the female graduate students. Then he tired of it — God knows why. Juggling a few Russian words with an audience of nubile females who adore you doesn't sound all that tiring to me."

"He thought he'd be the new Freud," I explained. "What *actually* happened, according to Dvorah Little's article about Konzak in *Metropolitan Life,* is that he got to listen to some professors' wives free-associate about whether their husbands would get tenure or their sons would get into dental school. To top it all off, the analyst is supposed to be silent and only let the patient talk — something that the flashy Konzak was not genetically predisposed to do."

"I can't imagine that everyone in the Freudian circle was so stupid. What's his con?"

"He's self-confident and very handsome in that 'Gatsby wannabe' kind of way. In terms of athletics he's a world-class windsurfer—even went to the U.S. Championships."

"I remember swimming at the public beach and really envying those guys who had mahogany speedboats. They never gave a shit when the lifeguard threatened to report them for water-skiing too close to the swimmers. I bet Konzak's old man would just tolerate that kind of thing with amusement. When you have that kind of family, it gives you more than looks." Jackie paused for a while. Looking out my tiny framed window into grey, dusty cloud formations, he added, "You can be lively and carefree. He wouldn't be afraid to point out his own weaknesses if they would serve to ingratiate him."

"I think he pretends he's really interested in everyone he talks to. Maybe he really is engrossed in them—long enough to get them to care for him. He wants to be adored as his mother adored him."

"How do you know he was adored by his mother?" Jackie inquired.

"I noticed his behaviour at the conference, specifically how he challenged others in the question-and-answer period. He didn't seem humiliated when he was off base, nor was he bothered by criticism from others. He seemed immune to it. The same has been true in the psychoanalytic journals over the years when scholars have written in some apt criticism to his articles. Konzak's written response is almost jaunty, rarely addressing the criticism that has been made."

"It must be amazing never to experience shame. That's like not having original sin. It could really free you up," Jackie said.

I didn't know how to respond, so I didn't say anything.

Ten minutes into the in-flight entertainment, Jackie said, "I want to get straight what everyone is so upset about." He poured four sugars into his Nescafé and said, "I got all my information from the newspaper and from the series of articles in *Metropolitan Life,* so let me know where I screw up. In 1895, when Freud's female patients told him they'd been sexually abused by the old man, he believed them and said, 'Wow, I've discovered that adult-onset hysteria is caused by incest in early childhood.' He called it the seduction theory. He held this theory for two years and then decided to call it quits in 1887. He said, 'Hey, wait a minute here. All of these female patients can't have been seduced by their fathers. I think they have imagined it. It is their fantasy.' Freud then asked himself why so many girls would fantasize incest. He had actually stumbled onto the idea that we all have a sexual longing for the opposite-sex parent. He decided to call this the Oedipus complex. This complex is the bulwark of psychoanalysis. That unconscious wish makes people neurotic or hysterical or whatever it is that keeps them on Freud's couch. So Freud goes on uncovering these so-called *fantasies* and when the patient makes enough slips of the tongue or has enough dreams that uncover Daddy and little daughter as husband and wife, the patient then realizes she hasn't *really* been sexually abused—she only imagined it. She then realizes it is her sexual longing for her old man that has caused the fantasy which she mistook for a realistic memory. At that point she gets up off the couch and is cured."

"Konzak has taken sociological information, used today's standards to judge Victorian Vienna in order to slander Freud, and then—"

Interrupting, he said, "I don't give a shit if that's right or wrong. You can thrash that out with Konzak. I just want to know what he's saying and who would care."

I gave him the most withering look in my repertoire, which indicated how sorry I was for having attempted a nanosecond of theoretical debate with such a hostile boor. Then I continued, "Konzak suggests that there was far more incest than Freud or anyone else in 1895 was aware of, and that many women, including his patients, were, *in reality*, sexually abused. That information is only coming out now. Konzak believes Freud was talking these women out of their realities — in other words, just slowly driving them nuts — and then what happens to his Oedipus complex? The cornerstone of psychoanalysis is shot to hell."

"In Freud's theory the father, i.e., the perpetrator, is cleared and the victim, the daughter, is guilty of unconscious sexual wishes," Jackie said while still writing in his notebook. "So, according to Konzak, Freud did just what society did — blamed the victim."

I nodded. "So Konzak calls every newspaper in town and says that all of the females who have been analyzed need to be recalled off the psychoanalytic conveyor belt like defective cars."

"The Ralph Nader of the psychoanalytic world," Jackie said.

"Konzak came up with the idea and it *is* interesting. However," I countered, "he muckrakes through the archives preparing everyone for the revelation and then he takes historical information out of context and makes Freud look malevolent. There's really no evidence to date that Freud *deliberately* did this. Konzak is right in that Freud probably didn't know how much incest was, in fact, out there. Classic Freudians say that psychoanalysis is about the patient's *perception* of reality, not reality itself."

Jackie raised his eyebrows. "You said there is no evidence *to date*. Konzak could have uncovered something big in the archives on Freud's seduction theory that you know nothing about yet."

"That's what he *says* he's done."

"So if Konzak is right, he is disproving Freud; if he's wrong, he is maligning him."

"The truth probably lies somewhere in between. Maybe Freud did see women who had sexual *memories* as opposed to sexual *fantasies* and he generalized the theory too quickly. After all, how large was his sample? Ten, maybe twenty, tops."

"The bottom line is"—Jackie interrupted yet again—"who cares enough to threaten Konzak's life?"

"First of all, one in three Americans have sought psychiatric help sometime in their lives. Freud's ideas become part of your life for that time period, and naturally everyone wants to gloat when he's found to have been wrong. Freud is the Big Daddy during analysis, and he's fairly authoritarian. It's no wonder those who have been in therapy might be gleeful now to think that they've caught him with his hands in the 'unconscious' cookie jar."

"Or else you might feel really angry that you spent years in analysis trying to resolve your Oedipal conflict and now find out maybe Freud made it up," Jackie offered. "What a colossal time-waster and mind-bender."

"It's no wonder it's such a big item in the East Coast papers, where so many people have been analyzed. I'll bet Konzak was offered plenty for that interview."

"Then he ups the ante and says his life has been threatened. Now he's making the world see his 'revelations' as a life-and-death issue. He's the hero struggling against the enemy in order to deliver truth." Jackie rolled his eyes.

"The same delusion he presented to me when I gave my paper—the rebel with a *cause célèbre*."

"They should have hired a guy they could trust, not an adventurer. If we're looking at his real enemies, then the Freud academy and the guys that hired Konzak would have to be at the top of the list. Then there are all those Park Avenue analysts who make their living saying 'hmmmmmm.'" Jackie said.

"What about someone high-profile who was psychoanalyzed by Freud and now is worried that Konzak has dug up his file? Who knows—maybe J. Edgar Hoover wore a different dress to each one of his sessions." I knew I was getting far-fetched, but hey, wasn't that the essence of brainstorming? "The other possibility is that *no* one has threatened Konzak's life. Maybe he just wants the attention. I think the death-threat take on the situation is a red herring. The guys in New York write about Freud's recent fall from grace, but the real people in America's heartland always thought Freud was crazy anyway. You know—childhood polymorphous perversity and all that."

"I'm with the heartland," Jackie said. "What's polymorphous perversity? Is that something I haven't tried?"

"Freud said that a child, if he had no rules from adults, would do whatever he could for gratification with any part of his body to any other object or person. He is saying that nothing is perverse until society tells the child it is perverse."

"Like sex with another man, a horse, a shoe—"

Interrupting this litany, I said, "Let's just say that a pervert is one who has refused to repress his childhood polymorphous perversity."

"So people don't like the term because Freud is really calling every civilized person a repressed pervert?"

Not wanting to get involved in a defence of Freud, since Jackie made it clear he didn't want to hear it, I said, "It seems egalitarian to some, but offensive to many."

"Don't get me wrong. I'm all for polymorphous perversity— always have been. The problem with Freud is he's a city-slicker momma's boy who never got out of the study. Shit, I grew up on Children's Aid industrial farms. I can tell you, I saw bisexuality among the animals, and the rubes told jokes about incest that I got when I was five. Freud acts like bisexuality is a big discovery.

I don't know what went on in your country club, but in my lock-up everyone eventually showed their bisexual side. After a few years half of us wore lipstick. You know why prisoners don't get together when they get out? It's not because they're following parole board rules, it's because they know they've done every uncivilized thing in the book. I've done it all myself, and the reason I don't give a flying fuck is because I know that everyone, at least every man, would do it if they were locked up long enough."

After about thirty seconds with no prompting from me, he went on. "The Oedipus complex. Give me a break! Of course everyone has the hots for their mother—it's the first piece of ass you see. Like, why is this some brilliant revelation? Your first love is your most important." Jackie's voice was rising. The businessman across the aisle had by now given up even a pretext of working on his expense report and looked our way. "I mean, what the hell," Jackie continued. "How is knowing this silly stuff—what every stiff who is in touch with human nature already knows—supposed to cure you? Consciousness is a spectrum, and Freud is only looking at a speck."

"You're raising your voice," I pointed out, in case he hadn't realized he was practically screaming. What the hell is he so angry about? If Freudian theory can make him this mad, it's no wonder he was in solitary confinement for so long.

"Well, it's so soulless and superficial," he mumbled, realizing he had attracted the attention of those around us. He leaned over and said to the expense account man across the aisle, "Man, if I have a sick soul, I don't need to go to some Freudian jerk who's going to take five years to let me know that I'm sexually as wild as the breeze and I've actually thought of doing mom. Only those guys on Fifth Avenue don't know that."

Much to my amazement, the guy in the Armani knock-off said, "Exactly. And it costs big bucks to hear it."

Maybe Jackie just scared the guy into agreement. The stewardess bustled down the aisle and asked, "Everything all right here?"

Not really.

The guy across the aisle ordered two whiskies. One for himself and one for Jackie.

Hours later, when we were descending over Vienna, Jackie spoke quietly, without an ounce of remorse or embarrassment over the scene he'd caused. "You and I need to be clear. It doesn't matter what I think of Freud, and for sure you're the Freudian expert. I'm along to do some sharpshooting in case anything gets rough. I've put in my time on both sides of the law, so I can stickhandle my way through that." He leaned forward so he could look into my eyes and lowered his voice so I could barely hear him. "Disagree if you want to, but don't tell me when I'm raising my voice or ever condescend to me again. If you want to say I'm full of shit, fine, but don't pull that patronizingly superior manner again or I'll show you what it *really* means to go slumming. By the way, remember you're not the only one with a prison library."

When had I been condescending? I guess whatever he perceived to be my heinous sense of superiority sent him into a rage that he then turned onto Freud. In the most egalitarian, calm tone I could manage I said, "When I attempted one line in Freud's defence, I believe you told me we were not here to discuss the validity of Freudian theory. At which point you proceeded to yell about Freud's inadequacies to whomever was within earshot. I would appreciate it if, in the future, when you feel the need to make arbitrary rules, you have the courtesy to follow them."

Surprisingly, he nodded, saying, "Fair enough." Then he quite cheerily moved on. "We have two mandates: to find out what information Konzak has on Freud that is scaring everyone, and to find out who, if anyone, might want Konzak permanently silenced. On the suspect front we have the following: the New York analysts; a possible disgruntled patient; and Von Enchanhauer, the past director who hired him, who must be kicking himself, and anyone else who actually cares if Freud is discredited."

After thinking for a moment, I said, "His daughter, Anna Freud, lives in London in Maresfield Gardens and is probably going to win the Nobel Prize before a permanent rest in Westminster Abbey, which could be any day now."

"I had no idea she kicked such intellectual butt. Was she tight with her father?" he asked while writing.

"She never married or had a family. She lived at home and devoted her life to her father. She stood up to the Gestapo for him, and later kept him alive for years when he had cancer. He is her life's work, and she is not going to take lightly to his being debunked. If Konzak has found some incriminating material on Freud in her own home, she's going to be as protective as a mother bear."

Jackie nodded. "That's it, then?"

Well, not exactly. I wanted to mention Gardonne but knew that he'd written to Jackie telling him I could be paranoid. I decided to risk it. "Just for the sake of completeness you may want to add Gardonne to the list." Jackie lifted an eyebrow, so I continued. "He says he is working for the North American Psychoanalytic, but remember, he hired two ex-cons for a reason. I have no idea what his agenda is, but I bet it's not what he says."

"My first bank accomplice offered me a simple rule from the wild: a wolf never shits where it lives."

"Meaning?"

"Gardonne is our employer. He pays our bills. Let's not start attacking the home base." However, after hesitating a moment, he did write Gardonne's name on the list of suspects.

I thought it best to move on. "What do you think about the threat issue?"

"Probably some group threatened Konzak as a precautionary measure. However, he's lived such a charmed life, if someone was playing for higher stakes, he'd never smell the danger."

"I don't predict getting information from him will be difficult," I offered.

"Look. A guy like Freud knows he's going to die in the limelight, so whatever personal skeletons he's got—and I'm sure he has plenty, because we all have something to hide—he's got them buried where even Sherlock Holmes couldn't find them. From what I've read of Freud, and granted it is very little, he has covered his ass completely. He's worked it out so that you can never prove him wrong. If you don't buy into his theory, he has fifty ways to Sunday to dismiss you. He says you're in denial or haven't accepted your own unconscious urges or some such horseshit. He was brilliant at sweeping away his footprints in the sand. You think a guy like that is going to leave some incriminating letters in his own home for someone like Konzak to unravel?"

"It's not as simple as Freud covering his own tracks," I said. "He had contemporaries, patients and students. All of those people wrote letters about their interactions with him. Academic letters are found all the time which reveal things about the great minds of the past."

"Freud strikes me as the kind of guy who you may get something on, but whatever you've got on him, he's got something bigger on you," Jackie added, "until finally you die with your mouth shut."

He closed his notebook.

5

—

HOME

—

Anyone who idolizes you is going to hate you when he discov-
ers that you are fallible. He never forgives. He has deceived
himself, and he blames you for it.

—ELBERT HUBBARD

WHEN I OPENED my eyes in Vienna, I took in the Franz Josef
room with toasty butter-yellow sunlight streaming in my windows. As I started into the bathroom, I caressed the brass
doorknob that was moulded into a leaf. It had been so long since
I'd seen an object of beauty that I felt as though I were thawing
from my frozen decade. I kept in mind that thawing too quickly
can cause severe pain, swelling and ultimately dead tissue. I
tried to hold myself back from taking in too much. I closed my
eyes, but then I smelled the familiar fragrance of the lemon-
oiled wood of the Biedermeier bed that reminded me of my
room when I was a little girl.

Gazing out the leaded glass window down at the busy
Fleischmarkt, I thought of the trips I'd made to Austria to ski
when I was a child and how my father had taken me to the art

gallery to see the Titians while my mother and sisters shopped for tablecloths. However, what I'd loved most were the Bruegels. My father, not one for impulse buying, actually bought me a 3,000-piece puzzle of my favourite Bruegel, *The Triumph of Death*, and over an entire winter we put it together at home.

As I walked to the lift to meet Jackie for breakfast, I remembered how in the sixties, when I was in England studying and my husband was in Germany, we would meet in Vienna. I smiled as I realized how, from our *Europe on $5.00 a Day* guidebook, we managed to do so much, from seeing Kokoschka's newly found drawings to hearing Yehudi Menuhin play Beethoven in the church where Beethoven wrote the violin concerto.

Upon entering the dining room I saw Jackie in jeans and a hooded sweatshirt with his Clydesdale legs stretched straight out under the table. I had to admit that with his wet curly hair pulled back from his face, you could see he had a commanding profile, however rough-hewn.

He barely grunted hello as he tossed me the menu. "Can't a guy get a coffee in this mausoleum?"

The coffees all had names that were some variant of the Hapsburg Empire—the *Joseplatz Koffee* or the *Maria Theresa*. In fact there was an entire page of caffeinated noble lineage.

Watching me read the menu, Jackie said, "In the good ol' U.S. of A. they don't have a *Thomas Jefferson* or a *Ben Franklin*. Just order one of these dudes that'll get me a black coffee."

"I'd suggest a Kurz."

It didn't take a detective to see there was something stuck in his craw. "What's with you? Wild night?"

"I don't call going to the British bookshop wild. At least, I didn't used to."

"Oh, the English-language bookstore on Weihburggasse? That shop has been there since I was a kid. Checking out Freud in English, or are you picking up a sequel on soul cleansing?"

"Not to get off the exciting topic of bookstores . . ." He paused, sneered and said, "Is *that* what you're wearing to meet Konzak?"

I ran my hand over my hair that was pulled back in one loose braid and looked down at my jeans, my lace-up mountain-climbing boots and baggy fisherman-knit sweater, and responded, "Actually, I thought of changing into spike heels, plastic wrap and a cowgirl hat before teetering over to the academy."

He kept reading for a minute or two before mumbling, "Well, it wouldn't turn my crank." He flicked his eyes at me. "Konzak is staying at a small apartment building around the corner. The lodging is owned by the Freud academy and is reserved for whenever the director is in town. He goes to the archive every day until about noon." He signalled the waiter for a coffee and told him not to put it in a thimble.

"How do you know all that?" I asked.

"Same way you know about Freud—it's my job." When I looked confused and slightly incredulous, he spoke in staccato blasts: "I own a detective agency. It has employees. They trailed Konzak." He shook his head, indicating he couldn't believe he was saddled with such a nincompoop.

"Sor-*ry*," I said. Most men who have tattoos and yellow teeth aren't incorporated. But I didn't say that out loud.

Approaching the door of 19 Bergasse, I saw the small historical plaque that said it had been Freud's home and office. I had a feeling of déjà vu. I'd walked these streets with Freud so many times in my mind. Like a milk horse, I knew exactly where to stop.

I hadn't expected to feel nervous, yet as I stood in the foyer my heart started pounding. I thought of all the years I'd been imprisoned, reading Freud into the wee hours, picturing all his patients and thinking about his writing to Berlin to share his latest findings with his only colleague, Wilhelm Fliess. I thought of Freud's own late nights when he was writing *The Interpretation of Dreams,* and of his loneliness as he built his theory of the unconscious all on his own, going months without sharing his discoveries, and finally of the gruelling schedule of seeing twelve patients a day.

Standing at the threshold, I realized how close I had felt toward Freud as a person. I felt the warmth of his smile as I entered. Of course he had his warts (even he admitted he never understood what a woman wanted, but then neither do I).

Although my heart was thundering, I realized as my face broke into an unexpected grin that I was more excited than anxious. I was actually climbing the stairs of a cellmate in whose study I had spent untold imaginary hours. I'd been afraid I would never see the fantasy house that had sustained me. I was finally coming home.

The rooms were tiny. It was hard to imagine that Freud lived, raised a large family and worked in this psychoanalytic doll's house most of his adult life. He didn't leave Vienna for England until 1938, to escape the Nazis. By then he was an old, sick man forced to cope in a new country and a new language.

In the waiting room, I could hardly turn around. It was so minute it held only a settee. Freud's office had a couch with a beautiful Persian carpet spread on it, and the desk and side tables teemed with antiquities. A small hallway led to Anna Freud's office off their shared waiting room. She was so lucky to have collaborated in intellectual life with her father, to have shared his *raison d'être.* How unique to have a father who wasn't disappointing in some gut-wrenching way. I was so moved that my composure began to slip.

I jumped when someone tapped my shoulder. Reflexively, I wheeled around for attack and saw a handsomely built man, an American judging by his broad shoulders and casual dress. He had on a sort of faded blue golf shirt with a tiny green alligator over one breast. The shirt hung outside of his jeans and was longer in the back. His narrow waist and hips were complemented by his boot-cut Levis. He must have just returned from somewhere sunny, since his lion's head of blond hair was straw-streaked across the top. The few lines around his eyes were enhanced by his tan.

"Hi," he said, as friendly and self-assured as could be. "I'm Anders Konzak." He seemed to be waiting for my reaction.

I thought I would have remembered him accurately, but I hadn't recalled that smile. He, like a surprising number of men, actually improved with age. "Oh! *The* Anders Konzak. Head of the Academy. You've had a lot of free publicity lately."

"Well, it hasn't been exactly free, but that's another story." He hesitated a moment and then said, "Kate, I guess you don't remember me. We met at a conference in Rochester."

"Of course! I *thought* you looked familiar when I saw your picture in *The Times*." I moved on quickly. "It is really amazingly powerful being here." Placing my palm on the manuscript of *Studies on Hysteria*, I continued, "I've imagined the man and his house, and read his letters—it's wonderful to see them here in the original."

"I know. I felt exactly the same way. Very few people get into this place on that level." He paused and shook his head in disbelief. "Wow! I can't believe this. A woman I've been dying to talk to for years walks in from a country I just left, a woman who is doing research, not just on Freud, but *early*

Freud—exactly my interest! Talk about karma! We've got to have lunch today."

"Sounds great."

"I'll meet you right here at one o'clock."

I was glad I hadn't wasted time in detective school. This seemed pretty easy.

Konzak appeared as promised at one and escorted me to a traditional Viennese restaurant called the Demel Café. Ignoring the hostess, he led me to a particular table, saying, "I thought you might like to sit at the exact table where Freud and Fliess discussed the origins of the theory of the unconscious."

As I looked around, I realized I was living a moment that I had imagined hundreds of times. In 1895 no one in the world believed in Freud except for Wilhelm Fliess, another neurologist, who travelled from Berlin to Vienna for their meetings. In an effort to let Konzak know how much I appreciated that he'd thought to bring me here, I said, "Imagining their encounters has sustained me for a long time. I can't believe I'm actually here." Then I added as casually as I could manage, "Particularly since my major interest is the Freud–Fliess correspondence."

"That's what I'm editing! Don't do another stitch of research."

"What do you mean? The collection of letters was published in 1954. It was Kris who edited them in '54 and called the book *Origins of Psychoanalysis.*"

"Remember when Ernst Kris—who was, by the way, only a mouthpiece for Anna Freud—said some of the letters are missing? They weren't *missing.* They were *expurgated.*" He leaned toward me and whispered, "I have them."

"Given what you said in *The Post,* I assumed you must have had some potent new information."

"Kate, now that I know you are interested in the Freud–Fleiss correspondence, let me give you some research advice. Be careful what you say in the archive. Be circumspect when requesting any documents. Anna Freud is the real keeper of the keys, and she has her minions guarding anything to do with that particular correspondence. Believe me, I've learned the hard way that all of the employees are mere drones for Anna Freud, the queen bee. I have to lay low for the time being, since, believe it or not, I actually stay with Anna Freud when I'm in London."

"Really? How come?"

"You probably know that to escape the Nazis she moved to London with her parents, to the house in Maresfield Gardens. Anna stayed on there with the original housekeeper. The collections are housed there, so as director of the Freud academy I have my own living quarters in what was once the servant's quarters on the third floor. Talk about dingy. I'm only at the Vienna museum part-time. Most of the best documents are in England. If you're in London, you'll have to come to the house."

"Isn't Anna Freud angry about the leaks to the press?"

"Furious, although she wouldn't know a feeling if she fell over one. They really want to fire me, but they can't until the board of directors meets next month. Then for sure I'll have to pack more than my psychological baggage."

"That's hard for you, I imagine," I said, trying to find out where his resentment really lay.

"You've read the early Freud. You know what he was up against. He dug his own grave recommending cocaine for general use, not knowing it was habit-forming for most people. He thought what was true for himself was true for the rest of the world."

"Imagine how Freud felt when his best friend Fleischl died from the addiction that Freud created. No wonder he specialized in everyone else's guilt," I said. Actually, I was thinking, for Christ's sake, the guy discovered the unconscious, dream analysis, the Oedipus complex and bisexuality, to name only a few. So he didn't know about the existence of the addictive personality in 1895. *Big deal.*

"As if that wasn't enough to make him feel like a permanent wipeout," Konzak said, "he decides to befriend Fliess, a doctor who leaves rolls of gauze in patients' orifices after operations, and believes that the nose is the centre of sexuality."

An old waiter approached with two cups of Schale Gold. Konzak placed his arm around the shrivelled man and said, "Rudolph, remember the post-Freudian bash we had here last year? Now *that* was a night."

"The best night since the thirties." Rudolph beamed as he tottered off.

"Back to the nose," I pressed on. "It is not quite as crazy as it sounds. I mean, Freud said that when we were in a previous evolutionary phase, we walked on all fours and the nose was a sexual organ, in that picking up the scent of female estrus and readiness for copulation made the nose an erogenous zone. Look at other mammals—they sniff everything as a form of sexual foreplay."

"No one wants to be reminded that we were once on all fours smelling each other's behinds. Advertisers are always the first to capitalize on human repression. That's why they invented FDS, deodorant and Odor-Eaters," said Anders.

"Fliess said the nose was an atrophied sexual organ in that Darwinian light. I mean, I know it's a bit crazy, but it makes *some* sense in that context. In fact, Fliess helped Freud to see that there are erogenous zones that are routinely repressed, and that's how he came upon the unconscious repression of bisexuality, for example."

I had to push ahead before we got distracted by lunch. I framed the big question as casually as I could while unfolding my napkin. "So, do you think that Freud had it right the first time when he described the seduction theory, and then went off the rails when he revised the theory and said the girls had fantasized the father's seduction?"

"I do indeed. These women told him that they'd been seduced and Freud chose to deny it." His voice went up an octave as he said, "I mean, we are talking about your basic fragile incest survivor here, who is no more responsible for her victim status than any other tiny, innocent child. In the world according to Freud, the fathers are innocent and the daughters are nymphomaniacs. That's why he had to see so many females, because the fathers didn't have this 'delusion.' *Right*. I mean, let's face it, Freud's female patients never got better."

"Who says?"

"Check the facts. Anna O., who was in real life Bertha Pappenheim, wound up in a mental hospital after Freud and Breuer got finished with her. She started out neurotic, was analyzed by Breuer and finished psychotic."

"If giving up the seduction theory was a mistake on Freud's part, do you think it was deliberate?"

"Of course it was, and that'll be coming out in the letters that will appear soon. Don't forget that Freud's former student Wilhelm Reich was out analyzing the *masses*. He refused to treat the elite that were Freud's bread and butter. He set up walk-in clinics to try to combine Freudian theory with Marxism. He tried to tell Freud how prevalent incest was among ordinary females, but Freud stonewalled him, said it happened mainly in 'the servant class.'" Reading my incredulous reaction, his voice became shrill. "I'm serious—*read* the letters."

"Why would Freud have ignored it?" I persisted.

"First of all, he couldn't risk becoming any more unpopular. He'd already made the cocaine mistake and couldn't allow his practice to dry up, which would have been the inevitable result if he were to accuse the referring physicians of seducing their daughters. The Viennese physicians would never have sent him another patient. What with Aunt Minna, a wife, five children and two sets of parents to support, he *had* to stay in the mainstream."

"That's pretty calculating."

"Remember, it wasn't all conscious. He had to bury his unconscious wishes toward Anna. Don't you think it's a little strange that he analyzed his own daughter? Anna was unusually attached to him, living at home, spending the last twenty years of her life with him, nursing him day and night during his cancer. Freud didn't want to take the rap for that Krazy-Glue bond.

"The real reason he severed his friendship with Fliess wasn't the sponge left in the nose. Operations were botched all the time in those days. It was that Fliess was diddling his own kid and writing about it and telling Freud all the prurient details of his research."

"Did Freud know Fliess was abusing his own child?"

"Naturally Fliess didn't say it was his own son, but Freud knew it couldn't have been anyone else. He just didn't want to face it. Years later Fliess's son Robert, who grew up to be a respected psychoanalyst, wrote about the whole incest episode, calling his father a 'psychotic.'"

"Well, I guess it would be hard to admit that your only supporter was in fact a psychotic child abuser."

"Exactly. Oh, by the way, don't tell anyone about Fliess's father–child scenario. It'll be out next month."

"Interesting!"

My response spurred Anders to further explanatory heights. "It's a male theory propounded by male analysts—all these poor hysterical girls needing to calm down. Why aren't there any more hysterics today?" Clearly this was a rhetorical question since Anders plowed ahead. "Freud *induced* hysteria in his patients. It's a beautiful misogynist theory that puts all the blame on the female, who is slowly driven hysterical—or nuts, if you like—when she tries to rectify the situation through analysis and is victimized again! Tell me, don't you think it's a little odd that statistics show that one-third of men commit some form of incest, yet *all* the women Freud saw imagined it? And not only imagined it but, according to him, were so obsessed by the *idea* that they became ill from their *wishes*."

Rudolph arrived with a little pile of pork on what looked like a cow pat and set it in front of us with a flourish. I rushed into my theory before Anders could swallow his first bite. "My version has a different twist. Hysteria is brought on by sexual repression, which was never more extreme for women than in the Victorian era. The hospitals were full of hysterics because of it. I agree it was a man-made disease, so to speak, but one of a different making. Women weren't allowed to express their sexual needs, and those females who found it too oppressive sometimes unconsciously opted out through hysteria or becoming neurasthenic, like William James's sister, Alice."

Interrupting with enthusiasm, Anders said, "Her diaries were fascinating. Alice was supposedly smarter than either Henry or William James. She was taught that sexuality was debased, and she wasn't allowed any occupation other than needlepoint. Eventually she became a neurasthenic who stitched herself onto a couch and never got up. Isn't that an unconscious way of saying, 'If you won't let me live a *real* life, I won't live a life at all'? It's self-destructive, but it does get the message across."

I said, "The hysterics of the nineteenth century were the first real feminist protestors, though of course they didn't know it.

Every century offers its sacrifices to the gods of 'progress,' progress being defined by those in power." I couldn't resist adding, "Anders, I think it's naive and historically inaccurate to say all that hysteria was due to Freud's misdiagnosis."

Konzak was leaning forward, ready to pounce as soon as I took a restorative breath. "Of course. I'm only trying to say that hysteria was aided and abetted by Freud. Some hysteria was a result of childhood sexual abuse, and no one was willing to point the finger at the males because so many males were guilty of those illicit thoughts. The men blocked it out. The reason hysteria occurred so much more frequently among women is that they were the victims of childhood sexual abuse. The power structure of bourgeois males pinned hysteria on women's anatomy. I mean, *hysteria* is Greek for 'womb.' The Hippocratic hypocrites actually perpetrated the idea that it was the womb wandering to other parts of the body that caused hysteria. Anyway, you know all about the wandering womb club. It was easier to blame the female anatomy rather than the women's victimized role in the family. Let's face it, these poor creatures who were Freud's patients were betrayed twice: once by their own fathers, through the incestuous act, and again by their analyst and father figure, Sigmund Freud, who refused to believe them when they confessed what had happened to them."

Anders was in full rhetorical swing. The waiters and the patrons at the other tables were beginning to listen, not because he was being too loud, but because his animation and star quality were beguiling—Elmer Gantry comes to Vienna.

"Let's say, for the sake of argument, that Freud did ignore the prevalence of sexual abuse in the family and assumed that these women were simply fantasizing. Wouldn't that make him a man of his time?" I inquired.

"That's not what the letters show. He didn't want to risk exposing the seduction theory to the powers that be."

"What 'powers that be'?"

"He needed referrals from the other medical specialists. He couldn't risk their censure. I mean, you can't start telling the male doctors that most or some of them have been incestuous. He did biological research until he was forty years old, then he slogged away at psychology for another ten years alone, without any university affiliation. At some point he had to acquire respectability. He practically said so to Fliess. Think of all the poor victims who were analyzed in this way! For God's sake, if women made permanently infertile by the Dalcon Shield could get millions for their infertility in a lawsuit, why can't those women who were analyzed by Freud and his successors file a class action suit against the Freud Foundation or all the psychoanalytic societies? All those psychoanalysts pay group malpractice rates—why shouldn't they be sued as a group?"

As Anders wound down, I realized how well he had mastered the sound bite. No wonder he was the darling of the press. He was speaking out for women and the powerless masses in general. To top it all off, what he said made some sense. However, I still wanted to see those letters before I was willing to believe that Freud was mal-intentioned or even wrong. Besides, telling Victorians that all children were polymorphously perverse hardly made it seem as if Freud was backing down from controversy.

I didn't want to go into some blind defence of Freud, yet I did want to establish how Konzak justified his theory, so I asked, "How do you account for the fact that people today who are victims of incest or other forms of sexual abuse aren't necessarily hysterical? Depending on the severity of the abuse, they suffer various dissociative states ranging from mild forms of amnesia to multiple personality, but not hysteria. If we subscribe to Freud's nosology, then hysteria is a rare diagnosis these days. The emotional excitability and excessive anxiety types are still as rampant as ever, but classic hysteria as Freud described it—the sensory and motor disturbances and the unconscious simulation of organic disorders—is rare."

"Hysteria is not even mentioned in the DSM, the bible of disorders," said Konzak.

"I'm sure you'll acknowledge that incest is at least as common now as it was in 1895. Shouldn't there be *more* hysteria now, in 1982, than there was in 1895? Instead, there is *less*. I hate to tell you this, Anders, especially since you're paying for lunch, but that refutes your main argument. There was more sexual repression in the nineteenth century and more hysteria. This supports my idea that hysteria was the result of prolonged sexual repression, not actual incest."

"Not always. Hysteria wears a new hat today. What about the so-called twentieth-century disease, chronic fatigue syndrome and fibromyalgia? Are these not psychosomatic hysterical formations of disease?"

"What about false memory syndrome?" I asked. "While every journalist is praising you for your intellectual work, Anders, no one is saying maybe Freud was right. After all, how do we explain all these women who claim they were seduced by their fathers and then it turns out to be false? I notice the press, *ergo* the public, blame the 'evil' therapists who tricked or coerced the patient into calling up false memories at a suggestible hypnotic moment. No one is saying, 'Yikes, maybe Freud was right.' *Some* women do fantasize these seductions. This takes us full circle back to Freud's idea that the unconscious makes no distinction between real and imagined acts. Somehow Freud got cut out of the loop and it's now called false memory syndrome and—"

"Oh no," Anders yelped, checking his watch, "I've got to get back. We've been here for longer than I thought. Frau Frakin, the lugubrious librarian of the Freud collection, has arranged for some frumps from England to come and look at archival pictures. They must already be waiting." He stood up, frantically signalling Rudolph for the check, and then said offhandedly, as though it were obvious, "We have to have dinner tonight. I was supposed to meet some snore-fest friend of Conrad Von Enchanhauer's—you must have heard of our arcane ex-director. I'll have to get out of it."

I nodded assent as he tossed shillings on the table. I smiled inwardly, thinking how funny it was to be trailing a guy who wouldn't leave me alone or shut up.

"Meet me in the dining room at the Palais Schwarzenberg in Schwarzenbergplatz at eight o'clock." On his way out he beamed a smile and said over his shoulder, "I've enjoyed smelling you."

After stopping in at the art gallery to see my favourite Bruegels, I returned to my room, where I found a cut-glass bowl full of tiny white flowers atop two gift-wrapped boxes. The card read:

Fräulein Kate,
Thanks for a great afternoon. I can't wait to talk again
tonight. It's amazing to connect with a mind that has been
studying the same fascinating, albeit arcane, material that
I have been so immersed in. You on one side of the globe
and me on the other. I'm glad our worlds finally collided.
I hope you won't think I've been too Vertigo with these
gifts, but I forgot to tell you today that the restaurant is
black tie, and I was unsure what you'd brought with you.
Yours in olfactory fascination,
Anders

P.S. The flowers are edelweiss, from the German edel, *which means "noble," and* weiss, *which means "white." Those woolly leaves and white heads remind me of your porcelain paleness.*

I opened the first box and took out a tailored, plain black Chanel silk dress with a scoop neck and small covered buttons down the front. There were also black lace stockings, small-heeled black suede pumps and a beaded evening bag. I felt the silk dress with its amber lining. Amazed by the gifts, and how perfectly he'd assessed my taste and size, I sat down on the bed and stared at them. After a few minutes I folded them into the boxes to send back, but paused, realizing it was my job to lead him on.

I jumped at a knock on the door. For some reason I expected Anders and was disappointed when it was only Jackie. "Oh, hi," I said, feeling like I'd been caught in some illicit act but wasn't sure what.

"I followed Konzak," he said, looking at the box on my bed. "Do you have any idea what these duds set him back?"

"Is this *The Price Is Right?*"

"Total bill $4,300 U.S. dollars. What's his angle? Picks up a woman at his job site, has lunch with her, leaves, goes out and spends nearly five grand on her for the evening. What's wrong with this picture?"

"We're obviously not seeing the same picture," I told him. "Maybe, just *maybe*, he thinks she's attractive—$4,300 worth of attractive in an outfit that doesn't turn your crank. Besides, thanks to Daddy, who turned Russian antiquities into American dollars, he's a multi-millionaire, so it's pin money to him. That's what's wrong with your picture."

"What time are you dining? And how did he know where to send the outfit?"

"Eight o'clock and I don't know," I said as he walked out.

That evening, while looking in the mirror, I was thankful for the pink Viennese shaded glass that added a much-needed rosy glow to my prison pallor. I hardly ever wore makeup but figured, since he'd bought all those fancy clothes, I could spring for some eyeliner and shadow. When the woman in the store asked me if I wanted sparkle or plain shadow, I chose sparkle. If you can sparkle at no extra cost, why not? I even bought some blush-on and mascara. I didn't want to get too Dolly Parton, always a risk for blondes, so I just wore my hair in a sort of French twist that was partially cascading down.

As I stood in the full-length mirror, I noticed the dress was short and the lace stockings made my legs seem to go on longer than I remembered. The shoes were a titch too tight, but I remembered my mother saying to my sisters when they complained about their shoes, "The best way to forget all our troubles is to wear tight shoes." The dress was more revealing than anything I would ever have bought myself—not in bad taste, but more of a statement than I felt comfortable making. As I tried to zip it up, the invisible zipper got stuck in the lining and I was trapped in a half-opened dress. Christ, no wonder I never wore girly stuff even when I wasn't in prison. What the hell was the point of invisible zippers? Were people supposed to imagine that you sewed the dress on while standing in it? I've never seen a male fly with an invisible zipper.

I could tell Jackie's sharp rap on the door. I took one last glance at my reflection. The woman who looked back was not the Kate who usually inhabited me. But then again, I was sick of living with her. Anyway, what the hell—it's a job. I'm sure Mata Hari had on-site party wear.

Opening the door, I said, "So?" glancing up from under my mascaraed lashes.

Jackie cocked his head to one side but didn't say anything. I had no choice but to ask for assistance with the zipper. His hands were the size of mine in oven mitts. I had no idea how he was going to fit his huge paw down my dress. However, he was surprisingly nimble and his long fingers had a certain grace about them.

When he touched my back, I jumped in the air. Embarrassed by my skittishness, I complained, "Your hands are cold."

He rubbed them together and then touched my back and reached down behind the zipper. Finally he said, "I think it's fixed." Looking a bit concerned, he added, "You're arching your back. Breathe normally and let's make sure it can take normal pressure."

I walked toward the door, stopped and twirled. "How do I look?"

"Like a judge's daughter on her way to a dance at the country club."

How did he know my father was a judge? I'm sure there had been no mention in Gardonne's letter of my father being a judge. I'll have to find out everything there is on this cracked Jack. I felt like I had exposed more than a broken zipper could reveal.

While I was still reeling, he was going on about getting information from Konzak. I only caught the tail end. "Don't focus on the Freudian details, but the political details. Why is he doing it? Where did he get the info?"

"I'm aware of what to ask," I said.

"Judging from what I saw, you were trying to be little miss smarty-pants instead of doing the job you were hired to do. Let him look smart and run off at the mouth. I know that goes against your grain, but just take off your armour and listen."

"Maybe you'd like to put on this getup and go yourself," I said, snapping my beaded evening bag shut.

"When you've been in prison since the age of nine, you've worn everything to get what you need." Checking his watch, he said, "I'll wait up for you so we can go over everything while it's fresh and you can write it down. If you don't get back tonight, call on this cellphone. The number is on automatic dial under San Quentin," he added, stuffing it in my big purse.

I wasn't sure what the hell he was calling me here, but I shot back, "Obviously, the women you've associated with are used to coming back in the morning with more than a cellphone in their purses."

"The judge's daughter returns with $4,300 on her back. The only difference is the price." He smiled slightly and closed the door.

As I stomped to the cab stand, I tried visualizing leaving my rage at the curb, a mind game I'd learned in prison anger-management class.

6

A VIENNESE WALTZ

—

The trouble with words is that you never know
whose mouths they've been in.
— DENNIS POTTER

WHILE SITTING IN the cab, I pulled that widget called a *cell-phone* out of my huge satchel-like purse. I couldn't believe I had to carry a satchel with this outfit, instead of an evening purse. How the hell else could I carry this stupid thing? It looked like R2-D2 without legs. It had no cord. Was this a joke? When did they start making these things? Maybe they were made especially for the detective industry. I guessed most detectives don't have to worry about large bags clashing with their formal evening attire. If they did, they would make these dohickeys smaller. I stuffed it away, figuring if I had to use it I'd remember how.

After winding around the busy rings of Vienna, we suddenly pulled into a magnificent quiet drive that was surrounded by lavish grounds trimmed by pink roses and filled with acres of lavender. We swung around a huge fountain that divided the road, and there before me stood a glorious baroque castle. The restaurant was apparently inside the Palais Schwarzenberg. The entrance was set off by two huge black iron gaslights. The doorman wore a green quasi-military outfit, perhaps a character from a Viennese operetta, but in reality he looked more like Jiminy Cricket.

When I entered and gave my name, the waiter bowed slightly, saying that Professor Konzak was waiting. He led me among the tables, and I felt everyone stop eating and stare at me.

I spotted Anders across the room. He looked like one of the boys at a debutante ball. The dinner jacket and pleated shirt absolutely suited him. He wore it with a casual air, yet he knew what a swath he cut as he beamed at me. "I knew that dress was made for you. You really look magnificent."

"I guess we can dispense with the idea that I'm going to tell you that you shouldn't have," I said.

"I'll always remember your entrance in that outfit. You're so transformed. You'd never think . . ." He paused.

"That I was a murderer."

"I was *trying* to say that no one would ever believe that dress was designed for anyone but you."

"Sorry. I guess I'm a little touchy. I was just released. You're the first real person I've talked to." I tried to smile, while telling myself to calm down. "I appreciate your not asking about prison life and how I got paroled and all the voyeuristic nonsense people can get involved in, misnaming it 'human interest.'" I looked down and added in as demure a tone as I could muster, "I'm not ready to talk about it yet."

"Not to worry. Topic closed." Without missing a breath he moved on, saying, "It's amazing what people make out of others—all based on their own needs. I think that journalist, Dvorah Little, was mad that I didn't come on to her, so she made me sound as though I were an imbecile. She misquoted me, and now she says she *lost* the tapes. How old is that ploy? What she doesn't know is that I have my own tapes. She'll find out in court."

"So," I asked as coyly as I could, "are you the Casanova she portrayed?" I remembered what Jackie had said about getting to the politics of the affair and not the ideas.

"I'm sort of a Casanova, in the same way you're sort of a murderer. I hope you don't mind me talking about this."

"No, it's fine." I actually hated it, and thought I'd made that clear thirty seconds ago.

"It's true I've been around the block, but Dvorah insinuated that I wanted to turn the academy into a bordello, or, given the predilection of some of the analysts I know, into a bathhouse."

"Well?" I prodded.

"I never wanted that. It was part of her own agenda to discredit me. Granted, I gave her plenty of ammunition. Sure I wanted the job at the academy, and I had to wine and dine Conrad Von Enchanhauer, the previous Freudian director, and Anna Freud, the real keeper of the keys. She's a harder nut than he is. He loved me."

"Really?" I asked, trying to look casual as I perused the menu.

"Well, it's sort of hard to explain out of context. You have to be steeped in psychoanalytic culture. Rule number one: the male analysts are usually castrated and the women are sexless neurotics. In terms of a personality profile, psychoanalysts are, generally speaking, a competitive, controlling lot who are basically unhappy and tend toward the obsessive end of the spectrum."

"Who else could talk about a dream for an hour?" I said, egging him on. I had to admit, Jackie was right. All I really had to do was be an adoring audience while Anders ran off at the mouth. I got far more information than if I debated with him.

"Exactly. They're terrified to appear vulnerable to each other. They're characters out of a *New Yorker* story, whose edges have been trimmed and the only emotions they express leak out as snide remarks."

"You must have been a bit of fresh air!" I said, thinking he was no more fresh air than Pine-Sol was the woods.

"Exactly! Both Dr. Von Enchanhauer and Anna Freud were sick of those mean-spirited philistines, yet neither was temperamentally suited for psychological battle in person or in print."

"Were they relieved when you came on the scene?"

"You got that right! Plus I was smart, interested in historical research, spoke three languages, and I truly admired Freud—and still do in a weird way. I got a standing ovation from the New York Psychoanalytic when I gave my paper on the Wolfman several years ago. Did all those analysts want to have an affair with me? I came on the scene and had what both Conrad Von Enchanhauer and Anna Freud needed, a real sexual identity. Then I blew everyone away by exposing the core of high-priced analysts for what they really are: opportunistic vultures."

"Vultures? In what sense?"

"They live off the misery of others for hours of unconscious titillation. Those analysts could lay any trip they wanted on their patients, since the only raw material is the patients' perception—never reality itself."

"Can you give me an example?"

"Let's look at Freud himself," he said. "He wouldn't have made the mistake with the seduction theory if he hadn't preferred the *unconscious* theory of incest to the reality."

"So Dr. Von Enchanhauer and Anna Freud wanted a hired gun to clean up the academy and to keep the vultures at bay, but they didn't want the gun turned on them or on Freud?"

"There's the rub," Anders said. "They wanted me because I had balls, but now they think I'm on a testosterone tear."

"Do they feel betrayed?"

"Of course, although they never said so. Betrayal is a feeling. They don't deal in the *F* word. They're *way* too neurotic for that. When I went to Conrad Von Enchanhauer with my interpretation of things, he told me the whole world would not understand what I was trying to do. He kept repeating his mantra, which is that we were here to elucidate Freud and not to destroy him."

"I guess you didn't want to genuflect in Vienna."

"But if I was interested in deification instead of intellectual truth, I'd return to the Catholic Church."

"When you took the job, did you feel this way?"

"No, how could I? I hadn't seen the unpublished material yet, and I hadn't recovered the letters that Freud wrote elsewhere. Most of those families or their descendants were willing to sell their letters, but they were waiting until Anna went to the big couch in the sky. First of all, the price would go up. Secondly, who wants to sell letters knowing only the ones that are flattering to Freud will be published while the rest will be labelled 'personal'? When I took over, the information flowed like hot lava. But of course it threatened to burn them. Finding the Fliess letters was a bonanza."

"Were you wining and dining them while you had the documents in hand?" I asked.

"No, not initially," Anders said while pouring more wine in our glasses. "You have no idea how depressing their lives were. Conrad Von Enchanhauer has never had five minutes of fun. His wife looked like a Hummel figurine, and he always seemed to be atoning for some imagined sin. I simply refused to adhere to all the restrictions he put on his life. I brought him kicking and screaming into the present, and he finally began to lighten up."

"Sounds like hard work," I said, sipping my wine. I wanted to watch my alcohol intake, but I also knew I needed a bit to carry off the passive girl routine.

"Miss Freud, as she likes to be called by her closest friends, had never even been to any of the great restaurants in London. I swear, I had to show her London as though she were a tourist. The house was left exactly as it had been on the day Freud died. It was more of a shrine to Freud than an archive. She'd never had a party, or even visits from friends. All of her clothes were left over from the days in Vienna. She clomped around in Wallabees and wore those waist-length boiled-wool numbers piped in black with silver buttons that reeked of mothballs. I stayed there on the third floor in an apartment that came with the job, but the place was relentlessly depressing. They must have shared a decorator with Dr. Caligari."

After what must have been a few hours of chatter, I had to admit that although he only talked about himself, he was engaging. I was shocked when the dessert table rolled our way. Where had the time gone? As I ate my chocolate-dipped strawberries, I leaned back and listened to a violinist playing works by Mozart. It would've been nice if he hadn't been wearing a powder-blue velour waistcoat, breeches, white stockings and, to top it all off, a peruke. As I drank my coffee, the violinist was replaced by a seven-piece orchestra.

"You can't come to Vienna and not waltz," Anders said, pushing back his chair.

I had no ready refusal, so I pushed my chair back reluctantly. I was in Vienna and it was time to waltz. Although dancing seemed to work for Tina Turner, it was a form of intimacy that made me wince. To me sex never seemed as weird as dancing. At least sex was hormone assisted.

I put it off for a few minutes by saying I had to go to the powder room. I couldn't believe I'd actually said "powder room."

As I walked away, I realized I would have to commit everything to memory. As I was going over the important exchanges in my head in front of the mirror, I was interrupted by a woman who was putting on lipstick. She had that aggressively American I-dress-for-comfort Tilley-unendurable look. She spoke into the mirror above the blast of the hand dryer. "I think I recognize you from the plane from . . . Toronto?"

"Yes," I replied with a Canadian reserve that I hoped would button her up. It turned out she was from Buffalo, so all subtle hint was lost.

"That man you were with is gorgeous. I wish I were travelling alone."

"Yeah, he's something with that tan," I conceded.

"I don't mean that guy you're with tonight, I mean the guy on the plane. What a body—and those cheekbones," she said over her shoulder while leaving. "They don't make bad boys like that any more."

Anders stood up as I approached the table and led me onto the dance floor. I'd been sent to dancing school as a preteen to prepare me for my danceless teenage years. I guess my mother had no way of knowing they wouldn't have dance cards in prison.

For a man of his reputation, Anders's dancing was surprisingly wooden. Thankfully, we sat the next dance out while Anders ordered a brandy. A waiter arrived with a little sterling silver blowtorch on wheels that fired up the glass. Then Anders made a big deal of sloshing it around and sniffing it. I knew it was time to get to the business I'd been hired for.

"You've really made some enemies in the Freudian world. You may never have lunch in Vienna again. Now everyone is breathlessly sitting on the edges of their analytic couches to see what you'll expose next."

"I could have made a fortune extorting money from the New York Psychoanalytic, if I'd not had integrity," he said, extending his hand for another dreadful dance.

Realizing I was getting somewhere, I pressed on. "Did they offer you money?"

"In the academic business it's called 'a lifelong study grant.'" He continued as we looped around the dance floor. "As for the analytic couch potatoes, are you kidding? They're shaking in their Gucci loafers. They make their livelihoods from Freud. You think they're going to go under for the sake of truth and — what — live in packing crates? These people know their practices are a sham. Look at the psychoanalytic outcome research. The studies have shown that in the long run patients actually *don't* improve."

"Interesting. How did they measure improvement?" I realized I was diverging from the topic of his enemies, but I didn't want to arouse his suspicions. At least that's what I told myself. In reality I'm a methodologist at heart.

"They measured symptom improvement. Does the patient have less anxiety, less depression and so on, now that the patient and the insurance-bearing taxpayer have invested five years in daily psychoanalysis? Guess what they found."

"No symptom improvement?"

"Exactly. Now guess how the psychoanalytic community handled the outcome of the research." Not waiting for me to answer, he continued, "Get this! They said, rather ingeniously, that the researchers were asking the *wrong questions*. They *should* ask, not if the patients are *cured*, but if they *know more about themselves* than they did before the analysis."

"That's a scream. Did they get away with it?"

"You bet they did. Of course, by changing the question, they had great outcome studies and continued to get more grants, academic appointments and, most importantly, health insurance money."

"*Anyone* would 'learn more' about themselves if they wrote a diary or talked to a wall for an hour a day for the same length of time," I added. "They didn't need psychoanalysis to learn more about themselves."

"I can't believe you're saying that, because that's exactly what those who opposed the research said. To prove their point they conducted a study of four experimental groups: one that had psychoanalysis, one that wrote a diary, one that talked to themselves for an hour, and one really hilarious group that worked with a computer program that alternately asked two questions—'What did your mother feel?' and 'Tell me more about that.' The program was originally written as a joke by an MIT undergraduate, and people began standing in line to use it."

"What was most successful?"

"The MIT program. People felt better in a shorter time, their symptoms were reduced *and* they felt they knew more about themselves." Anders threw his lion-blond locks back and laughed his contagious laugh. "Those people would kill to shut me up. Don't think those anally retentive psychoanalysts are the only ones shitting their pants. This stuff is big! It's the unconscious treasure chest of the last two centuries."

Hearing our laughter, the waiter bustled over to offer another brandy, and Anders got the bill. I offered to split it, but Anders dismissed my offer, saying, "Hey, it's on the academy.

I'll call this 'a conference on successful transference.'" As he signed, he said. "Now let's go for a walk. I really want you to see Michaelerplatz and the Hofburg. The lights on the winter riding stables are magical. Believe me, I'll show you everything worth seeing in Vienna. You have to block out the twentieth century and only picture the eighteenth and nineteenth." He effortlessly switched his boundless enthusiasm from Freud to Viennese architecture.

"It should be easy at this time of night." Actually, I didn't have that much trouble blocking out the twentieth century in the daytime, but I wanted to sound enthusiastic.

"There are some great walks I want to take you on in London when you're there. Let's get out of these clothes and we can meet at my place, number 8 in Wipplingerstrasse, in thirty minutes. I'm on the third floor."

"Well, it's already one-thirty in the morning," I said with far more hesitation than I felt, knowing that his tongue was now well oiled with wine and brandy. I didn't, however, want to wind up in a situation where I'd be expected to pay back for the dress and the evening the way women were so often expected to pay for things.

"So? What are you, Austrian?" he taunted.

"I'll brave it."

We agreed to meet at his place. As we parted, he said, "Be sure to wear hiking boots. We're going to walk till dawn on rough cobblestones, and there's often horse manure on the roads."

7

A FORCED SMILE

—

It is always possible to bind together a considerable number of people in love, so long as there are other people left over to receive the manifestations of their aggression.
—FREUD, *Civilization and Its Discontents*

AFTER CHANGING INTO hiking clothes, I barged into Jackie's suite. He was sprawled on his bed reading Edith Wharton's *The Age of Innocence*. I swung my leg onto his dresser to lace up my boot. "I'm meeting Anders in five minutes to go on a hike."

"Where?"

"His place. He said to wear hiking boots—so I think he's on the level."

He nodded the kind of nod that indicates you are so wrong it's almost funny. "Most guys that want you to come to their apartment at one-thirty in the morning are, as you say, on the level."

As I tightened my laces, I said, "Why would he tell me to wear hiking boots if he had other plans?"

"He strikes me as the kind of guy that could make boots a crucial part of his evening." As he stood up, he added, "I'll follow you approximately ten minutes behind and be outside his building if you need help . . . hiking." His smirk made me realize why people used lines like, "Wipe that smile off your face or I'll wipe it off for you." However, I didn't have the time to get into it.

While walking me to the elevator, he said, "You'd better write down keywords."

"I'll remember. Besides, he's been drinking, so I want to strike while his tongue is loosened. In fact, if his tongue was any looser it would fall out." Maybe I'd had a wee drop too many myself because as I buttoned my jacket I couldn't resist adding, "I met a woman from the plane and she said the man I was with was handsome. I obviously assumed she meant Konzak, but guess what . . . she meant *you*."

"I guess that's why I never had to lay out five grand," he said, still looking straight ahead as we waited for the rickety elevator. He closed the diamond-shaped lift-grate with one hand and smoked with the other, saying, "You'd better have the cellphone. Call me from a mountaintop if he wants you to do more than yodel." He smiled as the elevator lurched away.

As I cut through the Hofburg Gardens, the yellow buds of the forsythia caught the moonlight, shimmering like gold dust, lighting the pathway. Konzak's lodging was in the old Judenplatz ghetto where Jews were once locked in behind imposing gates, but the area had now become restored to Viennese chic. The building had perhaps ten units behind a huge double door that swung open on its ancient iron semicircle. Inside was a cobblestone courtyard with tangled old vines that had minuscule new maroon shoots emerging. Apartments jutted off a worn marble staircase illuminated by iodized copper hanging lamps.

I could see a light on the third floor.

Where was he? I was getting a sinking feeling as I realized he must be waiting for me to come to his room. God, I really had bought that ol' hiking-boots number. Must be the oldest trick in the Alps. Anders was probably in his room wearing nothing but thermal socks, and when I entered he'd scream, "Edelweiss!"

I was getting colder. It was early spring, but damp and clammy. I had no choice but to go up for him. As I trudged up the winding staircase, listening to my echoing footsteps, the light in the third-floor room flicked off. I actually laughed out loud at my own stupidity. How could I have questioned Anders's prowess as "a ladies' man"? Look at the work he put into it. Today alone he took me to lunch and dinner, and had indeed spent about five grand. Now here I am, a bit tipsy myself, climbing his stairs in the middle of the night. He'll say he didn't come out to meet me because he wanted me to see the moonlight peek through the wisteria vines into his room, or some such idiocy. How quintessentially Kate Fitzgerald of me to miss the point. This is yet another trait I had in common with Freud. If he never knew what a woman wanted, I never knew what a man wanted.

Anders had left the door of his lair agape. "Anders?" I called, poking my head in. There was enough light from the hall and the moonbeams streaming in the window for me to make out a lamp that I stumbled over to and finally managed to turn on.

What I'd actually stumbled over was Anders's body. He was lying on his back with his eyes looking straight up at me, his face contorted in a grimace that resembled a forced grin. His head had been almost completely severed from his body, except for the spinal column. It dangled like a bauble on a frayed cord. There was blood everywhere—on the walls, the light switch and especially the rug—so that when I walked, my boots made a squelching noise.

Suddenly everything went dark, and I heard quick footsteps. Jesus, the murderer must have been in the room, behind the door. I heard a creak in the hallway. I ran around the body, but slid and fell. I landed in something surprisingly warm and slippery. I held my hand up to the window, where the moonlight shone on it. It was blood, and I sat in a large pool of it. I felt steaming blood on my socks and legs.

I finally got to the door and looked out. To the right there was the empty staircase I'd ascended. To the left I saw a door close and a shadow pass the exit light on the fire escape. I ran toward it, grabbed the door handle and realized he had locked it from the outside when it shut. I heard footsteps running down the stairs. Remembering the cellphone, I reached in my pocket but stupidly forgot the code for the number. It had seemed so rinky-dink detective at the time. I dashed through the phone's directory. It was something like Quentin Crisp . . . a jail . . . San Quentin. The phone was now covered in blood, and my finger trembled so much I had trouble pressing the small buttons.

Jackie answered, singing "Climb Every Mountain."

"*Listen.* Anders is dead. I haven't touched him, but his head is hanging strangely and there's blood everywhere. I, uh . . . tried to stop the guy—the killer, I guess—whatever. I couldn't catch him. I think he was still in the room when I entered. He escaped down the fire escape . . . Jackie?" I realized my voice was quivering. My mouth went dry. My speech sounded thick and I could no longer formulate words clearly.

"Sit down wherever you are. If you faint, you're no good to anyone."

I slid down the hallway wall and took some deep breaths.

"I'm near the entrance. He can't have gone far unless there was a car waiting. I'll find him. Get inside the room as soon as you can."

My adrenaline thundered in my body to the point that I had staccato blasts for a heartbeat and felt a bungee cord tightening around my chest. When it finally slowed down to where I could do more than hold my heart, I had an almost overwhelming desire to hightail it back to my cell and swing the bars shut.

Finally, leaving bloody footsteps in my wake, I struggled to my feet and walked back into the room, refusing to look in Anders's direction. As I opened the bathroom door, I thought I saw a movement behind the shower curtain, an almost imperceptible flutter. I hadn't thought that there might be more than one guy, or that someone could still be in the apartment. Wasn't Jackie supposed to think of that . . . Christ!

I forced one foot in front of the other and pushed back the curtain. Was I summoning all my courage or was I simply doing what I thought I was supposed to do? Maybe courage is no more than the terror of humiliation. Anyway, all I saw was a soap dish. It must have been the draft from the door opening that had made the curtain flap. The doors were all opened—to the medicine cabinet, the vanity and the other closet in the small hall. The murderer must have been looking for something even if he also wanted to kill Anders. Maybe he was searching for something and Anders came home at the wrong time.

I jumped in terror when I peeked into a closet and there before me stood a terrified creature who looked like a fiendish red devil, the kind that lurks behind trees trying to tempt you in grade school catechisms. I blinked and then realized I was looking at my bloodied body in a full-length mirror on the back of the closet door.

I heard a sound and wheeled around. It was coming from the other room. A voice whispered, "Hello? Hello?" It got louder. "Kate?"

Jackie came to the bathroom door and saw me covered in blood. He put his arm around me and helped me to the bed.

"Where did he get you?" he whispered.

My head felt so heavy that I couldn't believe I'd held it up for so long. It fell on his shoulder like a bowling ball. "Nowhere, I slipped in the blood trying to run out. God, I've never seen anything like this, have you?"

"Never. It's not your professional-hit-man stuff." He leaned down and examined Konzak. "This killer is one *angry* man." He stood up shaking his head and looked carefully into my sunken eyes. "You all right?"

"Yeah. For some reason I think this is my fault. I shouldn't have agreed to meet him so late."

"That doesn't make any sense. Either someone didn't want him talking to you or he planned to kill him tonight anyway, having no idea he'd agreed to meet you later. Did you get a good look at the guy?"

"No. The fire escape door has shaded glass, so I only saw a shape outlined by the red exit light. The door locked automatically when it closed, or he locked it from the outside."

Jackie pumped air out of the side of his mouth, sounding like a deflating bellows. "Shit. I cannot fucking believe this!"

"Did you find anything?" I asked.

"Nothing. A car speeding away and I was on foot. He wasn't working alone. Someone held that fire exit door open, or maybe he propped it open with something. Did you see him bend down?"

"No. I arrived just as he was almost all of the way out."

"Take a minute now and try to remember anything about him that was distinctive. You may forget later."

"Nothing really. The silhouette was dim because the light was poor. Wait . . . I smelled something familiar in the room — a smell that's gone now. I also smelled it in the hall by the exit stairs where he escaped."

"Aftershave? Cigar? Pipe?" Jackie prompted.

"No . . . more of a house smell. I remember it from my childhood. It's very distinctive." I put my hands to my temples and pressed, willing that olfactory memory to connect with a name.

Jackie pressed on. "You came up the stairs and then what?"

"The light was on when I arrived in the courtyard, and then it switched off. I assumed Anders was pulling some kind of seduction stunt when I came into the dark room, until I switched on the lamp. I guess the murderer was behind the door the whole time. He turned off the light from the wall switch and bolted. I might have been able to catch him if I hadn't slipped on the blood, or if the exit door hadn't locked."

"Let's think for a minute," Jackie said as we stared at the mayhem around us.

"I've never seen this much blood," I said, holding my jeans away from my legs. My legs were starting to chill as the blood cooled.

"You sever an artery and it spurts," Jackie said as he paced, taking a deep drag on his cigarette and slowly exhaling.

"Shouldn't we call the police?"

"We can't. We're two ex-cons with a dead body in a foreign country."

I had to agree that was quite an albatross.

"We're going to have to find the murderer ourselves. When we do, we'll turn him over to Gardonne or to the police."

"I was the last person seen with him."

"No one knows who you are."

"I was at the archives, then lunch and dinner. All public places."

"So what? You're just another broad—he had three or four a week. You're nothing out of the ordinary. No one has your name. The cops will be looking for a robber, not a blonde Freudian." His eyes darted around the room. "We'll have to make this look like a robbery run amok—take his passport, wallet and a few valuables." He looked at his watch. "We gotta be out of here by dawn. That's a max of four hours to look for the tapes and read through the documents we can't carry out of here." Reading the fear in my eyes, he said, "It'll be a while before they'll find the body. Anyway, we'll be in London by noon tomorrow," he added, patting the tickets in his breast pocket.

Somewhere in the folds of my mind I knew that I was in big trouble. To avoid panic I told myself that Jackie could stick-handle around this kind of scenario. Things had become too serious to get into a power struggle with him.

Questions began dive-bombing. Even their shadows scared me. Is Jackie going to give me an alibi if I need one? Will Gardonne back me up? How bad does it sound that I've been out for less than a week and I'm involved in *another* murder? Anxiety began pouring into my body like molten steel. I tried to stay ahead of it, but it was spreading cell by cell and I could feel the heat. I hoped when it cooled it would reinforce my heart. I had to stop this line of questioning, overrule myself, or I'd be too panicked to go on. Best just to believe we would find the murderer if I followed Jackie's instructions. God knows I blocked out my husband's Judas kiss, then my father's renunciation at the trial, and I'd always suspected Gardonne's duplicity, but I really couldn't swallow any more. A person knows when she's reached saturation. Even one drop more of betrayal and I'd split at the seams.

Jackie didn't appear to be the least bit ruffled. "They wanted something from this place," he said while rolling Anders over and removing his wallet.

As Anders's arm smacked against the floor, all I could think was, Thank God for coagulation.

"He wanted the tapes that Anders kept. I'll have to remember what he said he recorded." I leaned against the wall and closed my eyes, trying to replay what had been revealed in the restaurant.

"He said Dvorah Little taped her interview with him, slandered him with phony quotes in a magazine article. Anders sued her for slander, but she said she lost the tapes. He said that he wasn't worried about the court case because he also taped the interview."

"Did Dvorah Little know she was being taped?" Jackie asked.

"I have the feeling she didn't, but I'm not sure." When I opened my eyes and the horror of the scene reappeared, I felt that ulcerated burning you get when you've had too much coffee and haven't eaten.

Jackie raised an eyebrow, saying, "You'd better remember that dinner conversation verbatim. As it turns out, that was his last supper."

"I'll remember it better than he does," I said, glancing down at Anders. I noticed, now that his face was blank, he really wasn't as attractive as everyone thought. Half of his charm was in his constant animation and in the self-love that drew people to him. Without it, he looked just like every other blond man in his forties who was starting to fade.

I was struck by his innocence. He had no way of measuring anyone's anger because he felt so loved. He never planned to hurt anyone. He assumed they would see him as bright and clever, if a bit impetuous. His throne of security had never been threatened, and he couldn't imagine ever feeling desperation.

Rifling through his other pockets, Jackie found a packet of Tic Tacs, a small package of Kleenex and a folded note on yellow paper carefully cut into a three-by-five-inch rectangle. In the centre the following phrase was neatly printed in black Magic Marker:

It's the name game.

We both shrugged, having no idea what it meant.

After searching every square inch of the entire living room and front closet, I went back into the bedroom and saw Jackie with his feet up on Anders's desk behind a mountain of correspondence. Everything he'd scanned thus far was in one big pile with yellow notes stuck in various pages.

Ignoring me while paging through the correspondence, he mumbled, "Anders has obviously been getting some crank notes. This one is quite threatening. It was on exactly the same yellow paper as the other one:

"ONLY THE FITTEST SURVIVE."

"When Darwin said that, it didn't sound so threatening." I paused for a second and then added, "Actually, Darwin didn't say it. Herbert Spencer coined the phrase and then capitalists used it to justify everything from child labour to debtors' prison in the nineteenth century."

"I don't know what happened in your joint, but in mine the meanest perpetrators used it to justify any bullshit they felt like pulling off," Jackie said.

"No wonder Darwin was sick with an unexplained malady," I said, shaking my head.

"I'd get sick too if my theory was used as a scientific justification for the big guys to squelch the little ones," Jackie concurred.

"Sure. Why do you think *Origin of Species* was a best-seller — love of insects? It blew out of every smokestack in England," I said.

"So this little ditty," he said, holding up the yellow rectangle, "is either a threatening letter or someone quoting or misquoting Darwin, or both," Jackie said as he placed a neon note on it, marking it *N.B.*

I breezed through one of Anders's old diaries, stopping at a strange yellow paper that looked like a pat of butter that Jackie had affixed to certain pages. "Are these strange yellow stickums only available in Europe?"

"No," he said. "I brought them from Toronto. Lots of offices have them. They're called Post-its."

October 28, 1980
Met the famous murderer-genius Kate Fitzgerald, hatched from well-known Toronto egg. Father—famous judge— leading intellectual in criminal law. Never met anyone who studied criminals who wasn't one himself. Usually they don't have the balls to be real criminals, so they study them or wheedle in court on their behalf. Smart psycho- paths become criminal lawyers while dumb ones become criminals. What would a great "authority" on the criminal mind produce but a criminal! She blew Daddy's cover— I love it.

She screams patrician elegant—understates her great ass, legs that go on forever, which even lumpen Birkenstocks can't fuck up, and tits that stand at attention. Imagine all that in a sexy black dress and black lace stockings and then seducing her—in stockings only— making her discover her sexuality only for me and wearing jeans and work shirts for the rest of the world. Everyone would notice how she transformed herself for me while she remained butch for the rest of mankind. Now there's a hard-on fantasy!

She gave a paper today at the Toronto Psychoanalytic Twit Institute (day-pass-escorted, armed guard). Almost a decade so far in maximum security. What could that do to you? Probably nothing the nuclear family hadn't a jump on.

Fitzgerald castrated my blow-hard analyst, Dr. Blasser, in his bit on how Freudian theory is really a science. While cleaning the floor with his dick (I'll bet that's a short broom!) Kate Fitzgerald pointed out that in order to be scientific, the theory had to be provable and disprovable. You cannot disprove Freud. Those that try, in the words of the sage psychoanalysts, are only resisting his theory. In what science do those who question the theory become the non-scientific ones, or the heretics?—for Christ sake!

I liked her example of the leechers in the nineteenth century. Doctors carried jars of leeches to draw out "sick" blood so the patient could recover. Oddly enough, no one ever got better (shades of psychoanalytic theory), but you couldn't disprove it, all you could say was it didn't work on a particular patient; or it's the patient who is resisting leeching or a family who has turned the patient against leeching. Didn't work—sorry, you're too old to leech.

Blasser was crossing his legs by the time she got to phrenology. Franz Gall and those deluded idiots believed that the size of the bumps on the head, mostly on the medulla oblongata, was the true test of IQ. I guess it's no weirder than the methods used today. When phrenologists were told Descartes's skull would prove him an idiot, they just said, Well, he was always overrated. (Got to remember these arguments when the assholes call me unscientific.)

Fitzgerald took questions, but refused to be part of the Toronto Psychoanalytic troop when it offered her a membership. The reason was some drivel about being unable to be objective if co-opted. Probably paranoid. Does fine in a rigid structure, but will fall apart when she gets outside (where the real enemies are), like that convicted killer Norman Mailer championed. Got paroled and killed a

*waitress on his third day out. His reason was great —
should be read at all Pizza Hut training sessions: she'd
brought someone else's food when he'd ordered first . . .
Now that's enough to make you believe in self-serve!*

*Fitzgerald's crime was interesting. Bit hazy on the
specifics. Think she claimed she killed her husband as a
form of mercy killing, or maybe it was self-defence, he may
have said he was going to kill her and then himself —
typical melodramatic depression bullshit. However, hubby
had written letters saying she was trying to kill him, and
he tried to get the police to wake up, but they let him fry.
I can just picture her getting fed up with some whiny
husband and shooting him, the way a normal person
might set a cockroach motel — they check in but they don't
check out.*

Obvious moral: monogamy kills.

*Did herself in at the trial. When his parents sobbed on
the witness stand, she yawned. Her parents put the final
nail in her coffin. Why would a jury believe you if your
own parents write you off? No financial support — had to
get legal aid. Forget the details. Tabloids made much of
the fact that the parents disenfranchised her. Parents
always say, "If you screw up, don't come crying to me."
Most parents don't mean it, but not so the Fitzgeralds!*

*Society loves killers. They have the guts to do what the
rest of us fantasize. Civilization has made us into wimps.
We've had to file away all our instincts and only leave
those that advance civilization. What a straitjacket. What
the fuck happened to the noble savage? How come all
other mammals get to fight to the death for a single
mate — after all, if they didn't, how would they transmit
their genes? Chuckles Darwin was hot on that trail. Sex*

and aggression are flip sides of the same coin. The more
aggressive you are, the more sex you get. (Ask any randy
walrus how he got his scars.) People are supposed to
sublimate by going to wrestling matches or watching
porn—snuff films or whatever. No wonder porn is a
billion-dollar business. Freud says in our primary process
we make no distinctions between good and bad, we just
want to follow our instincts. We've been bred to kill. I
mean, why else would we be so fascinated with killers?
That's what's great about war: you kill people for a
civilized cause.

When a woman kills, it tells you how sexy she really is.
Fantasy—be the man who tames the shrew. There's a lot of
male power in that. I wouldn't mind getting shot by Kate
Fitzgerald sometime. Who wants to fuck a woman by
jumping on top of her for five minutes and pinning her
down? That's for tsetse flies as far as I'm concerned. Give
me a sparring partner any day. If her killing instinct is so
powerful, imagine her sexual instinct!

I looked up to meet Jackie's scrutinizing eyes. "Well"—I let
out a deep breath I'd been holding—"I guess he met someone
who didn't sublimate his aggressive instincts."

If this is how most male *Homo sapiens* feel, it's amazing there
aren't more sexual and aggressive crimes. Civilization must be a
pretty powerful force to keep this stuff under wraps. Or maybe it's
all out there in an attenuated form and I simply don't get it, like
the way some people just don't get math. I remember when my
mother and sisters used to gossip, I thought it was so petty. Now
I realize that was their way of letting off a little steam so the whole
lid didn't pop off. I just went straight for murder. I guess I could
have used a bit of sublimation. Anyway, no point in going over all

of that again. I'll just pile my miscalculation about Anders on my mountain of human misunderstandings. I actually thought he wanted to talk to me about Freud. No wonder Jackie laughed.

"Look at the next entry I've marked. It's about six months later." Noticing my hesitation, Jackie added, "The rest isn't personal."

April 10, 1981
I got another clue from the paranoid today. He's really
getting on my nerves and applying pressure that I'm going
to have to deal with soon. I don't know what he's so irate
about. He didn't go to the Princeton Center for Advanced
Studies. There's a big difference between paranoid musings
and a well-thought-out theory. I've spun his paranoid straw
into golden scientific theory. Of course, he doesn't see that.

"Someone has been feeding Konzak info and not getting credit for it," I said.

"Interesting, isn't it? By the way, we have less than an hour before dawn. We'll take the diary and the two little weird yellow notes. Leave the rest. I took his Rolex and his Walkman as well so it looks like a robbery."

Before leaving Konzak's apartment, Jackie dragged his body into the bathroom and dumped it in the tub. I glanced in the hallway mirror. Now that the blood had dried, instead of looking like the devil, I resembled a rusty Tin Man. Gone was the willowy blonde; she'd been replaced by a tired woman of a certain age whose eyelids clung to their last bit of glitter.

Exhausted, we crept back to our hotel through the narrow Vienna streets. The city had a magical quality as the dawn reflected off the golden roofs. With no people to distract us, St. Stephen's church stood at its Gothic finest. It had been attacked by lightning, earthquake and man. The Russians burned it as late as

1945. The amazing structure has been repeatedly refashioned out of its own rubble since 1450. It even has two Turkish cannonballs buried within its walls. No matter how bad I felt, I tried to remember that it too had suffered its vicissitudes and was still standing.

Jackie said we had to shower and sleep for a few hours before doing any thinking. He alleged it was a big mistake to make crucial plans when in the throes of trauma. I wasn't exactly unglued, but I felt as though I had no neural activity, like those EEG machines that show the straight line in intensive care when they've lost the patient. I remember learning that when animals are traumatized, they lie low and don't move for hours or days. Apparently, in terms of survival, it is best to hibernate or become almost catatonic until danger passes. It was amazing how, despite my efforts to the contrary, I felt myself closing down as though someone were pumping me full of intravenous Valium.

I could barely crawl through the hotel lobby. Jackie had me take off all my clothes, including my boots, in the spa of the hotel so he could chuck them. I then went to my room in a bathrobe with the hotel insignia. When I asked him where he was disposing of them, he said it was better that I didn't know in case I was ever interrogated.

Again Jackie turned out to be right. It was amazing how, after sleeping for a few hours and showering, I felt the fog lifting. I heard a knock and, tucked into the spa robe, crept to the door. Jackie smiled, said "Compliments of expense account" and threw a shopping bag complete with new wardrobe on the bed. I unpacked black Ralph Lauren jeans, extra tall, a black cashmere V-neck sweater, a charcoal T-shirt and three pairs of socks, one thermal, one cotton and one cashmere. Not bad.

When I came out of the bathroom in the outfit, I opened the other bag he had brought and there were bright blue-and-yellow hiking boots. I said, "I can't believe you bought these." Reading the label, I quoted, "'Quick-dry Gore-Tex' boots. They look like the flag of Bosnia. Do they not have leather boots in Austria? What were those Nazis clicking together when they saluted—Gore-Tex? What did Mrs. Von Trapp wear when she climbed the mountain in her escape—Gore-Tex?"

"It's 1982. No one has worn leather boots since Madame Bovary."

As I walked through the Hoher market with Jackie on our way to lunch, I stopped abruptly and said, "I hear Haydn."

"You're stressed."

"Oh yeah? Look up." We saw the famous Anker clock that bridged two buildings and where, on the hour, a life-size historical figure paraded by in profile with music to accompany it. We were lucky to be there at noon when all twelve marched out in procession and presented themselves.

"They look like marching suspects in a lineup," he said.

After the prod from Jackie, and while I was at my most post-traumatic suggestible, the life-size historical statues that marched before us, did indeed take on the sinister characteristics of the murder suspects. As Marcus Aurelius ticked slowly past the window on the bridge and popped out to greet us, I said, "My, my, Marcus Aurelius bears an uncanny resemblance to Conrad Von Enchanhauer, major suspect—highly respected Freudian analyst, writer and thinker. German Jew who lived through the war and married the woman who hid him. He actually knew Freud and was analyzed by him. He's about as inner circle as it gets, in that he's one of the few confidants of Anna Freud. He had the ear of James Strachey, who translated Freud's twenty-three-volume collected works. We are talking here about the director of the Freudian academy for decades until he got too old, and he actually *chose* Anders Konzak as his replacement."

"Hope that wasn't his best decision," Jackie said.

"Konzak told me Conrad Von Enchanhauer 'loved him.' That's a quote."

"Some people throw the word *love* around like they're on a talk show. You haven't been around for a while. In the last decade, people toss intimate terms around like they're confetti. Nonetheless," he conceded, "it is an interesting choice of words."

As we stood looking up at the clock waiting for the next suspect, Jackie asked, "How do you know what Marcus Aurelius looked like?"

"I've seen this clock before when I was here many years ago. However, I particularly know the visage of Marcus Aurelius because my father gave me a poster of him when I was a kid for my bedroom wall. It had a quote from his *Meditations* at the bottom, which said, 'In the morning, when you are sluggish about getting up, let this thought be present: 'I am rising to a man's work.''"

"That was supposed to be inspiring?" Jackie asked.

The gold filigree clock doors popped open again. This time King Rudolf danced by with his consort Anna of Hohenberg. "Ah, here comes Anna Freud holding her father's hand, of course. Let us not forget that Konzak maligned her father, the man whom she adored. She stood up to the Nazis for dear ol' dad."

Then Empress Maria Theresa filed by in her finery accompanied by Emperor Franz I. I said, "Ah, here comes Dvorah Little walking down the Strasse interviewing none other than Konzak himself. Konzak was suing her for slander for the article she wrote about him in *Metropolitan Life*. I think the sky was falling for Chicken Little because, as Konzak said, she was reduced to the lamest of excuses, saying she'd 'lost' the tapes. Also, Konzak said he had his own tapes—whatever that means. She might have been on the hook for millions, unless Konzak had an untimely passing."

Next a strange little man who I think was supposed to be the poet Walter von der Vogelweide emerged from the clock for his daily foray. "He looks weird," Jackie added, "even for a few hundred years ago."

"We can't forget the sensitive scholar, perhaps paranoid, or crackpot who is playing games here. I don't know the details, but Konzak's diary reference to the 'paranoid musings' and the messages 'It's the name game' and 'Only the Fittest Survive' on yellow paper are codes of some kind. I think the 'paranoid musings' and the yellow messages are referring to the same person. I remember reading somewhere that paranoids are known for cutting up paper in weird ways for strange purposes. Have you ever heard that?"

"You're the expert on paranoids," he said.

I thought for a minute and then conceded, "Well, maybe the yellow scrap is only the name of a bar or something. Just the same, I'd start there. Check out if there's a bar or café called The Name Game in London, New York, Toronto, Vienna or even Rhode Island, since that's where Konzak's family is from. Truthfully, I have my doubts about the bar idea. People rip match covers or coasters to write down the name of a bar."

"Exactly. I've never met some gorgeous woman in a bar and said, 'Just a minute, I have to cut up some yellow foolscap into an exact three-by-five rectangle and then write down your number,'" Jackie said.

"That's my point: obsessive people don't pick up people in bars."

"Unless that's their obsession," he added.

Emperor Maximilian I crept along next. Getting into the spirit of the clock suspects, Jackie said, "Mad Max here represents a government or group of 'concerned citizens.' It wouldn't surprise me if this whole thing is on a bigger scale than one crazed murderer."

Agreeing, I said, "There are big guys in Washington who may have been analyzed by Freud, and they don't want their records coming out in the open."

"Yeah, remember that guy, Thomas Eagleton, who was running for vice-president for about five minutes in the early seventies until it came out that he'd been treated for depression. No one wants a guy holding the red phone who's been hooked up to jumper cables."

"Christ, how'd you remember that guy?" I asked.

"I'm a news junkie, among other addictions." After a few minutes of silence, Jackie said, "We have to be careful, though. Remember that Freud died in the forties. That was well over thirty years ago."

"How old are Bush and Reagan and Chip O'Neill and Ted Kennedy? Some of them were certainly adults thirty years ago." If they'd been analyzed by Freud, or Konzak found something on them, they'd have him silenced and call it a Freudian slip."

"What about those analyzed by Anna Freud? There is another whole generation. What about some kid of the rich and famous she psychoanalyzed who is now grown up and doesn't want the rest of the world to know he wore mommy's high heels?" Jackie added.

"To say nothing of the fact that Konzak was guileless enough to let them know what he was going to reveal," I said.

"Guileless or stupid."

Next Charlemagne brought up the rear, marching ready for battle. His fantastically carved wooden minions followed close behind. "Oh, here comes Gardonne and the North American Psychoanalytic Society. Konzak hinted at dinner that 'they' had tried bribery on him. He said they called it 'a lifelong study grant.' I don't think he took it for three reasons: one, he said he had too much integrity to take some academic payoff, and in a strange way I think he did; two, he wouldn't have told me about it if he had taken it; and three, he doesn't need money or a job. It's a bad idea to bribe someone with what he doesn't need."

Jackie asked, "Do you think the extortionist would have been Gardonne working alone or someone speaking for the society as a whole?" When I shrugged in response, he continued, "I doubt it was Gardonne trying to shut Konzak up. After all, he hired us to get him to talk."

"He may have chosen me to see if Konzak was willing to tell us anything because Gardonne knew he could keep me quiet." Looking at an incredulous Jackie, I added, "And you're an ex-con who spent half of your life in the pen and can easily be bought off. If not bought off, I bet he has stuff on you from prison."

"Think so?" Jackie asked, not betraying a shred of personal involvement.

"I have no idea what you would do, nor do I care personally, I'm just telling you what Gardonne would figure. Make no mistake about it—he chose two ex-cons for a reason. And it wasn't because he buys into John Howard. He buys into one major triumvirate, which is me, myself and I."

"I'm listening," he said, gluing his eyes to the doors to catch the emergence of the next historical figure. "That clock is amazing. Imagine carving those life-size figures and constructing the mechanism that keeps the whole shebang ticking along keeping perfect time." He shook his head in wonder as he watched the figures march by to the accompaniment of Beethoven, who wrote his greatest work a few blocks away.

"Gardonne isn't above bribery, he's just chosen a more conservative angle. Before he pays out big bucks, he wants to know not only what Konzak knows but what he's willing to spread around indiscriminately."

"What do you think Gardonne was going to do when he found out what info you could get out of Konzak?"

"Bribe him or—I know it sounds far-fetched—but maybe kill him," I suggested.

"I've met killers before. He doesn't strike me as one."

"Believe me, he doesn't shrink from unpleasant tasks, he simply delegates the job to professionals."

"A hit man?"

"Bingo."

"If it had been a hit man, Konzak would have been more neatly dispatched. Do you think you're over the top here?" Jackie asked.

"I know it sounds it, but what if I'd said to you yesterday that I didn't want to dine with Konzak because I thought he might be killed before the end of the night? That would've sounded over the top."

"Why would Dr. Gardonne hire us to investigate Konzak and then kill him on the first day of the job?" Jackie asked in a slow rhythm, as though he was testing to see how deep my paranoia lay.

I realized I was taking a big chance going on. If I told him what I really thought, he might think I was a true paranoid wing nut. After all, Gardonne had warned him in the letter he sent that if I got my emotional feathers ruffled, I could slip into paranoia faster than Son of Sam.

Deciding to risk it, I said, "Gardonne tried bribery to shut Konzak up, and I don't think it worked. What was left? Maybe he hired a hit man and then he could pin the murder on us, or more specifically me, the last person to see him alive. Strange it happened on the night we met."

Jackie nodded slowly. His face gave no hint of what he was thinking. He stood with his tree-trunk legs spread rooted to the pavement, his arms folded across his massive chest. We waited silently for the next suspect to march out of the clock. As we waited, he mumbled with his cigarette dangling from his lower lip, "These third-party payment schemes are ethical quicksand. Not only do you have to stay clean, but you have to worry about the ethics of the customer. You can bump into corners with that many angles."

"I can't believe you always buy into what every one of your customers wants done," I said.

"I know what they want done, and if I don't always agree with it, at least there's no hidden agenda. I have no desire to be an unwitting accomplice in Gardonne's crime—if there is one," Jackie said, rubbing the back of his neck.

"Would that make us accomplices to a crime in the eyes of the law?"

"Depends on all kinds of things. Let me ask you something. Why did you sign up for this task if you distrust Gardonne so much?"

"Because if I hadn't 'signed up,' as you so euphemistically put it, he would have denied my Temporary Absence and eventually my parole."

"How did he let you know that?" he asked in a tone that told me he suspected I was exhibiting the paranoia he had been warned about in the letter.

"He never said it. It was implied. He's too smart to come out in the open with a threat like that." I knew having no hard evidence sounded pathetic or even paranoid.

The clock stopped ringing. All the figures had returned to their shelves, and the face went dark.

PART II

—

FINE CHINA

—

8

A TICKET TO RYDE

—

Come, . . . to the Isle of Wight;
Where, far from noise and smoke of town . . .
You'll have no scandal while you dine,
But honest talk and wholesome wine,
And only hear the magpie gossip
Garrulous under a roof of pine.
—TENNYSON, "To the Rev. F.D. Maurice"

JACKIE AND I boarded the first plane out of Vienna, relieved to be going to London, which was crawling with suspects. First was Freud's trusted archivist, Dr. Conrad Von Enchanhauer. Then we would move on to Freud's daughter, Anna, who lived in the old family home that was the site of the largest Freudian archives.

The stewardess, dressed as Mary Poppins, handed me the London *Times*. I couldn't believe that on the front page was the third excerpt from Dvorah Little's article, with the following headline:

ANDERS KONZAK, THE FLASHY DIRECTOR OF THE FREUD ACADEMY, REFERS TO HIS OWN LEGION OF INFIDELITIES AS A SICKNESS

It was jarring to read about him in the present tense. Pointing to the caption, I nudged Jackie and asked, "Why did he cause such a sensation?"

"Blow the whistle on Freud and have sex with thousands while doing it—sounds pretty interesting to me," he said, pointing to the headlines in the *Tribune*. "He's in here too, similar spread."

"I think his hold on others was his ability to ply them with unlimited adoration or whatever it was they needed until they were hooked, and then they returned the attention in spades. It's a bargain made with the devil in the form of Eros—no wonder he has arrows. When dancing with Konzak, I realized it had little to do with sex. Those sexual conquests are just a way of quantifying his hits." Jackie was still looking at the paper and not responding, so I said rather pointedly, "You know what I mean?"

"I know more about real sex than you know about Freud," he said while perusing the sports section.

"I wasn't delving into *your* sexual proclivities. I was just trying to figure out why someone with the intellectual clout of Von Enchanhauer would say he *loved* a lightweight like Konzak."

Jackie shrugged. He then opened a folder labelled *Von E.* and read aloud: "'The good doctor is married to Sofia Von Enchanhauer, a major player in the Austrian aristocracy. Her father was one of the most powerful manufacturers in Europe and the family still has substantial land holdings in Vienna, Berlin and New York. Conrad Von Enchanhauer was Jewish and she was the perfection of Nazi youth. Her family disapproved, but they came around. They have two children, both World Cup sailors.'"

"Sailing isn't the usual activity for children of survivors. They feel threatened enough on dry land," I offered.

"I guess it isn't the Jewish half that sails."

Circling Heathrow, we glimpsed a patchwork of perfectly furrowed fields and my old affection for England flooded back, the kind of feeling we reserve for the place where we lived in our early twenties, when only challenges lay ahead and failure seemed destined for others. The years I'd spent happily ensconced at Oxford, unspoiled by the shadow of family, washed over me. The memories of languorous hours debating in low-ceilinged pubs when ideas could keep you up at night, and nosing in second-hand bookstores along narrow, winding streets, made me turn to Jackie and exclaim, "Don't you just love England?"

"Too old and too cramped. I prefer Canada's West Coast. I'm not a rolling-hill kind of guy. I prefer the jagged Rockies."

After unpacking in his adjoining room, Jackie knocked as I unbraided my hair. His first piece of news was that we had just missed Anna Freud. She was travelling, giving lectures and fundraising for her Hampstead clinic. She was expected back in two days. To top off Jackie's investigative tour de force, he said Conrad Von Enchanhauer wasn't in his London home in Kensington, but at his stone cottage on the Isle of Wight.

Don't detectives call ahead or have some idea if people are going to be home before they fly across the ocean? Anyway, this was Gardonne's nickel, not mine, so I said, "No problem. I know Wight, it's only a few hours from here off the southern coast near Portsmouth. It's gorgeous, and the heather and wild daffodils should be in bloom since it is so far south. I hope we're not too early. Buy some hiking boots in London today and then we'll take a train down to Portsmouth and hop a ferry to Ryde, interview Von Enchanhauer and then catch Anna when we get back to London."

"You're hooked on hiking boots," he said.

As I unpacked, the thought of the wildflowers and sea air that awaited us made me so happy I couldn't help but sing "Ticket to Ride." Jackie actually sang along in harmony and I couldn't help wondering how he'd learned harmony in solitary confinement. "The Von E.s probably have a slip at Cowes. It's a famous yachting centre. No doubt they're there to watch their sons race."

"I wonder if their yacht is called the *Freudian Sloop*."

"Tied up in the *Freudian Slip*," I said as I continued to unpack. "Cowes is only half an hour from the mainland, but too crowded and 'hail fellow well met' for my taste. The southwest part of the island is rustic and lovely."

"Spare me the thatched-cottage number."

"Sorry, it ain't San Quentin. You'll have to put up with the coast sparkling from white chalk cliffs with wild pyramidal orchids and the sea breeze carrying its fragrance for miles."

"All in a day's work."

"I'll take you to the spot where Tennyson wrote *In Memoriam*."

"I can't wait."

"We'll stay in Shandy's Manor. It's a centuries-old house that was last remodelled in the nineteenth century and made into a country inn. I'll book us into two of the most inspiring suites, the Lord Tennyson and the Keats. They have copies of the original works displayed in the actual rooms where they were written for the visitor to read, with all of the original crossings-out. I once stayed in the room where Keats had looked out the window during a storm and wrote:

> "It keeps eternal whisperings around
> Desolate shores, and with its mighty swell
> Gluts twice ten thousand caverns—"

"Speaking of 'ten thousand,'" Jackie interrupted, "I'd better let Gardonne know we're riding to Ryde in case someone else loses their head."

"What did Gardonne say when you told him about Konzak's untimely demise? I'll bet he barely lifted a tweezed brow."

"I sent him a fax at his office. I didn't go into details. If what you think about him turns out to be true, I don't want him to use the fax as Exhibit A. I told him to fax me through my office and I'd contact him again from London. I wrote that I assumed he would want us to continue to search for what Konzak will be publishing, since it may have gone to the publisher already, or to find out who would have wanted Konzak killed. I said if he didn't want us to continue, he could let us know in London and we could settle up."

"Do you think he'll want us to carry on?"

"Who knows? I only know that I keep getting my per diem plus expenses till someone tells me to stop."

Standing on the deck while the ferry docked on the Isle of Wight, we felt the temperature drop. The air tasted salty and cool. The hardy flora had to withstand the island storms, and the result was that the heather was purpler than on the mainland and the cowslips more deeply yellow. Nature seemed to have decided that if you made it through the wind and the storms, you deserved to be more resplendent in your own beauty. After docking we drove in our dinky rental car along roads that were so narrow we had to get out at one point and pull back the flowering shrubs in order to see the road signs.

The inn was more magnificent than I'd remembered. The huge curved window and the carved mouldings framed a view of grand rhododendrons that were as big as willow trees and bowed after the rain, burdened with swollen clusters of vermilion blossoms. Only shortly out of my cinder-block cell, I luxuriated in my own room and antechamber, spreading everything out comfortably. I folded myself up on the pale celery-coloured, cushioned window seat and looked out at the countryside as I read from the copy of Tennyson that was left in every room, a refreshing change from a Gideon Bible.

Jackie rang to say, "I've called for dinner reservations and guess what—the attire is jacket only and you should dress accordingly."

"Sorry. I don't remember that. In the height of tourist season we could have gone elsewhere, but we're a few weeks early. I guess we have no choice, unless we travel on those ribbon roads for an hour at night, driving on the wrong side."

"Well?" he pressed.

"I only have that black outfit from Konzak." I didn't relish putting that on.

"Well, I'm hungry. Let's get on our gear and go."

I stopped dead when I saw him in the lobby. He was wearing a soft moss-coloured Italian suit with a black turtleneck underneath. He smiled the first unguarded smile I'd had from him. He walked up to me and took my arm in a formal way, wrapping it around his. While waiting to be seated, he said, "If you don't have a break on a long case, you get stale. We need to relax tonight."

I glanced into the empty, palatial dining room. We, like the daffodils, had arrived about two weeks before the official spring opening. The maître d' indicated that we could sit where we liked. I chose a round table in an alcove surrounded by curved windows with a bowed floor-to-ceiling window draped in Venetian-cream silk curtains. The bow was furnished with two curved gilt-and-marble console tables on which stood elaborate candelabra. Behind the candelabra were eight-foot gilt-framed mirrors that reflected the candlelight. The flickering candles danced around the room and bounced off the walls, which were stippled in yellow, apricot and grey. A bowl of grape hyacinths stood on the white damask tablecloth. Behind Jackie's chair there was a large stone fireplace that, although it looked medieval and had what appeared to be ancient carvings of St. George slaying the dragon, was surrounded by nineteenth-century William Morris tile. Not only was the fireplace taller than Jackie, but the oversize andirons were the first thing I'd seen dwarf him.

When the waiter poured wine from a Waterford cut-glass decanter, Jackie lifted his glass and toasted, "To a night off the job and each other's case."

I was overcome with the beauty of the place and the brilliance of James Adam's architectural design. Although I'd been there decades earlier with my parents and sisters, I, like most teenagers, had paid little attention to the hotel, being more concerned with where I could get a hamburger and fries and ride horses. Today it seemed magical to me. Maybe it was because, for the first time, jail and all of its monochrome indignities seemed so far away. I looked over at Jackie and knew that he knew what I was thinking because he'd been there too.

Something had come over me that I didn't recognize. The room looked enchanted and Jackie, of all people, looked stunningly handsome in his captain's chair, with the fireplace behind him casting shadows on his sharp features. I had never known someone who could look quite so altered in different circumstances.

The moonlight made the purple wisteria vines outside of the window look like they'd been dipped in silver. We both sat sipping our wine. He smoked and leaned back in his chair. The silence was companionable and not the least bit awkward. The waiter asked if we wanted a menu, and Jackie, like me, seemed to want to savour the moment, telling him we'd wait a bit.

Maybe it was the combination of the wine, the Konzak trauma, the return to a country where I'd been so free and the dress, or maybe it was having had Jackie take my arm after so long without real human touch, but I felt something loosen inside of me. I told him how beautiful the room was and how amazed I was that Tennyson had written his famous poem *Maud* in this very manor, and may have been inspired in this exact seat by the bow window.

"You were right to bring us here. It's nice to see you so happy," Jackie said.

"Don't you like it?"

"Sure. But I like it more seeing it through your eyes. I love how you know about all the tiles and the window frames and who made what—the Bristol blue glass—the whole thing. I travel a lot on expense account, but I never look for anything but under-ground parking. Seeing all the features come to life as you explain them makes me realize there's a hell of a lot more to see than I've paid attention to. Sometimes it's nice to meet people who have a different background and see the world through a new lens."

"We also have a large chunk of shared history," I said.

"Yeah, but you just stopped in as an already formed human being. Really, jail is all I've ever known. For the life of me I can't figure out where the last fifteen years went. It feels like I just walked out of the joint. The four-year university stint is a vivid and great memory, but the rest is a fog. My Toronto apartment means no more to me than a jail cell."

"How old were you when you were first sent up?"

"Young. Eight, maybe nine. A lot happened before that. My mother was an Italian immigrant. She got pregnant at fifteen and my father married her. My father bailed before I could talk, and my mother, who had two kids by sixteen, drank her meals and smoked in between. By the time I was five, I was already stealing food for me and my four-year-old sister. My mother would give us peanut butter, but my sister was allergic to peanuts and almost died. She eventually OD'd anyway, so I guess I could have saved her twenty rotten years and let her eat peanuts."

"Is stealing how you wound up in jail?"

"No, I was really a good thief. My sister and I did it together. She was the lookout. She had the curly blonde hair of my German father and really didn't look the part. My mother said she needed to work and couldn't afford to keep us. To be fair to her, it was before relief had kicked in. Anyway, she dumped us in foster residences, but we kept running home — you know, following the bread crumbs, but there was no Hansel and Gretel ending. She finally said she couldn't control us, so I was labelled 'recalcitrant' and my sister was called 'unmanageable.' I was put in what was then called 'industry' — jail for kids.

"I wanted to get out. I started a fire in an empty barn on the property when I was nine. I thought that would make them let me go home, or else my mother would see that I needed to be home. What they did then was put me in adult lock-up."

"How did you get stuck for decades?"

"I bought in. I was the only kid at the prison. I did what you did for your dad. I picked the most respected members of the prison population. The ones that parented me and showed me the ropes became my family. They looked out for me. I'd never felt that before. I wanted them to be proud of me. I became more and more outrageous, did more time in solitary than anyone else, moved into the big stuff — wholesale drugs, bank robbing. I thought I was the cream rising to the top. I had no idea that shit floats."

"Did your mother ever visit you?"

"Never. Neither me nor my sister. We looked like my father and she hated him. She married again at twenty-five and had three more kids. She was still a head case and mean as a snake, but she'd grown up enough to know she had really screwed up with us. I mean, she was fifteen, you can't really blame her, she was just a kid herself. She didn't want me or my sister around as reminders of her past or as bad influences on her new, stupid but well-behaved children and janitor husband. We were the signs that she'd had roller heels as a teenager."

"What happened to your sister?"

"I introduced her to heroin. I was doing it. Told her it helped the pain. She was dead before she was twenty."

"Sad story."

"I made it out."

"Was Gardonne your shrink?"

"No. I got labelled uncooperative. You just have to flip a few shrinks' desks for that to happen. Besides, he was more interested in the stock fraud kind of guy."

"How did you know him?"

"They give all prisoners some IQ test when they are assessing you for work within the prison system. He liked my score, so he wanted me to be a spokesman for some TV show they were doing. I worked with him on that since it beat whatever other bullshit they had organized. It was early on in my career and, truthfully, he wasn't bad to me."

As we ate dinner, we talked and laughed with a real gallows humour about jail and its proclivities. He howled when I told him how I'd broken into the computer and read the files and, once in a while, added things to people's files depending on whether I liked them or not.

During my dessert trifle I was laughing hard at some of the stories he told about scams in the yard when a piece of my hair fell out of my hair clip and flopped on my face. He took the lock and gently placed it behind my ear, saying, "You look beautiful in the candlelight." He said it as a kind of fact with no emotional overtone, which scared me to death. My face heated up and my neck felt flushed from rushing blood. I was unable to respond. I knew that I was blushing as only a blue-eyed blonde can, with deep wine-red colour spilling over my face.

Looking up as the waiter took away our plates, I caught a glimpse of something at the entrance to the dining room that I hoped was an apparition. Gardonne. I shot Jackie an incredulous glance. He flashed back a look that had already gone steely and said the previous moment was over, and maybe never really happened.

He smiled with the understated nod of a detective, stood up, shook hands with Dr. Gardonne and motioned toward a chair, sweeping anything he had shared with me off the table like a crumb.

Dr. Gardonne offered no explanation as to why he would be halfway around the world on this island. As usual, he broke the silence. "Kate, you look lovely." He paused, which was unusual for him. "Remarkably content under the circumstances." I glared at him, feeling less content by the second. He continued, "I know that you've been working terribly hard, so I'm happy to see that you have found time to enjoy yourselves."

I felt caught out, yet was furious at myself for my emotional nakedness. I glanced at Jackie, who looked perfectly composed.

Getting nowhere with me, Gardonne turned to Jackie and said, "I received your fax about Anders Konzak's . . . mishap. Although I understand why you chose not to go to the police, it does place us all in an awkward position." Feeling the chill at the table, he offered, "I was at the Tavistock Institute in London at a conference on the schizoid personality and decided it would be easy enough to take a train down and meet you. The less in print the better."

"I understand your concern," Jackie said. "We have a tight list of suspects and we feel fairly confident that we can wrap this up quickly. When we've got the murderer in our sights, I'll inform you and then we can decide on how to involve the police."

Gardonne's intonation went dead flat, something I'd never heard from him before. "Jackie, I don't feel reassured."

"I know you're thinking that Kate was last seen with him and you hired her, so you are implicated. However, you have less to worry about than you think. No one knows her name. I think it will take a while to find the body. Despite being high profile, Konzak had no fixed job or address. His mail could pile up in Vienna and they would simply assume he was in England. Eventually the smell will go into the hall, but you'd be surprised how long that will take. He's in the bathroom with the window open. Everything is under control."

Gardonne turned his glower from Jackie to me. "As usual, Kate, you're guided by brevity." When my brevity continued, so did he. "Kate, I feel badly involving you in what I thought was an intellectual challenge but has turned into something quite grisly. This is the last thing you need at such a vulnerable time of your reintegration to the outside. I came partly to see if I could be of any help and to inform you that if you want to leave the case, I would understand."

"I can hang in."

Clearly frustrated by my lack of response, he said, "We need to be prudent. The reality is, I hired you to investigate a man who was murdered on the first day of the investigation. Naturally I would like my name to be kept out of it. I understand that may not be possible, and I don't want you to do anything illegal. Kate, I would appreciate it if you would co-operate with me in this relatively honest request." He leaned his arms on the table in his let's-talk-turkey mode. "I hear what Jackie is saying. However, what are you going to say if you *are* implicated by the police?"

Jackie broke in. "I can always say that she was in my room at the time of the murder. Your name will never come up. They can't trace it, since you paid me in cash."

Gardonne leaned back. Mission accomplished. He poured himself some wine while asking me, "What was your impression of Konzak?"

"A lightweight with a bigger ego than brain. However, he wasn't stupid and could get people to reveal information against their better judgment. His lack of discretion had the ring of refreshing honesty when you were with him."

"What about his book, which will, no doubt, be published posthumously?" Gardonne inquired.

"The book, as far as I can tell, is rather nebulous. I'm going to check for the manuscript at the London archives when we get back from interviewing Von Enchanhauer. I don't know if it's gone to the publisher yet. Konzak said something about getting it together to be out in a few months."

"What's going to be in it?" Gardonne asked.

"Supposedly it's a new edition of Freud's correspondence with Wilhelm Fliess. There has already been an annotated Freud–Fliess abridged and incomplete correspondence published a number of years ago, which became the first volume in the standard edition of Freud's collected works. Konzak says it's time for a new edition because he has unearthed more letters and has information which will place the letters in a new light. I suspect, from what he said to me, that he's already blown his whole wad to *The Washington Post*. His annotations will be his simplistic interpretations of Freud's motives, which have about as much validity as a Ouija board."

"Can he carry it off?" Gardonne asked.

"There's no doubt he could have sustained a talk show with his animation and conviction, but a book of 'revelations' would be thin indeed. To say nothing of historical context. He could never imagine an era where he didn't exist. If the book comes out, his public will scatter like church mice when his intellectual nuggets spin into intellectual straw. You need more than adolescent rebellion to sustain a book."

"So you're saying we have very little to worry about when and if the book is released posthumously."

"Once you've read Freud, you realize he has thought of more contingencies than his critics have given him credit for. What he doesn't cover in one volume, he'll mention in the footnote of another edition added fourteen years later. There's no doubt that Konzak knows how to dig for material, but Freud was smarter."

"Thank you, Kate. I knew I picked the right person for the job. I'm relieved we're not at odds on this, as there is so much work ahead that has to be carried out quickly and with no conflicting loyalties."

What a terrifying thought. I managed to say, "It's a fortuitous accident that you want Konzak to be in an intellectual wasteland and that is, in fact, where he is permanently marooned." Realizing I no longer had to spend fifty minutes with Gardonne, I reached for my clutch bag, saying, "I rise at five a.m. to run, and for the first time I can do it outside among the heather, so I'll say good-night."

Dr. Gardonne stood up formally and shook hands, while Jackie stayed seated and nodded.

No one answered when I called the desk to arrange a wake-up call. These historical inns are great on atmosphere and low on service, just like the rest of England, I groused as I stomped down to the desk.

I stood in the small lobby waiting for the decrepit proprietor, who clearly felt that in the off-season he could afford the luxury of slumber. I had noted his posh accent when we arrived, the kind of guy who felt guests were somewhat of an intrusion in his regal residence—but had acquiesced to becoming part of the National Trust when he realized someone had to pay the outrageous taxes. I counted only three of the fourteen keys had been taken, and that had to be Jackie, Gardonne and me. The proprietor's checking the register to see if he had room when we arrived was a scene out of *Fawlty Towers*. He'd acted like he could squeeze us in and would not have to send us to the stable.

The baronial living room where the front desk was located jutted off a large, ancient, stone-flagged entrance hall that was empty except for some huge blue-and-white Chinese ginger jars. The small bar, which must originally have been a study or parlour, jutted off the other side of the entrance hall. As I stood at the front desk, the voice of Dr. Gardonne, a psychiatric foghorn, echoed in the empty hallway. As I inched out of the living room and into the hallway, I figured Gardonne and Jackie were the only people in the bar besides the young bartender, who doubled as the bellhop. I slid into the hallway and tiptoed on the flagstones, realizing I was practically alone in a large mansion and could eavesdrop at will.

As I crept closer, I heard Gardonne say, "Without saying anything which would betray our confidentiality, I know Kate quite well. After all, I've been her therapist for nearly a decade." Jackie's response was an inaudible murmur, but Gardonne continued to blast forth. "I want to warn you that she can become quite paranoid when she's faced with an emotional attachment. She has been known to decompensate—"

Jackie interrupted, saying, "Leave the jargon in the shop, will ya, Doc?"

"Sorry." Dr. Gardonne went on to explain, "She can lose contact with reality. She has been considered dangerous, even in the prison milieu." There was a brief silence where they both must have been drinking. "She was placed in solitary after pulling a knife on a woman in her cellblock. She cut her to the point where she needed medical attention."

Christ, he's bringing up that stale tale. As if Jackie is going to even blink at that diddly-shit. Again Jackie's voice was muffled, so I edged closer to the bar door, slithering along the wall, but I could still hear only Gardonne. "Jackie, I feel that I need to be frank with you. The reason I came down here is that I wanted to ask you in person if you believe that Kate had anything to do with the murder."

"I thought of it. I'd be a fool not to. Since there was no sign of struggle, I'll put my money on Konzak having been out of commission—stun gun or poison—before his throat was slit. Kate could have poisoned him in the restaurant, where the dishes went through a high-power dishwasher so there will be no trace. Konzak made it back to his apartment. She came back to the hotel to change her clothes because she knew there might be a struggle, one she could never carry out in high heels. Also, her presence in my room would give her an alibi. She could always say he was killed when she was changing. She went to Konzak's apartment, found him comatose, slit his throat, folded the knife, the small kind they smuggle into prisons, flushed it down the toilet, threw things around to make it look like a break-in and then called me. One thing she didn't count on was that I'd be so close behind and she wouldn't have time to change her bloodied clothes. She said she tripped over the body and that the murderer got out the fire exit door.

However, when I got there two minutes later there was no one in sight."

"Oh my God. Why would she do it?" Gardonne asked.

"She's killed before. When men get too close and simultaneously betray her trust, she could lose it and kill again. Who really knows? You're the shrink."

I had trouble holding myself up. I looked around the lobby and found room in an apse that was meant for statuary—which was perilously close to what I was at the moment. I crawled in behind a Ming Dynasty pot and leaned on the blue patterned cover for support.

"I thought this project would be an intellectual task that would be perfect for her. My desire to help her overshadowed my judgment. I should have analyzed my motivation more clearly." He ordered another Glenfiddich. "Does Kate know that you think she did it?"

"I don't think she did it. You asked me if she was a suspect. I'd be a fool not to see her as one. She was the last to see him alive and she has a history. Problem is, she has no motive."

"You just explained the motive."

"Sure it's a motive. It fits, but not like a glove. I don't believe Konzak was ever an emotional issue for her. She had a good time and was flattered and all that, but he never really pushed her buttons." Gardonne must have looked at him askance, because Jackie said in a tone that indicated he'd been challenged, "Listen, you know what *decompensate* means. Congratu-fucking-lations. However, I know when a man is under a woman's skin."

There was a long silence until Gardonne came at it from another angle. "She can be a good actress. People without consciences are very rarely betrayed by anxiety related to guilt, because they have no guilt. That's why they're so convincing."

Without consciences? Holy shit. I rested my face on the cool porcelain.

"She would have, if what you say about her acting talent is correct, put on a better show when we found him."

Gardonne isn't trying to find out if I was the killer; he's trying to implicate me, or else scare Jackie out of forming an alliance with me against him. I wondered what I could possibly find out about Gardonne if I did align myself with Jackie against him. Gardonne was coming perilously close to framing me. Jesus, I'd better tap into his agenda before I'm scratching my head on death row in a foreign land. I edged as close to the door as I could get without casting a shadow in the doorway, to hear Jackie's response, but he was silent.

Gardonne hesitated and then said, "I don't want to be indelicate."

"Then don't," Jackie said, and I heard his ice chips jingle.

"May I ask you one thing?" Jackie didn't say anything. "Are you attracted to Kate?"

I wanted to run away but knew I was rooted.

"No aging, skinny ex-con who fancies herself an intellectual is going to bring my pecker out of my pocket on or off the job."

Gardonne pushed. "Some men find intelligent women a turn-on."

"Yeah? How come Madam Curie isn't a pin-up girl?"

I turned tail and tiptoed across the stone floor like the mice in *The Nutcracker* who realize their short night of coming alive has ended. I scurried up the grand staircase fearing I was not headed for the palace of the sugar plum fairy but a big house of another hue.

After bolting my door, I waited for the tears. None came. I guess people cry over sadness, not emptiness. I was just right back where I started.

I wondered why I had been so taken with Jackie. Christ, even his teeth looked like they'd been worn down. He'd begun to metamorphose into someone who was appealing—handsome, manly in the sense that he didn't have anything to prove. He had also been through his own hell and wasn't whining about it, and that felt like a bond. Of course, it wasn't a bond, it was only common experience. He was probably a born psychopath and was only manipulating me. But then again, Gardonne says I'm a psychopath, so that may be another bond.

If I didn't pull myself together and fight both of those guys, I'd wind up back in prison saying, "I *knew* they were framing me, but I tucked away this atom of hope that they were on my side."

The first thing to do when you smell mendacity is to remember that you have to be your own agent. Who the hell else can you trust?

I had to check out Gardonne's room and see if I could find anything that would give me any leads. I slunk down the stairs to the unmanned desk. With Jackie and Gardonne still droning on in the bar, I skulked behind the desk and took the spare key to Dr. Gardonne's room off the hook.

I felt more like a detective than a genuine burglar while unlocking Gardonne's door with the big old-fashioned key. Inside, it smelled like his office—a combination of pipe smoke, dry-cleaned clothes and shoe polish. He had ordered one of those suit pressers that he'd plugged in and his Brooks Brothers sat in its little hot stockade.

I rummaged through his toilet kit and found his Clinique-for-the-active-man astringent. His suitcase had the usual boring socks, underwear and psychological journals where he hoped to find his name in a footnote. He had a leather zip sewing kit, the kind of accoutrement they might sell at an upscale men's store for Father's Day. As I unzipped it, I noticed a rusty medal or medallion pinned to the top of the black satin. If he had something old, it was usually refinished. This looked like a piece of junk, too oxidized to read. I pinned it to the lining of my dress in hopes of cleaning it up later. There was a phone number written next to his bed, so I jotted it down and tiptoed out.

As I was about to enter my room, Gardonne came down the hall and said, "Oh Kate, I'm glad I have you alone for a moment." He looked up and down the empty hall and hesitated, looking more unnerved than I'd ever seen him. "Kate . . . Kate . . . I don't want to betray any confidentiality, but for your own protection I think that you should know that Jackie is a sexual predator."

"*Please*, who isn't? Read Darwin. Go to a singles bar."

As my door swung shut, his voice squeaked under the wire, whispering, "Ask yourself why he did so much solitary."

The door locked automatically. I leaned against it, realizing we had all dispatched the heavy artillery.

After I scrubbed the medallion with toothpaste, the words *Woodsman of the Year* appeared. There were smaller, less decipherable letters on the other side. Finally, with the help of nail polish remover, I made out *Onondaga Troop No. 189*.

A knock on the door startled me. Quickly tossing the medal into a drawer, I asked, "Who is it?"

"Tennyson." He tried the door, saying, "It's Jackie. I want to make arrangements for tomorrow."

I tightened my robe over my dress, unlocked the door and ignored him while walking to the vanity to brush my hair.

Jackie sauntered in with his confident sexy walk and beamed that mercurial smile my way.

"Save the leer for the strippers' runway."

Not missing a beat, he nodded. Jackie had perfected the loco-motion of the amoeba—when he hit an obstacle, he could effortlessly reverse direction. "Fine," he replied as he headed back toward the door and said evenly over his shoulder, "We have to go to Conrad Von Enchanhauer's at eight in the morning. I'll meet you after breakfast." He closed the door firmly behind him.

9

ENGLISH MANOR HOUSE

—

The ego is not master of its own house.
—FREUD, A Difficulty in the Path of Psychoanalysis

WE DROVE TO the Von Enchanhauer cottage in silence. As we pulled onto a dirt side road, Jackie said, "I sent a fax to Von Enchanhauer telling him that Konzak has been threatened and that we've been hired by the psychoanalytic task force to investigate. Because these guys stand at attention if there are letters after your name, I also told Gardonne to send him a note on the official association stationery thanking him for his co-operation."

"He is going to know he is a suspect. I mean, we are all suspects."

"Oh," Jackie said with no perceivable expression. "I didn't know I'd been added to the suspect list."

"Really? Isn't it possible that Gardonne hired you to get rid of Anders Konzak? You run to Konzak's apartment while I walk, kill him quickly—after all, you're twice his size—go down the fire escape and wait for me to call. It's a perfect set-up. You and Gardonne pin it on me since I was last seen with him on the

day of the murder, and I am coincidentally a previously convicted murderer. If I recall, it was your idea not to call the
police."

"It's possible," he said, nodding as he pushed in the lighter.

"I'm surprised that you agree with the intellectual fantasies of
an aging, skinny ex-convict," I said.

Jackie nodded as though he understood the change in mood.
We drove along in silence above the chalky cliffs looking
toward Tennyson Down. Finally he said, "I wondered why, when
Gardonne had me alone at the bar, his emotional emphasis was
not on Konzak but on you."

"He might be nervous that he's hired an ex-patient, which is
contrary to the code of conduct for a psychiatrist, and is now
sweating bullets about it," I suggested.

He leaned back on his headrest and slowly let smoke escape
through his nostrils. He looked like a burned-out dragon. Finally
he said, "You're a big package, but Gardonne had always handled
you alone. Either he's got something to hide and is trying to use
the divide-and-conquer technique, or he's romantically interested in you and is anxious now that you're outside of his reach."

Knowing the romantic angle was way off base, I quickly
responded, "He's never shown any personal interest in me in
nine years."

"Maybe you just didn't get it."

"Isn't that thing kind of hard to miss?" I asked.

"Not if that part of your brain is atrophied or if some part of
you wants to miss it. I have the sense that you have no idea how
people feel about you, which, as far as I can see, is the basis for
most of your problems."

"I've already got one bad psychiatrist—thanks."

There was quiet in the car as the bushes on the narrow road
threatened to scratch the windows. I felt an inner quaking and

my mouth tasted as though I'd been chewing aluminum foil for breakfast.

"I don't know if you eavesdropped on the rest of the conversation I had with him, but as soon as I referred to you as unappealing, using prison vernacular, he returned to the details of the case and seemed far less agitated."

"It seemed to have done the trick." I couldn't resist adding in the tone of a scientific lab report, "I had no idea that peckers were kept in pockets—quite a stash." As we rounded the final curve, I added, "I understand they put you in solitary if yours sees the light of day too often."

Jackie nodded smugly, as though he'd been expecting me to say exactly what I'd said. "You can take this wherever you want, 'cause I've already been in that big house and wiped my shame on the mat." After he smoked a cigarette and ground it into the ashtray, he said, "For example, I told you what I chose to tell you last night about my life because for me they are only facts about my life. There is no longer any shame attached to them."

As we drove along with open fields of purple blooming heather, I had this gnawing feeling of wanting to believe him. I knew I'd better shore up my defences. The stakes were too high at this stage to risk getting sandbagged by Gardonne or Jackie.

Von Enchanhauer's "cottage" looked like an English manor. Built with ancient fieldstone, it had bow windows threaded in clematis vines. The deep thatch was cut out on the second floor to make rounded dormers. An aproned housekeeper who stood in stark contrast to her exquisitely detailed surroundings answered the door. In her full-length orange apron slick with ground-in dirt, she resembled a carved pumpkin whose pulp has been hollowed out for a jack-o'-lantern. Her accent was from one of those Balkan countries that kept changing their borders.

She invited us in, saying Dr. Von Enchanhauer would be "down soon." Then she muttered "Down soon" again and backed out of the foyer.

Dr. Conrad Von Enchanhauer smiled as he entered the room. He made a slight bow to greet me and shook Jackie's hand. He was old and craggy. There was something overplayed about his demeanour, almost as though it were a parody of the aging Jewish Freudian intellectual who hovers over a desk all day combing through obscure tomes. As Jackie began producing our credentials, the professor said in a thick Austrian accent, "That will not be necessary, Mr. Lawton. May I offer you some tea before we commence."

Jackie declined. I knew that I should as well, since accepting would turn Von Enchanhauer into a host instead of a suspect. However, I was sick of playing Jackie's private dick game, so said, "Earl Grey, please."

Tea was delivered by a clean-aproned Tefonia. The pot was a beautiful hand-painted blue, with a lid in the shape of a ceramic snail and a mushroom handle. The steam came out of holes in the snail's antennae. I said, "Oh, this hyperventilating mollusc is exquisite. Isn't it Royal Copenhagen?"

He nodded, smiling.

"I noticed the collection in the cabinet. I also observed those large pieces of Wedgwood hung in the embrasures. The English country garden plus the pagoda is a wonderful mix. The Chinese orange is a magnificent touch. I never knew that Wedgwood did anything that urbane."

"The Wedgwood family was one of England's most influential in many areas," he said rather formally.

"They were an amazing family," I said, still looking at his china collection. "They began the Industrial Revolution and had the money to prove it. They built their own railway to carry their china. Have you been to the Wedgwood Museum in Stoke-on-Trent in Staffordshire? I bet the curator would die to have some of this china on loan."

"What sparked your interest in the Wedgwoods?" he asked.

"I tripped upon the Wedgwoods in a former lifetime, when I was doing a Ph.D. in the philosophy of science on Darwin's later works. I'm sure you know that two generations of Wedgwoods married their neighbours, the Darwins. Charles Darwin's mother and his wife were Wedgwoods. If it hadn't been for the wealth of the Wedgwood side of the family, Charles Darwin might have had to get a real job and wouldn't have had the time to amass his theory of evolution.

"The confluence of wealth and genius in that family left quite a lineage. I'm sure you are aware that Francis Galton, the great statistician, was also the Wedgwoods' and Darwins' cousin," he said.

"I know. I love how he collected people at fairs to participate in his studies—in a tent, no less. Still, he came up with 'regression to the mean' and about a dozen other statistical canons."

We discussed ceramics for a while and he told me that in his London home he had some original Worcester, Derby, Coalport and Spode. I had a weird pocket in my brain that loved fine antique china. Even as a little girl I prized those doll tea sets. I used to throw out the dolls and keep the tiny china sets. Von Enchanhauer had a fantastic collection—and this was only the summer home.

Jackie sat silently during this interlude of tea talk, ignored by both of us. I was impressed with how well I could block people out when I set my mind to it. Some people could cook, some could sew; my specialty was burning off threatening people as though they were warts on my psyche.

Finally Jackie broke up the Wedgwood détente with the subtlety of a jackhammer. "Dr. Von Enchanhauer, as you are probably aware, there have been some threats made on the life of Anders Konzak."

"Yes, Anders mentioned that. He tends to exaggerate, so I must admit I didn't pay them much heed. Now that you have decided to investigate, I will revise that opinion." Looking from Jackie to me, he asked, "Is there something I don't know?"

"We don't know what you know," I said.

"Touché," said the doctor, adding, "Anders told me that someone has been sending him threatening letters in the mail."

"Did he ever mention anyone he suspected?" Jackie asked.

"He suspects that many people are jealous of him to the point of madness," Dr. Von Enchanhauer said, smiling as though this was somehow an endearing trait.

"Are they?" Jackie asked.

"Not to my knowledge."

"Why would anyone want to harm him?"

"Anders doesn't have any sense of how much he pushes people. He knows he has enemies, but he is unaware how he made them or how intense they are."

"Do you count yourself in that legion of enemies?" Jackie asked.

He sat for a long moment with his head cocked to the side, choosing his words carefully. "I'm disappointed in him and incensed at myself. He's like a kitten who frolics and has no idea that he is annoying others. I should have seen this facet of him, but I didn't. He had me under his spell."

"Can you tell me a little about that?" I winced, knowing that I got that pathetic line from Dr. Gardonne.

"Well, let's see. He has a way of being totally sincere. He's always enthusiastic, and nothing is ever dull. He sees truth and beauty everywhere. The problem is, he has created his own truth and then admired the beauty of it. For many years I searched for the right person to run the academy. I needed someone with great intellectual depth and dedication to Freud. He had all of the credentials and background knowledge. He was an analyst who also knew how to do research, and he spoke several languages. He had an enthusiasm that I believed he would apply to the job. Unfortunately, the whole did not equal the sum of the parts."

"Do you think he's right about Freud?" I asked.

"That is a complicated question. I believe that somewhere along the line Anders wanted fame but settled for notoriety, since his unconscious need for recognition superseded his need for the truth. The theories that he hatched made him appear to be a maverick, and he went through Freud to find verification for these theories. Unfortunately, truth is discovered the other way around."

Although nothing Dr. Von Enchanhauer said was untrue—in fact I agreed with him—I needed to pin him down. I dove into the heart of the debate. "Konzak's major argument, thus far, is that Freud should never have given up the seduction theory he held from 1895 to 1897. We both know he held the theory that the etiology of hysteria lies in childhood seduction, or as we would say today, if you are an incest victim as a child, you may grow up to be hysterical." I began pacing on the flagstone floor with my hands behind my back, thinking of the best way to present these issues without being condescending to a man who already knew all the details. "Then, in 1897, Freud changed his mind. He said that he had made a mistake in thinking that fathers seduced their daughters. What Freud said he had mistaken for real seduction or incest was really the patient's sexual fantasies about the father. Freud said he had stumbled onto the Oedipal complex." I walked over to the fireplace and leaned on the mantel, saying, "I have two questions for you. One, do you think that Konzak is right when he says that Freud made a mistake when he gave up the seduction theory? Second, do you think Freud gave it up because he found another, more in-depth theory to replace it, or did he give up the theory, as Konzak suggested, for reasons of self-interest?"

Jackie felt the need to clarify what I said by adding, "Freud knew that if he blew the cover on the bourgeois incest-perpetrating fathers who doubled in the daytime as the referring physicians, then the doctors wouldn't send Freud their patients and he'd go belly up? By self-interest, Konzak was suggesting Freud knew where his bread was buttered and he needed to make a living, so he went on letting daddies diddle their daughters."

I glared at Jackie, giving him the look that said he didn't have to opt for puerile explanation just because he didn't know the theoretical details of Freud or the history of English china; no one expected him to. I had begun to realize that when he felt insecure, which usually had to do with class or education, he opted to strike out, be as vulgar as he fantasized everyone thought he was. He'd done the same thing on the plane and in the dining room in Vienna when he didn't know what coffee to order. Christ Almighty, now I had to deal with an ex-con who might be framing me and who, in addition, metamorphosed into a boor whenever he felt insecure.

Dr. Von Enchanhauer ignored Jackie and didn't seem the least thrown by my questions. He sat looking at the beamed ceiling, presumably thinking. He was clearly not a man given to spontaneity or ill-thought-out ideas. I had quite a while to study his face, which was off-kilter in some way. His hairline was straight and his nose looked like it had been borrowed from Pinocchio. Not that it was large, but it didn't fit the frame of his face. I wondered if Jackie had noticed how odd he looked, almost as though someone had stretched him on a rack in the basement.

He began slowly. "I think whenever anyone, particularly a great mind, gives up a theory, there is often much that is correct within it. The reason it gets replaced isn't that it is totally wrong, it simply doesn't suit the data as well as another, more elegant theory. When Freud gave up the seduction theory, he missed some real incidents of incest within his patient group, and that is unfortunate more for the patients than for the future of psychoanalysis. Denying a patient's reality is never advisable. His sample was small, maybe twelve to fifteen, and quite homogeneous in that it was mostly bourgeois Jewish women. There was probably more incest at the time than he knew about. Whether there was as much as in the present time, I doubt it—particularly in that particular patient population.

"Perhaps it would be better to ask what would have happened if he *hadn't* given up the seduction theory. He may have become a family reformer, but that was not his interest or his forte. Had he kept the seduction theory, he would never have moved on and made what I believe posterity has labelled his greatest discovery—the unconscious. Freud said he was led by the hand from his patients' seduction fantasies to the unconscious. The fantasies were the unconscious intruding into conscious life, which was the cause of the illness. Hysterics can be terribly hard on themselves, believing they should have no sexual or angry thoughts. Humans act on their *perceptions* of reality, not on reality per se. It was tracing those sexual fantasies of the female patient for her father that opened the door not only to the unconscious but to its extensions, such as dream interpretation, defences and the whole foundation of dynamic psychology as we know it today."

He stopped for a moment, had a sip of tea and then continued. "I now believe that Konzak has never really understood psychoanalysis. It is about how one balances one's unconscious needs or learns to accept them. It is not about the mishaps or degradations of everyday life. Of course appalling things happen in everyday life and those things need to be dealt with, but that is not the job of psychoanalysis. Konzak isn't wrong or lying; he is expecting something from psychoanalysis that it wasn't designed to give. Freud was never interested in happiness. He said that through analysis a person could expect to rise from a state of abject misery into one of everyday unhappiness. Freud discerned in human nature a series of animalistic urges and drives kept in check by a merciless taskmaster, the superego. The fight in psychoanalysis is within the individual, not between the individual and society." Looking over at Jackie's furrowed brow, he said, "Konzak took a drive in a car and expected it to fly, and then suddenly became angry when it never left the ground. If one wants to fly, one must board a plane."

I nodded, indicating that he should go on. We both left a long silence, hoping he would fill it.

"Miss Fitzgerald, your second question is much easier to answer. I do not think that Freud gave up the seduction theory for reasons of self-interest. If he was interested only in the advancement of his career, he wouldn't have gone on to have a replacement theory that was as upsetting to the society at large as the first. He said all children were polymorphously perverse, and he said that our unconscious minds were perpetually seething cauldrons of sex and violence. It may not seem like much today, but remember, you live in a post-Freudian era. I don't think, if Freud wanted to be presented to the archduchess, he would have moved on to another theory that scandalized the Victorian era in Vienna. If Freud was the opportunist Konzak portrays, then he would have given up his Jewish identity, something that was commonly done to get a university or public appointment, married for wealth, fraternized with the wealthy in order to cultivate clients, and opted for the now-obsolete treatment plans of the day. He did none of the above. Therefore, I am at a loss to find the opportunism to which Anders so confidently alludes."

"Often wolves see only wolves behind every tree," Jackie offered.

"This is a sad but perceptive remark, I am afraid, Mr. Lawton."

"So aside from some theoretical differences, you and Konzak are disagreeing on the character of Freud," Jackie said, his little spiral notebook opened. "It sounds to me like you and Konzak just saw images of yourselves in Freud."

"Thank you, Mr. Lawton." He smiled for the first time at Jackie and added, "I take that as a compliment." He put his cup down, clasped his hands together, sat on the edge of his wing chair and said, with more emphasis than he'd used earlier, "I have no doubt that Freud occasionally imposed his theory onto his patients. He would not have been human if he had not. However, if Freud had been the man that Anders is portraying, he would never have made so many discoveries. He was a scientist who tried several theories and techniques and then utilized what he found worked best. He often wrote about his self-doubts to others who were close to him, and he expressed, as well, his frustration about the lack of precision in analytic theory. He, like all of us who have used the analytic method, wished it were otherwise. We are not historians or sociologists, but we must let the mind show us, the analysts, its own circuitous route, unfettered by our own reality. Psychoanalysis is the study of the unconscious mind, not the practical therapy of social work."

"You think that Konzak is not lying, he just doesn't understand psychoanalysis?" Jackie clarified aloud as he wrote in his notebook.

"I would say that Anders is not lying about certain facts, but he is slandering Freud because, firstly, he is committing the sin of presentism, judging the past by present standards, and secondly, Freud was not in any way dishonest. He confronted the polymorphous perversity of the child in the Victorian era—is that not a love of truth?"

Jackie said, "You've got a point there. That was definitely swimming upstream."

"Of course, I take responsibility for this public humiliation. My only hope is that Anna Freud can forgive me. I was analyzed by Freud and I believe that I owe him my life. I know he was a man of honour and genius. Yet it is I who allowed this to happen."

"Why?" I asked, ignoring his agonized plea for understanding.

"Ms. Fitzgerald, have you ever been taken in by someone and thought you were being objective, but because of your own poverty of spirit at the time, you were not seeing the person but instead a projection of your own needs?"

His question had the effect of a psychological stun gun. I was instantly immobilized and a series of pictures took over. In the first I was about five years old, holding my father's hand on a glorious fall day as we walked along the Precambrian Shield in Ontario's Bruce Peninsula. I can still smell the wild leeks and sorrel and feel the water dripping off the rocks as he explained the process of fossilization while we examined a salamander embedded in the limestone.

In the next image I'm a freshman in college standing next to my husband late at night in the computer science department. He is sorting out my programming cards to feed into the voracious IBM monster that was as big as a room.

The brightest picture of all is of me in my prison cell in the wee hours of silence, reading my pale blue edition of the collected Freud. Together Freud and I were hacking at the undergrowth of the unconscious.

I had a sudden feeling of déjà vu. Had I overestimated Freud, deified him like I had my father and husband? Had I been seduced by all three? How humiliating to have this cast of cardboard heroes fluttering down upon one another. I didn't feel that I had the inner resources to take another crushing disappointment.

"Kate?" Jackie prodded.

Blinking away the images, I refocused on the room. How long had I been blown away by Von E.'s question? Gathering all the tatters that remained in my left brain, I said what any interviewer says when caught out. "Dr. Von Enchanhauer, we are not here to discuss my needs but yours."

"I have tried to analyze them. I believe the years of hiding and the war took away my joy and spontaneity, and Anders Konzak has enough to share. He lives a charmed life, and if you manage to fit under his umbrella you may share in his version of truth and beauty. He is always happy, and he sees as dull and plodding those who rake through his theories searching for their factual underpinnings. I longed to roll back the clock, to have something of his carefree self-love."

Jackie waited a moment and then said, "Before we leave, we would like to know who you think are his enemies."

"Konzak's enemies? I can think of no one who is dangerous."

"We'll decide if they're dangerous," Jackie said.

"I would, of course, be at the top of the list. I was seduced by him in front of the entire Freudian community and then the world in the newspapers. My poor judgment has been 'hung out to dry,' as the president of the New York Psychoanalytic Association has so succinctly put it. Next there is Anna Freud. She does not seem to blame me, but rather holds Anders responsible. She feels more than I do that he was duplicitous. I think he is deluded. Anna is a magnanimous person and says that our lives are too short for vendetta. Eventually Konzak will show his true colours and we must let him do that. I wanted to write a piece for the journals in order to set the record straight. She convinced me that her father would have handled it by ignoring it. She has already moved on and is working on a new book on the defence mechanisms. Of course, she was never as taken with Anders as I was." He looked to the bottom of his empty teacup. "She hired him on my recommendation."

"Next?" Jackie prompted him.

"Then there is the North American psychoanalytic group. They are less forgiving and less mentally healthy than Anna Freud. They would lose their patient base if Freud were discredited. This group is spearheaded by a Dr. Gardonne. He's called me several times."

"We are looking into him already," Jackie said, glaring at me to keep me from interupting.

"Then there is Dvorah Little. She stands to lose a lot in a lawsuit. She's a New York journalist whom I've heard Anders is suing for slander or some such thing. She—" He looked up, feeling the presence of someone else in the room, and glanced toward the entrance. A woman, who must have been Sofia, his wife, hesitated in the archway. "Oh, dear, do come in and meet my guests."

She was tall and statuesque, and must have been beautiful in her day. She had pale grey hair pinned back in a chignon and an ice princess quality, although she was not haughty. Konzak had been way off in describing her as "a Hummel figurine." I imagine she froze him out of her world when she saw he was seducing Von Enchanhauer to get the director's job. Instead of feeling her distain, Konzak chose to see her as a lifeless piece of porcelain.

The doctor stood several inches shorter than his German spouse. She looked past him and was very formal during the introductions. "My dear, these are some authorities who are investigating Anders Konzak," the doctor said.

She smiled as she shook hands. "It's a bit late, isn't it?"

"Apparently Anders says he has been threatened."

"By whom?"

"They're here to find out by whom," he said without a trace of impatience.

"Oh. I see."

"I've given a list of anyone I might suspect," he told his wife.

"*Suspect*—that sounds terribly American," she said in the clipped, tutored English she must have learned as a child in Germany.

Jackie shot me a glance indicating the interview was over.

While the housekeeper got the coats, I strolled over to the mantel and looked at a framed photograph of two princely young men leaning on the mast of a yacht with an old woman seated gingerly in the bow. "Oh, are these two handsome men standing with Anna Freud your sons?" One of the two was holding up a huge silver cup. "They look as though they're in great shape. What a magnificent boat. Is it mahogany?"

"Yes, all but the hull, which was oak. Unfortunately they had to trade it in for something lighter to race with," Mrs. Von Enchanhauer said.

"Those smiles are radiant. Who do they look like?" I took a step back and assessed the picture. "Not you or your husband."

Mrs. Von Enchanhauer came over and beamed at the picture, obviously adoring her boys. "I feel they look like my husband," she said with maternal pride.

"Really, my dear, our guests will think you're deranged. The boys are tall and blond and I am short and dark. They are quite the ladies' men, and I have not been known for my captivating appeal."

Sofia looked straight ahead as though her husband hadn't spoken. Jackie and Dr. Von Enchanhauer walked ahead to the car as she and I followed, discussing porcelain. She said, quite warmly when she discovered my interest in ceramics, "I had no idea that young people were interested in collecting these things."

I guess when you're really elderly, anyone hovering around the big four–oh seems young. "I admire utilitarian objects that are also beautiful." I mentioned the teacup I'd seen on their mantel that was cobalt blue and gold. The handle was the arched, entwined necks of two herons whose heads lay gently on either side of the handle.

"Oh well, you will have to come to our home in London and see the entire collection of Rosenthal. You strike me as someone who would love Rosenthal, where the beauty is all in the line."

Jackie tapped my arm and said, "We want to get to London before the roundabouts start spinning."

One thing male detectives didn't seem to understand was that you get more out of people if you warm them up. If women genuinely share an interest, they'll share everything else. As Jackie was starting the car and I was putting on my seat belt, Sophia leaned into the car and said, "I have some Wedgwood in my London home which was commissioned by a Russian count who wanted a thousand pieces with a different English scene on each piece. You're welcome to come and see it." She stood up and, as though she had just remembered something, leaned over the top of the car and, addressing her husband, said, "Oh, Conrad, did you mention that pesky man that Anders got those silly notes from—you know, that American vagrant of sorts?"

"Oh, I don't think that was anything, my dear," her husband said. "Just one of those Freudian scholars who ought to be a patient," he said, smiling through thin lips.

Jackie turned off the motor and asked, "What was his name?"

"It was a type of circus name," she said. "Wasn't it, dear?"

"I thought it was Italian," Dr. Von Enchanhauer acknowledged. "He isn't affiliated with any institution. Well . . . he is a sort of detective, as it were. He coveted Anders's director's position and occasionally called and left messages. Anders is, of course, interested in everyone, and this man was quite interesting."

"Didn't Professor Konzak mention him?" Sofia inquired.

"No, he didn't," I said. "If you do remember his name, call us. Where did he call you from?"

"He didn't call us. He called Professor Konzak." Sofia Von Enchanhauer looked directly at her husband for only the second time during the interview, and continued, "Remember when Professor Konzak met him and said he was a genius but—not quite right?"

Conrad Von Enchanhauer blinked a number of times and said, "Oh yes, I do remember him telling us that, but he would have no reason to threaten Anders. I believe Mr. Lawton and Miss Fitzgerald are asking me who would be angry or want to threaten him." Turning to Jackie, he said, "Mrs. Von Enchanhauer is quite right. Anders should know his name. If he is unbalanced, he could have his own set of delusions. I suppose anyone who is delusional is potentially dangerous."

"It depends on the delusion," said Jackie, leaning out of the window. Then he jammed the car in reverse and sped out the long winding driveway. "Jesus, every time I make a turn I have to concentrate on which side of the road I want to end up on. Let's go straight to the ferry. As I drive, get out the clipboard and write all the information from the interview. It's important to get everything. You'd be amazed at what minutiae will be forgotten by the time we get to the ferry." He paused to light a cigarette as I opened the clipboard. "So what did you think?"

"The housekeeper is as old as the house and looks like no one's home."

"Those country types don't like any authorities," Jackie said.

"That's not so in England," I assured him. "Any authority is treated with reverence."

"She's not English, although I can't place her accent. She's not German or Austrian. The vowels are not reminiscent of a Romance language either. The words have a staccato quality that is Eastern European."

"I noticed that the doc went out to order the tea—Tefonia didn't come in to ask if we wanted something. Sofia must have gone into the kitchen and told her to change her apron and to keep quiet. That maid must know something. Do you think we should go back there after the Von E.s have gone to London?"

"Come on—so she looked a little blank, even for the English. Anyway, I imagine she travels with them."

I turned to him and said with incredulity, "Didn't you notice she wasn't playing with a full deck? There is something wrong with her. She repeats phrases—sort of echolalia, or parroting."

"Didn't notice it—didn't notice it," Jackie mumbled with an autistic lilt.

"And she didn't even change that filthy apron until someone in the kitchen told her to."

"Maybe she's just messy and dumb. Not a rare combination, judging from my childhood. I think she's repeating what the Von Enchanhauers told her to say."

Writing madly, I continued, "That British porcelain collection has to be one of the world's finest. Those English antiques are incredible. That curved mahogany desk was magnificent."

"So?" Jackie asked.

"Why would a European Jew and a transposed German replicate such English authenticity? Why bother? When you were in Vienna, did you have an overwhelming desire to go home and redecorate with Biedermeier, to wear lederhosen and yodel?"

"I did have an urge to buy one of those green felt hats, you know, the kind with the mini shaving brushes on the side." While driving in the drizzle, watching for the Cat's Eye fog lights in the road, he added, "I never wanted the lederhosen, though—the pockets are too small."

I just shook my head, saying, "I think when someone parodies an identity it's because they're desperate to hide their own."

"So if they collected beer steins named Shultz, they wouldn't have identity problems?"

"You don't get it," I said while writing. "Let's move on to Conrad Von Enchanhauer, possibly the ugliest man since Quasimodo. He was out of proportion. His torso didn't match his head. He has such translucent skin, and then that strange hair."

"Strange?"

"Didn't you notice that he looked like an aging Ken doll?"

"No, I can't say that I did."

"His hair was in tufts with perfectly straight lines across the forehead and at the back of the neck."

"Tufts?"

"Yeah, like lots of little hairs stuffed in one hole. It was a cross between Astroturf and indoor-outdoor carpeting." Jackie ignored me as I continued. "His Pinocchio nose isn't supported by his face. It looks stuck on with playdough. The rest of his features are fine, but his nose is thick and large. His whole face looks like someone cut it in half and then put it together with a slice missing."

"What?" Jackie said, moving from a tone of incredulity to one of annoyance.

"It's like a CAT scan in which someone removed a slice and then put it back together and left a view on the radiology floor . . . Didn't you notice that?"

"That there was a slice of him on the radiology floor? No, I can't say as I picked up on that missing slice of life," Jackie grumbled.

"The longer you know me, the more you will realize I am the queen of deformity detection. I can spot a wandering eye from 20/20."

"Are you getting to the facts?" Jackie wondered aloud.

"Quiet, I'm trying to remember something," I said, dashing off some notes. "This is how I work. I write down every little thing and then later, when I'm stumped, I go back for info that becomes clues."

"Ironed out a pretty good system after all these years in the trade, eh?"

I barely heard him, my writing trying to catch up with my brain. Looking up, I said, "Facts, what the hell are facts, other than things you notice and write down? Cicero's opinions have become today's facts. Scientific facts change when there is a necessity for change, not because the facts are untrue—they are just no longer useful."

"This is like facts from *Ladies' Home Journal*, but go ahead," Jackie said in as withdrawn a tone as one could use and still be talking

"Von E. was perfectly dressed to replicate the English country gentleman in his plaid Viyella shirt, except for one little thing," I announced.

"I give up."

"His sleeves were too long. Why?" I asked.

"You're the deviation queen."

"Because he has scarring on that arm. Whatever it is, I can tell you right now that he was hiding it. He drank his tea awkwardly so his sleeve wouldn't ride up. There was no way he could hide it when I shook his hand so vigorously. I saw it."

"Hiding scars doesn't imply anything," Jackie said.

Ignoring him, I said, "Are you aware that hair does not grow over scar tissue?"

"Yes," he said, pointing to a scar on his eyebrow.

"He has black curly hair and his scarring has no lighter pigment on the scar tissue. Strange, don't you think, since dark-haired people have lighter scar tissue? What is stranger is that he has hair growing out of the scar."

"So? He has a hairy scar."

"Next," I continued with my litany, "it was clear to me he didn't want his wife there. He stood up when she came in the room, which forced us to our feet, and then he remained on his pins to get either her or us out."

"That *was* a bit awkward," he agreed.

"Now let's move to the obvious," I said, starting a new page.

"Let's."

"When Von E. had time to prepare his answers, he seemed diplomatic and truthful. However, the more I talked to Sofia, the frosty wife who thawed out during the china tête-à-tête, the more anxious he became."

"With good reason," Jackie said. "She came up with the idea of the Italian circus performer. Strange he hadn't mentioned it. Although he didn't freak out when she did. Von E. just dismissed him as crazy."

"That's the way psychiatrists freak out. Besides, crazy doesn't mean stupid."

Jackie, having seen as many crazies in the prison yard as I had, nodded vociferously, saying, "Usually their craziness had a grain of truth. If you could cut away the craziness, you could usually find a more intelligent person than the guards ever could have been."

"Exactly," I said. "The staff chose to be there—how stupid was that?" He nodded agreement as he downshifted and pulled onto the I-5. "Another major slip," I continued. "When the Italian circus clown was mentioned, why didn't Von E. say 'Ask Anders,' the way Sofia did?"

"You want me to say because he already knew Konzak was dead. Sorry, but my take on that was that he assumed we had already asked Konzak and we were just seeing what he would say. I do, however, agree we should red-letter it. You finished yet?" Jackie asked.

"No." I was still scribbling. "Then Sofia looked at her children's photograph—who, by the way, looked like the archetypal Nazi youth. The boys definitely looked like brothers but bore no resemblance to her. She has a long narrow forehead, theirs are both wide. The wife said they looked like her husband. That was strange on two counts. One, they are tall, blond and thin and look like the Aryan dream. Their father looks totally Semitic. There is nothing of him in the boys."

"You're grasping at straws now," Jackie said.

"According to genetic theory the kids could look like their great-uncle. It would be only mildly unusual. The strange thing is that when the wife said that they looked like their father, she seemed to warm toward her husband and she glanced over at him for the first time during our visit."

"People who've been married for well over fifty years don't always gaze into one another's eyes, judging from the marriages I've seen." Jackie added, "Or was I just brought up on the unromantic side of the tracks?"

"You're right. The unique bit was his saying we would think she was *deranged*. Strange use of a word, I thought, especially for one who refers to his wife as 'Mrs. Von Enchanhauer.' She was shocked, but recovered quickly. If Konzak used the word *deranged*, I wouldn't think so much of it. It was not a word she was accustomed to hearing from him. Psychiatrists have a range from A to B. *Deranged*, when referring to his wife, is right out of his obsessive ballpark. And, by the way, why would we think she was deranged for seeing her husband in the children? It was part of the fierce denial people use when they are anxious or need to hide something. Methinks the Jewish man doth protest too much." While scrawling on, I said, "I am now inputting a summary that says, 'Von E. did well on all of the items that he could rehearse and not so well on the spontaneous things.' He originally planned to see us in London and to have his wife in the country, I'm sure of it. It was a good thing to catch him off guard by coming to the Isle of Wight." I stopped my screed and glanced over at Jackie. "Your turn."

"What's left? The two substantial things are the Italian circus performer and the picture of the sons. I also picked up that Mrs. Von E. finds the good doctor beneath contempt and their life is dreary together. The rest is amateur sleuth stuff, in my opinion." He must have realized how condescending he sounded and immediately reframed it. "Listen, I mean that I can only follow up on two of those leads. Let's find out who the kids are, or, more precisely, whose kids they are, and also who the Italian clown is. Tufts of hair are hard to follow up on. Where do you go? Mattel?"

While we were making a list of what needed follow-up, Jackie said, "We're going to have to work quickly from now on. Konzak's body is getting as mouldy as John Brown's and someone is going to find him."

We circled the roundabout and sped to the ferry terminal.

10

—

FREUD ON ICE

—

I only wish she [Anna Freud] would soon find some reason
to exchange her attachment to her old father for
some more lasting one.

—FREUD

AS WE PULLED up to 19 Maresfield Gardens, I gazed out of the
car window at the lugubrious house that Freud had lived in
while suffering a torturous death from mouth cancer. The man
who invented the "talking cure" died of cancer of the mouth
and jaw, a literal slip of the tongue. Freud would have made
much of that had he been analyzing anyone but himself.

His daughter, Anna, had stayed on alone in the house since
his death and had made part of the home, the psychoanalytic
chambers, into a small museum. Though I'd suspected
Konzak of hyperbole, I was struck by how accurately he had
described the dreariness that pervaded the place. Roots were
knuckling out the cobblestones, the bushes were overgrown
and the bald earth sprouted only the occasional clump of
grass. Shade had mildewed the ground and mushrooms sprang

up as though they were the only plants that could survive in the sour soil.

Jackie rang the doorbell several times, until a Teutonic-looking housekeeper wearing a black uniform and white apron opened the door. The hall was dark and the wainscotting was varnished a crackled, shiny brown. The rug looked as though it had last been vacuumed by Franz Josef.

"Miss Freud waits for you in the study," she said. She moved only her bottom jaw when she spoke, like a ventriloquist's dummy.

The study, at least, had a look of being in use. Handsome leaded glass windows stretched from the floor to the ceiling. A small austere elderly woman put down her pen, stood up and reached over her desk piled high with books marked with those futuristic Post-its to shake our hands.

She wore a simple wool suit, a white blouse, thick stockings that wrinkled at the ankles and Hush Puppies. Her naturally curly hair was hastily tied back in a bun. Her face had a lovely bone structure, and her penetrating eyes of intense green were set against skin that was colourless and translucent.

She motioned us to have a seat in two metal office chairs in front of her desk. She sat behind her huge mahogany desk on her swivel chair, folded her hands, smiled and asked in a thick Viennese accent, "How may I help you?"

"We're here to ask a few questions about Anders Konzak."

Anna Freud looked at us, waiting for the questions. Her businesslike manner made it clear that although she was willing to be co-operative, she had work to do and wanted to get on with it.

"I believe Anders Konzak is presently the director of the Freud academy?" I asked.

"That's correct," she said, and awaited my next question.

"When I talked to Konzak last week, he said that he expected to be fired from the academy as soon as the board met next month."

"That is possible. You'd have to interview all of the board members in order to ascertain that."

"To come straight to the point, Miss Freud, since you seem a no-nonsense kind of woman and I'm that kind of man, Konzak has stated that his life has been threatened. We've been assigned to investigate those threats," Jackie said.

"Yes?" she said expectantly.

"You must have been offended by Konzak's attacks on Sigmund Freud, particularly since you were the person who hired him." I knew, in fact, that Anna hadn't hired him, but I wanted to jump-start her.

"You have asked me several questions," she said. "I will attempt to answer them separately. I was certainly distressed by Professor Konzak's blitzkrieg upon my father. However, it was tempered by two things. First, I am used to censure. My father was attacked for his work by much of the civilized world for all of my life with him. I was interrogated by the Gestapo in 1938 for twenty-three hours, so I have learned to temper my expectations. I anticipate a certain amount of trouble and then I am not as distressed as I would otherwise have been." She walked out from behind her desk, looked directly at Jackie and continued. "Another reason I was not too upset was that I am not close to Professor Konzak. I'm afraid that I, like my father before me, do not share the enthusiasm of some others for that certain type of American brashness. I was never in favour of hiring Professor Konzak. It was Dr. Von Enchanhauer who felt that he was suitable for the job. Since I'm so busy with teaching, writing and with my practice, I'm afraid that most of the paperwork fell on his shoulders and he wanted some respite, believing that Professor

Konzak was intelligent, a devoted Freudian and energetic. I agreed only with the latter." Anna Freud spoke with the same precision found in her writing. Although she had a heavy accent, she did not hesitate or need to search for words in English. It was not hard to see her point when, after all, she had the same view of Konzak that I had.

"Yes, Dr. Von Enchanhauer told us that it was a question of his own bad judgment. However, Konzak lives here with you, so you must know him somewhat better than anyone else on the board."

"We dine together on some evenings when Elsa makes a meal, but surprisingly few. His work frequently takes him away in the evening, as does mine. Very often I work late at the institute and dine on a cold supper in my study. His apartment is separate. I believe he's out of town at the moment."

"Dr. Gardonne has obtained a 'writ of entry' from Anders Konzak allowing us access into his apartment," Jackie said as he rummaged around in his tattered file folder searching for the document.

"That won't be necessary. You are most welcome to see it at any time. I'll have Elsa take you up." Anna spoke as she walked toward the door.

"Thank you. We would like to see it before we leave," Jackie said, implying that we weren't ready to leave yet. He walked over to an alcove in her office that was clearly the section of the room used for play therapy. It had toys, games, a farm set and a large doll house. It also had a child-size desk with two mini chairs. Jackie immediately went to the yellow Tonka trucks on the shelf and began rolling them back and forth. "Wow, what a great room. Look at all the toys, Kate." Looking gleefully at Anna Freud, he said, "I forgot you work with children."

"I can see you have no problem with male identity," Anna Freud said, returning his smile.

As Jackie cranked the elevator on the Fisher-Price gas station, he said, "You've acknowledged that Konzak may be dismissed by the board next month. What has he done that's so offensive?"

"I have not had the opportunity to discuss this at length with the other board members. I have had the advantage of seeing the letters and papers that he intended publishing next month, and I believe he has misinterpreted certain things. I believe Professor Konzak has defended his theory by publishing some facts taken out of context. He advised his readership, or perhaps I should say audience, to wait until the letters are published and then they will agree on his perspicacity. Only the serious scholars will actually read the letters when they are published. For the rest of the world the damage has been done. The newspapers and magazines all ran stories without the facts to back them up. Everyone who has ever been psychoanalyzed or taken part in any therapy wants to catch Freud out as having done something wrong."

"Why?" Jackie asked.

"Because it's titillating," she replied. "Because Freud has 'caught them,' as it were. Very few reputable journals would publish an article of scientific slander. They would demand to wait until the letters were published and then give Professor Konzak's paper to at least three reputable experts in the field, then wait to hear the referees' opinions before publishing it. If the article were at all disputed, standard practice would be to run it with a rebuttal or mention in an editor's introduction that the findings were not agreed upon by several of the leaders in that particular field. Yet newspapers think nothing of publishing this theory without any evidence to back it up, and no one is calling it slander."

"I guess *The Washington Post* must have thought the director of the Freud academy was a reputable source. I mean, he isn't Charles Manson," Jackie pointed out.

"Why is this happening now to such a towering figure as Freud?" I asked, genuinely perplexed. Since we were in the play room, I began to build with large wooden blocks.

"Freud is often subjected to less careful scrutiny than others because his insights are so threatening," Anna Freud said. "People unconsciously want him discredited. No one is immune to unconscious motivation—not even the editor of *The Washington Post.*"

"Speaking of slander, what did you think of Dvorah Little's series on Anders Konzak in *Metropolitan Life?*"

"Of course, it rivalled the British tabloids. I had no idea whether the slander originated from Dvorah Little or from Anders Konzak. He insisted that she lied about what he'd said. To his credit, he had his misgivings about her before the article appeared. At dinner one evening he referred to her as 'Devouring Dvorah' and described her interviewing techniques as somewhat provocative."

"In what way?" Jackie pounced on the salacious.

"I didn't inquire."

"Do you think Konzak was wrong in his assessment of your father's work on the seduction theory?" I asked.

"This question requires a long and complicated answer, which I don't want to become embroiled in. You began by asking me who would have threatened Professor Konzak, and I have no idea. He has enemies in several walks of life, from forsaken lovers to professors of Russian literature. One makes enemies when one does not gauge one's effect on others."

"Do you think Konzak is psychopathic?" I asked.

"No, psychopaths enjoy manipulating for its own sake. Konzak is defending what he believes is true."

"Do you think there are secrets that he is going to reveal that will have devastating effects on anyone?" I persevered.

"No, or I would never have given him the material. There is

nothing damaging to anyone in the letters, especially to anyone alive. Wilhelm Fliess's letters reveal elements of the unscientific nature of his work, but that is something that has already been well documented. Fliess's fame is only related to his friendship with my father. I have spoken to Fliess's son about it and shown the unpublished letters to him. He felt that there was nothing any more damaging in them than had already come out when Kris edited the selected correspondence and Strachey included them in the collected works of Freud many years ago. Also—"

"Fliess!" Jackie interrupted, barely hiding his delight. "Is his daughter or granddaughter Heidi Fliess, the Hollywood prostitute?"

"Madame, I believe," Anna Freud corrected him.

"I've followed her career," Jackie said enthusiastically as he began parking several Matchbox cars on the top of the toy gas station. I shot him a withering look to which he replied, "Well, she was a good businesswoman." Since neither Anna Freud nor I shared his enthusiasm, he was forced to move on. "All right," he asked, changing tack entirely, "do you know of any Italian-American person, described as a hippie or free spirit, who corresponded with Konzak?"

"What was his name?"

"We don't know. His name had something to do with the circus."

She thought for a moment. "No, I can't think of anyone who matches that description. One thing I can say is that Professor Konzak had friends from all walks of life. When he moved in here, it took two weeks for his phone to be connected and he used mine for that duration. He had calls from waiters, ambassadors, academics in subjects ranging from Russian to women's studies, Finnish drywallers, chess champions from Iceland, American jazz musicians and Australian windsurfers. It would not surprise me if he had an Italian-American friend in the circus."

Jackie exchanged a let's-get-out-of-here glance with me as I was putting the final touches to my blocks. I said to Anna Freud, "We would appreciate looking at Konzak's quarters, and in order not to disturb you again we'll have the housekeeper show us out."

Anna, who was sitting on a bentwood rocker behind us, rang a tiny bell that looked like a Christmas tree ornament. As we waited for the housekeeper's arrival, Anna and Jackie crowded around the wooden edifice I had built as we were speaking. Anna smiled and said, "Ah, Miss Fitzgerald, I see you also have no problems with sexual identity."

"Wrong!" Jackie said.

As we laughed, Anna surveyed my building-block home and said, "You have built a house, as girls almost always do. You see, men build structures with open spaces and women build them closed. I notice, however, that instead of one door you have allotted four. I suspect confinement has been an issue for you."

Before I could respond, the housekeeper bustled in and swept us out of the study—far more efficiently than she swept the rest of the house. She seemed to be ushering us to the front door, so Jackie reminded her that Anna Freud had said we could look in Konzak's room. "I know that," she barked, and stomped up the dark staircase ahead of us.

On the third floor the hallway was lined with closed doors. It looked more like a rooming house than a home. She unlocked one door with a key from her apron pocket.

"Must be hard having Professor Konzak here now, with all that's happened," I ventured.

"He keeps to his self more now, don't he?" Elsa said with some satisfaction.

"Nice to have someone to cook for?" I asked, hoping to elicit the woman-to-woman thing.

"Oh, he had his complaints, he did. Too much red meat, too much mutton, wanting greens with every meal. He made me a lot of extra work, he did." She seemed pleased to have the floor. "He would pull things out of closets and then leave the rest for me to tidy up. He may have charmed people outside of these walls, but he never made an impression on me. Saying them things 'bout Herr Freud showed no respect. Most of my life I know Professor Freud, but no one care to ask me nothing, but some oily upstart from America they asks. People believes what they want, I says."

"We'll let you know when we're leaving," Jackie said, closing the door.

"Fine," she said, and turning abruptly, clomped down the stairs. I thought we might have learned more from her if Jackie hadn't interrupted, but decided not to make an issue of it.

We went through Konzak's rooms but came up with nothing unusual. Then, Jackie found a little trinket in a drawer, carefully wrapped in yellow paper. It was a key chain with a miniature 45 rpm record replica attached to it. The title on the record read, *The Name Game*. We looked at each other with a "Eureka" eyebrow lift, recalling the murder scene.

"The note on the small three-by-five yellow lined paper we found in Konzak's pocket said the same thing! It was the one he was wearing when he was killed," I said.

Jackie said, "Keep your voice down. It said '*It's the name game*,' but you're right, it's the same thing."

"You were supposed to find out if it was a bar or book or whatever," I reminded him.

"Nothing checked out in terms of bars—"

"Hey, wait a minute. You know, now that I see *The Name Game* written on this miniature record, I remember that it was a song from the sixties."

"I don't remember it. How did it go?"

"It presented an algorithm that enabled even a dimwit to make a rhyme out of anybody's name."

"Just sing it and cut the bullshit," he said as he went through Konzak's pockets in his closet.

"We played it at riding camp. You snapped your fingers and sang variations on someone's name, all of which had to rhyme, like, *The first letter is J and the second letter is A and it rhymes with 'wacky'—JACKIE.*"

"Gee, I sure lost a hunk of civilization when I didn't remember that song," Jackie said as he searched Konzak's in-box. "Here's a whole list of questions from his publisher in New York. We'll call him when we're there," Jackie said, writing down the number.

"Here is his real key chain. It matches his leather wallet. It's made of sealskin. That's more Anders-ish," I offered.

We could hear Elsa skulking in the hall. I whispered to Jackie, "Why does she make that clomping sound when she walks? And those shoes are weird, even for the Germanic type. Her shoes look like golf clubs with laces on the side."

"She has a club foot, Little Miss Deviation Queen."

When I opened the door to leave, she seemed flummoxed and said she was afraid that if we'd called her she wouldn't have been able to hear us.

"Professor Konzak has quite a reputation as a ladies' man in the press. Do you think it's true?" I asked, again feigning girl talk as we walked down the hall together.

"I keeps out of other people's affairs, that ain't my concern. What peoples do behind closed doors is their business."

As we walked to the car, Jackie said, "Elsa's cute."

"How would you like to go to a housekeeper convention in England? If the rest are like Elsa and Tefonia at the Von Enchanhauers', they'd be quite a group."

"They make female prison guards look like pin-ups," Jackie agreed.

"Her accent is an interesting combination of Austrian peasant and Cockney glottal stop. Really strange that someone should employ her so long. She obviously wasn't hired for her outstanding housekeeping skills. I thought Germanic types cleaned their Meissen knick-knacks with toothpicks. That stereotype was obviously made up by someone who never met Elsa."

"Must be her personal warmth, then," Jackie said, lighting a much-needed cigarette.

"How many housekeepers don't clean, complain incessantly and, the ultimate final shot, refuse to gossip about Anders Konzak's multitudinous infidelities?"

"One—Elsa. Or was that a trick question?"

Once safely ensconced in the car, pen at the ready, I turned my gaze expectantly on Jackie. "Well . . . your turn."

As he started the car, he said, "Anna's a hard read. Tough . . . sensible. She doesn't seem too upset about the whole Anders betrayal. After all, she didn't hire him, Conrad Von Enchanhauer did. She agreed to hire him to be polite, and now she's saying 'I told you so.' Professor pudding-face Von Enchanhauer corroborated it. She did make one big mistake, though."

"She sure did," I agreed.

"'Konzak *had* friends.' Interesting use of the past tense," Jackie said, blowing smoke rings.

"Exactly. However, she may be referring to the fact that he no longer has friends as opposed to the fact that he's no longer with us."

"Possible," Jackie allowed.

"Although we agree she was cool, let's remember, when you've been interrogated by the Gestapo we must seem like Cheech and Chong."

Jackie lifted an eyebrow in agreement and added, "Even if you haven't been interrogated by the Gestapo, we might seem like Cheech and Chong."

"As a point of interest," I asked, "why did you choose to ask about the Italian American?"

"I wanted to see her reaction. It seemed relatively normal. Interesting she never said, 'Why don't you ask Konzak?' But that could be because she didn't want to presume to tell us how to do our job. She didn't seem to have any attachment to Konzak, as Von Enchanhauer did."

"I wouldn't put a lot of weight on that. Konzak is attacking her father, who was her whole life. She stopped living the day he died. The house looked like Miss Havisham's. Only the study had some life in it. At least Dr. Von Enchanhauer is married with a few kids. She's living in a time warp."

"Are you saying single women are suspect?" he asked, glancing over at me. "In that case, look no farther."

"No, it's not her singleness but her asexual quality. When you wandered into her play therapy centre, it was interesting that the first thing she evaluated in you and then in me was our sexual or gender identity."

"I nosed around in there to see if she was going to be defensive about her space, but she wasn't. I thought she just did that tongue-in-cheek."

"Read Freud on the psychopathology of humour," I said. Knowing I was grasping, I added, "Don't you think she seems devoid of sexual identity?"

"Does that make her a killer?"

"No," I snapped, looking up from my clipboard. "If that were the case, look no farther. I'm only writing my impressions."

"Did you notice that 'Devouring Dvorah' bit?" Jackie asked. "She must have thought it was important to let us know that

Konzak didn't like Dvorah and had said nasty things about her on a personal level."

"I don't know if I would go so far as to say 'important.'"

"It's the only thing she quoted."

"True enough."

"You may know a Freudian slip, but I know a cat fight when I see one," Jackie said. "Tight-lipped Anna Freud couldn't help but let us know that Anders Konzak didn't fancy Dvorah Little. Why do you think she said it—if you're so smart?"

"I don't know, but you're way off on that one. You've been in too many cathouses."

As we drove in silence for about twenty minutes along the crowded London streets, I thought of the landscape of the Isle of Wight and the crashing waves at Freshwater Bay, where Tennyson wrote,

> Sunset and evening star,
> And one clear call for me!
> And may there be no moaning of the bar,
> When I put out to sea.

It would be so wonderful to feel that you've accomplished something, or just to feel no "moaning of the bar" when you "put out." Maybe accomplishment isn't the issue; maybe it's just achieving peace. Finally I asked Jackie, "Didn't Anna Freud's life have an enviable sort of order and serenity to it?"

"I felt I was surrounded by a crusty death. She was good at managing her little world, which was no more than manipulating words on a page that she defends and polishes. She's never had to deal with anything real or taken a risk."

"You don't feel that being the first analysand, or being interrogated by the Nazis, was real?"

"Neither was a risk or a choice. She *had* to do both. Real life is when you make choices to enlarge your world. Anyone can look serene if she makes her world small enough that she can control all of it."

"Who are you? Mr. Expansive? Mr. Stop-the-world-I-want-to-get-off?"

"I didn't realize you were inquiring about *my* life. I was trying to answer *your* question. You don't have to defend Anna Freud— I'm not attacking her. I'm just saying what her life looked like to me, or, as you would say, my *perception* of her life."

I nodded.

Buoyed up by my concession, he said, "I mean, really, the woman wrote on childhood defences. Anyone who spends her life doing that is defending against big stuff! Jung is right about those Freudians. He says that they carry on about sex, Oedipal complexes and all that shit. While Freud grew up with neurotic city slickers who lived in rarefied intellectual circles cut off from nature, Jung lived among Swiss peasants. Jung is on to something when he says that Freud was a prude. Freud made a living on what he'd repressed, and then when he finally remembered what every working-class man, prisoner and truck driver from Königsberg to Kalamazoo knows, he called it a discovery." His voice had escalated to the point that he was yelling, slamming the gears and swearing at drivers on the M4. "I mean, is incest always so terrible? Jung says it has a highly religious aspect."

I had no intention of wading in on this one, so I sat it out and about ten minutes later he continued as though there had been no gap in the conversation. "I remember on my one and only visit to my father, when I was five—Children's Aid tracked him down while my mother was in the drunk tank—my father's girl-friend sucked my dick in the bathtub. It was the only nice moment I can remember from my whole childhood. I felt she really liked me, and it felt great."

Jackie was using Jung in the same way Konzak was interpreting Freud, to meet his own needs. I guess he didn't want to seem like a victim. I felt like saying look at prostitutes, nearly all of whom have been victims of incest or some form of childhood sexual abuse. They're still re-enacting it, and I doubt that they think they're performing a "religious ritual." His sudden impulsive anger seemed to come from nowhere. If this was the rage he could express over an *idea* at the age of forty-two, when his testosterone was on the wane, I could only imagine what he was capable of at age eighteen as he bent bars in solitary, screaming down the empty corridor.

I waited about fifteen minutes, until his face was less purple and his breathing had calmed down, before I even glanced his way. In an effort to move on, I began a new topic, saying, "Our first priority is that Italian circus character."

"I'm on it. We're landing at LaGuardia in the morning," he said with perfect equanimity. "We're registered at the Plaza so we can interview the American psychoanalytic crowd and the journalist Dvorah Little."

11

A GLIMPSE OF SKYLINE

—

What Joy Ambition finds!
—MILTON, *Paradise Lost*

NEW YORK IS always magical. Glancing out my window at the Plaza onto Central Park, I saw the virginal white cherry blossoms littering the pathways as nature's confetti heralding the spring. You can't stomp on New York; homelessness, violence, bankruptcy and muggings can take a run at it, but no one ever really knocks it over. It's like those Bobo dolls that rock but always bounce back before the next punch.

I'd stayed in this exact suite many years ago, when my father brought the family for what he referred to as "our annual educational bite of the Big Apple." At the UN the only thing I really liked were the flags. The highlights were the Guggenheim, the anthill gallery where the worker bees wore headsets, and the stock exchange, which my father referred to as an example of American greed. He said, indicating the men who were running around the floor shouting and holding up white bandages of paper, that these were the sons of the men who jumped off the

Empire State Building in 1929. My father must have considered himself above this particular vulgar fray since he only invested in blue-chip stocks.

My father and I walked through Central Park, where we watched the speed-chess games and the black man who walked on his hands in a green zoot suit, to the drinking fountain. My most vivid memory was that my father held my hand as we strolled through the city. However, he was quick to point out that he was clasping my little paw because New York could be dangerous and it was his job to protect me.

After our day of sightseeing we met my mother and sisters at the Russian Tea Room so they could be revived from shopping for the theatre. My father made my older sisters listen to everything we'd learned in the day while they'd been burning their brain cells at Bergdorf's. My father acted as though my mother had taken my sisters to the Bowery instead of Bonwit's, hinting that their ultimate moral and intellectual turpitude would have to fall on her conscience. She shouldered this burden blithely while opening her shopping bags and slowly unwrapping the coloured tissue paper, displaying all of her new acquisitions. I wondered if, in later years, she had ever reminded him of all those moments and that in fact it was me who turned into a murderer while my sisters married and continued shopping. Actually, I doubt it. She wasn't that type.

I put my hand on the rolltop desk that I'd loved opening and shutting, yet today it stuck halfway up and I couldn't get at the stationery I'd so loved writing on. The suite had a living room and a bedroom. The rooms had been redone since my last visit, the twin beds replaced by one king-sized and the spread matching the Brunswig & Fils wallpaper and drapes. The bath was a Jacuzzi rivalling those in *Bride's* magazine. The bed was turned down and a wrapped chocolate truffle was centred on the pillow.

I thought I'd luxuriate in this room I remembered so vividly, but for some reason I just felt like I was in an Ethan Allen furniture window.

The phone rang. When I answered it, expecting Jackie, I had Dr. Gardonne dangling on the line.

"Kate?"

"You got her."

"How's it going?"

"Not bad. We interviewed both Anna Freud and Von Enchanhauer. They seemed clean, but they didn't squeak. We need thorough investigations done on both of them. She's foxier than he is, but they're up to something."

"Done. Jackie has already got one of his employees to look into it."

"There's an Italian-American weirdo who hung around the archives and may have sent threatening notes to Konzak. For some reason Von Enchanhauer didn't mention him."

"A clown's name in Italian—Jackie ordered a search for him. He's having all of the psychoanalytic newsletters and mailing lists searched. The two or three large libraries with world-class early Freud collections that have interlibrary loans are under surveillance. He'd have had to order his material from one of them. Jackie has had all the mailing registrations for the psycho-analytic conventions and congresses searched for Italian names. He is also checking out all letters to the editor with any Konzak content that have been sent into the newspaper since the big media pieces came out." Gardonne rattled on, "He is ferreting out all Italian Americans in those groups. Jackie says their names can turn up through interlibrary loans. Jackie is correct in assuming that paranoid personality disorders typically siphon off the big cities. He is also investigating all the places where those record key chains are sold, and that particular grade of yellow paper."

When had Jackie had time to do all this?

"There was also a strange yellow note that said 'Only the fittest survive'," I added.

"Correct. Jackie believes it might have to do with Darwin. He's traced all Visa receipts and cheques of anyone who has bought any Darwiniana in the last six months in Toronto, New York, London or Vienna . . . Where's Jackie now?"

"Don't know. We're going to Dvorah Little's later today."

"Jackie told me he had a library search done and a private detective detailing her already while you two were in Europe. Oh, lest I forget, Jackie mentioned how well you interviewed Von Enchanhauer and Anna Freud. It was clever how you engaged Mrs. Von Enchanhauer through the china diplomacy. It seems you've accomplished quite a bit."

Jackie said that?

"Another day, another dollar, as my ex-roommate used to say, but she was in another line of work." I said "Over and out" as I hung up.

Where the hell was Jackie, anyway? I paced around the room trying to block him out of my mind. Best to assume that he had been bullshitting when he said he believed in my innocence. Who cares if some tattooed bank robber who uses toothpicks as dining utensils thinks I'm innocent? I was getting paid to think about Freud. If I could blot out the horrors of prison, I should be able to blot out Jackie. But for some reason he just kept leaking into my mind. His face had turned into mercury and slithered under the doors of all the wrong compartments. I tried desperately to catch it and squelch it, but the more I tried to grasp it, the more it divided and multiplied.

As I was strapping on my heart rate monitor for a jog in Central Park, I heard a knock on the door. I opened it to see Jackie in jogging shorts and tank top. What had looked like beefiness were in fact thick muscles that protruded across his chest and wound down his arms and legs.

"I forgot my toothpaste," he said, walking past me as I did my stretches. He passed me again on the way out, not saying a word, just flashing me the toothpaste. (It wasn't like he'd need much.) After the door closed, I glanced at my heart rate. It had risen into my training zone. I guess that's what Descartes meant by the mind–body problem.

I ran into him again waiting for the elevator and said, "I hope you aren't under the illusion that we're jogging together. With the amount you smoke, you couldn't catch up to me in this elevator." He just shrugged and jogged in place.

We headed down in silence and crossed to the park. It was one of New York's sunniest days. This was the New York everyone wants to remember, the first official day of spring when everyone literally lightens up by dumping their three-pound winter coats. The grass was pleading to be green and the blossoms were waving from the trees. Fathers were out with their sons in Yankee baseball caps with thick red plastic bats. Kids trying to learn to ride their shiny new bikes were weaving in and out of picnicking lovers while anxious parents puffed alongside. As I picked up speed, I couldn't help but smile at Jackie, knowing he shared my love of fresh air and movement. We ran abreast in long-legged strides of perfect unison, the ex-con Carlsberg-Clydesdales in Central Park. We double-timed to the rhythm of the South American quartet who played under the bridge with their weird woodwinds and multicoloured pointed hats.

After about a half-hour I felt transported as we passed the black street performers in front of the museum who did their hyper calisthenics accompanied by their ghetto blasters. Even the glue sniffers had given up their plastic bags for the day and opted to sit on the grass and sniff the perfumed air. Jackie held up a hand showing five long fingers and I knew he meant five minutes full out for interval training. I saw a snow fence in the distance that was still up to protect the new grass seed and I signalled that I would jump over and keep going. We vaulted at the same moment and landed in the outfield of a Lubavitchers baseball game. The wigged wives in the stands gave us a hand as we waved and kept moving. Even the crack-manic poets who sold their poems on scraps of scruffy paper stepped back as we sprinted by. No one I knew had ever kept up with me before and Jackie didn't even seem winded. I couldn't help but notice that his running style matched his personality; it was strong and smooth and he never looked as though he was going as fast as he was.

After forty-five minutes, Jackie caught my eye and pointed to his watch. We stretched under a row of purple-flowered Judas trees. As we held our ankles, straightened our legs and pointed our butts to heaven, we glanced over at each other—two horses that finally got out of the barn.

Thirsty as hell, we stopped at a bicycle cart in Washington Square and had Slush Puppies. We watched a wide-eyed Marilyn Monroe transvestite admire a baby in an English pram pushed by a Wall Street mother. Jackie looked at me and raised his Slush Puppy to mine in a toast to a rare but wonderful moment when everything on this tiny island of Manhattan was in sync.

An hour later as we waited for the elevator of Dvorah Little's Fifth Avenue apartment, I asked Jackie if there was anything I needed to know about the upcoming interview. As the elevator door opened, he stepped in and said, "I have a few ideas, but I'll save them for the strippers' runway."

The old red-nosed doorman placed a tiny kryptonite look-alike key into an elevator button that said *P*. The double doors opened onto the foyer of a penthouse apartment that was an ode to square footage. He said, "They used this as a set for some of the William Powell–Myrna Loy movies. Those were different times."

A black cleaning lady sporting a weave, a Calvin Klein T-shirt and major attitude said, "Who you here to see?"

"Miss Little, little miss. She's expecting us," Jackie said.

The cleaning lady said, "You watch who you callin' little, Mista Big." She dropped her central vac and called up the winding staircase, "Dvorah, there are some folks to see you. I think they from Amway or somethin'."

"Thank you, Delphinia. Why don't you take a break now? It's time for your programs."

Dvorah sashayed down the staircase, Loretta Young style, gracefully pointing each of her E-width shoes and dressed in a black pantsuit that must have been meant to underplay her Wagnerian frame. She had a bone structure such that, no matter how much weight she lost, she would still have the shoulders of Rosey Grier. Her dangling silver earrings, combined with her predilection for black, her designer yet sensible shoes, and hair that, although carefully coiffed, still had a thrown-together Virginia Woolf academic insouciance, signalled her as a card-carrying member of the psychoanalytic crowd. I suspected she might originally have been from Brooklyn and attempted a makeover, but even the best pantsuit at Pennington's wasn't going to hoist her over the Brooklyn Bridge.

As she hoofed it downstairs and smiled at us, I was momentarily blinded by gleaming silver bands on her teeth. Who the hell gets braces at forty years of age? I guess the kind who always wanted their teeth fixed but whose parents couldn't afford it, or else said, "You never smile anyway."

Dvorah told us that she had a publishing deadline and,

although she had thought she'd have more time, she was behind and could only give us about fifteen minutes. Quickly, before we could react, she added, "Are you two related? There's something about you that looks familial."

"We're identical twins. I'm the one with the mole," Jackie continued without missing a beat. "I believe you've written an exposé"—Jackie pronounced it without the accent—"for *Metropolitan Life* on Anders Konzak and his trouble with the Freud academy and now he's suing you for libel."

"It's turned so ugly," she said, rolling her eyes.

"Is it true that you tape-recorded every session but that the tapes have been lost?"

"That's right so far," she acknowledged.

"Were they stolen?" Jackie asked.

"I have no idea. They may be genuinely lost. I only wish I had them to avoid this entire legal harangue. It's absurdly time-consuming, and the lawyer's fees are ridiculous."

"Do you think Konzak really has anything of interest, intellectual or otherwise, that'll come out in the book?" I asked.

"I think he's bluffing. But I also didn't think he would sue me for writing exactly what he said to me, so what do I know?"

"That article you wrote put him on the celebrity circuit and gave him his fifteen minutes of fame, but"—here Jackie paused for emphasis—"it also cost him his job."

"*Excuse me! He* was the one who was publishing the, quote"—Dvorah made quotation marks in the air with tastefully manicured red talons—"'complete' Freud–Fliess correspondence with annotations that supposedly maligned Freud, not *me*. I was quoting what *he* said. I didn't give an interview with *The Washington Post* condemning Freud—he did."

Jackie pressed on. "Did you know that there have been threats made on the life of Konzak?"

"No. But it doesn't surprise me," she said.

"You would, of course, benefit if Konzak died."

"So would the rest of the urban landscape."

As Jackie was questioning her, he began ambling around her apartment, mumbling about the fantastic view. "This apartment is great. The view of the park is amazing, and the roof garden—wow! I'll bet your parents were happy when you moved here from your fifth-floor walk-up on the Lower East Side."

"Of course I never would've bought it if I had known about these legal expenses."

"You must have made some prudent investments to afford this place," he said while moseying from room to room. "Oh Kate, look at this solarium. Wouldn't you kill to have morning coffee out here? Is this spectacular or *what?*"

"I'm sorry that you're here too early to see the roof garden in bloom," Dvorah said.

"Who's your broker? You couldn't afford this place on the pittance of a freelance journalist," Jackie said. Dvorah feigned laughter by silently tossing her head back. "No, seriously," he said, "how did you pay for it?"

I thought this was getting embarrassing. It was no wonder that Dvorah's *joie de vivre*, however brittle, clouded.

"Hey, you want to ask about Konzak's enemies, fine. I'm not some welfare mother that you can push around. I don't have to tell *you*, a schlemiel from nowhere who the psychoanalytic association hired to cover its ass, my broker's name or what I paid for anything," she snapped.

"You're right, except for the schlemiel part. Because I know you have no broker. You don't even have investments or any personal inheritance. Your parents live in Levittown. You made no claims on your income tax for any investments last year. You actually paid cash for this penthouse in a private sale eleven months ago. Strange thing to do when the bank interest rate is lower than inflation. Money burning a hole in your pocket?" Jackie asked.

"My finances are none of your concern."

"They're interesting, though. Four months after your interview with Konzak you had over one million dollars in cash."

"So what do you think, Einstein, Konzak paid me a million for writing *bad* things about him in a magazine?"

I could see why Gardonne hired Jackie. He had a detective network with tentacles that could reach into any pile of muck and grab hold of some, as they so euphemistically say in the CIA, "intelligence." Clearly Jackie learned in prison how to get contraband off the black market. And what is intelligence, if not verbal contraband?

"Ever heard of a Canadian psychiatrist named Gardonne?" he asked.

"No."

"Strange." He paused. "You must have an obsessive-compulsive disorder, because you've been dialling his number at least once a month for the last few months."

Speaking up for the first time, I said, "You have a similar disorder to Dr. Gardonne. Maybe you both have Tourette's syndrome and you both have the same symptomatic tic of calling each other's phone numbers. Dr. Gardonne had your number on a pad beside his bed in his room on the Isle of Wight."

Dvorah sank down into her Ultrasuede loveseat with its plumped raw-silk throw pillows and let out a long breath of surrender. She looked at the ceiling and said, "So sue me! So I'm having an affair with him. Gee, I wonder if I'm the first working girl in New York to have an affair with a married man. It may be a touch seedy, but hardly worth an investigation."

I doubted that Gardonne would have an affair with this Kate Smith look-alike. Besides, sex wasn't one of his bargaining tools. Nine years with someone tells you something.

"Kate, you look dubious," Jackie said in a jocular tone. "You know something, Dvorah? I too share Kate's shock. We would never expect sexual impropriety from either of you. Rabid upward mobility would be more your forte."

Getting progressively more agitated, Dvorah said, "Look—" but Jackie interrupted her.

"We have looked, and guess what? We have the following coincidences. Number one, you're a starving journalist. Two, you interview Anders Konzak and *lose* the tapes of the interview. There is talk of him suing you. Number three, you're in contact with Dr. Gardonne in a flurry of activities, sexual or otherwise. Number four, you suddenly 'come into money' of the cash variety. Enough to catapult you from the East to the West side. This is a dot-to-dot drawing where the numbers don't connect. I'm listing facts, but the word 'coincidence' suggests they are somehow related." He talked while walking around the solarium smelling spice plants on the windowsill.

"I don't know what the hell goes on in that frozen tundra where moose outnumber people, but here in the good old U.S. of A. we don't shake in our boots over coincidences," Dvorah said.

"Oh, you New Yorkers, with the fine-tuned judicial system, want connecting links. *Fine.*" His voice shot up an octave and each word burst forth like a missile. "You interviewed Konzak and you found out some dirt that was harmful to Gardonne personally. You agreed to lose the tapes that incriminated Gardonne if the good doctor would come up with some dough—big dough, judging from your domicile. This is known where I come from, in the northern hinterlands, as blackmail."

"That's crazy. But to play along with your little scenario, why would you care? Wouldn't that be known in most circles as a business transaction? So what if Dr. Gardonne gave me money for a tape—who's complaining?" Her tone was jaded even for a New Yorker. When no one answered, she continued, "May I be so crass as to inquire what my motive might be?"

"Sure. I would too. Whatever dirt you got on Gardonne from Konzak, you had to be sure that no one else got hold of it as well. How can you blackmail someone if everyone knows the secret? What if the secret appeared in *The Washington Post*? Now let me see—how can you get Gardonne to give you money but assure him that Konzak will never open his mouth again? *Eureka!* Permanently silence Konzak."

"What am I missing here?" Still clinging to her this-is-ever-so-amusing voice, she pressed on. "Are you arresting me or something?"

"Not at all. You asked for the linchpin of coincidence," Jackie pointed out.

"I can see how you might misinterpret things in the way that you have. It is, however, an unfortunate misunderstanding."

Jackie interjected, "Now that I've seen you, I can see how you could easily have knocked off Konzak with one mighty backhand as long as you put all of your weight behind it and bent your knees."

The Miss Congeniality face clouded and her voice lost its light warble as she bellowed, "Get out or I'll call the doorman."

"Kate, she might call the doorman," Jackie said.

"Oh no, not the doorman," I echoed.

"Don't come back here without a warrant or a subpoena or whatever it is that you assholes need to get it up." She flounced through the foyer to the elevator and spoke into a gleaming brass intercom. "Rodriguez, my guests are leaving. They're salespeople and I'm not interested in buying."

"One stop at twelve and then I'll shoot right up, Miss Little," the intercom replied.

"Interesting that when you accuse a woman of murder she doesn't raise an eyebrow, but when you suggest she might be one big momma she kicks you out," Jackie said to me as we walked toward the elevator. The word *murder* hovering in the whirring air purifier, Dvorah turned to me and said, "Believe it or not, I find Anders Konzak rather charming. When he turns up, please let him know that I wish I'd been able to get across more of his personal charisma in the article I wrote. I'm not allowed to talk to him now that we're involved in litigation."

Walking behind us, Jackie piped up with "I think he'll be surprised to hear that you feel that way, although his charm may have come off better in the Danube Hotel than it did in the article." In a purely conversational tone he added, "I know other things did."

She didn't miss a beat. "That's quite true. When we were at the Demel Café, Anders was quite right when he said we were getting too much mike interference. The tape quality was much better in the hotel."

"Oh God, Mike was there as well! That would account for all the noise. Now the breakfast for two was a nice touch, after that all-night *chat*. No wonder you ordered so much orange juice, you must have been parched."

"I did fifty-eight hours of taping. When and where didn't seem important to me. Fifty-eight hours is a lot of time."

"Well, now we know he didn't have premature ejaculation," Jackie said reassuringly.

She smiled, looked at the red elevator light as it crawled through the numbers and said, "Nice try."

"We know about the missing tapes, and we know that Konzak has his own set of tapes. Or used to have them. Konzak taped the wailing and howling that came from that room. We all found the howling of anthropological interest. There was some speculation that you were the original wild child raised by wolves, as in Dvorah Wolfwoman—or would that be Wolfperson? Anyway, you can settle your origins in court because those tapes will be admissible in your big libel case."

"I think I would know what was taped. Why would Konzak have me to a hotel room, have . . . his way with me, and tape it?"

"As an ace in the hole, so to speak, in case he needed some leverage in the *unlikely* event that you misquoted him and then you lost those tapes. Let's face it, Konzak was no genius, but he's enough of a card shark to know how another will play her hand. After all, it's his stock-in-trade." Jackie then pulled a micro-cassette out of his pocket and slowly lit a cigarette.

"Well, how do I know that is real?" She was still using her cocktail party voice.

"Kate, which part should we play? The part about the high heels or the line I like best, the one that covers modern technology? When Mr. Konzak says his mind is a computer and Ms. Little says, 'What I like most is your hard disk.'"

"Beats a floppy," I had to agree.

A thin line of perspiration appeared on her electrolyzed upper lip.

The art deco elevator doors opened, Jackie bounced in and I followed. "Bye," Jackie said in his usual throwaway tone, "but listen, my little girl Friday, remember the headlines, 'Konzak Breaks His Own Record at 2001 Sexual Conquest.' The article reads something like this: 'Konzak sues the 2001, a Ms. Dvorah Little, in a libel case for millions. She claims she "lost" the tapes of their interview, but he was less careless. Exhibit A, taped in Konzak's boudoir at 2:30 a.m., reveals wolf calls, high-heeled staccato dancing and a more technical discussion of Konzak's software.'"

"Don't worry, the public is never interested in this type of thing," I added, getting into the spirit.

The doors closed and we rode down in amused silence. As the elevator approached the lobby, Dvorah's voice, which had now returned to her Brooklyn roots, blasted statically over the intercom, "Rodriguez, please bring those salespeople back up."

"We made a sale. She couldn't resist our software," Jackie said, slapping my hand.

We tumbled off the elevator to see Dvorah Little's drained face. We filed into her high-tech study, one of those great rooms with built-in hanging file drawers that pulled out with just a slight nudge, perfect lighting over her expansive desk and in her built-in bookcases. One whole side of the room was a full-length window framing the New York skyline.

Grabbing a cigarette from Jackie's pack, she stared straight ahead and said, "Let's make the best of a bad situation. I am willing to be perfectly honest in return for that tape."

"We'll corroborate the information and then return the tape," Jackie said, taking an uninvited seat in a leather chair. "What is your relationship to Gardonne?"

She took a long breath, walked over to the window, placed her hands flat on the glass, taking in the city skyline, and mumbled, "When I was a kid living in my parents' tiny, claustrophobic house, I used to listen to *Rhapsody in Blue* and look at the album cover. It had exactly this skyline. I was determined to own that view someday." A tear streaked her makeup. "It didn't last quite as long as I'd hoped. But hey . . ."

As she turned away from the window and faced us with smudged mascara and tired hair, I saw the girl in high school who had to dance with the gym teacher because no one else asked her in "social dancing" class.

Jackie must have sensed the same hollow sense of failure

because his voice had more compassion in it when he said, "Let's sit down and get this over with as fast as possible, preferably with no bullshit on either of our parts. What's your relationship to Dr. Gardonne?"

"I met him a few months after I did the interview with Konzak."

"How did that come about?"

"During the interview I mentioned that the North American Psychoanalytic had recently elected a Torontonian to its ethics board. As lunch conversation, since Konzak was from Montreal, and was also a psychoanalyst there, I asked him if he knew the new Canadian board member, a man named Dr. Gardonne from Toronto, who, it was said, carried a lot of clout. Konzak laughed and said he knew of him but that it was the ultimate irony that an unethical man should head an ethics committee. It was like Roy Cohn, still in the closet in the McCarthy era, condemning homosexuals. Life imitating bad art. You can imagine how Konzak carried on about it."

"What had Gardonne done that was immoral?" Jackie asked.

"Used confidential information from a patient for his own financial benefit. He had a patient in the 1970s who was the Ontario minister of parks and recreation, or held a portfolio or whatever people hold in Canada. The minister was an honest man who came into therapy because of his anxiety. While in analysis the minister told Gardonne that he was anxious about making some decisions about the ownership of the Toronto Islands. There were four islands three miles off the downtown shore which were poorly serviced by a ferry system. These islands were originally used for summer residences at the turn of the century. The government bought the islands in the 1950s and leased out the property and cottages on five-year renewable leases until they could decide what to do with the land. Most of the cottages had become dilapidated over the years and were leased out for a pittance to what became an artists' colony. There was a proposal by the government to repossess the islands for parkland, as they were already government owned. They would make the islands into a huge connecting park system and build a causeway out of landfill from the mainland. The minister wanted to make it a tourist attraction with an aviary and boating. No cars would be allowed, and it would be a safe place for bikes.

"Anyway, there was only one store per island and they were all rundown one room convenience affairs that were badly managed by island ex-hippies, mostly American draft dodgers who stayed after the Vietnam War ended. The proposal entertained by Toronto city council was that the owners of all of the present facilities would have first crack at buying the concessions for the public park. With the proposed causeway and new facilities, there would be thousands of people every day in winter for cross-country skiing and in summer for boating and the amusement park.

"While the minister was telling Gardonne how anxious he was about expropriating the few island residents, Gardonne crept out from behind the analytic couch and bought out all the facilities on the island he could, before the takeover was made public. Needless to say, he got all of this for a song, using his wife's inheritance."

"Those restaurants are now a gold mine. I think they're run by Helen of Troy Concessions," Jackie said. "I go over there to fish in the summer in the stocked pond. Helen of Troy has a monopoly over there, so you are forced to buy an overpriced white bread sandwich."

"That's a holding company for Gardonne," Dvorah responded.

"How did Konzak become involved in this?" I asked her.

"Totally inadvertently. About five years after the minister finished his analysis with Gardonne, he still had anxiety attacks."

"Surprise," I said, exchanging glances with Jackie.

"The minister had been transferred to Montreal and his daughter was an undergraduate taking a course on 'Nabokov and Psychoanalysis' from Konzak at McGill. She told Konzak about her father's anxiety, and Konzak, not one to dine on humble pie, said, 'Send him to me and I'll cure him.'"

"As if anxiety isn't enough, he gets Gardonne and then Konzak for *help*," Jackie said, shaking his head.

"In his analysis with Konzak, the minister talked about high government wheeling and dealing. He asked Konzak why he wanted to focus on his childhood instead of his immediate business transactions as Dr. Gardonne, his other shrink, had done."

Jackie said, "So even Konzak put two and two together."

"Konzak began to ask what the minister had revealed to Gardonne and found out the analysis took place during the Toronto Island purchase. Konzak found out that Helen of Troy Concessions was really a puppet organization run by Gardonne."

"Why didn't Konzak do anything about Gardonne's unethical behaviour at the time?" Jackie asked.

"Small potatoes," Dvorah replied. "The minister died suddenly from an aneurysm. Gardonne was nothing to Konzak but a two-bit boring analyst who was making a tarnished living in a boring burg. No different from what he already suspected about analysts in general."

"Konzak is more into fame than justice," I agreed.

"Anders told me this whole *histoire* only as a piece of juicy gossip. He never thought or didn't care that if I repeated it verbatim, it would completely ruin Gardonne professionally."

While Dvorah was lighting another cigarette, Jackie continued her tale. "However, you, the ever-opportunistic host, realized how important this bit of information was in terms of blackmail, and you had it on tape. You, unlike Konzak, were not the rich golden boy. You struggled to write long intellectual exposés on almost unknown feminist photographers. Your work received a smattering of acclaim, but financially you were paid less than a store clerk. You went from walk-up to walk-down until you decided that you had carried your last grocery bag up five flights and smelled everyone else's gefilte fish for the last Friday night. You decided to sell that tape to Gardonne for a tidy sum, which you immediately plunked down for this *Thin Man* movie set before he could put a stop payment on the cheque or take the money offshore."

Dvorah blew smoke in a French inhale that in no way resembled Simone Signoret. "Gardonne was up front with me. I said I knew about the island and wanted the money. He was upset but paid up within a week, and he said he was going to make sure that Konzak was not planning a Tet Offensive on him."

Jackie stood up and said, "Well, Dvorah dear, we're departing."

As we walked toward the elevator for the second time, Dvorah implored Jackie, "What's going to happen to me?"

"Blackmail is a crime, my dear, even in New York."

Pulling herself together, since she could see wheedling was getting her nowhere, she asked, "Can I give you my take on this 'crime,' as you put it?"

"Sure." Jackie could do flippancy better than most I'd seen.

"Gardonne is dishonest, and he ripped off the government of Ontario. That's no different than tax evasion. I mean, it's a soft crime. I tapped into some of it because I was in the right place at the right time." She pressed the elevator button and said, "Do you think bribes aren't an everyday occurrence in journalism, particularly *investigative* journalism?" Pushing what she hoped was her address to the jury, she said, "You don't think Deep Throat sang for nothing, do you?"

Forever the bloodhound, Jackie said calmly, "At the risk of redundancy, Dvorah, there have been maybe three crimes committed here. Let me spell it out for you: A, blackmail; B, Konzak has been threatened; C, Konzak is now missing."

"Jesus, I honestly don't know what happened to him." She lit one cigarette from another. "I wish I still lived in my walk-up." As she cradled her head in her hands, she mumbled, "This is fantasy run amok."

"Well, I'll tell you what, Dvorah," Jackie said. "Things will be a lot easier for you if you never see or hear from Gardonne again. Never let him know that we know about the island affair."

"I swear I never will." She was now addressing the floor.

"We will know if you tell Gardonne, and if you do, the police will be called faster than you can say 'Dvorah Little gets busted big.'"

As we stood in the vestibule, she asked, "I've been fully cooperative. May I have the tape now?"

"Dvorah," Jackie said, putting his arm around her and holding the tape in his other hand, "I want to help you to avoid temptation. Lucifer can take many forms, so I'm going to hold the tape just to be sure that you don't contact Gardonne in the immediate future."

"When am I getting the tape?"

"As soon as we find Konzak alive and well. Shouldn't be long."

In the elevator, we exchanged the smile of the Cheshire cats and didn't say one word until we hit the deli next door, slid into the Naugahyde stalls and ordered coffee with edible oil.

"Jackie, there was no tape in Konzak's place, unless the murderer got it. We tore the place apart. Where did you get the info?"

"That was a hunch. My assistant interviewed everyone that stayed at Konzak's place the night of the meeting-of-the-minds-and-body interview. The man in the suite under them heard the constant click of high heels. He even called the management at three a.m. and made a complaint, which, thanks to the obsessions of the Austrians, was logged so the morning shift could follow up on any problems.

"Next, we interviewed everyone who knew Konzak in Vienna. We came across a waiter at Demel's who said that he and Konzak spent many a night picking up women and discussing their past sexual exploits. Sandwiched between a thousand dick-brain stories about the Viennese damsels and what they *really* do with their blonde braids, Konzak mentioned that he was interviewed by a journalist who compared his dick to a hard or floppy disc or some such crap. I read all of the interviews with him in the last year and only three were by women. The complaint about the high heels matched the dates of the interview with Dvorah. So I knew I had a stiletto edge on a one-in-three chance.

"Good work, Kimo Sabe." I leaned over and shook his hand.

He nodded and said, "You were right, Gardonne was exactly what you said he was. He may have hired you to see if Konzak would reveal the Gardonne island rip-off caper during your interview. If Konzak blabbed, then you would tell Gardonne and he would know that Konzak was more than a loose cannon. You would have to tell him what Konzak said, but you could never blow the whistle to the rest of the world because Gardonne had power over you. He could deny your parole."

I nodded in relief. As Jackie took a giant bite of a pastrami sandwich, I said, "Jesus, why don't you just plug your veins with cholesterol?"

"Couldn't expense-account it."

"So? Did either Dvorah or Gardonne murder Konzak?"

"I think Dvorah is telling the truth. She has no idea Konzak has gone to the academy in the sky. She bought into a blackmail number that may have been more than she bargained for. Smart girl, went to the Bronx School of Science. She wanted a piece of the pie and no one was giving her more than the crumbs on the plate. Ambition grew like frost on a window until she could no longer see out. She let the martoonies-in-the-drawing-room-and-madcap-antics-with-handsome-men fantasies get the better of her, but I don't think she's a murderer. I think she wrote that crap about Konzak because he was 'toying with her affections.' Did you miss that pathetic moment when she wanted you to tell Konzak that she had found him charming? She's needy," Jackie said through a mouthful of coleslaw, "but way too high on the guilt meter to have killed Konzak."

"Gardonne?" I inquired.

"I've met my share of killers, but I don't think that he's one either. That's not to say he's not a lying, conniving, psychopathic piece of shit."

"Okay, but how many upper-class murderers do you know?"

"One. She's sitting across from me." He said this nonchalantly, between bites.

Clearly, if I was going to focus on the class differences between us, he was going to let me have it between the eyes. "I can't believe I asked that question" was all I said. Christ, I'd forgotten that I was a murderer. After all these years, consciously or unconsciously, I still didn't put myself in the killer category. Refusing to get derailed by my own repressed garbage, I pressed on. "I don't believe he would kill someone with his bare hands, because they're too manicured," I said, gulping my cold coffee. "But he could pick up a phone and have it done in the same way he orders a pizza."

"A hit man?" he asked, while putting an astonishing amount of salt on his pastrami.

"It's known as delegation," I answered.

"You're right about that," Jackie said, "but he has no motive. He's already rich. Konzak wasn't at all interested in exposing Gardonne. He only blathered about it because Dvorah mentioned his name and Konzak's tongue was flappin' in the wind. Konzak was gunning for Freud. I don't think Gardonne has delusions of grandeur. Really, no one cares about him, a small-timer from Toronto, and within a few months no one will care about Konzak. I'm inclined to believe the Freudian contingent that thinks Konzak will be old news when he gets tripped up in his own fantasies."

"I think you've got the wrong take on Konzak *and* Gardonne," I said, holding up two fingers. "Konzak is going down as unbalanced. But really, he was as honest as the day is long. He was like a young puppy that everyone thought was a hunting dog. It wasn't his fault. You could have given him a lie detector test and he would have come out clean."

"That's one down," Jackie said.

"Secondly, Gardonne is more ruthless than you think. Sure he has money, but we have no idea how much. He didn't have so much that he didn't want more when he got involved in the island scandal. He got lucky with Dvorah. He met his moral equal. All he had to do was pay her off. Since Konzak mentioned the damaging information to Dvorah, and we both know his mouth was a scattergun, then he could tell someone else. What if the next person he tells turns Gardonne in to the board of ethics? Gardonne would lose his licence and be humiliated in front of colleagues and his golf club. With Konzak six feet under, he wouldn't have to worry about public shame. He wants a green light from old wealth and he isn't taking chances. There is some desperation around his class status. He plays the part too well."

"You know more about the details of those social mores." He pronounced it with a silent *e*. "It's one strange world to me."

"Your vocabulary doesn't indicate that it is a strange world," I pointed out.

"Your manners don't indicate that you could murder someone." He sipped his coffee and then added, "Except for how you're looking at me now. Actually, I'm flattered that you noticed my vocabulary. I was locked up at such an early age I missed most of school. All I had were porn books I borrowed from the older prisoners. I got hooked on smut, eventually read it all. I then began reading higher-quality porn, stuff like Henry Miller. Every time Miller or Lawrence mentioned another writer, I got that author out of the library. Eventually I'd read a lot."

"How did you understand the words?"

"I kept notebooks. I had twenty-six of them. Whenever I ran into a word I didn't know, I copied it down and the sentence it was used in and then, when I ran into the same word again, I would try and figure it out from the context and write that down. Once, a Mennonite minister came into my cell to try and convert me and saw my word books, as I called them, and he told me about the dictionary. That sure lightened my load. Besides, at age twelve I'd use any book with the word 'dick' in it. I was amazed when I found it, and have used it as a sacred text ever since."

"Have you always loved language?"

"No, but I found out that I was a fair writer and girls loved my letters and wrote back and visited, so I saw it got pussy, which was then my main goal, so I perfected it. You need words to do that. Finally the other guys saw the steamy mail I got. They paid me to write the kind of thing women like. You know—emotionally dripping erotica."

That explained why he missed some obvious pronunciations and why there were some strange lacunas (a word he'd pronounced with a soft *c*) in his knowledge.

I looked over at him and realized he'd told me this because he knew he'd gone over the line by harping on about my murder rap again. Most people would apologize for offending me or they wouldn't bring it up, but when Jackie went over the line, he divulged a truth about himself. I had to hope he would hurt my feelings often for that was my only way of learning about him. For some reason I found learning things about him quite interesting. Of course, at some point he will have cashed in all of his chips when I know all I need to know.

As he was getting the check, he said, "Well, now that we know about Gardonne, we need to reassess. He has only perfunctory interest in psychoanalysis and Freud being maligned. It looks legitimate because he's head of the psychoanalytic association. He chose you to find out if Konzak would tell an alluring woman about his island caper when she announced she was from Toronto. He had to have a female from Toronto and she had to be someone he could control. You were perfect—except for the alluring part," Jackie said, sliding out of his booth.

As we waited at the cash register, I said, "His whole Isle of Wight visit wasn't really Freudian diplomacy as much as it was to make sure we were alienated from each other."

"Why is that so important to him?"

"If we got together, we might start investigating him. Or even scarier, if he decided to frame me in the end and pin this murder on me, he doesn't want you to have formed a loyalty to me. Any loyalty to me is loyalty against him."

"It seems to have worked," he said jauntily, then added in a more serious tone, "There is a big leap between blackmail and killing someone. I'm willing to list him as a minor suspect. If he was a major one, he would have had Konzak killed before he forked over big bucks to Dvorah. However, I'll put a few detectives on Gardonne and let's see what crawls out of his background."

Knowing Gardonne's well-honed chameleon qualities, I warned, "You better get your best bloodhounds."

"I've never been enamoured by his John Wayne psychiatric prowess number, but really, let's not lose focus here. Gardonne is peripheral to the reason we were hired. Sure he's a suspect, but we're here to unravel the whole Freudian house of cards — which is, by the way, sitting on a fault with a rising Richter."

I looked askance at Jackie.

"I'm going to outline my priorities. One, we were hired to find out why Konzak turned against Freud. Two, we need to know where he got his information and from whom. Three, we also have a murder case on our hands that we have to solve or, if it is turned over to the police, we may swing for it. We need to solve the first two in order to figure out the third. Now, fourth, we know Gardonne may be involved in the whole thing somehow, but I'm still going to work on my top priorities and eventually, if we are hit in the face with Gardonne as a suspect, then we'll deal with it. Till then, I'm not putting him at the top of my list."

Once I heard that Jackie thought Gardonne was innocuous, or not a high priority, I knew I had to keep quiet about the Boy Scout medal I'd acquired on my break-and-enter in Gardonne's room on the Isle of Wight. It had not escaped me that Jackie had all kinds of information on Dvorah that he hadn't shared with me beforehand. I was convinced that Gardonne was far more than a psychological poseur. Not only was he using me, he might even be framing me for Konzak's death. I had to gain some personal control of the situation. The bottom line was, I had no way of knowing what side of the fence Jackie was really on. He could be working with Gardonne to frame me. It was best for me to keep the Onondaga badge to myself until I had time to investigate Gardonne on my own. He was way too smart, or canny, for most detectives.

As we went through the revolving door of the deli, Jackie held up two airline tickets and mimed the face of a clown. On the street, I said hopefully, "The Italian-American circus clown?" as I grabbed the tickets, which had *Toronto* emblazoned in red.

"A man named Robert Bozzetelli has an outside reader's registration card for the Robarts Library at the University of Toronto. He's well known to the biomedical librarian who's in charge of the psychoanalytic collection. He borrows books on the early Freudian years and has obtained the Freud–Fliess correspondence in its original German through interlibrary loan. The bottom line is, he's borrowed more esoteric Freudiana from all over the world than any professor ever has."

"An Italian clown. Who needs a detective? We'll probably spot him right away because he'll be the only smiling man in Toronto."

12

A THREE-RING DETECTIVE

—

Innocence is ashamed of nothing.
—JEAN JACQUES ROUSSEAU

JACKIE AND I landed in Toronto for the first link in what later became known as The Italian Clown Odyssey. I was happy to have my feet on home turf even if I knew it was really toxic landfill. At least Canadians as a group, I guess I should say excluding myself, use their guns for hunting *other* species.

The cab driver, a Rasta from St. Vincent whose dreadlocks resembled a cat-vomited furball, asked where we were going. He looked at the paper Jackie handed him and smiled, displaying two gold incisors with diamonds discreetly placed in the centre. When I leaned over the front seat, I noticed he was wearing a T-shirt that said *My boss is a Jewish carpenter.*

"Yeah, mun. It downtown, off Queen Street—near Bellwoods Park."

"Is that the Queen Street strip area?" Jackie asked.

"That it be." He started laughing uproariously.

Jackie and I failed to see what was so funny—but it did sort of cheer us up.

"What goes on at Queen near Bellwoods Park?" I asked.

"Lots of white druggies down there, and punks in the roomin' houses near Parkdale. Some artist types." He looked at the paper again and said, "303 Crawford. That be in the action. You goin' to see the city, you go there."

As we drove down a tree-shaded street that was lined with old red-brick Victorian row houses that were now mostly rooming houses, the cab ground to a halt in front of a tiny patch of scruffy lawn. In the middle was a strange sculpture that looked vaguely scientific—a homemade Stonehenge, casting no shadow at all. Maybe this guy knew more about time than we did.

Jackie and I took deep breaths as we approached the cracked front walkway. We tottered gingerly up the wooden stairs since the porch had a few missing planks. There was an overstuffed old couch, covered with flyers, that clearly doubled as lawn furniture. A typed sign in Gothic print on the centre of the door read

𝔖𝔬𝔩𝔦𝔠𝔦𝔱𝔬𝔯𝔰 𝔴𝔢𝔩𝔠𝔬𝔪𝔢— 𝔍𝔲𝔰𝔱 𝔪𝔞𝔨𝔢 𝔦𝔱 𝔦𝔫𝔱𝔢𝔯𝔢𝔰𝔱𝔦𝔫𝔤

No one answered my knock, but I heard a tape deck blaring the McGarrigle Sisters singing "Talk to Me of Mendocino," so I tentatively opened the door, whispering to Jackie, "I feel like Goldilocks."

"The cops call it B and E," Jackie said as we tiptoed down the narrow hall that was lined with bicycles and smelled of old cooking—a mixture of everything from curry to bacon. We followed the music to a big old kitchen. As we entered, we saw a girl, or maybe a woman, who was standing at the speckled Formica counter pouring tea from a lovely raku earthenware pot. She was dressed in a version of Hare Krishna robes cum 3HO member. Upon second glance I decided she was probably unaffiliated, and had most likely come up with the downtown deconstructionist chic all on her own. Her skin looked pale, as though it had not seen the light of day since the last eclipse. Remarkable earrings dangled from half-exposed ears under a white turban. On one ear, on what would normally be the post of the earring, was a small lamb. Dangling from the lamb on a small chain was a lamb chop. On the other ear was a cow, and dangling from it was a hamburger. She had a lithe, slender figure under her gauzy pants, with Birkenstock sandals on her feet over Christmas socks with a moose on one foot and the words *Merry Christmoose* written in holly-print on the other. Aside from her earrings and socks, her outfit was white.

An East Indian man, who looked new to the country, stood at the stove stirring some sort of soup in a large pot. The turbaned Canadian woman strolled over to the kitchen table and flopped into a chair as she was telling the man how she couldn't get another cent from unemployment and that she believed they discriminated against jewellery makers.

"Hey, how you doin'?" Jackie said from the doorway as though he were a welcome guest. Both occupants of the kitchen looked up without surprise. "We knocked but no one answered." They both smiled as though it was normal to have people enter the house uninvited. Maybe that's how things worked in a rooming house.

"Do you know a man named Robert Bozzetelli?" I ventured.

The turbaned woman thought for at least a full minute and then said, "No. Sounds like he's in trouble with a dealer?"

"No, we want to talk to him about his work," I said.

"We do not know him. Very sorry," said the man.

At that moment a Canadian Native with long braided black hair wearing a blue Levis shirt and jeans sauntered into the room. I'd lay money on his being a Cree. (You live in the Canadian prison system long enough, you learn to distinguish tribes.) Ignoring us, he said to the turbaned woman, "They mean Bozo, you know, who lives in the basement."

"Oh, *Bozo*," the woman said with a sudden look of recognition. "Yeah, he hangs out with The Wizard."

"Who's The Wizard?" Jackie asked.

"He's a professional wizard. You know, he rents himself out as a wizard for parties and stuff."

"You know, a wizard is like to England as a guru is to India or a medicine man is to the Cree," the Native offered in further explanation.

"Yes, yes," added the East Indian man as he stirred his pot, confirming the Native's explanation.

"Shawna, I haven't seen Bozo for like, a day and a half, have you?" the Native asked.

"No, but when he works, he usually types for days and then finally craters. Once he told me he lost eight pounds writing a paper."

"What's he write about?" I inquired.

"Well, let's see, he calls himself a Freudian dick."

"What's he like?" Jackie asked.

"Intense, really intense. Like, don't ask him a question if you don't have a lot of time," the Native said.

"Does he work?" Jackie asked.

"Yeah, in a record store where they sell oldies, like it's called . . ." The woman's voice began to trail off. "Ye Old Shoppe or something."

"Shawna, *Jesus*," the Native said, banging his hand on the counter, "it's called the Vinyl Museum."

"Relax, Edgar. So that's what it's called—should I throw myself in front of a totem pole or what? Holy moly."

The East Indian looked as though he didn't understand much of what was going on, but he tried to be helpful by indicating the way to the basement.

We went down a narrow, rickety staircase and beheld the strangest decor I'd ever laid eyes on. It was one of those old dungeon numbers that hadn't been updated in ninety years. There was a big oil tank in the corner and a huge octopus of a furnace in the centre where laundry was hung to dry on its duct-taped tentacles. Floor-to-ceiling shelves graced the wall in raw old wood that had obviously been brought in from wrecking sites and looked half rotted. The shelves were separated by bricks that had fallen out of the basement wall, or they might have been pulled out, since there were gaping holes in the wall where raw earth was visible. The shelves were packed from floor to ceiling with books, many with notes sticking out of them. I pulled out one of the notes from Freud's *Psychopathology of Everyday Life*. It said, in big red childishly printed letters,

IS THAT SO, BUDDY?

I carefully replaced it and pulled out another from a volume of Darwin. It said,

TELL IT LIKE IT IS, BROTHER!

The basement dweller had obviously run out of room for books and had begun piling them on the floor, on newspapers. The entire floor was laid out with old *New York Times Magazine* covers. They were set out like tiles in an interlocking arrangement and had then been shellacked to the floor. Actually, the barrage of colour was quite beautiful; a collage of current events is a welcome variation on the rag rug. Some of the shelves had little three-by-five cards bearing the names of different congresses: *American Psychoanalytic, New York Psychoanalytic.* One said *Idiots.* On the idiot shelf were papers by Sulloway, Lacan and Konzak. I nodded to Jackie, letting him know we were in the right place.

The small rooms were divided by piles of books that went three-quarters of the way up to the ceiling pipes. The overall apartment was, in actuality, a maze of books, more fantastic than anything described in *Alice in Wonderland.* In one unit, or "room," there was a single bed made neatly with an eiderdown duvet, and a night light beside it. Next to the furnace the occupant had lined up cans of vegetables with tiny air holes drilled in the top. I leaned down and felt one; it was hot to the touch. Around a corner was a living room with an old couch, a chair and a reading lamp on an old vinyl table. Then we followed the book-lined maze around farther and came to a desk of sorts, an old door lying horizontally on top of two rusted double-drawer file cabinets.

Something moved. I jumped back. There was a man sitting with his back to us at the desk. He wheeled around in his old leather office chair and said, "Hello, I'm Bozo, a Freudian dick at your service."

He was slight and had a long red wavy ponytail and a face of fading freckles. On his nose sat a pair of granny glasses, and there was a barrette in the shape of a Milk-Bone dog biscuit holding back his Botticelli hair. His faded jeans and flannel shirt, the latter with a picture of Roy Rogers's show-off face twirling a lasso, were neat and clean. He looked about thirty-five but might have been older. Freckles are deceiving. Everyone who has them looks like Tom Sawyer or one of his buddies.

A voice wafted from upstairs. "Buzzie Bear my darling?"

"Yes, Shawna?" said Bozo with patience.

"Bozo, oh my little Bozo?"

"Yes, Shawna?" Bozo said, moving toward the stairs.

"You have some guests. Should I send them down?"

"Thank you. I believe they've found their way."

"No problem-o. Glad to help."

They spoke as politely as Ozzie and Harriet. It seemed unreal to me that people would speak this courteously. I must have got used to prison life, where people were rude to one another most of the time. It saddened me to think that I'd become acclimatized to coarseness. When I first went to prison I was shocked by the constant disrespect and crudeness, and now I was shocked by the use of basic manners.

Jackie rolled his eyes at me, indicating that the woman was a space cadet. It had been, after all, at least five or ten minutes since we had left her in the kitchen and descended into the basement.

"Too much Xanax, Shawna darling," Bozo said to himself, and then looked up as though he was shocked to see us yet again. "How may I be of service?"

I shot Jackie an I-can-handle-this look. I had a sudden brainstorm and pulled Jackie's arm back, restraining him, effectively pushing him to the background.

"We represent a certain benefactor who, for the time being, wishes to remain anonymous," I said.

"John Beresford Tipton?" asked Bozo.

"Who's he?" I asked.

"The million-dollar guy, the anonymous donor on the 1950s TV show," Jackie said, incredulous that I hadn't heard of him. "I used to hope he'd come to our door, but it was always the cops."

"Oh," I said. I hadn't been allowed to watch television. My

father said it rotted one's brain. Yet, this weirdo and this jailbird had the freedom to watch as much TV as they wanted and neither turned out stupid. Forging ahead, I said, "We've read of your research on the Freudian detective front."

"Where?"

"Dr. Von Enchanhauer gave us a few of your articles," I said, fabricating.

"That's amazing. I didn't think he would ever refer to me in public. I thought I was his id."

"We work for a publishing company, which will be identified when and if you're interested in the deal that we propose." As I was talking, Jackie glanced over at me with a this-better-be-good expression. Undaunted, I continued. "We want you to do your version of the Freud biography. We think the reading public is just about ready for your revisionist view of Freud." This got no reaction whatsoever, so I thundered on. "You're a thorough scholar and you have something new to say. We'd be willing to give you a generous advance and then pay you by the chapter, as long as you agree to syndication."

"Like Dickens' Bozo stories?"

"Exactly."

"Well . . . you know, I used to be a trusting little earthling, but I've learned the hard way not to affiliate myself with any particular group because that group's ideology insidiously creeps in and slowly strangles the truth. As you may notice from my humble abode," he said with a gracious sweep of his arm, indicating a panoramic view of his subterranean book maze, "I have had to take pecuniary measures. I am in the precarious position of wanting to publish but having no benefactor. Look at that poor boob Anders Konzak. He has to toe the party line or Anna Freud and Von E. are going to cut off his dick. In fact, it's on the chopping block as we speak."

"You see Konzak as someone who's on the right track in the search for truth but has been muzzled by the Freudian establishment?" I asked.

"He has been muzzled, but then again, so have other rabid dogs who foam at the mouth. Of course, what he has had to say is gibberish anyway. He's not entirely wrong, but he has nothing between the ears and sees the world through his gonads. Therefore, he presents only sensationalist trivia."

"You know Konzak, then?"

"We've met a few times," he said, closing some open books on his desk.

"What do you think of him?"

"That's a matter of public record. I've written an article of seventy-one pages chronicling his errors." Snapping into action, he moved his feet sideways like a crab and drove his chair down one aisle, around a corner, and then slammed his feet down, braking when he reached his destination in front of his rotting wood bookshelf. He pulled off a thick bound pile of paper entitled "A comedy of errors, or The Freudian slip is the only one Konzak has not lifted."

"I am sorry that I have to charge for my papers, but the price only covers the Xeroxing and the office work. That will be $6.80 each."

I offered to buy copies of all of his work to date. Bozo didn't seem flattered or even surprised, but politely scuttled around his maze, standing sometimes on a milk crate and pulling papers from various shelves. At last he collected a pile of hand-bound Xeroxing that was about two feet high and said, "There you go. A veritable Tower of Babel."

"I think your intellectual independence is a good idea. You're a Freudian entrepreneur."

"That's the only way to stay honest. Most private detectives have their expenses paid for by their employer, which is, of course, corrupting."

"I can relate to that," I said, glancing at Jackie.

"I would prefer to charge nothing, but unfortunately that is not the nature of the human condition."

"But wouldn't it be easier to find a publishing company that would pay you? They handle all of the secretarial work and distribution, and then you'd be able to concentrate on your intellectual endeavour. They have whole marketing departments to advertise and handle the dogwork."

"Yes, but they have the E-word."

I thought for a moment and then said, "Editors?"

"You got it. Give the lady a cigar, because sometimes a cigar is just a cigar."

"So?" I said. "Don't they only give suggestions?"

"Hah! Read the contracts. They can make a publication shorter, more 'popular,' 'ease the prose,' make it 'more readily accessible' or 'appeal to a broader readership.' These are all euphemisms for making intellectual nourishment into fibreless pap. Ever heard of the *Reader's Digest* condensed book? I have chosen my lifestyle for a certain reason. I don't want to be affiliated. Every time I do, I feel that some part of me gets devoured."

Nodding in agreement, I said, "I've had my moments of feeling like human remains."

"I could have finished at MIT and become a 'scientist,' to use the term loosely. But they only wanted hypotheses proven. You couldn't get a Ph.D. if you *disproved* something. That's just opportunistic science. It prepares people to work in drug companies or, worse still, universities. Someone becomes an aerospace engineer and he has to prove that space travel is good, which in government terms translates as 'worth the tax dollars,' or the engineer is out of a job. Professors have to push students through to get their government subsidy per student. They say the easiest way to a Ph.D. is to replicate a study. What the hell, if Einstein did that, we'd still be suffering through Newtonian physics. He had to work in a patent office in order to *not* be in the system."

Bolstering Bozo's opinion, I added, "Do you know what G.E. Moore said about Wittgenstein's Ph.D. thesis? 'Gentlemen of the committee: This thesis is most definitely a work of genius, and what's more I believe it *may* meet the requirements for a Ph.D. from this university.'"

"Bull's-eye," Bozo bellowed in agreement as he punched the air and continued, "I work in a record store two days a week, live frugally and have more intellectual freedom, which is the only kind that matters, than the president of General Motors."

Jackie nodded assent and turned to me with a glance that said I'd hatched this whole publishing scenario without clearing it with him, so now it was up to me to advance the plot.

"Let's have dinner together and we can talk," I said, buying some time. "Can Jackie and I take you out to a Queen Street club? Maybe hear some jazz later? We'd love to persuade you to do the book with us. However, if it falls through, so be it. I'd still like to hear more about your research."

"Sounds good, but this is a co-op house and it's my turn to cook tonight. Why don't you two join us for vegetarian curry and we can go out for an *après*-dinner concert? The jazz scene never heats up until late anyway."

"Oh, I love curry," I said.

"Shawna is doing dessert and Edgar is responsible for prep."

"That *is* co-operative."

Jackie inquired, "Bozo, do you have a phone book and a scrap of paper? I want to write down the number and call the jazz club for reservations."

"Sure," he said, producing yellow paper dissected into perfect three-by-five rectangles.

Holding up the yellow foolscap, Jackie said, "Kate, we should save our old foolscap and have someone cut it, like this."

"Right, boss." I mimicked the voice of Rochester.

Bozo laughed and, picking up on my festive mood, said, "Hark, Shawna heralds."

The squeaky voice emanating from upstairs was unmistakably Shawna's. "It's time for dinner, Buzzie Bear."

Bozo went to the foot of the stairs and called up, "Edgar, I'm having two guests dine with us this evening. I made copious quantities of curry, so just add a little yogurt to the raita, please. Oh, and turf on two more chapatis."

"Not to worry, Bozo," Shawna replied. "Hari had to go to some relatives for a Muslim prayer thing." There was a long pause with the Native grumbling something and then she shouted down, "Oh, I mean Hindu."

Jackie inhaled deeply suggesting he'd rather dine in the sewers of Calcutta. I shot back a stop-being-so-finicky-and-pipe-down look in reply. I wanted to get all I could from Bozo, the dispatcher of three-by-five bits of yellow wisdom, and I wanted to strike while Bozo's surprise was our advantage.

Before dinner, Bozo introduced us. The woman in white was Shawna Barker; the East Indian, who was on his way out, was Hari Persad; the Native was Edgar Divided-Highway. As we were being seated—believe it or not, Bozo had a seating arrangement—a man with dark curly hair dashed in the front door and came bounding into the room. "This is the one, the *only*—The Wizard!" Bozo said by means of introduction.

"Is it *The* Wizard or just Wizard?" I asked.

Jackie shot me a look that said, *Knock it off.*

"It is very astute of you to notice the first and last name," The

Wizard replied. "I am indeed called *The* Wizard on my passport. Unless in formal circumstances, very few call me The Wizard. Virtually no one calls me The. I, like Cher and Jesus, opted for a single moniker." Still panting from rushing, he said to the group at large, "Sorry, I'm a tad late getting home."

Everyone assured him it was no problem and he then said, "Bozo, guess what? I was just down at CBC and the producer said that the radio show *Ideas* might be willing to do a three-part series on my Darwin angle. I'm submitting an outline entitled *Darwin's Morality: The Thin Edge of the Wedge*," he said, flashing a set of stained teeth. He was unremarkably dressed in T-shirt and black jeans. Across the chest on his shirt was the legend *Honk if you believe in magic*.

"Wizard, these people want me to publish a book on Freud."

"Interesting," Wizard said as he heaped his plate with food, "but haven't we circumvented that route?" .

"That was precisely the stand I took." Looking over at me, Bozo asked, "Would you mind if we all went to the jazz club?"

"Our pleasure," Jackie said.

"Hot dog," Shawna squealed. "Let's go to Aardvark."

"They're missing a major prerequisite for jazz—a band," said Wizard.

"Gee, it's great to live with a scientist, Wizzy," she purred. She had a way of speaking that bordered on self-parody but was at the same time somehow enchanting.

Taking my first bite of vegetarian curry, I couldn't believe how good it was. Jackie beat me to the punch by exclaiming aloud how delicious it tasted.

"Fresh coriander with a pinch of asafetida is the answer," Bozo answered with pride. "I eat my dinner with the co-op house, but I dine independently for my other meals. I usually throw an air-holed can in the furnace and pull it out with tongs.

It's important not to let little routines eat up your life. I don't mind dinner, but three times a day puts your physical appetite in the driver's seat."

Shawna produced some kind of squares for dessert, probably brownies, presented on antique Wedgwood black Asiatic pheasant plates, and said, "I hate walnuts because they look like tiny brains, so I put in another kind of nut. You munchkins have to guess."

The squares were great and tasted like thick chocolate cake. Jackie ventured, "Pecans?"

"Right! Wow, you're a pecan-on-the-first-bite kinda guy!" Shawna continued in a tone of mock awe, "I'm going to save a dance for you."

"This Wedgwood china is exquisite," I said to Shawna, lifting a plate to the light. "I can tell by the colour it must be really old—like 1770?"

"Shawna, a true utilitarian, has chosen to dine upon my Wedgwood collection. Kate, you are very close in your date," The Wizard acknowledged. "The colour was perfected by Edward Singer in 1773."

"That must have been after the factory moved back to Etruria."

"Wow, you're right. Within the same year," The Wizard said.

Jackie lifted one eyebrow as we made eye contact indicating he had very little idea why a character like The Wizard would have this china and why I knew about the dates of the glazes. I returned his gaze, letting him know it was no weirder than being a Darwinian by day and a wizard by night.

As they carefully cleared the finery, Shawna said, "Let's go to the Aardvark."

"Shawna, do you have like a cavity in your brain where your memory is supposed to be? It has no band." Edgar continued, "Read my lips, *no band*."

"Oh right, you mentioned that. How about the Kit Kat?" she suggested.

"Too tiny."

"How about the Bamboo?"

"It's big and loud and not exactly jazz, but it borders on it. I believe I Want to Shoot Ted Kennedy is playing there," The Wizard said.

"No, it changed tonight to the Anna Bananas," Edgar said, glancing up from NOW magazine.

Suddenly The Wizard opened his mouth and spit fire across the room.

"Hot curry, Wizard?" Bozo inquired.

"It's a tablet he puts under his tongue and then he strikes it by rubbing it on the roof of his mouth," Edgar told us in a tone of galloping ennui.

"I love that, Wizzy," Shawna cooed. Marilyn Monroe could have learned breathing and intonation from Shawna.

"Shawna, you may love it, but I don't want to wind up a piece of charcoal. Save that crap for your suburban birthday parties. Plus it's really fuckin' up your teeth. Come on, you guys, let's go," Edgar said as he pushed himself away from the table.

13

THE WHITE RABBIT

—

The theory determines the observation.
— EINSTEIN

AT THE BAMBOO CLUB, each waitress wore a different ensemble. The one serving us wore a T-shirt that said *No Mere Deadhead* and, to top it off, a McDonald's visor. With her ample figure stuffed in her purple stretch pants she resembled an eggplant. "Howdy Mouseketeers, what's happenin'?"

"This is Daphne, my soulmate," Shawna said by way of introduction. "And this is Jackie. Oh yeah, and Kate, his sort of woman-workmate. Hey, *woman-workmate*, that's a good name for a new pink sparkly Bic."

I began to feel, for want of a better word, strange. I didn't know why, but the music was in some way different from anything I'd heard before, or maybe I was just hearing it differently. Usually music was just background for me, yet now my entire body was moving, my heartbeat in sync with the drum's rhythm, and I could hear each instrument separately. The dancers looked as though they were at the end of a kaleidoscope held to

the light. The Frida Kahlo bright colours were flying, resembling a paper dragon fluttering at Chinese New Year. It must
have been one of those prison deprivation moments that creep
up on you and make everything you have not seen or heard in a
long time become larger than life in colour, volume, stimulation and, best of all, enjoyment. As I looked around I felt
inexplicably predisposed to liking everyone I was with. Knowing
they were weird didn't take a detective, but it was more fun than
I'd had in a long time.

I tuned in again to the conversation at the table. I had the odd
feeling of zoning in and out. Usually I was hyper-attentive. Not
that I ever got the lay of the land, but I always listened. Now
there just seemed to be so much going on, and the selective
attention feature of my brain had checked out. Maybe this was
one of those reintegration-into-society, kind of depersonalized
moments that they talk about in prison outtake interviews.

Daphne came over to our table, slapped down a bowl of chips
and flopped into a seat. Usually I don't like junk food, but
tonight the chips looked tempting. I put one in my mouth. I
couldn't believe that it went down my throat like a penknife, and
the salt crystals on the chip felt as though they were dice size. I
had forgotten to chew. As I choked on my chip, Shawna said,
"They aren't even barbecue."

People started dancing, but no one danced with anyone in
particular, each did a sort of interpretive number *à la* Isadora
Duncan. I joined in, and for some reason was not embarrassed
about this performing. It seemed far preferable to dancing with
a partner.

When I sat down, I was so enthusiastic I just had to announce,
"Dancing alone is fantastic."

"It's the only way to travel," said Bozo. "Otherwise you have
all the folderol about who leads, when to stop, who else to dance

with, whatever. Look at primitive tribes—they don't dance with partners."

"So you don't believe in partners at all?"

"No, not really. People are only together for procreation, which I think is overrated."

"You mean the sexual act or producing offspring?" I asked.

"Both. I mean, really, it's a total compromise, isn't it? You try to get him to communicate and he tries to get you to have intercourse. I mean, read Darwin. He's where it's at. Wizard is a Darwinian who writes for *The Evolutionary News*."

"How do they have news? I thought there was news only every two million years."

"Yeah, well, that's why he's a wizard on the side," Bozo said.

Winded after doing a magician's version of the watusi, The Wizard flopped into his chair. Hearing his name mentioned at the tail end of my conversation with Bozo, he joined in, saying, "You know, I love Chuck, but he had no balls. He couldn't face telling the truth, made himself sick and then blamed his cowardice on his century." The Wizard then mimicked Darwin's upper-crust English accent. "'Oh those poor chaps can't handle it.' True, Freud was a bit sleazier, but he had more balls than Chuck. Darwin had to say it all about birds and work his way up to humans. By the time he crept up the Linnaean ladder to the *Homo sapiens*—or down, as the case may be—he had vomited his brains out, literally. Then—"

I was so enthused I interrupted, grabbing his arm, and said, "I know *exactly* what you mean. Darwin was sick for nearly his whole career. I mean, he vomited every day for thirty years. Some scholars believe that he permanently suffered from some tropical disease that he contracted when he went around the world on the *Beagle*. No doctor ever got to the bottom of it. I agree with you that his illness was probably psychosomatic.

Confronting the creationists was too much for him. It's ironic that a man who loathed controversy managed to change the world view. However, the hullabaloo it raised literally made him sick. By the time he began to explore human emotions, he knew he wouldn't be able to weather the storm."

Our conversation was interrupted by a seasoned, mellow yet beseeching saxophone that sounded more beautiful than an ode to a nightingale. I looked up to the stage and was shocked to see Jackie blowing the horn. His Germanic precision made him hit each note exactly. However, his Italian heat gave each note a twisted, sensual quality. In fact his playing was a microcosm of his personality, which was pretty well a perfect combo if you were willing to overlook his mountain of pathology. However, I had to admit, tonight that mountain didn't seem insurmountable; it wasn't even an anthill.

I was clearly not alone in finding the music arresting, since people from the dance floor crowded around the stage to hear him. I could tell he'd listened to twenty years of Coltrane's arrangements as he blew out "Night in Tunisia." As he hit the first few notes of "Smoke Gets in Your Eyes," everyone in the club clapped. What on earth was Jackie doing onstage?

It was really sweltering in the Bamboo, since it had started filling up. Jackie had taken off his shirt, exposing his powerful shoulders in his Stanley Kowalski–type undershirt. My mind produced a full-blown Instamatic of his jogging in Central Park. I wondered why I'd always seen that type as so Brutus. Now I understood why Olive Oyl made such a fuss as I watched the sweat sliding down Jackie's neck, the stage light hitting his muscles at different angles. Everything from my neck down crackled to life, giving me some idea how much I'd been overusing my brain and letting everything else atrophy.

When the riff was over, our eyes caught. I heard my heart

pounding and the slosh of blood running up my legs like spiders. Did anyone else hear this? This sure gave "the telltale heart" new meaning.

The surging was so overwhelming I was sure I had screen doors instead of heart valves, so I choked to Shawna, "God, I feel like I'm having a heart attack."

"Really? Have a diet Coke." Shawna yelled out to Daphne as she went by, "Overdose here. Could we have a diet Coke?"

Overdose. The penny began to drop. "What was in that bownie?" I gasped.

"Oh, it's my mix of coke and hash. And I soak the pecans in my own little concoction. The Wizard calls them creeping carob. I call them bomber brownies, because they kind of dive-bomb down and get you when you least expect it. Just ignore the speediness—it passes. The outside goes first, you know, like the coating of gumballs."

Now that I knew I wasn't having a heart attack, I relaxed and went with it. I asked Shawna, "Does every man here look handsome or is this only affecting *my* erogenous zones?"

"*Duh.* Like why do you think people take drugs? They make everyone look better."

"And the music is so clear," I added.

"Why do you think Gracy Slick had a white rabbit?" Shawna knocked on the side of my head, indicating my denseness. Everyone was doubled over in laughter now.

Even Daphne, the waitress, said, "Uh-oh, Dorothy's in from Kansas."

"But hey, guys," I felt I needed to point out, "lest we forget, that white rabbit can morph into a monkey on your back before you can say 'little yellow pill.'"

"Drugs are not addictive. Some personalities are addictive and some are not," Bozo piped in. He'd just slid back from the dance floor, where he had done a Dorothy Hamill routine sans skates. "Look at Freud."

"Before we get going on Freud, I have to get some fresh air. My eyes are killing me from this smoke. Bozo," I asked, "do you want to come outside with me for a few minutes and get some fresh exhaust fumes?" I knew that if he was going to get onto Freud, it might be important information and I also knew I had to have some quiet and some cold air to straighten me out.

"It really can get oppressive. Let's go up to the roof bar. It is too early in the season for it to be open, but they leave the bar stools there."

The roof garden bar was huge and empty. The stools were chained together and two raccoons were staring at us indignantly from one of the far corners. We sat at the bar, which was housed in a faux grass shack lean-to, and looked over the edge onto Queen Street.

We sat quietly for a few minutes until I said, "I've never been stoned before in front of two raccoons. I feel how angry they are that we have walked into their home. Drugs can make you so much less species-specific. Or is it that you are just more aware of your surroundings?"

"I think it makes you less territorial or self-involved, so you notice others in a more real way for what they are instead of who you want or expect them to be," Bozo replied as he waved to the raccoons.

"Speaking of drugs and perception, you were starting to talk about Freud and drugs as you emerged from the dance floor — at least I think that is what you were saying — or was that a long time ago?" I took a deep breath and filled my lungs with bracing April night air.

"Oh yeah, right. Freud used cocaine for investigative work because it sharpened his mind and staved off mental fatigue. He didn't have an addictive personality and only used it once a week and only in moderation. His cocaine work was published before he realized he had to change his image. That's when the subterfuge started. I got onto it one day when I was doing cocaine myself. I allow myself to do cocaine every other Saturday night to feel what Freud felt. I never drink liquor because it dulls the senses. If I wanted my senses dulled, I would have gone into insurance."

"What subterfuge would he have used?"

"He had a mother who wanted a famous son and he was willing to do anything that would catapult him to prominence. We all spend our lives fighting for our mothers' love. Freud surrounded himself with lackeys who wanted to protect him, because underneath they knew the truth. I mean, unconsciously they knew."

"Who knew?"

"Well, some of the people who read him have figured him out, but Anna Freud and Von Enchanhauer know for sure. Talk about denial. They're constantly talking about his integrity and how he wasn't even interested in sex with good old Martha. Does it strike you as odd that a man who's not interested in sex would devote his life to exploring it?"

I nodded and he went on. "Now that you've had some idea what an aphrodisiac cocaine is, do you really think that Sig was only interested in *theory*? He wanted to write it all up but still protect his reputation, so he did what any normal man would do—he went underground."

"What do you *mean* by 'underground'?"

"His first obfuscation was writing about his own psyche through 'fictional patients.' I've checked it all out."

"That's a difficult thing to prove a century later," I pointed out, "even for a Freudian detective. Can you give me one solid example?"

"Certainly. There are myriad examples. Let's look at the 'patient' in *The Psychopathology of Everyday Life* who had the affair in Italy and then had anxiety about the possible pregnancy of his mate."

"The famous *aliquis* association?"

"One and the same. Allow me to reiterate the details to make my point. Freud says that a 'man he met on a holiday trip' consulted him about how and why he could have forgotten a familiar phrase from Virgil's *Aeneid*. The patient knew the poem very well since his adolescence, had recited it many times, and yet he forgot the phrase '*Exoriar (e) ALIQUIS nostris ex ossibus ultor.*' This lapse gave the gentleman great consternation, and Freud, assuming the gentleman's lapse was an unconscious act of repression, suggested the gentleman free-associate to the phrase. In the patient's free associations he divided *aliquis* into *a* and *liquis*, which translates to 'a liquid.' His next association was to a church in Italy where he had gone with his lover on a recent vacation. In the church there had been paintings of all of the saints of the calendar year, which he and his lover had admired. If one considered the two associations together, one would have a liquid that appears every month of the calendar year, which is obviously a woman's period. The patient was astounded by his own associations and confessed to Freud that upon return to Vienna from Italy with his lover, the classic situation arose: the woman missed her period — *a liquis* so to speak! This caused great anxiety in the patient, thus making him 'forget' a phrase from the *Aeneid* that he had previously committed to memory."

That case had already been written up by Freud. "Tell me something I don't know," I said, genuinely disappointed.

"The 'gentleman' in question was Sigmund Freud and the lover was none other than his sister-in-law Minna."

"The sister of Freud's wife, Martha?" I asked. Dubious, I continued, "Do you mean the single sister who moved into the Freud household after her fiancé died and stayed for forty years?"

"One and the same," Bozo said.

I couldn't help looking askance as I asked, "How do you know that?"

"Easy. He travelled with his sister-in-law Minna to Italy and left Martha at home to mind the shrink shop while he gallivanted around, screwing Minna from Naples on down, so to speak. There are postcards and letters from the trip. It was no secret. Freud actually had the chutzpah, as he would have called it, to send a postcard to Sandor Ferenczi, his close friend. I have found the card. It is a reproduction of the miracle of St. Januarius, proving that Freud was in the church of the calendar saints. Then three months after his return, Minna must have missed her period."

"How do you know that she missed her period?"

"Three months after Freud and Minna returned home from their trip, I have found records that Minna Bernays was sent away to Switzerland to have an abortion. The cover was that she was taken to a spa for the treatment of tuberculosis.

"When I visited Freud's old high school, who do you think had won a plaque in a public speaking contest for a recitation of exactly that poem? Sig himself. Three months to the day after his return from Italy with Minna in 1906, a trip he describes in his letters, he wrote the *aliquis* memory."

"Interesting," I said.

"Exactly. I've written an eighty-page paper with the *aliquis* story as only one example of Freud's masquerade. Even though I have no specific credentials, I'd racked up enough publications to present a paper at the Western New York Psychoanalytic Association conference last year." He added, "That's where I met Konzak and Von Enchanhauer."

"Didn't anyone else figure this out?"

"Sure, but they were silenced and their letters were withheld. Freud's friend Fliess was a perfect example. Even Ernest Jones, the official, not so earnest Freud biographer, quotes Fliess as saying that Freud read his 'own thoughts into his patients.' Carl Jung, no psychological lightweight, guessed the whole thing and said that he thought the psychological-mole number was unnecessary and that people would accept Freud's theories anyway. Jung was a generation younger than Freud, and it was already the 1900s when Jung confronted him aboard ship on the way to America, where they were both delivering lectures at Clark University. As I piece it together, he said, 'Siggy, listen, it's a new century. It is no longer turn-of-the-century Vienna. Come clean. I've figured it all out. *I've* been up front about my infidelities and other peccadilloes. Why aren't you?'

"That's when Freud fainted. Bonk! Flat out on the deck. Jung walked over to him and said, 'Don't worry, I'm not going to tell anyone. I'll keep your pathetic cover-up, but I'm no longer interested in being *your* disciple.'

"If you want more facts, in 1957 Jung gave an interview in which he said that Minna Bernays told him she had had an affair with Freud. Naturally, Jungians believed him, since why would he lie, and Freudians dismissed it as Jung, the rebellious son, having an Oedipal temper tantrum."

I sat dumbfounded as Bozo continued. "Look at a lackey like James Strachey. Don't you think choosing a translator and editor for your collected works who was also your former patient shows a slight conflict of interest?"

"I agree. Even back then it would have raised a few eyebrows."

"Strachey said in a footnote to the *aliquis* association, added in 1924, 'This short analysis has received much attention in the literature of the subject and has provoked lively discussion,' blahbity blah blah. Not only did he cover for Freud, but he also skewed some of the translation, whitewashing Freud. If you want to read it, it's in the Tower of Babel I gave you earlier today."

Excited, I said, "This new slant is riveting. I can't wait to read your entire Freudian gestalt." Thinking aloud I said, "That, of course, explains why he surrounded himself with men of such a diminished sense of independence. They were only pedantically intelligent, such as Jones, Abraham and the others who shuffled the cards on Freud's ideas but never changed or added to the deck." I added, "I always wondered why he didn't pick more original thinkers to be in his circle. I read Freud alone, so I could never discuss him with anyone."

"Right, the heavies like Jung and Reich and eventually Ferenczi were kicked out when they said, 'Hey, wait just one minute here. Freud's the joker in *this* deck.' He then got involved with some sycophantic women whom he analyzed and worked his Svengali transference number on until they were stuck in the Freudian sticky web. If they complained about him, they would be 'rebelling against daddy,' and they really wanted his approval. What regressed female doesn't want her father's love? No one on this planet who is locked into the dynamics of the nuclear family."

"Exactly." I knew this only too well.

"For Christ's sake, look at Anna Freud. Not only was she locked into the dynamics of the nuclear family with dad, but she was locked into an *analysis* with him. That regression and that transference were a permanent psychological chastity belt, man. But that's a whole other story." Bozo got off his stool and started to run in place to warm up.

"You used the phrase 'before Freud went underground.' Have you published—sorry, I should say distributed; I forgot about the E-word—more revelations than we've just talked about?"

"Sure, I've got stuff in cold storage, it's so hot!"

"Such as?"

"Well, I shared some of it with Konzak and in return he was supposed to get me a grant to continue my work. People in the nineteenth century had to cover their asses. Freud chose writing underground."

"Wait, this is moving too fast for me," I groaned, holding my head, hoping he would elucidate. He was stoned and the timing was perfect. Unfortunately, so was I, and I needed forceps to pull out my own ideas, let alone follow his. Someone had oiled my synapses. My brain was jumping from idea to idea like a monkey in a Jungle Gym.

"Look, Freud had one lifetime," Bozo said. "He had to get the ideas out somehow. He didn't have the scientific evidence he needed to move ahead, but he was sure of his theory. So he didn't fudge the data, he just fudged who it came from. He made subjective material look more objective by saying he'd collected the data from his patients. In fact the data was mostly from him. I'm just trying to get the full picture out there. He seduced the reader, but that doesn't mean he was wrong. Let's face it," Bozo said. "He was a genius who was way more right than wrong."

"I agree. I understand you're far more interested in Freud's metapsychology. In the long term who really cares if Freud got his sister-in-law in the family way?"

"Exactly." At this point he slid across the roof floor, doing a Smokey Robinson and the Miracles, Motown dance number. It was so cold we could see our breath.

As he danced back toward the bar stools, he said, "The bomb is going to drop. The big wave is coming soon, Moon Doggie." As he boogied around my bar stool, he asked, "Aren't you cold?"

"No, I've spent some time up in the tundra, so this feels like the Caribbean to me." He was starting to shiver in his thin flannel shirt. Realizing I had little time left before we would have to go inside, I asked the big question. "How does Konzak fit into this?"

"I was willing to share the information with him in a reciprocal arrangement, but I was taken to the Freudian cleaners. Konzak sucked me in—no wonder he's an expert on the *seduction* theory. He took my information and peddled it as his own. But it was so stupid, because I was going to tell him the rest, like the corroborating evidence, and he blew me off, labelling me as paranoid or something. Now he had the right information, but as soon as I realized he was going to steal my research and my theories and then label me as crazy, I wouldn't give him the corroborating information. So what does the brainless twit do? He thinks he's a heavy-duty thinker, so he wings it. From the wings will fall bird shit, especially when the letters, which are soon to be released from the archives, splat in the eye of John Q. Public. I can't wait to hear Von Enchanhauer and Anna Freud make *bubkes* of him."

"'Bubkes'?" There was a Freudian term I'd missed.

"I love that word *bubkes*, it's Yiddish for 'lamb shit.' You know, those little pebbles. What a perfect put-down, not even meriting the status of 'crap'—having to settle for the diminutive version. Yiddish is great for put-downs. I use Italian for *amour* and English for schizoid precision. I like German to pontificate."

We were sliding from one topic to another like snakes on hot pavement. I kept forgetting what I was saying when I was in the middle of a sentence, and sometimes even in the middle of a word. I suddenly realized how wide the space between nerve endings could be. Drugs made that synapse longer than the Brooklyn Bridge. I had to mentally run to get from one idea to another, and got lost if another idea intervened. Before I ran out of electrical stimulation to get from one thought to another, I managed to croak, "Bozo, listen, what is the Freudian bomb?"

"Hey," he said, holding his T-shirt away from his chest and waving it, "man, does my T-shirt say *Dupe?* Making a mistake once is ignorance, twice is stupidity. I am a Freudian dick and I get paid for my work."

"I don't blame you for that. Konzak really burned you."

"He killed the goose when he called me paranoid, and now he has egg on his face," Bozo said with surprisingly little rancour.

"Who else knew that Konzak had this time bomb?"

"Who the hell knows? He was Mr. Galloping Garrulous. He was probably insensitive enough to tell those who would be most levelled by it and then wonder why they were freaking out."

"Who would be most affected?" I tried to concentrate, but I began sinking on my bar stool as though my spine were made of tapioca.

I heard a voice from the bottom of the wrought-iron fire escape stairs wafting up to the roof. It was the unmistakable squeak of Shawna. "Buzzie Bear! Have you gone through the roof? We're all looking for you and Kate, you know, Jackie's workmate from the publishing company. We miss you. You promised me a dance." She popped her head around the door and said, "Wow, you could have an ice wine up here."

"I'm on my way down with one of the punctilious publishing partners, Shawna my dear," Bozo said as we walked down the stairs.

As we entered the main dance floor, we were hit by a blistering wall of heat. Jackie's face lit up when he saw me and he actually picked me up, saying, "Dance and save me from Shawna."

"Yeah, man," Bozo corroborated Jackie's trepidation, "Shawna needs to be locked up after a brownie. We all need full-body condoms. Jackie, my man, you're in nymphomaniacal peril."

I smiled and this time I didn't look away from Jackie's blue eyes.

Shawna came tooling up to the table and purred, "Kate, it's no good to have relationships with co-workers. So they say at the Workmen's Compensation Board's course called How to Get a Job and Keep It."

"This is just a dance, Shawna," I said over my shoulder as Jackie drew me to him and Aretha Franklin's version of "(You Make Me Feel Like) A Natural Woman" began with its long, sensuous notes.

Shawna turned to the others at the table. "Wanna watusi?" She persisted, waving in front of their faces. "Hello? Wizzie and Bozo, hello?"

"Not to Motown, thanks, Shawna," The Wizard said.

She turned to Edgar, who was peacefully rapping his hands on the table, entranced by the music. "Come on, Edgar."

"Shawna, quit bein' such a queen friggin' flake," he said with his eyes closed as he continued drumming.

She went over and pulled out his chair and said with a great deal of patience, "Don't be such a Chief Thundercloud." He stood up and took her arm in the courtliest of manners and off they spun like Kathryn and Arthur Murray.

We began to sway with the music, Jackie's body pulsating with mine. The sweltering temperature of the room made his face glisten. "Isn't the music exquisite?" I asked, wondering if it was just me.

"Incredible." Jackie added as an afterthought, "Great night."

"I know. I can't remember when I've had so much fun. These people are wacky but, in another way, they have a good time."

"You wouldn't believe what that guy, The Wizard, knows about science. I've been talking to him about Darwin. I went outside in the parking lot with him for a cigarette and to cool down. He lit my cigarette by spitting fire at it. I almost lost my nose."

We laughed so hard I was almost crying. After a few minutes

he said, "When you have your whole day to work on the things you enjoy, it's astonishing what you can learn. What's incredible is how he has made all these connections between biology and psychology."

People were clapping. We looked up, suddenly realizing the music was over and we were the only people left on the dance floor. Laughing, we quickly scuttled back to our table.

Shawna came barrelling toward Jackie and tried to grab him, while Daphne chuckled on.

"Kate, the dance floor is yours for the picking. Jackie, you get me," Shawna said, offering herself up.

"No thanks, Shawna, I'll stick to Kate." He added, "She's more my speed."

Jackie was certainly more effusive than usual as we careened around the dance floor, and said, "You look pretty tonight with your face so shiny and your hair falling down."

I looked away. I knew I was supposed to say something, but I felt as though I'd just slid into an iron lung. Jackie must have picked up on my suddenly stiff ramrod back, for he precipitously returned to the case. "We have to check out Von Enchanhauer. Kate, I've decided you're right, he's hiding something."

"People who are good at detecting certain traits in others usually have that trait in spades, but it's gone underground. For example, have you ever met a detective who doesn't play the same part in real life?" I asked.

"What do you mean?"

"You know, plays a role in life, pretends something. That's why we're so good at it. There is no one real character that we are violating. We are emotional chameleons. That's why 'false identities' work so well for us."

"Why *us?*" Jackie inquired, not in a hostile way but just exploring the topic.

"Defence mechanisms, I guess. You had to go under cover, become a juvenile delinquent, grow muscles, be a heroin addict, rob banks, make yourself invincible and eventually get yourself locked in prison. You're not stupid, yet you've been in and out since you were nine. What are you hiding from, I wonder?" I noticed that this concoction, whatever it was that Shawna had made, actually lowered one's inhibitions and made defences seem like odd, inconvenient cubbyholes to be hiding in. While the psychological fences came down, unlike with alcohol, the analytical ability barely faltered—or so it seemed at the time.

"It's too difficult to gauge relationships . . ." Jackie said, letting out a long, frustrated breath. "Love—wanting it, having no idea how to get or give it, having to settle for sex. Actually, sex was only a little bit of it. However, it opened the love door just a crack, enough to keep me on the merry-go-round of sexual obsession. I was a sex addict not because it was perfect but because it was so imperfect. It let me look through the keyhole. The pain of not having love, or not knowing how to get it, was so overwhelming that I did everything in my power to block it. First came the sex, then the drugs, then the crimes, then prison. I could then be locked away from the pain."

I was fairly shocked by this revelation, but I'd noticed that this "brownie" was a bit of a truth serum. I remembered that on previous occasions, when I asked him something directly, he could be surprisingly open about his feelings if he was in the mood.

"How did you end the cycle?" I asked.

"I just turned off the sex. It had jump-started the rest of the cycle." He looked down at me wrapped in his arms and asked, "And you?"

"Me? I couldn't be the perfect emotionless intellectual that my father wanted, so I went underground with it all. The real me never comes out, because there isn't one. It's an optical illusion. It's like an onion, and you just keep peeling away the layers and finally there are no more layers."

"Even onions have centres," he pointed out.

"Bad simile, then. Maybe it is like a permanent house of mirrors. Everything is a distortion. You never see a true reflection."

Jackie put a finger to my lips to silence me. "Kate, all of this is the drugs talking, and they may be letting us say more than we would want revealed when straight. I've been there before, hundreds of times." He added, slightly pressing my head to his chest, "Let's just dance, be in this moment and not analyze things any more tonight."

I loved the large headrest of his shoulders. They were so broad that I had lots of cushioned space for my head. Our sweat glued us together. The room was spinning slightly and I had to hold Jackie tightly just to stand up. His arms were long and his chest was wide; it was the first time I'd felt totally enveloped in an embrace. I felt his heart pumping against my ear.

The ticking of his heart reminded me of the time our family got a tiny puppy when I was a little girl. The breeder said the puppy was a bit too young to be separated from the mother, so she should sleep with a clock wrapped in a blanket to calm her at night by replicating the mother's heartbeat. My father scoffed at this idea until the puppy howled and cried for hours the first night, keeping us all awake. Finally, defying my father for the first time in my four-year-old memory, my mother quietly got the clock and put it under the puppy's blanket. To my amazement the puppy then immediately curled up and went to sleep with her ear to the ticking clock.

The song was over, but I couldn't face breaking away from him when he made a slight movement to go back to the table.

We held on to one another for a long moment, and I had the strange sensation of wanting to get closer and closer to him, moving my feet onto his. I felt like crawling up his body and wrapping my legs around him. My head flopped on his neck and I lightly licked his neck as a horse welcomes a salt block. He held me so tightly he was lifting me off the ground. He rubbed the side of his head in my hair and I heard his quick stabs of breath. I was sliding slowly up and down against his body, fitting into every crevice of his anatomy.

The Anna Bananas began a fast reggae, breaking the spell, and we snapped apart. The bamboo world around me still looked as though I were viewing it through a telephoto lens, but at least it was returning into focus. I held Jackie to help myself deal with what I perceived to be a steep uphill slant as we returned to the table. He helped me stay upright and get oriented again. The drugs were wearing off, and I felt the old Kate was coming back. I wondered how long we'd been dancing. A minute? An hour? The ability to judge time had been lost in the lobes of those soaked pecans.

The table was empty. I looked at the dance floor and then we rushed over to the bar. No sign of our party anywhere. We returned to the empty table and found a note written on a coaster:

Dear Publishers Bearing Gifts:
   Edgar was a little under the weather so we toddled home. It's going to take more than one of us so . . . 10-4. I can't believe it's after 2:00 a.m. Let's talk soon about the work. Thanks for a great night.
                    Your Freudian private dick,
                              Bozo,
                              et al.

"Shit." I crumpled the coaster and flung it on the table. "Jesus Christ. I was getting so much info from him, and then *you* had to undulate over to dance!"

"Ever heard 'Tomorrow is another day'?" Jackie asked.

"No, but I can learn a lot of original thinking with you."

"He would have become suspicious if you'd asked too much. Stoned or not, he's not an idiot."

"You might be right." Never one to notice that milk has already been spilt, I couldn't help but add, "I still think I should have graciously declined and you'd eventually have gotten the drift."

"So might he have." His voice softened and he said, "You can't force a relationship. Let it grow, and as he trusts you the material will pour out. If he wakes up tomorrow and is leery, it's game over . . . Christ, I'll bet you're the type that has fast sex and then wonders why it wasn't satisfying," Jackie added.

What the hell is he talking about? He interrupts me at a crucial moment in the case with some dancing idiocy and then accuses me of being a bad lover. Jesus H. Christ. I gave him a look that said if I wasn't so tired I'd wring his neck like the Road Runner. I also wanted to get home and safely under my covers before Jackie made any allusion to the fact that I wasn't "gracefully declining" a hell of a lot on that dance floor. Rereading the soggy coaster, I said, "Let's go home and meet at his place at noon. If we go any earlier, he might get suspicious."

"Right," Jackie said as we walked toward the exit.

"I want to get home to get everything down before I forget it."

"You'd better dictate it in the car, because this dope is like catnip. I've already forgotten everything The Wizard said," he confessed.

He listened all the way back to my place as I mumbled into the recorder, and when I flicked off the switch he said, "That's a lot of good stuff . . . Do you think Bozo's crazy?"

"I don't know. For sure he's smarter than Konzak. I'll read what I can of his papers overnight and I'll tell you more in the morning."

14

—

THE MARCH OF THE MAGGOTS

—

A little sincerity is a dangerous thing,
and a great deal is absolutely fatal.
—OSCAR WILDE

AT EXACTLY NOON I sauntered onto Bozo's front porch. The
magnolia tree was in full bloom, its pink art deco coffee-cup
buds poking their way through the rotting porch spindles. The buds
hadn't been out last night but were in full bloom today. Some of
the flowers had dropped off already and lay spent on the lawn.
How long was it actually in *full* bloom? Maybe only a moment.

"Hi," Shawna said while lugging out a garbage bag. As it hit
the curb I heard the clang of Bozo's charred cans. She plunked
it on the curb. "Holy Toledo, spring came so fast the magnolias
didn't last a day."

"I was just thinking that. Things are heating up too quickly."
As we walked through the front door, I asked if Bozo was up.

"Don't know. He and Wizzy keep weird hours. I have to keep
regular hours to go down to the unemployment office. Want to
buy some jewellery?"

"Sure, let's see it."

"I'll bring it down to the kitchen. My room is a little messy."

Eventually she sashayed in with a Greb boot box and joined me at the kitchen table. Picking through the box, she pulled out some half-inch-long thin yellow plastic sticks that were covered in red glitter. They weren't even straight.

"Hmmm," was all I could muster.

"These are called moon dust on bananas."

"Neil Armstrong would like these. You should send him a promotional pair."

"He's probably not pierced," she said absent-mindedly as she poked around in the box, pulling out a wrinkled brown stick the size of a match. Holding it up, she trilled a drum roll and then histrionically announced, *"Presenting!"*

As she rummaged for its mate, I took the opportunity to inquire about Bozo. "You really live in an interesting house. How long have you all been together?"

"The Wizard and Bozo were the founding members, I was next—that was four years ago—and then came Edgar. Hari's the baby."

"Long time."

"It's a chunk."

"They're a tad weird."

"You know what Buzzie Bear says is weird?" I couldn't imagine, so I was glad when she filled in for me. "Weird is lining up at IKEA to buy particleboard covered in white plastic called Billy. What's that about? I love Bozo and The Wiz, that's for sure."

"Communal living sounds hard to me. Have you guys made it work?"

"We've never had a fight," she said proudly, still grubbing in her Greb box. "We had a few guys before Hari, but we decided on Hari because he was quiet and not part of the going-out crowd." (She held her hands up making two quotation marks as she said "going-out.") "He does his cooking and his one day of cleaning. Bozo doesn't pay any rent on account of he fixes things for the landlord, who owns a slew of rooming houses. The Wiz and Bozo can fix anything. They even wired a renovation down the street, just by getting a book from Canadian Tire called *So You Want to Be a Live Wire*."

"Do Bozo and The Wizard ever fight?"

"Never, that I've seen. They're both really into talking about the civilization thing, you know, and sometimes they argue about their buddies, Darwin and Freud. Buzzy and The Wiz set places for them at Christmas dinner."

"For Darwin and Freud?"

"Yep."

"Do they have girlfriends?"

"Darwin and Freud?" she asked, still rummaging in her shoebox. "I think they're married. Like who's into the sugar daddy thing anyway? Although it looks better the longer the unemployment line gets."

"No, I meant Bozo and The Wizard."

"Oh. Bozo's not interested. He says sex is enslaving just like a job. It's momentary and overrated compared to the mind. The Wizard prefers magic, but really his magic tricks have made his teeth look like little stubby pieces of charcoal. Like, those teeth are kind of in-your-face glowing like Indian corn—who's going to be his girlfriend?" She pulled out a little piece of white plastic with a raised yellow dot. "Aha, here's the egg." I couldn't think of a thing to say about this ridiculous little trinket. "Ta-dah," she said with a flourish. "Now you have bacon and eggs," she said, lining the brown stick earring up with the yellow dot with the white edges. "Although now I've moved on to double yolks. You see, I'm like not into Bobbsey-twin earrings. I'm into concepts.

That's why we have two ears, you know, for a continuing theme. *Now*," Shawna said, continuing in her theatricality, "I have 'Donkeys from Different Lands.'" She pulled out two tiny donkeys no bigger than a thumbnail. One wore a vest and sombrero, which Shawna said was a play on the "Mexican donkey idea," and the one wearing a tiny Blue Jays baseball cap was "obvious."

"Oh, perfect!" I was certainly more enthused about these than the bacon and eggs. Reaching for my purse I said, "Give me the two donkeys. They're essential to any wardrobe."

"Well, *I* think so, but tell that to Holt Renfrew. They said there was no market for Donkeys of the World. You know, their customers are into animals in their natural habitat and not moon-dusted bananas. But I'm not selling out."

Checking my watch, I decided to go ahead and interview Bozo myself since Jackie was uncharacteristically late. Before forking over the money, I hesitated and then said, "You'd better throw in the bacon and eggs. They'd be perfect for breakfast meetings." Thirty dollars poorer, I headed down to the basement, leaving Shawna to explore her shoebox of "concept earrings."

Standing at the top of the dark, narrow stairs, making my hands into a megaphone, I craned my neck down the winding staircase and whispered so as not to frighten the somnolent scholar, "Bozo . . . Bozo, it's Kate." As I descended, I smelled something like barbecue starter fluid. "Bozo," I said more loudly. I felt an eerie silence. Finally I yelled, "Bozo!" When I got to the bottom of the stairs, I saw papers ripped apart and Bozo's walls of books collapsed to a pile of literary rubble in the middle of the room.

The book mound was damp, and as I got closer I smelled kerosene. Someone had been looking for something he couldn't find and then had tried to burn down the place. But the fire had quickly burned out. Books are hard to burn because there's no air between the pages (except in the ones on the best-seller list). Whoever started the fire wasn't a practised pyromaniac; that eliminated the idea of a professional job. God, Bozo was going to be upset. This subterranean library was his life.

Then I realized he wouldn't be upset about it at all—because he was dead, looking straight up at me. He had been killed in the same way as Konzak. His shirt was drenched in blood and his neck was sliced from ear to ear, his whole head hanging over the back of his old-fashioned wooden swivel chair. The blood had pooled on the floor and had run toward a drain in the basement. There were maggots in an endless lineup marching confidently out of the drain in pairs like Bonaparte's men crossing Russia. How did they get here so quickly? Maybe being so close to the sewer.

Moving as far away as I could from the body, I backed myself right up against the cold, damp earthen wall. I slunk to the floor, leaned forward on my haunches and lowered my head. I felt weak and saw little dark spots in my peripheral vision as though the sight had somehow torn holes in my retina. Later when I thought about the scene I realized how much less shocking it was to see such mayhem the second time, third if you count my husband. I remember studying "habituation," the decline of a conditioned response following repeated exposure to the conditioned stimulus, in a behaviour modification class in first-year university and realizing how much lessened my physiological response was after each murder.

I walked upstairs and asked if I could use the phone. Getting Jackie's answering machine, I suddenly realized that Bozo's line was probably tapped, so I concocted a cryptic message. "Hi, I've got a joke for you. What's black and white and red all over? . . . Wrong . . . A dead zebra. Hey, you're supposed to laugh, you bloody Bozo." I hung up, trying to think of what to do next. If I told Shawna, the police would get involved and our identities would be revealed. There would be no choice in this situation, because he would soon be discovered when the Maginot line of maggots marched upstairs.

"Bozo still asleep?" Shawna asked.

"Uh-huh. Dead to the world."

"He must have been working all night on his revelations. They're goin' to be big, rock the whole community."

"Do you know what they are?"

"No, I'm more interested in astrology and tarot cards, but The Wizard might."

"Where's he?"

"Upstairs, first door on the right. Tell him B'nai B'rith called and wants him to swallow fire in a Passover skit at Holy Blossom Temple."

Walking up the stairs, I felt my legs shaking like a newborn calf's. I teetered toward The Wizard's room and swung open the door. He wasn't in his room that I could see. A homemade desk of wooden planks wrapped around two sides of his room. The long shelf-like desk was crowded with scientific displays. The Wizard had a few empty animal cages and a big fish tank with two large, hideous turtles scratching at the sides. Old electronics parts were scattered about. He had wires in bright colours suspended from the ceiling and bound to the wall with electrical tape. There were all kinds of scientific books on shelves that went from floor to ceiling. One whole wall was devoted to Darwin's books and letters. There were thousands of Xeroxed pages piled high on top of the books.

Obviously the murderer had been in the room fairly recently. He had rummaged through all the books on the lower shelves but for some reason had not touched the top shelves. Either a short murderer, one in a hurry or one who found what he was looking for on a lower shelf.

Where the hell was The Wizard? I opened a closet door and something fell out on me. I batted it away frantically, remembering what it was like to be covered in Konzak's steaming blood. It was, however, a large backpack that had been stuffed in the closet. Maybe The Wizard returned earlier, saw the murderer and ran. Or maybe he came home, saw his room and went to Bozo's room, saw him dead, realized he was a hunted man and ran. Maybe whoever killed Bozo killed The Wizard and carried his body away. No one would pay any attention to noises in the hall in this place. Jackie and I had sauntered in from the street without anyone even looking up.

All of these thoughts raced through my mind as I ran downstairs and asked, "Where is The Wizard?"

"Not sleeping? He's a nighthawk—I've never known him to be up this early. I didn't hear him going out. But stranger things have happened. After all, he *is* a wizard," Shawna said, and returned to exploring in her shoebox.

"Is anyone else home?"

"Edgar is at Indian Affairs trying to get someone to pay for his drum lessons, and Hari is working. He has an illegal job driving airport limousines. It's a good way to learn the city, if you're into learning the city."

"I think I'll meet Jackie and have breakfast, show him my new donkey earrings and come back when Bozo is more awake. I'll just go down one last time, check if he's up."

"Okey-dokey." Shawna looked up and said, "Those earrings look great on you."

I went to the basement again, descending to the now ripening odour of Bozo's body. I forced myself to look at his thin frame. I knew I had to work quickly. What had the murderer

wanted from Anders Konzak that he hadn't found there and
hoped to find here? Was he someone who wanted the big break-
throughs that would rock the psychoanalytic community? Did
he find them here?

I started with a pile of books and worked my way through
things. Unfortunately, the intruder had removed all of the cards
from the books and taken them. Now it was going to be next to
impossible to put together Bozo's theory. I had to reconstruct his
mind and figure out the revelations he was threatening to release.
I would have to see Freud as Bozo had seen him in order to solve
this case. But someone else wanted Bozo's revelations, and we
were in a race, a race where he had a head start. If I solved the
intellectual mystery that Bozo must have solved, and if the murderer knew that I'd figured it out, I would be the next in line for
a surgically enlarged smile.

On top of the desk was Bozo's diary. The last entry read:

*I met some lovely people named Jackie and Kate this
evening who treated us to the Bamboo. They work for a
publishing firm and have offered me a book contract which
would pay in instalments. It actually sounds interesting.
I don't want a repeat of the scandal I had with Anders
Konzak. He must have sex appeal because I'm immune
to that kind of thing and when that's stripped away you
have a peanut brain. I actually like the woman, Kate,
enormously. I think she really knows her Freud and I felt a
kind of kindred spirit. She is more mainline, but I believe
she has similar circuitry, although we did have some
excellent concoction provided by our bejewelled roommate.
Chemically induced or not, I felt so akin to her that
I almost told her about A*

The bottom of that page and the next page were ripped out.

Hearing footsteps upstairs, I realized I *had* to go before Homicide got dusting. As I closed the door, I said, "Goodbye, Shawna."

"Party on, Kate the Skate."

As Shawna spoke, my heart went out to her. From this day forward her life would be irrevocably altered.

I felt lonely as I walked to the corner, and far sadder than I had felt over Konzak's death. The communal home had been eccentric by anyone's standards, but they had been warm and welcoming to both Jackie and me. Bozo had the most interesting mind I'd collided with in a long time. I had stayed up all last night reading as much of his work as I could. It was argued from a mind like a Venus flytrap. You would have to get up pretty early in the morning to pull the logical wool over his bloodshot eyes. Whether his theories were correct or not I had no idea, but I felt a pit in my stomach at the loss of a man of originality and integrity.

As I was walking home from Bozo's, I heard footsteps behind me. It became more eerie as I took several more turns and the steps were still right behind me. Looking around, I realized I was in a desolate part of town as I walked south of King Street among deserted factories and waste disposal plants. Finally I was within sight of Lake Ontario, with rusty shipyards and junked Liberian oil tankers propped on cradles along the shore.

Was the man behind me the murderer? Had he seen me return to Bozo's house? He had killed Konzak, Bozo, probably The Wizard, and now he was going to kill me. I didn't let myself turn around or he'd probably kill me on the spot if he knew I was on to him. After all, he was following me instead of killing me for a reason. Call me picky, but I'd rather be trailed than nailed.

Where was Jackie? I'd called his Toronto apartment and his office and left messages. Things about Jackie began to dawn on me, things I'd unconsciously filed away. He was the only one who had known that Konzak was going to be alone in his Vienna apartment at the time of the murder. He had also known that I was going to go to Bozo's at noon today. He knew enough about Freud to know what to destroy. He was strong enough to carry out The Wizard. Now, when Jackie was supposed to meet me, he hadn't shown up.

My saliva turned into acetone, and my heart was pumping nitroglycerine. As I walked faster, the dynamite went off in my brain, the depressing facts exploded. The one that finally dive-bombed me was the infamous "pecker in his pocket" speech I'd overheard him having with Dr. Gardonne at the bar on the Isle of Wight. Maybe I had fantasized Jackie on an "as need" basis. I needed a strong, no-nonsense man of action and authenticity when I got out of prison. Probably the real Jackie was that cold bastard I'd overheard. After all, that one matched his history: the solitary confinement, the violence. Gardonne even said he'd been a "pervert." I wonder if Gardonne and I would call the same things perversions. I know he'd been a sex addict. Was that a perversion? Who knows? Who cares? What was important was that I needed him to be good, honest and strong. Why did I keep focusing on his strong shoulders? I guess I was sick of carrying my own load.

When you really got down to it, though, what had Jackie said that was so bad in his tête-à-tête with Gardonne on the Isle of Wight? Objectively, nothing. The only thing he'd done was to drive an axe through my irresistible female spy fantasy. He hadn't been interested in me sexually since I was old and skinny and . . . whatever. Why remember the rest? He was just rubbing my nose into the reality that I was a fading blonde, creeping, maybe galloping, over the hill. Even the Con Ed men weren't going to get conned by me. God, ego can build a stone wall around an aging woman, allowing her to stonewall about her age, her desirability, her precipitous decline in the pecking order of the universe. She's cashed in all her chips and still has to stay in the game. I shook my head and plowed on.

I had heard undercover agency stories before, in fact several that were remarkably similar to this one. The CIA or FBI hires someone to run the operation, a front like Gardonne. Then the front hires some patsy, like me, to get all of the information. Then the agency gets rid of the investigator if he knows too much after he's done the work.

I was in jail with a woman who worked for the FBI as an infiltrator in the Students for a Democratic Society. She knew that the pipe bomb that blew up the SDS members in a townhouse in Greenwich Village in 1970 was not, as reported, set off by some SDS dodo who supposedly crossed wires while making the bomb in the basement, but was set off by the FBI. The infiltrator found out the SDS were going to set off bombs in strategic New York spots, told the FBI, and the FBI blew up the whole house, killing almost all of the SDS members inside. Eventually some messy evidence arose and, rather than take responsibility for the blow-up, the FBI tried to pin it on the SDS infiltrator. Fearing a frame-up, she took off for Canada, was caught and was jailed with me for a year awaiting extradition. At least that's what she told me, and I never had any reason to doubt her.

This Konzak file unfolds the following way. The FBI, under the guise of Dr. Gardonne's APA umbrella, hires me and Jackie. One is the undercover for the agency and the other unravels the plot. (Maybe the FBI wants to destroy Freud. J.E. Hoover was weird enough to have made it into the Freudian annals, or, in his case, anals. He probably wore a dress while reading *Three Essays on Sexuality*. If I knew he was gay, wore Givenchy and had more high heels than Imelda Marcos, Freud probably knew it before me.) I lead them to victims and they knock them off one by one and then in the end blame me, a convicted murderer.

My thoughts galloped as fast as my feet. Shit, it just struck me. Maybe they weren't going to blame me; maybe they were going to kill me. I ran so fast that I didn't think even Jackie would be able to catch me. Someone was so close behind me I heard his breathing.

As I saw my condo in the distance, I knew I had to make my break now. I dashed home, knowing I could outflank him in a final sprint. I darted into my lobby past the bewildered doorman. Only then did I feel safe enough to look behind me. I saw nothing other than a mongrel dog barking at something that had darted between the buildings.

Turning to the doorman, I practically panted, "Did you see who was following me?"

"Sorry. Wasn't looking."

"Why is that dog barking like that?"

"Don't know. Dogs bark sometimes. Oh yeah, now that I see you, I just remembered. A guy was here today and said it was really important to give you this note before you left the building this morning. But . . . I guess I forgot," he said, shrugging as he handed me a sealed envelope.

Exhausted, I leaned against the wall between the elevators and read:

Dear Kate,
I gave this note to the dozy doorman. Didn't want to
phone in case it was tapped. It is now 9:30 in the morning

*and I just went to Bozo's. I wanted to get there a few hours
early and wire the place before anyone was up. I entered
through the basement to find the main line and tripped
over Bozo—dead. Killed with the same finishing touches
as Konzak. Wizard's room had been rifled through, but
no evidence of a struggle or a body. Clearly the killer
was looking for something—he's getting frenzied—less
careful than he was at Konzak's—things thrown around
indiscriminately, etc.*

*Do not, repeat, do not under any circumstances go
there. You don't want to be seen at the scene of this crime.
Sorry I couldn't wait but I had to act quickly. I'm only a
few hours behind The Wizard—if he's out there. I'm
trailing him (airports, train stations).*

*Freud and Darwin material is left in boxes for you. Get
it from the doorman. No one saw me there this morning
and I don't think that anyone got our last names last
night. Hopefully the whole house is too paranoid to call
the police.*

*Burn through the books as fast as you can and while
you're at it burn this note. I'll fax you when I know
something.*

Kate [something was heavily crossed out]

  Keep dancin,'

  J.

I turned all of my frustration into rage at the doorman and
screamed, "You know, that message was important for me to
receive *before* I went out this morning."

"I think I was getting Mr. Lebowitz's car out of the garage
when you left."

"I fucking passed you at eleven-thirty standing *right here*."

"No need to use language like that, *Miss* Fitzgerald. It is no longer *Mrs.*, is it?" He feigned confusion while letting me know he'd followed my murder trial.

I had to talk myself down before I leapt over his veneer podium, ripped off his epaulettes and stuffed them down his throat. I took some deep breaths and stretched my arms over my head. What was the point of taking this wreckage called my life out on this dork doorman?

He held the door open as I piled my legal-document boxes in the elevator (he said he had a bad back or he'd have helped). I pressed the button for my floor and the door was grunting to a close as he stubbornly held it open. Finally I asked him in as calm a voice as I could muster to let go.

He hesitated and then muttered as the door was three-quarters shut, "Come to think of it, that dog only yaps when someone goes between the buildings. Bye."

The door shut.

15

—

A PSYCHIC STAKEOUT

—

Crime, like virtue, ripens by degrees.

—JEAN RACINE

THE BEST WAY for me to concentrate was to replicate my prison day in my Harbourfront apartment. I woke up at 4 a.m., put on my "concentration clothes unit"—sweatshirt, sweatpants and slipper socks—and went to work until noon. Then, like a diligent rodent, I jumped on my wheel for exercise, got off my rowing machine in an hour and went back to work until 5 p.m. I had dinner sent in, worked again until 9 p.m., and then went to bed. I have no idea for how many days I did this. One thing I do know is that as the duration increased, so did my concentration. I left my answering machine on with the sound turned off. I did my best work in solitary. No one has attention deficit disorder if there is only one thing to take your attention.

I was determined to infiltrate the minds of Bozo and The Wizard. I began by going over the conversation I'd had with Bozo. I paced up and down my apartment trying to remember exactly what he had said to me. I am blessed with a great memory. (This of course can be a curse, for I can remember all of my mistakes in Technicolor.) I decided to distill its essence on my computer.

BOZO SUMMARY

—

1. Freud was into sex and cocaine.

2. Freud was not an observer of neurosis; he analyzed himself and inserted his own pathology into his cases.

3. Freud's entire theory was an effort to normalize his own behaviour. *Example*: Freud's sense of propriety, etc. (what eventually became known in his theory as the superego) wouldn't permit him to be in love with his mother, even though his mother was closer to his age than she was to her husband's. (Good Jewish boys love their mother. They are not *in* love with them.) Instead he normalized his feelings in order to deny that he himself had incestuous desires. He defended himself by saying that he was trapped in something larger than that—he suffered from the "Universal Oedipus Complex."

4. Method: Freud discovered, when he wrote the cocaine papers, that Victorian Vienna wasn't able to deal with his experimentation, so he went underground. The real discoveries were about himself. Freud was foxy. He was playing with his readers, waiting for the one person who could figure it out after his death. He confessed to some innocuous yet tantalizing nuggets in his autobiographical sketch. The connecting links are left to the self-proclaimed "Freudian dicks" such as Bozo.

5. Possibility: Maybe there were never any patients; all of Freud's research was on himself. Maybe that's how he ascertained the nature of bisexuality. Freud was both the male and the female patients. It was still brilliant, because it obviously had universal application. Freud gingerly brought his unconscious onto the thin ice of the public pond, guarding against a sudden thaw with the qualifier "I had a patient who . . ." That phrase is the psychoanalytic equivalent of the cliché, "I had a friend who . . ."

I typed pages of possible ideas based on Bozo's theory that Freud was the master of obfuscation. After hours of frustration trying to break the Freud code, I decided to make a chart of all the hardcore evidence, such as it was.

Once thing I knew about Bozo was that he had a scientific mind, and that type usually knows the demands of the scientific process. He may have correlated evidence in a strange way, but he was far too rigorous in orientation not to base his theory on some tangible facts. Konzak had been a professor of literature and he only had to have "interesting interpretations," while no one gets into MIT physics without knowing that you better be able to back up a theory with more than a few bon mots. (If force couldn't be predicted by Newton's laws of motion, he'd have had to count on Fig Newtons for fame. Without black holes, Einstein would still be toiling away in a patent office. If the world had been square, Columbus would be working for a cruise line.) I wrote out all of the following points on a large sheet of bristol board and tacked it above my desk.

EVIDENCE

1. A word beginning with the capital letter A is ripped out of a notebook. (Check to see if I can obtain an imprint from the page below.)
2. A small piece of yellow lined paper that has one line on it that says "**It's the name game**," and a key chain that says "**The Name Game**" on a miniature record platter.

3. The Darwin collection. Wizard was a Darwinian and his library was trashed. There had to be a reason. Someone wanted to kill him. Maybe someone did and had him taken away, but he also wanted to destroy or confiscate evidence from the Darwin collection. There was a top shelf he didn't reach and there were still notes in it. The murderer must have been scared away by The Wizard or someone in the house because the job hadn't been completed. This means there may be evidence in The Wizard's Darwin collection, particularly on the top shelf. Konzak is connected to Darwin and The Wizard in some way because there was a yellow note in Konzak's effects that said "**Only the Fittest Survive**."

4. Freud published twenty-four volumes, not including correspondence. Konzak was interested in the seduction theory and he mentioned Fliess. Bozo also focused on Fliess, the use of cocaine and the seduction theory. It is interesting to note that both men with exactly the same, somewhat esoteric research interests are dead. The seduction theory, Fliess and Freud's cocaine period were all before 1895. The answer must, therefore, be in the

first few volumes (Fliess 1890) and couldn't be past 1895, the year volume five was published, entitled *Studies on Hysteria.*

Now the secret is lodged somewhere in this room, in these books. Why else would the murderer try to get rid of them and pull out the notes stuck in them? I was relieved to see that in haste the murderer had missed the notes that were not protruding from the volumes. I began by reading all the notes that Bozo wrote in the margins of the collected Freud.

After days and days of work, I faxed a note to Jackie:

Dear Jack fruit, or do you prefer Jack ass,
Great idea leaving the dozy doorman with your note.
Why didn't you just entrust it to a sea slug? He gave it
to me when I got back from Bozo's, where I thought I
was stood up by my former dancing partner. I saw
Bozo's lost and yet undiscovered mind at noon. Ran
into Shawna and bought some earrings—so I truly have
been earmarked for the lineup. Anyway, more on that
later.

    Please go to the record store where Bozo worked and find
out if they had those record key chains now or ever. If so,
what were all the titles, and what ones did Bozo buy?
Next, I want to know everything about Bozo's family—if
he ever had any mental problems of any kind and if there
is mental illness in the family. Also trace The Wizard
(clearly an alias unless his mother named him The) for the
same thing. Find all of their transcripts and talk to all
teachers and professors.

    I am afraid that The Wizard got away and the killer is
stalking him. Please step up the manhunt. I'm going as

fast as my brain will take me, but I'm beginning to
smoke.

        Woman in need of rubber brain insulation,
        Kate

I crawled into bed and fell asleep and began dreaming in black
and white. I saw teenagers dancing in a canteen or on the 1950s
TV show *American Bandstand*. Actually, it was Annette Funicello
wearing Mickey Mouse Club ears dancing with a blond teenaged
boy whom I knew I'd seen before but couldn't place. They began
dancing to the idiotic song "The Name Game." It was sung by the
Anna Bananas and introduced by Bozo, the MC for the evening,
as a sort of clownish Dick Clark. He started singing into the
microphone, "*Bo-na-na fanna, fo-fan-na. Fee-fi mo-man-na . . .*"
The dream was interrupted by my alarm.

I dutifully jotted the dream down in my diary, where I stored
my unconscious time travels. Annette Funicello, my God, what
grey matter was she stored in? I marvelled at the boring minutiae
that the mind was willing to store.

I did agree with Freud's well-known line "Dreams are the
royal road to the unconscious," so I knew I had to take this
dream seriously. I tried to free-associate to it, but I couldn't get
much. I excavated my mind trying to find the face of the
teenaged boy. Although I knew he was stored deep in the folds
of my grey matter, I couldn't place him. And what the hell did
Annette Funicello have to do with Freud? When I thought
of Annette, all I could think of was the song the Mouseketeers
sang on *The Mickey Mouse Club*. They introduced themselves
by jumping out at the audience and singing their names—
Cubby, Cathy, Annette, Doreen, etcetera.

The miniature record on the key chain that we'd found in
Konzak's apartment was titled "The Name Game." Maybe the

dream had something to do with *Studies on Hysteria*, which I'd been reading yesterday before I went to sleep. All of the cases were titled by name. I got out the book again, looked at the names and brought the cases to my mind.

Freud's "name game" titles were Emmy, Lucy, Katharine, Elizabeth Von R. and, the most famous of all, Anna O., which was not written by Freud but by the co-author, Breuer. I started at that point and continued to reread *Studies on Hysteria* for the rest of the day.

A few days later my fax grunted a shiny scroll from Jackie:

Dear no-date Kate (unless pecan-inspired):
There is something wrong with the Gardonne inquiry.
Everything checks out too easily. I'm excavating another
layer right away, but I'll give you what I've got. First of all,
his name is Gardonne and he comes from Portland,
Maine. I have yet to find anyone there who remembers
him. I did find a birth certificate for him there. He
attended medical school at the University of Cincinnati
and was listed in the top half of the class.

He moved to Toronto in 1961. He attempted the
medical boards three times and passed on his last
attempt. He married a wealthy woman, daughter of a
well-known lumber baron turned wholesale papermaker.
Not one for letting the chips fall where they may, daddy
took some of his best British Columbia timber (just a
toothpick to him) and built his dear daughter a house
next door to him in Toronto in an exclusive section of
Rosedale as a surprise wedding gift. Gardonne and
Mrs. Junior League have four children, all of whom are
in private schools and, if they have not yet distinguished
themselves, pass as normal.

*The wife still seems thrilled to have snagged the handsome
doctor from the U.S. when she was a 21-year-old candystriper.
The usual story. She could be married to Charles Manson
and she wouldn't notice as long as he played golf.*

*You were right regarding his grey matter. He's never
written an original paper and, although he has an
impressive résumé in terms of girth, he has never been
any more than third author. He compiled papers from
conferences into a book and then got someone to write
an introduction. Your doorman could do that.*

*Speaking of which, I'm sorry about the doorman
disaster. I guess slipping a guy a twenty and thinking the
job will get done no longer has the cachet it once had.
Live and learn.*

> *Forever,*
> *J. Fruit*

*P.S. I'm following a lead on The Wizard to Butte,
Montana. Seriously. My dicks have unearthed a guy who
is lighting fires at some expensive dude ranch. Anyway, it
gives me a chance to practise my lasso. Stay chained to
your desk. I'll think of you when my spurs get dull.*

I got a sinking feeling that Gardonne was going to outsmart
everyone as he always had and I would be left holding the
prison term. I realized that the moment had come for me to
unpack the Woodsman of the Year award and do my own metal
detection in Onondaga, New York. In my trial I had trusted
lawyers to make my case, and I learned the hard way that
"expertise" is only a lousy college degree and a job. If you want
something done, do it yourself. No one ever cares as much
about you as you.

I was torn on this one. I really wanted to get that research done because I knew it would eventually find the killer. But I also knew that Gardonne had the potential to be more lethal to me than any killer. A murderer would just shoot me, while Gardonne would frame me, stash me back in the slammer and make Chinese water torture look like a refreshing drink.

Jackie was tied up for a few more days looking for The Wizard out west. I could get to Onondaga in six hours by train, lose one day of work if I read on the train, and get back before he knew I was gone.

PART III

—

ROOT CANAL

—

16

—

A BOY SCOUT

—

If you do not tell the truth about yourself,
you cannot tell it about other people.
—VIRGINIA WOOLF

I SETTLED INTO watching through the grimy window of the train as it chugged through the ghost towns of upstate New York. As I flashed past each pillaged place, I began to wonder what had happened to small-town America. Not only were the factories vacant, their broken windows stuffed with *For Lease* signs, but even the tall smokestacks had graffiti at the top. Who in his right mind would risk his life climbing to the top of a tall, skinny smokestack to spray-paint *Ronald Ray-gun Sucks the Fat One?*

As my lonely little coach nosed into the dilapidated Onondaga station, I gazed around at what was clearly a dump. Although some people were milling about, they didn't seem to be going anywhere. While searching for a cab, I noticed that the whole station, and downtown for that matter, looked like a vacated Hollywood set. Clearly Onondaga had just rolled over and died.

— 261 —

I took one last glance at the Boy Scouts pin and a picture of Gardonne from one of the prison newsletters. I couldn't believe that was all I had to go on. I'd called the Boy Scouts of America, which was almost as defunct as Onondaga. I told them I was a journalist who wanted to write an article on the difference Scouts had made. I led them to believe I was just going to focus on one typical troop. They were only too happy to search their records. Troop No. 189 was a group of eight-year-old boys run by a Mr. Robert Stone beginning in 1939. Mr. Stone still renewed his Eagle Scouts newsletter at an Onondaga address.

It was absurd to look for a cab where there were no pedestrians. However, what were my choices? There didn't seem to be any public transport. In the phone booth that was littered with broken beer bottles and looked like it had last been cleaned by Alexander Graham Bell, I attempted to search the Yellow Pages, but they'd been ripped out of the book, leaving only yellow stubble, so I walked up to the stationmaster's desk and asked for a taxi. He looked a little shocked by the request, as though I'd asked for a pumpkin driven by mice. He recovered slowly and dialed the phone, saying into the old-fashioned black receiver: "Marge, it's Harold. I'm down here at the station and there's a woman blew into town needs drivin' every which way."

About forty-five minutes later, an older woman pulled into the train station in a wheelchair access bus. She leaned out of the driver's-seat window and hollered, "You call a cab?" Picking up on my incredulous look, she continued, "I wear two hats. I'm the wheelchair access and the cab company all wound up in one vehicle."

I had never heard the word *vehicle* pronounced with the accent on the middle syllable other than in *Oklahoma!* "Do you know this address?" I asked, handing her the scrap of paper.

"Sure do. That's Bob Stone's place. He's solid as a rock." She spoke between spasms of laughter that sent her body rolling in waves of undulating blubber. "He lives out on the Ridge Road. By the by, I'm Marge. Hop in," she said, opening the wide door with one quick turn of a lever below her steering wheel. She manoeuvered the vehicle around and headed away from town. She was a pretty feisty driver and had a cigarette dangling from her dry lower lip. "So what's old Bob up to?"

If he was older than Marge, it couldn't have been by much.

"That's what I'm here to find out," I answered.

We pulled into a long gravel drive and faced an angel-brick bungalow. I thanked the woman for the ride while walking toward the door.

"You going to be here long?" she asked. When I shrugged, she said, "'Cause I might's as well wait on you. It would take me a while to get out here again picking you up. I'll pop in and see old Bob. The world needs more like 'im, but there ain't none left."

"What's so good about him?"

"Oh, he was the high school principal here for years, and worked with the boys' clubs and all manner of things to help the young ones grow up straight. He so old now he even lost his own son. Must be nigh ninety. Lost his missus nearly twenty years ago to the cancer."

Bob appeared at the door, looking thin and weathered but clean-shaven, and he carried himself as straight as an arrow. The cab driver stepped right in the front door, dodging the dried flower arrangements, turned toward me and said, "Bob, this here woman's from the government and is doing some serious investigating and I'm in charge of taking her round town. Mind if we come in?" Then she strolled into the living room and flopped down on the 3-D brocade couch.

"Not at all, Marge. Would you like a Bosco?"

"Fine by me, Bob," Marge said.

Do they still make Bosco or does he have a forty-year-old bottle?

Marge could be an asset. She seemed to have cottoned on to the idea of "official business," which gave me a legitimacy I could use. Bob never questioned my authority to stroll into his house and ask questions. He seemed tickled pink that anyone thought to ask him anything.

While he was in the kitchen, I looked around at the walls covered with pictures of a younger Bob with the graduating classes and basketball teams of various bygone eras. In one he was kneeling in front of a smiling team holding a ball that said *Class of '53*. There was a picture of him cutting a ribbon at what looked like a retirement home. In another one he was wearing a button that proclaimed *I like Ike*.

While I was getting out the medal, I asked if he had ever met anyone named Willard Gardonne. He thought for a long while and shook his head. "No, that name doesn't ring a bell."

"Well, I can tell you one thing," Marge piped up, clearly determined to be part of the proceedings, "Bob Stone never forgot a face of anyone who went to his school—not in this lifetime."

Bob rubbed his face and still shook his head. "Sorry I can't help you."

"This Gardin fellow do something wrong?" Marge asked hopefully.

"Marge, I'm not sure that's our affair," Bob said in his principal's voice.

My heart sank, but I decided to bring out the medal anyway. I showed it to him and he said, "Well, I led twenty-three Scout troops and some I led even when they flew up to Eagles." He looked at the medal for a long time and then out the window as he said, "You know, the young people today just aren't interested."

"Bob is the town reeve and historian. He keeps track of every prize anyone ever won. If someone dies, it's Bob who can give you his vitals for the paper."

"You've got Troop 189. Let's see." Bob rocked on his bentwood rocker for a minute and then said slowly, "That was around 1935–40. They changed the numbering system after the war. Excuse me, let me just get some things from my nook."

He climbed the stairs, and then descended several minutes later with four huge scrapbooks with yellowed newspaper clippings hanging out the sides that dried-out Scotch tape could no longer hold. He set them down gently. They were well dusted and had Saran Wrap around the covers like old-fashioned book jackets. Not only had Bob devoted his life to service organizations, he had kept a perfect chronicle—the Rosetta stone of small-town life. I was struck by how hard I was trying to wipe out the last few decades while old Bob cherished all of his.

"Let's see, I'm looking for Troop 189." He opened one album gingerly and turned the yellowed pages. He found the 1939 troop picture of cowlicked boys with chipped teeth and knock knees in their khaki shorts and red scarves. I read the names at the bottom. There was no Gardonne. I looked at each child and, as far as I could tell, no one resembled Gardonne. On the opposite page was a newspaper clipping of a boy who chopped more wood in three minutes than any other boy in Scouting history. The caption under the smiling face read, *Young Ned Mapple axed the competition*. I hadn't caught the smile in the group photo, but it jumped out at me in the enlarged picture. It was the same Mr.-Deeds-goes-to-prison smile that peeped out into the prison hallway and said, "Next please."

I couldn't contain my excitement as I knew a salaried government employee should. "That's him," I shouted.

"Young Ned Mapple?" Bob asked.

"Wouldn't surprise me if he was in trouble, being from trash stock. He probably went the way of the other Mapples. Ain't seen him in a coon's age" was Marge's unsolicited opinion.

Bob looked at the picture and said, "Poor Young Ned Mapple," and shook his head. "I remember him well. A great ball player. I have other pictures of him. He was a draft choice for one of the farm teams for the National League. If I recollect correctly—I'm getting a bit rusty upstairs—it was the Padres."

Marge leaned back on her rocker, folded her hands on her bevelled stomach and said with soothsayer's certainty, "Nothing but trouble—them Mapples. A root canal couldn't help that family tree." Exchanging glances with Bob, she continued, "Helen got hers after what she done. That Young Ned cut from the same bolt."

Bob leaned back in his rocking chair and began what seemed to be for him the painful experience of relating Young Ned Mapple's family history. "The Mapples are one of those tragic families who have suffered generations of chronic alcoholism and all the sorrow that accompanies it. Ned Mapple Senior, known as Old Ned, was a diabetic who never monitored his illness, loved his cups. The poor bugger gradually lost his legs and eyesight. He became a permanent feature begging on the already impoverished streets of Onondaga. It was terrible for the Mapple children and the mother. Marge, did they have twelve children? My memory fails me."

"She had eleven but lost one of the little ones to polio—letting them swim in that quarry. Some of the others died young too—is my recollection anyway."

Bob picked up the story. "It was in the era before public relief, and Helen Mapple had to turn to other ways to make a living. She used to clean houses, but as Onondaga declined economically, people did their own cleaning. With eleven young ones behind her door, life became progressively more sordid for her."

"She's a bad woman and always has been," Marge chanted. Who needs a Greek chorus when you have Marge?

"I take it she's still alive?" I asked.

"Nothin' kills vermin," Marge replied. "She's crippled up with empty semen at this point."

"That's *emphysema*, Marge," Bob offered.

Undeterred, Marge continued, "Lives over behind the bank—second floor above the old fish store. It's been a dollar store comin' up a year now."

"She still there, Marge?"

"She ain't goin' nowhere with them lungs. She'd all of her brood early, so I put Young Ned at around fifty. She can't be seventy yet. Looks a hundred. Old Ned, her husband, was always cursing the Lord and screaming at people who walked by. He used to park hisself right down at the gazebo there on River Street and turn his head and call people bad names out the side o' his mouth. Why he did that carryin' on is beyond me."

"Korsakoff's syndrome," I told her. "Alcohol related. Usually in older chronic alcoholic males who have pickled their brains. One of the symptoms is screaming obscenities." I'd read about it in another lifetime when I was studying brain physiology.

"Land sakes, what they goin' to come up with next!" Marge shook her head

"That's our Old Ned," Old Bob said sadly. "Poor Young Ned never had a chance to live that down." Turning to me, he added, "Small towns look uncrowded, but reputations are packed closer than sardines."

"Old Ned's not so bad. It's her carryings-on with that brood to look after."

Bob gently reminded her, "Marge, 'But for fortune there go I.'"

"I'll tell you about a fortune! She made and lost plenty in her day, and none of it went to the children."

"Was she an alcoholic?" I asked, wondering what the hell else could be evil in Onondaga in the 1930s.

"Worse. She made her choices. She was a harlot right in her own home. Had two or three children that way. She turned poor Old Ned out. I used to say to my daughters, 'You go out and park with some man and you'll wind up like Helen Mapple.' That put the fear o' God in 'em, I can tell you."

Bob just sat there rocking and finally asked, "What did you want to know about Young Ned?"

"What was he like?" I thought this was pretty lame but couldn't think of anything else to ask.

"A quiet boy who was always on the outside. Didn't have clean clothes or even a Kleenex. He never had his Scouts fees or a uniform, and the others would have to take up a fund for him. Something happened to him as a teenager. He began to have money and nice clothes, and even a car, which was strange given that they lived above a fish store with eleven kids in two rooms.

"He had great hand-eye coordination and was a good batter and moved up in the Little League. He got a baseball scholarship to a local state college and I never saw him after that. He kind of disappeared. I don't think he has any ties to Helen, or his brothers or sisters, most of whom have stayed around town and basically been tarred by the same brush as their mother."

"It sounds as though Young Ned may have been the Mapples' success story. At least he got a college education. Why do you see him as tragic as the rest?"

"His dad asked him for money and he laughed at his own father, who sat crumpled up in the River Street gazebo. Young Ned would adjust the collar on his casual golf clothes as he sauntered by Old Ned, ignoring him. He tried to hobnob with the rich boys and girls from the country club, but they wouldn't have any part of him. Even when he tooted around in his convertible, he just rattled around alone," Bob said.

Marge piped in, "When he was in grade school, the kids in the playground used to chant, 'Your mother rattles her Mapple' till he'd cry his eyes out and the nuns would pull the hecklers in by their ears."

"Bob, you mentioned that 'something happened' and Young Ned was suddenly flush and had a convertible?" I left this open-ended, hoping Bob would pick up on it. However, he just sat there until Marge jumped in.

"He's the craftiest of the Mapple brood. No one knows for sure what he was up to. Some say he made it bringing in carloads from the races at Saratoga Springs to his mother's place and got a cut of that action. My sister-in-law heard tell from a woman who was a chambermaid at one of the good hotels near the race-track that Young Ned used to arrange for rich girls from New York City to come up and stay in that fancy hotel to have abortions. She heard he later blackmailed a few of the rich ones."

"Marge, the unvarnished truth of the matter is no one knew where his sudden windfall came from," Bob said, staring straight ahead as he rocked on his creaking chair.

Marge shook her head and said, "Why, I got more respect for Art Mapple, the youngest. At least he makes a dollar cleaning septic tanks. It's an honest living. Young Ned is destined for a life like his mom's. Peas in a pod."

I managed to squeeze a few words into Marge's monologue as she took a moment to blow on her steaming Bosco. "Marge, would you take me to see Mrs. Mapple?"

"I ain't in the habit of travelling in that neighbourhood, but I'll do it for the job."

While Marge was parking the wheelchair bus outside Helen Mapple's building, she said, "She's too laid up to run her bawdy house now. What goes around comes around."

As we walked across the street, a man with a bottle of Electra Shave sticking out of a paper bag said, "You pickin' up old Helen? She ain't goin' out, ya know. She used to get me to go to the Stop 'n Shop."

Marge marched on, dodging his weave, but did turn to me and whisper, "If she's cranky, it might be best to have some Hostess Twinkies, some pop and a large pack of Marlboros."

After detouring to the convenience store, we entered the narrow, dark staircase and the spring sunlight vanished. There were dozens of flyers that had been dropped through the mail slot, some of which advertised last Christmas's specials.

Helen Mapple's door had a paper sign taped on it that said *No Soliciting*. "That's a good one," Marge said as she knocked loudly on the unfinished plywood door.

There was no answer.

"It's Marge. Got a fare here wants to talk to you."

Still nothing.

Marge's voice became more entreating. "Come on, Helen. They want to talk about old times." I found Marge's use of the pronoun *they* interesting. She turned to me and nodded toward the bag of carcinogens we'd brought. "Helen, we brought you some treaties. Thought we could all have a Coke and a smoke together."

After a long silence Marge tried the door. It was open. She entered and I reluctantly trailed behind. The apartment was too dark to make out anything. After stumbling over chairs, we followed a wheezing and gurgling sound that led us to a doorway. From the abyss we heard a hoarse whisper. Helen croaked, "What kind o' smokes you got, not them low-tar shit-sticks?"

"Large Marlboro," Marge answered.

When my eyes were finally dark-adapted, Helen came into focus. She looked like an anorexic Mae West. As she leaned up on an elbow to reach for the cigarettes, she began a low, rumbling cough that quickly escalated. I could almost hear her tiny air sacs tearing one by one. The area above her lip had turned blue as her bronchi fought for oxygen. "You can't even breathe in this town."

"For God's sake, Helen, turn on a light!" Marge admonished.

"No lights." Just saying this racked Helen's body with spasms to the point that I wondered if she'd ever get another breath. Between gasps she managed to say, "Marge, why don't you make yourself useful for once and plug me in."

I stood back in horror as Marge held the oxygen mask up to her mouth and her chest rose and fell like a bellows. Helen then sank back on her filthy pillow. All around the bed there were empty bottles of various sorts, from wine to prune juice. I'd never expected anything like this. On a bare mattress lay a woman with withered limbs and faded blonde hair matted in the back, giving her head a permanently dented appearance. With her barrel chest and atrophied limbs she looked like a cartoon ant. Marge was right about one thing: she did look a hundred. Her eyes had faded to the point where I doubted they could adjust to light any more.

The desiccated form spoke in a gravelly whisper. "What you want?" Then she added, "It better not be much for a lousy pack of smokes." She glanced my way for the first time and continued, "Who do you want the dirt on? I didn't use to sell information for such a small price." As she turned her head away from me, I noticed she had grey roots. How the hell did she manage to dye her hair when she could hardly sit?

"Actually, Helen, I want to know about you," I said.

"I'm touched."

As she smirked, I saw that familiar ironic smile that had infuriated me for nine years.

"Tell me about your marriage in the early days, Helen."

"What's it to you? Doing some TV show on those that ain't found the Lord or something?"

"Hey, you get your Twinkies, Helen?" Marge said.

Helen took a long drag, coughed up phlegm the colour of a boiled lobster and whispered, "No one ever made a living for me in this lifetime, so I made my own."

"How?"

"It weren't easy in the 1930s to be out of harm's way from some drunk you married when you was no more than a high school ignoramus . . . But, I managed."

"I imagine anything you'd do would be an improvement on the life you were living."

"Both the job and the money was better when I was a call girl."

"'Call girl'—that's rich—like saying I drive a white stretch limo," Marge said, folding her arms in front of her.

"The only white thing you stretched is that arse of yours. Why, it's grown to the broad side of a barn." Marge looked as though she'd been hit with a wrecker's ball. With her temporarily out of the running, Helen turned to me. "You bet I was, and a high-priced one at that. I had eleven children, but I never lost my figure till I got laid up."

She was getting paler and her lip was turning blue and dusty-looking. I knew I didn't have much time before she'd have to be plugged in again. "What happened to your children?"

"The boys mostly run to Thunderbird wine."

"I heard that Young Ned did well?" I said it as though I found it hard to believe.

"He got the Macquire brains." She took a deep drag on her Marlboro. "That's my maiden name."

"Is Young Ned still successful?"

"Put it this way—he never hooked up with no bad women like I did men."

"What ever happened to him?"

"Don't know. Went to college on a baseball scholarship. We're both good with our hands."

"Did he graduate?"

"Don't know."

"You never heard from him again?"

"Nope."

"That's kind of sad."

"I raised them with food on the table and did better than my own kin did for me, so I don't mind. They don't owe me nothing."

"What if something happened to you? Does anyone have a way to get hold of him?"

"No."

"Where did he go to college?"

"Started out here and downstate, I heard."

"Is he in touch with his brothers or sisters?"

"He was always closest to me."

"What did I tell you?" Marge chimed in, clearly having recovered, and, since she had the floor, continued, "How many of them is left now, Helen?"

"Uh . . . six to my reckoning. Two died as youngsters. One died in Vietnam. One got the diabetes and drink like Old Ned. I lost track of the rest. The only girl dead is Jen. Drank some Clorox . . . " Helen began to breathe as though she were underwater trying to swim to the surface. Marge fumbled with the oxygen mask, trying to sort out how to hook it on. The old woman whispered, "I want some peace here. What more info do you want for a pack of cigarettes and a lousy lunch? Marge, get me two aspirins and a Percodan from the back of the toilet and then get out."

Her eyes were closed. She was too tired even to finish her cigarette. I leaned close to her ear and said, "Thanks for talking to me." I hesitated. "Is there anything you want to know about Young Ned?"

She seemed to be struggling to speak, so I pulled the mask away from her mouth. She opened her eyes, which were now glassy from too much steroid, as she rasped, sounding like metal scraping on metal, "You know, I'm from Troy, New York, just down the next throughway exit. I was so beautiful they called me Helen of Troy." She fell back on the pillow and I let her mask snap back on her face.

17

LONGING FOR A LOCK-TENDER

—

With memory set smarting like a reopened wound, a man's
past is not simply a dead history, an outworn preparation of the
present: it is not a repented error shaken loose from the life: it
is a still quivering part of himself, bringing shudders and bitter
flavors and the tingling of a merited shame.

—GEORGE ELIOT

As I STUMBLED out of Helen's dark apartment, I was blinded by
even the pale Onondaga sunshine. Marge asked, as though we
were on a Better Homes and Gardens tour, "Well, where to now?"

"A good hotel," I mumbled, and stretched my seat belt around
my giant wheelchair seat.

"There's only the Gauntlet—old local tavern with a few rooms
upstairs. Even Holiday Inn couldn't make it here—nothing to
come for. Used to be the glove capital of the U.S. till Hong Kong
fingered it. Now travelling salesmen just keep on travelling. They
even took away our exit on the New York State Thruway." Marge
was interrupted by another call on her beeper. "This is the busiest
day I've had all year. I'll just drop you off at the Gauntlet."

— 275 —

I entered the old tavern with knotty pine walls and a blinking neon light over the bar that flashed *Stroh's is spoken here*. (I should have assumed it wasn't English.) A sea of male faces lifted their hooded lids to look me over. I couldn't face the "special," a hot roast beef sandwich 'n' gravy, so negotiated a grilled cheese off the lunch menu.

My room smelled of old beer and disinfectant. The bedding was dingy, with burn holes on the spread. I was too exhausted to care. Besides, whom was I going to complain to—room service? As I climbed under my clammy covers, I pictured myself old and alone, dying at the Gauntlet—my Helen of Troy days long gone.

Something jolted me awake. How long had I been asleep? I heard sounds in the hall—footsteps hovering at my door. No one else could possibly be staying in *this* dive. There was fumbling with my lock. Then the door slowly creaked open, allowing only a glimmer of light from the dim hallway, just enough for me to see an advancing shadow. I didn't move a muscle, pretending to sleep. I hoped it was a robber who would take my backpack and flee. But my gut knew better.

The figure closed the door, locked it from the inside and walked toward me. A huge hand passed before my eyes and loomed over my body. He was going to strangle me. If I screamed, who would hear? He reached over my head. I heard a click as he flicked on the reading lamp behind my bed. Momentarily blinded by the glare, I heard the menacing figure say, "Kate Fitzgerald?"

Christ, they found Bozo already, someone identified me from the Bamboo Club or they got my name from Shawna or Hari. Or it's the murderer thinking I know more than I do, or that snake Gardonne. I'd been followed. One of those guys in the tavern wasn't there for the "daily special"—or was he?

My heart was pounding and my arms felt like rubber. I finally recognized the voice. Waiting for my stabbing breath to finally subside, I managed to say through my dry mouth, "Well, Jackie, this is quite a coincidence, having the same hotel room at the Gauntlet in Onondaga. Everything full in Montana?"

"Save your repartee for the country club, Kate. You're in violation of your Temporary Absence. You know, if you have unauthorized travel on a TA, you'll never get parole. They could slap you back into the big house and put duct tape over your mouth for the better part of your menopause. You're goddamn lucky I'm a better detective than Gardonne."

"I certainly feel lucky, privileged even."

"I had to fly in from Montana to handle this so there wouldn't be anything in writing, and now I have to turn around and go back to Butte." He looked at me, genuinely puzzled, and said, "If you wanted to come here—which is, by the way, another country—why didn't you tell me?"

"I had to save my own ass. You made it quite clear that you weren't putting yourself out for a 'skinny, aging ex-con.'"

"There is no point clarifying what I said to Gardonne that night. You have your own delusionary suppositions that have become your own lonely little creed."

It *was* lonely, but less dangerous than believing him.

He walked over to the window, opened the plastic curtain, and the pink fluorescent martini glass with its olive in perpetual motion blinked in the room. "So let's get out of this depressing hole."

As I got dressed in the bathroom, he yelled through the door, "What the hell did you go to bed so early for? I knocked, but you must have been fast asleep, so I let myself in."

"What else was I going to do in Onondaga at the Gauntlet Hotel? By the way, how did you find me here?"

"*Please.* I followed the bread crumbs, okay?"

He had to have a tail on me or he never would have known I'd come here. If I confront him with that, he'll just say I'm paranoid and we'll have another go-round of my "pathology" and how hard I am to work with. Anyway, he didn't turn me in to Gardonne. Instead, he chose to take a long flight from out West to sort it out himself. I guess that says something.

As I tied my hair back in front of the bathroom mirror, I said, "I thought you might be the police coming to get me for the Bozo murder."

"Clearly no one in the house mentioned either of us."

"What are you, clairvoyant?"

"I have a buddy in Homicide who told me that they know it is one of two people, either a crazy couple who suspect Bozo of poisoning their cats, or The Wizard, who they think was involved in a drug deal gone wrong, killed Bozo and fled the scene. They have an 'all-out' on him. There is one detective on it who is two years from retirement and who I was told was, quote, 'not bucking for the Chief's job.'"

"What does that mean if you're not at the policemen's ball?"

"No one really cares who killed Bozo. They assume it is one low-life guy with rotted teeth who killed another crazy guy who wears a dog bone. The motive: drug deal gone bust in a druggy neighbourhood. Happens with frightening regularity. They are vaguely looking for The Wizard—the name alone was enough to make him a suspect—and have foisted off the case onto the laziest old guy on the force who can barely hold a pencil, let alone a revolver."

As I walked out of the bathroom, he was standing by the door. "Come on," he said impatiently, as though I should have some idea where we were going. "We're going for a walk along the polluted canal. At least it's water, and I'll tell you what I uncovered."

———

As we strolled along the towpath next to the Erie Canal, Jackie began, "Well, my guys checked with the University of Cincinnati. Gardonne *was* enrolled there. We checked on his mailing address and it was correct. I checked with the parents' address given in Gardonne's first year. They live in Columbus, Ohio. Their son, Willard Gardonne, killed himself the day after completing his psychiatry residency. The university never knew. Our man was waiting in the wings, sent in a change of address, got Gardonne's degrees in the mail and remains on the mailing list for the alumni newsletter. He even makes contributions to the medical school bursary fund. The certificates from the University of Toronto that we, like the rest of his clientele, assumed were degrees in a residency were really for an eight-week refresher course taken after he moved to Toronto.

"After scanning every medical school picture, I finally found his in the graduating class of some dumpy medical school in British Honduras where you could practically buy yourself an MD in the early sixties. The name under the picture was—"

I interrupted, asking, "Could it be Ned Mapple, Rumpelstiltskin?"

Jackie raised an eyebrow in approval. I then gave him a thumbnail sketch of Young Ned Mapple and his diseased family tree.

I had never seen Jackie shocked, but Gardonne's roots caught him by surprise. Finally he shook his head and said, "Well, Young Ned found the perfect route to upward mobility in Honduras. If you flunked out of another med school or you could buy your way into any place, this was the school for you. In fact, they even had the classes in English. It cost a fortune, but you could recoup in three years of hard work. Also, rich doctors who wanted their sons to follow in their venerable footsteps but whose sons had considerably smaller feet were shoo-ins in

British Honduras. All their daddies had to do was pay and give some guest lectures. *Voilà*—a prestigious faculty. They have since lost their accreditation."

"How do they stay in business?"

"They set up in a country until they have a whole group of graduates who flunk their U.S. medical boards and the College of Physicians and Surgeons gets after them. Then they quickly move to another country and set up all over again."

"I guess where there's a buck to be made, someone will make it," I said, marvelling at capitalists' ability to fill a niche.

"Gardonne got into college with a baseball scholarship. He went to Onondaga Community College and then transferred to the state teachers' college and played baseball for them. Then, with tax-free blackmail money growing at compound interest, he bought his way into medicine." Jackie made it sound as if the scam had been somewhat worthy.

I said, "Remember, no one ever said he was stupid. He was just disadvantaged. His mother was probably smart. At one point she had employees and a real going concern. She had a business that ran all the way down the state into New York City. Sure it fell apart, those kind of businesses almost always do. If she'd been from some other family, she probably would have had an MBA. She must have adjusted herself to any clientele, just like Young Ned learned to do. If you read *Reader's Digest*'s 'Word Power' every month on how to build your vocabulary, and went to a Dale Carnegie public speaking course, you could carry it off. Let's face it, he was good at the act. He stayed out of jail— neither of us managed that."

"Hey, I've been straight for fifteen years. You've barely smelled the flowers, so watch it." He then nodded and said, "You're right, though."

"He has elaborate, well-honed resources. There were moments

when I almost believed in him. No one ever said he didn't know anything. Look, when he moved to Canada, he had to have passed the medical boards and the qualifying exams in psychiatry. Whether he did it on his first, second or third try, he did it, which is nothing to sneeze at."

Jackie saw me rub my hands together to warm them up and reached into his pocket and gave me his gloves. As I put them on, I said, "You know, you can take the Dapple out of the Mapple, but as his mother said, 'he got the Macquire brains,' and you can't get rid of them. He was a blackmailer then and he's still one now."

"Some things you just can't change," Jackie agreed.

We walked along the windy canal as the stars shimmered on the water and light darted around us like broken glass when a big boat left a wake. I'd almost forgotten how big-city lights diminish the stars. I felt so at peace listening to the water lap the sides that I slid my arm through Jackie's and leaned a bit on his leather jacket.

Ignoring the gesture, or else just assuming it's how friends behave, he continued on about Gardonne. "He didn't want to take the risk of living in the U.S. where he might be recognized or traced by Social Security or Internal Revenue. He looked around for someone who lived far away and he came up with Gardonne in Cincinnati. He changed his name, then left the country so he would never have to 'dapple in Mapple' again."

"He didn't have to deal with his family worrying about him."

"If someone knew Gardonne from Cincinnati," Jackie said, lighting up a cigarette, "he would simply say he was a different Gardonne and went to the University of Toronto. If they went to the University of Toronto, he would say he went to Cincinnati. If he got caught, he could say he went to both universities, one for his meds and one for his psychiatry residency."

"It worked."

"I can't see how he passed as Dr. Gardonne. Maybe I'm just so out of that upper-class professional world I don't get it, but wouldn't *someone* realize he didn't know anything—that the emperor had no clothes?"

"No. He was dressed in his new persona, which accounts for ninety percent of most professional aura. He was born handsome, just like his mother was born pretty. He has inherited her looks and her wily savvy and psychopathic personality."

"Maybe he learned it," Jackie suggested.

"I don't want to get into the boring nature-nurture debate at this point."

"Fine."

Jackie had a way of expressing monosyllables that packed a wallop. He was sensitive on the word *psychopath*. I'm sure his file was peppered with the term.

I pushed ahead, saying, "He's dapper and he married up, so everyone assumed he had money."

"But don't you have to make diagnoses? And isn't there some skill involved?"

"Sure there is, and if he'd been a surgeon he would have been caught. There would have been a whole operating theatre watching him. Psychiatrists work alone for the most part. There are no checks and balances unless the patient complains."

"I know I had brain-numbingly stupid shrinks in the pen," Jackie said. "But I thought the good psychiatrists were on the outside. Don't people who aren't locked up complain about incompetence?"

"Psychiatric patients are usually the disenfranchised. The schizophrenics who complain are dismissed as fruitcakes and the neurotics rarely get better anyway, even if the best psychiatrists in the world treat them. Even Freud said, 'Psychoanalysis changes everyday misery into common unhappiness.'"

"Not your basic cure," Jackie said. His face looked thoughtful, even wistful, and he added, "I always imagined that on the outside everything worked—like psychiatry. Childhood fantasy, I guess. You'd have thought I'd have been cured of it with college and my government work and all that. I guess not."

"A psychiatrist can parrot about ten phrases and make a living. You can always lay the responsibility on the patient. He was particularly wise to move to Canada, where there is socialized medicine. Psychiatrists are perceived as free. If you, as the patient, get nothing out of it, you haven't spent anything. You aren't ripped off *personally*, so you don't sue. You drop out of the therapy and the taxpayer picks up the tab."

"You get what you pay for," said Jackie.

"Exactly. Gardonne got rich on the Toronto Island concession scam and by nabbing a rich wife. Most psychiatrists aren't independently wealthy and need to have consecutive fifty-minute sessions with patients all day long. Seeing patients is paid like piecework. No one pays you to go to meetings."

"What about his job in the prison?"

"All staff positions, no matter how prestigious they look, are salaried. They pay less than a psychiatrist can earn working piecework in a shelter for the homeless. Of course, the medical profession doesn't call it piecework, they call it 'fee for service,' but it means exactly the same thing."

"He chose a prison because he was least likely to be caught out. He was in the safest place he could possibly be in," Jackie said.

"I think he felt at home there. He works in prison because he knows that is where he belongs. Psychologically, it's perfect. He is psychopathic as well as imprisoned in his own life. He has to act twenty-four hours a day."

"At least prisoners can be their pathetic selves." Jackie shook his head as he continued, "His life must have been hell for him to go to this much trouble. He must have assumed no one could love him, or even like him if they knew he was Young Ned Mapple."

"If you want to get really Freudian, you could say his job at the women's prison was a return to the Mother, the woman he was closest to until he realized she'd rather have a few bucks, a cigarette and compare herself to Helen of Troy."

"Who wants to get *that* Freudian?"

"Obviously not you," I laughed. "Helen did say she was closest to Young Ned. There is some evidence they worked together, and let's not forget, he named his concession company Helen of Troy."

Jackie held his hands up in front of his face as though I had held him at gunpoint and said, "Stop with the mother stuff. You're giving me the creeps."

As we walked along, we came to a lock in the canal. The lock-tender waved to us from the window in his little house. We stopped and looked at the lock mechanism and all three of its tiers. I used to enjoy watching the boats go through the Welland locks when I was a child. Seeing the locks open and the water rush in was something we tried to recapture as kids when we built stick dams during the spring thaws. As a child, safely ensconced on the towpath, it comforted me to know that there were engineers navigating so you never scraped bottom or hit rough waters.

As we gazed at the lock's giant gates, Jackie said, "It's so sad. There are so many kids that just get thrown in and somehow they have to make it. Gardonne never had any help. He had to make it up as he went along."

It was after midnight as we walked for miles along the locks of the Erie Canal on this early spring night when winter's chill could still rise out of the earth and catch you unawares. On our way back to the Gauntlet, I snapped up my Patagonia as I looked around at the vacant parking lots littered with broken beer bottles and at the nameless old warehouses that had nothing but shattered windows.

"It's cities like this that let you know what's happening outside of Manhattan and San Francisco."

Nodding his head, Jackie said, "Let's not stay here overnight. It's already the middle of the night. I swore after prison I'd never stay in another dump unless I had to. We can take turns driving and get back to Toronto by morning. I can catch the first flight back to Montana."

As we turned back to the hotel to get my stuff, I said, "Helen was pathetic. Jackie, you should have seen her. She was all used up. She didn't want to be a victim, but all she knew how to do was victimize. With all the people who have touched her life, she has to pay a rubby to get her junk food."

"There is nothing sadder than an old whore," Jackie said.

"Forget the whore part. I wouldn't expect the johns to give her oxygen. But she did have nearly a dozen kids, and there is a church in town. What ever happened to 'good works'?" Answering my own question, since Jackie hadn't, I said, "I guess they left with the thruway exit."

"You feel sorry for Dr. Gardonne?"

"No, he only wasted my time, but I bet there are some women he really hurt. You know, the female-desperado-for-love profile."

"Aren't we all that type at some level?" We continued walking for a few minutes. He threw his last cigarette into the canal and added, "Some risk asking for it more than others is all."

I shrugged and kept my eyes on the ground, stepping on cracks in the cement. As we walked back to the Gauntlet, we kept pulling up our collars to keep out the chill.

—

18

ADJUSTING TO THE LIGHT

—

> Although I have suppressed a large number of
> quite interesting details, this case history of Anna O. . .
> was not in itself of an unusual character.
> —FREUD AND BREUER, *Studies on Hysteria*,
> "Case of Anna O."

AFTER COMING BACK to Toronto, I seemed to have calmed down. I now knew I wasn't crazy where Gardonne was concerned, and Jackie now had to agree that Gardonne was up to no good. I could tell that Jackie was shocked that Gardonne had so successfully conned him. Jackie had a lifetime of seeing the unsuccessful psychopaths in jail—the losers who got caught. He was taken aback by the successful psychopathic suit on the outside, the professional flim-flam man who truly deserved the title of con artist.

I also made a mental note that he was willing to cover my ass when he had to. Although he must have had a tail on me, he'd come back from Montana to get me in Onondaga before Gardonne or anyone else found out I was gone. He'd seemed concerned about getting me back into Canada without a TA violation.

Now that I wasn't looking for knives in my back, I could concentrate on the investigation of Freud. On our way from Onondaga we agreed that I would shut myself in until I solved the Freud puzzle or decoded Bozo's work. In the meantime Jackie would travel until he found The Wizard alive or dead. Of course, as Shawna had reminded us, disappearance was an occupational hazard for wizards.

Jackie was right: a division of labour had been far more productive for the case. Or to put it in prison vernacular—we both did our best work in solitary. Now, after a week alone, I needed to send him an update via air mail special delivery:

Dear crazy as a jay bird:
I've thrown all the information into the funnel and come
up with something to do with seduction between 1895 and
1900, probably in Studies on Hysteria.
I need you to get us on the first plane to England as
well as permission from the archives to go through
Freud's letters. (I won't ask how you'll get it, but I'm sure
you'll manage.) I want to see everything that Konzak
saw. I'm particularly interested in the daily calendars in
order to see all of Freud's appointment books from
1890–95. I have most of the Bozo part put together, but
I still have to work on The Wizard.
Speaking of the magician himself, how was Montana?
I know you were busy in Butte, but did you have fireside
chats with The Wizard?
I believe that whatever the intellectual secrets are, it's
too much for someone or something. I'm convinced that if
I can sort out the intellectual side of this, the murderer
will be obvious.

I agree with you that we should get more info on Von Enchanhauer's past and also on Anna Freud. Let's do that while we're in London.

Finally, what is happening on the little record chain front? You said you were going to check for fingerprints and match them with everyone's who lives in Bozo's house. I doubt it turned up anything, but if it did, let me know.

> *Old, skinny and still truckin',*
> *Alias*
> *Mata Hari from the tundra*

Within two days I got a telegram delivered with a return address of the Custer Country Motel, Montana. On bright yellow stationary was printed the following:

Dear slender and seasoned,
Well, Montana was an information drought. The magical cowboy was nothing more than a prairie oyster who listened to the Doors' "Light My Fire" on one too many acid trips. Too bad 'cause even the teeth were a match.

Speaking of hides, I hope you realize, my little Freudianette, I have saved yours with Gardonne. I headed off the psychoanalytic posse with some bullshit about why you were out of town during your Onondaga odyssey. Stick to the New-York-City-Psychoanalytic-library number if he asks.

Booked our flight to England—Last Minute Club. We leave at 6:10 a.m. See you at the airport.

I'm taking some heat here, but I managed to get tails on everyone.

> *Hanging up my spurs,*
> *Jackie*

———

I ran into a bedraggled Jackie with two days' beard growth in the customs lineup. His road-map eyes let me know that he had flown in from the West Coast just in time to change planes for London. I didn't look much better since I'd been up into the wee hours attempting to back up my theories with facts.

As I flopped into my orange connected plastic chair in our gate, I said, "God, this airport is hideous."

"Where do you think they got the phrase 'terminal illness'?" Jackie said over his shoulder as he headed in the direction of the coffee wagon.

"Get me one, will you?" I asked.

"I planned on it."

"How do you know what I take?"

He rhymed off the following litany in a monotone. "Decaf if it's brewed. If it's instant, stick to high-octane—with milk only, preferably two percent. If they only have non-dairy whitener, you'll take it black. If there's only tea, first choice Twinings, second Bigelow."

About ten minutes later, when he handed me my coffee, he said, "You know what kind of woman I like?"

"I can't imagine," I said, not looking up from the paper.

"The kind who just says, 'Get me a coffee.'"

"If she was that undiscriminating, how could she have chosen you?" I said as I opened the lid carefully marked *decaf, 2 percent.*

After boarding our British Airways flight, Jackie said, "I checked, and Freud's appointment books for those years are in London in storage. Only a few years got left in Vienna. Who're you looking for?"

"Anna O."

Jackie looked confused. "Wait a minute. Wasn't she Breuer's patient? Didn't Freud and Breuer write *Studies on Hysteria* together? Don't we need to check things out with Breuer's archives to see if they have his appointment books or if they're still in existence?"

"Jackie, would you start thinking like Bozo."

"Let me have a coffee first," he said, prying open his white plastic lid.

"Here's the index of *Studies on Hysteria*," I said, bending back the spine of the well-thumbed volume. "All of the cases are by Freud except one, Anna O., which is by Breuer."

"Am I supposed to get this?" he said, blowing loudly on his coffee.

"Did Freud ever collaborate before or after?"

"No."

"Then why did he do it with *Studies on Hysteria?* Why? I'll tell you why."

"I counted on that," Jackie said, stretching his arms in the air and making a loud yawning noise.

"Well, Bozo would say that Anna O. was someone that Freud was trying to hide, so he fobbed her off on Breuer, then an old man. Breuer agreed to put his name on one case if he could get second authorship to the entire volume. That case was Freud's and no one but Freud's." I turned to Jackie and said, "Have those computer linguists analyze Freud's other writing and I bet the syntax will be the same. Remember what leaked out about Anna O. in the authorized Jones biography of Freud?"

"It isn't on the tip of my tongue," Jackie said while making an abortive attempt at stretching his legs and banging into the seat in front of him. "Christ!" he bellowed. "Solitary was preferable to the way these airlines cram in the passengers. And they call *me* criminal." The guy next to him looked worried. "Anyway," Jackie said, once he'd caused a rumpus, "wasn't Anna O. the real founder of the free association method? She was able to get rid of her physical symptoms by talking about them. She told Breuer to forget the hypnotism hocus-pocus and to shut up and let her free-associate. She called it her 'chimney sweeping.' If she had a chance to 'sweep' on a regular basis, she could keep her symptoms—I think one was paralysis—at bay. Breuer cured her, and said he owed the technique to her."

Sometimes Jackie surprised me by what he could learn in a short period of time. I said, "He didn't cure her and close the case, he ran out on the patient. Breuer lied or obfuscated in the text of Anna O. by suppressing some of the details of the case. He does give Anna O. the credit for the technique of free association. What he doesn't tell you comes out fifty years later in the official Freud biography. The reason Breuer terminated the case is that Anna O., the woman whom Breuer described as being devoted to her sick father and having 'remarkably little sexual interest,' had a psychoanalytic bundle of joy for him one day. Breuer arrived at her house, back in the days when they made house calls, for their session and found Anna O., who was then probably, at the most, in her early twenties, in the throes of a hysterical childbirth, technically known as pseudocyesis, a phantom birth. There she was, fully dilated, and the married Breuer ran out of her house, never to return."

"I'd keep going," Jackie said.

"Okay, we know that Jones, Freud's *official* biographer, gives us that scenario. Now let's look at this from the point of view of Bozo, the *unofficial* biographer. First of all he would say Breuer is a cheap cover for Freud; second, the pregnancy was based on something real that happened between Anna O. and Freud; and third, no one gets pregnant on her own except for the one and only Blessed Virgin."

"And my girlfriend when I was in doing my second ten," Jackie added.

"I did a little research on the 'real' Anna O., who was Bertha Pappenheim. She was an amazing woman in her own right. She spent many years in a mental hospital, yet when she got out she became the first social worker. Vienna even minted a stamp after her. She started a home for unwed mothers."

"Being one herself, unconsciously, right?" Jackie said, and nodded, impressed by his own psychological acumen. "You know, you were right about one thing—it really isn't so hard to do this psychiatrist gig."

"Well, thinking in Bozo style, I would say that Freud hid the real Anna O.'s identity and thought Bertha Pappenheim would fit the role perfectly. She had mental problems and high scruples, the Freud family knew the Pappenheim family, and Breuer had in fact analyzed the real Bertha Pappenheim. She was intelligent enough to come up with the free association method, and he could pin the unwed mother on her. What must have happened, thinking Bozo style, is that someone got on to the fact that it was really Freud who analyzed Anna O. By the time Jones wrote the Freud biography, Breuer was dead and Bertha Pappenheim was too old to fight. Since neither was in any shape for denials, Freud leaked out the tidbit about her so-called 'true' identity. The Freudian circle could be thrown off the scent and at the same time be titillated with this 'inside' knowledge. Needless to say, Bertha Pappenheim's relatives denied the whole thing, and the records show she had been in a mental hospital at the time. No one listened to her, though, because she was a nutbar at one point. Anyway, if you were an unwed mother in Victorian Vienna and gave birth, real or imagined, wouldn't you deny it?"

"Definitely," said Jackie. "But hey, don't listen to me, I used to lie about everything." After gulping some coffee, he continued,

"The problem is—*who cares?* Is she still alive, this big Bertha?"

"No."

"Who cares what happened to a patient of Freud's, or if he wanted to say it was Breuer who analyzed her?" I just looked at him, refusing to answer anything so obvious, so he said, "Like the person who murdered two people by poisoning them and then slitting their throats."

"The killer is one of the following: either the patient who really was Anna O., or Bertha Pappenheim's relatives, or the Gardonnes of this world, or the passionate Freudians, like Von Enchanhauer or Anna Freud, who can't bear to see his holiness's name besmirched. Or . . ." I had a flash of insight looking through my tiny window as we rose above the clouds, "a person who fits into several of these categories."

Jackie handed me a twenty-five-page computer printout, saying, "Here is the unauthorized Von Enchanhauer biography. I'm still spinning my wheels on Anna Freud's. I think she's a little like Ralph Nader—everyone has been trying to get dirt on her for years, but she's as dull as a drink of water."

"I thought that's what Gardonne looked like at first," I said.

As Jackie flipped through the pages, he said, "A real snorefest. Not one tiny detail has crawled from under any rock."

"I'm willing to bet that you lift the right rock and you'll find slugs packed with personal dirt. No one, I repeat, *no one* would write the best paper in the world on defence mechanisms unless they're defending plenty of their own. There's a rule of thumb that's always served me well. I think I may embroider a sampler for my kitchen: *Everyone Has Something to Hide.*"

"Have you ever *been* in your kitchen?" Jackie asked.

Before opening my backpack stuffed with Bozo's papers, I took a deep breath and said to Jackie, "Book me into a bed and breakfast in Maresfield Gardens. I want to be close to the archives."

Lest I relax for a minute and watch the in-flight entertainment, Jackie handed me some leads he'd got on Von Enchanhauer and Anna Freud in New York by interviewing the psychoanalytic geriatric set who emigrated from Europe after the war.

After thirteen hours of restorative sleep, I rang the doorbell of Anna Freud's house. Elsa, the club-footed housekeeper, galumphed to the door, opening it a crack. As she stomped up the stairs, leading me to Anna Freud's study, she muttered to no one in particular, "You're attacking an old woman, you are, and stealing her peace of mind. She's been through enough. You once will be old, and who will care for you, eh?"

"If you're speaking to me, probably who cares for me now— no one," I answered in a matter-of-fact tone with an edge of English chipper.

As I stepped into Anna's study, I was again struck by its contrast with the rest of the *Sunset Boulevard* house. The desk was backed by a beautiful bay window that looked out on masses of rhododendrons with trailing wisteria as a background. All the windows were dormered, with window seats cushioned in soft Liberty prints. The books in the cherry cases were askew from constant use. Behind her desk, Anna Freud looked so content that I thought if *only* I could work in a study like this, even I might feel her equanimity and serenity. She was the first female Freudian. No one could take that away from her. All she wanted was to do her work. She felt no other pulls.

Then again, I had to be careful not to be seduced. This serene woman, who sat in this tranquil study, was calmly composing ways that human beings took their volatile feelings and stuffed them back into their heads because those feelings were too terrifying for civilization to witness. The form was serene, the content was not.

"Hello, Miss Fitzgerald," she said, looking up from her writing. "I hope your journey was satisfactory."

"Yes, thank you. I regret any inconvenience this may cause you. We have reason to believe that these threats to Konzak need to be thoroughly investigated."

"Those letters can be incredibly upsetting. I regret that I have not saved all the puerile mail I received over the years that threatened my father. I am afraid that there were more than I care to remember."

"May I ask you a few questions before I go upstairs?"

"Certainly. Would you like some tea?"

"That would be great. Earl Grey?"

"That is my favourite. I feel I've left my Viennese coffee roots for the land of the bottomless cup of tea."

"Me too. I went to university here. Tea time was great. You know, I tried to lay it on when I got back to Canada. I even bought clotted cream and scones, but it was never the same."

"Yes, I tried that too. I gave up in New York and had deli."

"You've got to admit, though, only the U.S. can provide a decent shower with normal water pressure. You can't even get a decent shower at the Savoy," I said.

"It has always struck me as singular that England is an island surrounded by water but it only dribbles from the taps."

"I want to assure you that I'm a great admirer of your father, and I would never deliberately tarnish his reputation. I need to see what Konzak was on to in order to try to enter the mind of the person who has threatened Konzak and understand his motive. Otherwise we'll never solve the case. Also, a man who calls himself The Wizard is in danger."

"The Wizard?"

"Yes, he had his name legally changed to The Wizard, with The as his first name and Wizard as his surname," I said, rolling my eyes as if to say that she as a psychoanalyst did not have the corner on strange people. "If he's not dead, he's in hiding or has been kidnapped, and I believe he's in danger. Dr. Gardonne assured us you'd be co-operative."

"I understand. Dr. Von Enchanhauer called and he assured me it was all necessary, and I appreciate your offering to sign the press waiver. I'll avail myself of that if you're still amenable. I had my lawyer draw up the document." As Anna Freud came out from behind her desk and handed it to me, I was struck by her animated step and piercing blue eyes. Her eyes looked young and engaged with everything around her, compared with the rest of her decrepit body.

We went through double French doors into the part of the study used by the secretary, which looked comfortably efficient with sleek ergonomic furniture. All the latest technological accoutrements that make communicating a snap were within reach. Although I loved the Dickensian warmth of the first room, there was a part of me that admired this room, with all the latest technology that gracefully brought it into this century. I realized that these studies united the two sides of my nature, as they had Anna Freud's. If I hadn't screwed up my life so much, I would have had exactly this combination for my study.

"I'd kill for this study," I said, regretting my choice of words as soon as they were out of my mouth. She must know that I was convicted of killing someone. She was probably thinking that I'd killed for far less than a study. Anyway, the cat was out of the bag. There was no way I could now say that it was only a figure of speech.

Upstairs, I went through the cupboards and boxes, retracing Konzak's steps. It was easy to see what he had looked at because everything else was covered in dust. There were cupboards full of papers in elastic bands and letters stuffed in old Viennese hat boxes that had been thrown together when the Freuds fled the Nazis. It was two-thirty in the morning when I finally tiptoed down the stairs and saw Anna's study light on. I popped my head in and said, "Sorry I was here so long. I hope I don't wear out my press-gagged welcome."

Anna Freud smiled and said that she had to work late or she would lose her train of thought. I assured her that I did the same thing. "I am finished now and have just put a cozy on a pot of Earl Grey, if I can interest you in a cup," she said.

"Oh, that sounds great," I acknowledged. "I've been reading for a number of days now and my neck is in knots," The tea steeped on the window seat as I sank comfortably into a corduroy wing chair. I thought I'd try a gambit or two to see where they led. "You know, I can't get over the absurdity of this. Konzak's 'great revelations' are based on innuendo scantily dressed as facts. When his book is published posthumously, there's really very little to say. It's a tempest in a teapot. He'll have put himself in more disrepute than Dvorah Little put him in."

"Posthumously?" Anna Freud asked, looking puzzled. "Has Konzak agreed to wait until his death to publish his work? I find that hard to believe. He's usually chomping at the bit for fame, even if it's no more than notoriety. Dr. Von Enchanhauer must have found some way to reach him."

"Anders Konzak was murdered in Vienna a while ago," I said.

Anna looked at her teacup and placed it very carefully on her desk. She said nothing for a long minute. She folded her hands under her chin and rested her elbows on her chair. She twisted slightly in her swivel chair. I waited for her to respond. Finally she said, "Professor Konzak would have enjoyed the attention this will bring."

"Ironic, isn't it? An exhibitionist getting attention when he's too dead to enjoy it?"

She shook her head in disbelief, saying, "It's so tragic and unnecessary. The murderer has inflated notions of Professor Konzak's intellectual capabilities. He was really harmless."

I nodded. "He's been hunted by his own PR."

"I know. I tried to tell him when he was staying here and we dined together that he was putting his own theories before the evidence. Nothing would convince him. I wanted to save him and Dr. Von Enchanhauer the embarrassment." She looked more pained than shocked as she said, "Poor, poor Dr. Von Enchanhauer. He cared so much that I didn't have the heart to tell him all of my grave misgivings."

"Did you ever tell Konzak, no holds barred, what you thought of him intellectually?"

"No, I didn't. For some reason, he put me in mind of my nephew's eighth birthday. I was the adult in charge and tried to get the children to calm down, but eventually one gives up and lets chaos reign."

"That's an interesting analogy. Do you have a lot to do with children?"

"Not now. But remember, I used to teach. Also my sister and brother-in-law died young, so I assumed the care of their children until more suitable arrangements could be made. I suppose my nephew's eighth birthday party was so chaotic that it has stayed in my mind for over fifty years."

"That's a lot of chaos," I said, leaning back on the headrest and savouring my tea. "It's interesting that we're both single. Why has everyone made such a big deal about your marital status?"

"I suspect that people wanted to know about Freud's life and, since he's no longer with us, they settle on mine—a poor substitute. Also, because Freud delved into the unconscious, which can be quite threatening, people have a desire to find unhealthy parts in him and in his family so they can discredit his ideas through discrediting him."

"Like there is something wrong with you, his daughter, because you have remained single? That's weird, since there was something wrong with me when I was married." As I drained my teacup, I added, "To me your life looks idyllic. You've been in on the ground floor of the discovery of a movement that has changed Western thought, pursued your own career, founded the study of child analysis, started the war orphanage and done meaningful work every day. People talk about you as being 'alone.' Haven't you preferred it to what you see mothers and wives doing? I know I would."

"It's hard to explain that to people who don't share your sentiments. People think it's simple denial. I would never ask for any other life. It's been one of true challenge in an unforgettable journey of the mind and of the political arena."

Getting more animated, I leaned forward in my chair, saying, "There is no moment like the one when things become clear intellectually—when all the pieces fit. You must have had that moment in your paper on defence mechanisms. It's like giving birth to an idea."

"Yes, I've had that feeling"—she nodded, smiling, sharing my enthusiasm—"in giving birth, as you say, to ideas. Of course, sometimes when you write a difficult paper it feels like a breech birth. Then when you read it over, it may be a stillbirth. But I have also had that wondrous moment when solving analytic cases, finally understanding how a patient's persistent symptom is fed by a particular unconscious need, eventually seeing the amazing transformation when he begins to address the real world."

"I read your father's work when I was in prison. Perhaps I had a heightened sensibility while there. My existence was so barren that I began drowning in the shame of prison futility. I reached for the floating identity of the more successful. After reading Freud's volumes while holed up in an eight-by-ten sensory deprivation box, I pictured his every movement, and I often conversed with him in my mind. I know it sounds strange, but at times I felt I was Freud. I *felt* his joy in discovery, and also his fatigue after seeing so many patients, knowing he still had to write them up. Did he keep notebooks of his daily cases, the ones that were not case presentations or pieces for writing, just cases in progress?"

"He wrote up all of his findings in a daily diary so he could go back to the dates if he formally wrote up the case histories. But unfortunately, he really only kept the notes if he was going to hand the case over to someone else. He could commit the details of his own cases to memory. You will notice that he hardly ever crossed out and has made only one draft."

"That's what I do—don't you? I keep everything in my head until it spills out in my dreams and in slips of the tongue and I finally pour it all out on the printed page."

"No, I work quite differently. I take notes and plan and write several drafts and then file it away, and then I bring it out in a month and have a fresh look at it."

After warming up our teas, she settled herself and, changing the subject, asked, "Going back to your time in prison, if I might, you sound as though it was not truly dreadful?"

I realized no one had ever asked me directly about my time in the penitentiary. "It was horrendous in some ways, but in others it was a time to learn in an uninterrupted way. Intellectualization was my defence and it worked surprisingly well. I decided since I was there that I could thoroughly learn from at least two minds who are cornerstones of Western civilization."

"Who was the other?"

"Darwin. I had done extensive work on him in graduate school, but there was so much more to read, especially in the light of what I'd learned from Freud. I didn't get as far as I'd planned since I was given a Temporary Absence — emphasis on the 'temporary.' In a way, prison gave me freedom from everyday life. Many women decide to be mothers not really understanding the job description, and are imprisoned for years in domestic drudgery without time off for good behaviour. The harder you work at it, the worse it is. The more responsibility the mother takes, the less responsibility the child takes. I used to watch the mothers at prison when their children came to visit. They were usually more upset after the visit than before it. Maybe that's an exception, but my sister's teenage children treated her as though she was a burden, and a heavy one at that. I guess kids have to leave their parents eventually, and they accomplish it by pushing them away."

"Yes, it's like an eagle pushing against its mother to get into its first flight. The eaglet is airborne, but the mother feels the wings pushing against her chest and no one tells her the supposed gossamer wings are in fact made of iron."

"I think Lepidoptera have it figured out. Butterflies never see their mother. After mating, the female never sees the father again, except maybe socially, and then she lays eggs and never sees them again. The eggs turn into caterpillars, then they pupate and emerge fully formed and fly away, free from bonding issues, Oedipal complexes or tired mothers." As I poured my Earl Grey over the sterling strainer, I added, "No wonder they call it metamorphosis."

"Did you know that the Greeks believed that the soul left the body after death in the form of a butterfly? Their symbol for soul was a butterfly-winged girl, interestingly named — Psyche," Anna said.

"Rousseau was pretty on top of it when he said the best parenting was 'benign neglect.'"

"Speaking of parenting, how did your family respond to your incarceration, if you don't mind me asking?"

"My father took the side of my husband's family. I guess you could call it neglect of the non-benign variety. He said that even if the murder or my husband's death was a mistake, his family had lost their son. My mother followed suit because she always does. And my sisters both did what my mother did because they always do. My father doesn't allow emotion to creep into his rational thinking. He prides himself on that."

"What about unconditional love, the idea that you may not like what your child does *but* you still love the child, otherwise you are abandoning her?"

"Rationally, there is no unconditional love. If your child commits an unacceptable act then, well, you shouldn't forgive him or her if it offends your sense of reason. If you believe that, you *have* to abandon your child if you find yourself in that circumstance."

"Your father sounds as though he cannot handle his feelings and has taught you that his ineptitude in the field of human emotions is really an exercise in rational control."

All of a sudden my heart had been punctured and was leaking anguish into my pericardium. Why would a few words shoot through me like that? I mean, it's not a news flash that my father had problems with love and empathy. There must have been a roped-off area of my brain that housed the little girl who idolized her father's *rationality*. Before this moment I'd never understood that area as a defence.

Through the white noise of anxiety I heard Anna talking, but I could only focus on the tail end of a sentence, " . . . I hope you don't follow in his footsteps."

I said, "Naturally, I've thought about this a lot. That's probably why I chose to study Darwin and Freud. Although my temperament is more suited to the hard sciences, I needed answers for life, not for science. Sometimes I think that unconsciously I committed my crime to flush my father's rejection out in the open." I heard myself saying these surprising words, but as they hung in the air, it felt like someone else had said them.

"Well." Anna smiled wryly. "It worked."

"Hey, I did something right."

"Maybe you also had the unconscious hope that your mother would stand up and be counted."

"That doesn't ring true to me. I had two sisters who were already ten and thirteen when I was born. I was a mistake, or else my father's last hope for a boy. My mother had burned out by the time I came along. A former Ford model, she and my sisters loved shopping and all forms of female endeavour. My father, who was over a decade older than my mother, had retired by the time I was two years old. He had been too busy with his career on the bench to have had much input in my sisters' lives. I became his pet project, entitled The Making of a Rational Woman. A pedagogue at heart, he devoted himself to my home-teaching. While I had little in common with my mother and sisters, I shared nearly all the academic and athletic interests of my father."

"John Stuart Mill was the product of that same hothouse of education," Anna said. "It left him brilliant but impaired. He never consummated his marriage. The sexual longing was extinguished within him, obviously crushed by an exaggerated emphasis on intellectual development."

"I think Mill's asexuality had more to do with early social isolation than too much loading on the intellectual side of the brain. Fortunately, my father believed in sports and I was allowed to be on all kinds of teams, which offered me social development in the form of female bonding, or at least enough to give me an orientation. Sex is of interest to me, but I'm not interested in relationships."

"Fascinating. That's the opposite of John Stuart Mill."

"Too bad we're of different eras," I said. "I could have had sex with him and he could have had a relationship with me." I warmed to Anna's unguarded laugh and realized how she sprang to life like a thirsty sponge when engaging in intellectual conversation.

"Life is shorter than you think. There is never a way to tell people how fast the years go by after sixty-five."

"Do you wish you had done things differently?" I asked.

"No, not really." She hesitated for a moment and then continued, "Sometimes when I see my friend Dorothy with her now adult children, I feel slightly dejected, but I have had a unique intellectual journey and the joy of all of the children who have been close to me. I was able to give my father all my time when he was ill, and that was a choice, one I would never take back. When he died, I wanted to know that I had done all I could to make him comfortable and to keep a brilliant mind working under torturous physical conditions."

"We have quite a bit in common. Sure, I'm the North American après-feminist brash version, you're the European pre-feminist model. But both of us have been made into rationalists by our fathers and have in some ways been irretrievably altered by it." Comparing myself to Anna Freud sounded ridiculously pompous, so I added the qualifier, "I mean on a personal level. I'm infamous and you're famous. You've made intellectual contributions that will live on and I'm yesterday's news. Yet I feel that we share a past. Not many women have been raised by their fathers in your or even my era."

"Yes, both men do sound deterministic and strong in their own ways. However, I would like to think that mine would not have abandoned me in a moment of dire need."

"Well, he did analyze you. Do you think that was fair?"

"Fair . . ." Anna said, pausing. "That's an interesting choice of adjective. Advancing science is not always *fair*. Sometimes it can be ruthless. I try not to talk about my analysis now because people don't understand that psychoanalysis was in the founding stages. No one knew what problems could arise. Let us not commit the sin of presentism."

"It would be the least of my sins, but not to belabour the point, the papers on transference had already been written. How can an analyst remain the good, all-loving *idealized* father when he is your *real* father?"

"This is a problem for another evening. I'm not trying to be obscure, but one should never discuss one's analysis or its emotional intensity becomes diluted. There were no other analysts at the time that would have suited my needs."

"It reminds me of my own father, who raised me to be unique, what he fantasized as superior, then when I did something, like kill my husband, which you must admit was unique, he was outraged. Over what? Over the murder? No way. It was over the fact that his experiment to raise a girl to be unemotional didn't work. He thought it would make me more rational, less like my simpy mother and sisters. What it *in fact* has done is make me dismissive of the whole psychological cesspool frequently referred to as *emotions*."

"I wonder if 'dismissive' is the word that you want to use. Might 'fearful' be more suitable? You were in a classic double bind. You wanted your father's love, which was a feeling, but he made it clear that he would *love* you only on the condition that you never showed your *love* for him. In fact he would *love* you if you always denied your feelings and only used your intellect." As she said this, she watched my face closely, waited a moment for it to sink in, then continued, "It's no wonder your marriage blew up. Your husband required love, and in order to give it you would have been betraying your father, or the strictly rational image your father created."

My heart was hammering. I'd never come close to having this kind of revelation with Gardonne in nine years.

After a long silence I began packing up to leave, realizing I had gained all the insight and emotional Catch-22s I could take for a day. As I zipped my backpack, I decided to move away from the less than delightful dyad of my father and me, saying, "Let's face it, if a woman was logical, she wouldn't bother with a mate and a family. It's all give and no take. I realized that when I was in grade nine and my mother said, 'Why don't you ask Bobby Wells about his fishing expedition with his father? Boys love to talk about themselves and they love girls who listen.'"

I stood up and stretched. "Anyway, you're right," I said to Anna, "these are all problems for another evening." Looking at my watch, I said, "God! It's after three in the morning. I usually get up an hour from now."

As she walked me to the door, I said, "Please don't mention Konzak's murder to anyone, and that includes Dr. Von Enchanhauer. I know it is a big favour to ask, but I probably shouldn't have told you about it. It's just that it seemed so false to be discussing his possible reaction to this or that. Besides . . ." I hesitated but decided to blunder on. "I have enjoyed our conversations and would feel compromised if any emotional dishonesty crept in. I've done enough of that in my psychiatric dealings."

"I understand, and thank you for extending the courtesy of telling me privately." We shook hands at the open door and she said, "I don't envy you the arduous task of going through all of Freud's writing and the correspondence looking for clues."

"Of course it'll be like finding a needle in a haystack if it's a random killer. But I have my doubts about that. Killing a man who has gleaned information about Freud and his practice between 1895 and 1900 hardly sounds random to me."

Anna nodded in agreement as the door closed.

The next day I sat waiting for Jackie in the Duke of Gloucester, a smoke-filled English pub, eating Stilton and some kind of shrivelled baby gourd that only the English would call a pickle. As he sat down, I was already going at him about what I'd found at the archives. "I'm eighty percent there."

"I'm not used to women who are only eighty percent there," he said, flinging two Xeroxed reports on the table. "Here's our darling Dr. Von E. His résumé reads like a charm. Not one missing moment or one shady act. Was hospitalized only once, for appendicitis in 1945, and had a slow recuperation."

"What hospital?" I asked.

"Royal Vic," he said as he waved to the waitress while pointing to my ploughman's lunch and nodding.

"Did you get the records?"

"I tried. They're missing. The folder is there, but the report is torn out. That's the only suspicious thing."

"We should get an X-ray to see if that appendix is gone," I suggested.

"That's not going to be easy."

"He'll co-operate. He's already cowed by having chosen Konzak. He doesn't want to look even more ridiculous."

"I don't think he committed the murder," Jackie said. "A few missing hospital records, one month after the end of the war when everything was in chaos, isn't so far-fetched." When I looked dubious, he said, "I'll admit there is something weird about him. I actually think he's a homosexual," then he bit into his gourd.

"Where did the kids come from, the head of Zeus? Those boys don't look like the result of turkey basting to me . . . Actually, now that you mention it, they do look like artificial insemination, with Albert Speer as a sperm donor."

"Having kids doesn't mean anything. You can be gay and still fake it."

"As in 'Lie on your back and think of Jan Morris'?" I inquired.

"Yeah, women fake it all the time—or else only get eighty percent there," Jackie concurred.

I had my doubts about the homosexual orientation. "Why would you say he is gay?" I asked.

"A feeling," Jackie said with dismissive nonchalance.

"The last time you said 'a feeling,' you were in your crib," I pointed out.

"Ever heard 'You don't have to be a weatherman to know which way the wind blows'?"

"Oh, that's interesting. I thought we were working on this case together and risking our pathetic, but all we've got, lives, and working sixteen-hour shifts for what has turned into an entire spring—that's a lifetime for a tulip. But Jackie Lawton wants to talk about the way the wind blows. *Fine.*" I nodded, plowing through my ploughman's lunch.

Realizing he was cornered, he said, "All right, here it goes," and took a long pull on his dark ale. "He never once looked at your ass when we were at his cottage on the Isle of Wight. You wore cowboy boots, jeans and a turtleneck. When you looked at the crockery crap with the wife, he never once looked at your body."

I was so embarrassed once I realized I'd trapped him into saying something about my body that I started laughing and said,

"Now I've found it, the electric Kool-Aid acid test for heterosexuality: looking at my ass! Jesus, the U.S. Army could have used that test years ago."

"Actually, I wouldn't list your butt as a dangerous weapon. Remember, I've been in jail since I was nine. Anyone in jail has to have a sixth sense about that kind of thing. It's part of the culture."

I heard myself asking, against my better judgment, "Did you have homosexual affairs in jail?" I was going to add *not that it's any of my business*, but that was fairly obvious.

He looked at me for a long time, considering, and then said, "I was there for all of my teen years and my twenties. Of course I had homosexual affairs, non-consensual at first and then later consensual. When there are no women, you make do. Everyone did." I just looked at him, regretting that I'd ever asked him. Reading my expression, he said, "Didn't Freud say everyone is bisexual?" He shrugged and continued, "I've had some wild sexual experiences in jail and some real relationships. I have just chosen to leave it behind. I refuse to be burned by shame any more. You keep that stuff in and you only do more things that you consider shameful. I'm beyond thinking of my past as shameful."

I nodded. Shame sticks like napalm and keeps burning. I felt a kind of respect for him. In spite of—or maybe because of—what he'd been through, he was really more secure in himself than a lot of men, who can't express the feelings of a gnat. He seemed rock-solid at this point. If he says Von Enchanhauer is a homosexual even though there is no indication of it, I'd place money on it.

There was laughter and good cheer all around us in the pub, and I realized that despite my usual difficulty in getting along with people, I liked Jackie, and the realization didn't scare me as much as I might have expected. I began to know what people meant by the concept of *friendship*. It felt like the first day you take off your winter jacket, as your driveway thaws and you get out your bike. I imagined myself basking in a field of yellow daffodils, soaking up the sun like a lizard.

I looked up, and despite the toothpick between his teeth he managed a warm smile. He slapped his hand down on the table decisively and said, "One more Guinness and we're off." He continued between long gulps, "It's time to hit up Dr. Von Enchanhauer, and remember, he never mentioned Bozo until his wife horned in. He's hiding the fact that he knew Bozo and we need to know why. I checked the registration records of that conference that Bozo mentioned in western New York. Von Enchanhauer, Bozo and Konzak were there exactly as Bozo described it. I agree with you there's something altogether weird about him, but I can't quite get it. I'm ninety percent there — you know the feeling, man?"

We laughed and stumbled out of the pub, adjusting our eyes to the light.

19

UP HIS SLEEVE

—

Jews and homosexuals are the outstanding creative
minorities in contemporary urban culture. Creative,
that is, in the truest sense: they are creators of
sensibilities. The two pioneering forces of modern
sensibility are Jewish moral seriousness and
homosexual aestheticism and irony.
— SUSAN SONTAG, *Against Interpretation*

DR. VON ENCHANHAUER'S London flat was an elegant
Kensington condominium in a handsome old building
covered with an orange trumpet vine. The windows overlooked a beautiful *jardin anglais* bursting with perennials of
every colour.

As Jackie rang the wrought-iron door buzzer, he mumbled as
an architectural aside, "Leave it to the English to make modern
technology look old and rusty . . ."

"I love that about the English. They value tradition and they
never fall into that Hollywood period-piece mode. They have a
real sense of their own history."

"Christ, I didn't mean to start 'Rule, Britannia!'" Jackie said as he rang the bell again. "Yesterday I told Von E. we wanted to ask him a few questions, so he could stew for a day."

The housekeeper, Tefonia, opened the door and stared. Jackie asked, "May we see Dr. Von Enchanhauer?"

She nodded her assent in an exaggerated way, as though she were a marionette, but then stood there as blank as a wood chip.

Dr. Von Enchanhauer called from upstairs, "Please invite our guests up, Tefonia." She turned tail and plodded up the stairs.

Jackie whispered, "She looks like something from *Deliverance*."

I made the Ozark banjo sound "*de-de-de-de*."

Dr. Von Enchanhauer greeted each of us formally, as did his Margaret Thatcher–coiffed wife. Mrs. Von Enchanhauer smiled, saying, "Miss Fitzgerald, I thought, since you had been so taken with the china, I would take the liberty of getting out my Minton bone china when I heard you were coming."

Despite the detective air I was supposed to maintain, I was thrilled to go to the dining room to see it. Her slender fingers massaged the raised decoration on the plates, in which each flower was slightly more open on each plate until it was in full bloom on the largest platter. It was a magnificent cobalt-blue glaze that was never replicated after the eighteenth century; the technique died with the potter. I picked up one of the plates and held it to the light to admire the detail on the moulding. "These are so beautiful you must enjoy them every time you glance their way."

"Dr. Von Enchanhauer and my sons are not interested, so I had them in the back of the sideboard. Your interest revived mine, and I got them out and I'm enjoying them again as though they were new. They are delicate, they remind me of easier times. I'm so delighted to share their beauty with you."

After I'd rejoined Dr. Von Enchanhauer and Jackie in the sitting room, I said in what I hoped would be an official "Just the facts ma'am" kind of voice, "Dr. Von Enchanhauer, we have only a few minutes, so we must come directly to the point. When were you analyzed by Freud?"

"Once when I was a teenager in Vienna and once again right after the war in England."

Jackie piped up, "Doctor, I understand you were in the hospital in 1945."

"That's correct."

During their interchange I watched Mrs. Von E. carefully. She looked down at her teacup and began to finger the edge. Then she sat on her hands. People do things they hope others will do. The first thing you do when someone has food on her teeth is run your tongue over your own teeth. I was sure the operation had to do with his hand, the one with the scarring on it. Why else would his wife hide her hand when they mentioned the hospitalization?

"I had an appendectomy," Dr. Von Enchanhauer said.

"I see. You were in hospital quite a long time—four weeks in the hospital at a time when so many people were sick?" Jackie queried.

"Yes. I developed an infection. The appendix had ruptured. Antibiotics were not yet in general use by any means, and there was a shortage after the war. I know that is hard to imagine when you're all from the era of the broad-spectrum."

"It's odd," Jackie said, "that you would be in an English hospital when you were still living in Vienna with your wife. With a stabbing pain in your appendix, I can't imagine you saying, 'Ouch, darling, I have an excruciating pain in my side. I think I'll go over to England right away.'"

"Vienna was in a terrible state and there was a huge waiting list. My wife's father used some business connections and managed to get me referred to the Royal Vic. However, the whole trip took too long, as you have suggested, and the appendix burst before the surgery."

"May I ask what happened to your hand?" I inquired.

"Yes," he said, never hesitating or making any attempt to cover his hand. "Before the war broke out I was Sofia's tutor, and we had agreed to marry after I finished my medical degree. I'd gone back to university after studying metaphysics. During the war I, like the rest of the Jews in Europe, no longer had the luxury of continuing my education or developing relationships. My sole occupation became eluding the Nazis. Sofia's family kindly offered to hide me for what turned out to be a number of years in a well in the barn, an actual underground silo, which was no longer in use, where I won't say I lived, but I existed." He was quick to add, "I am very grateful to them. Otherwise I would have perished in the camps along with the rest of my family."

"Your wife's family had a huge home. Why did you have to stay in the barn? It must have been freezing," Jackie asked.

"You must remember this was Germany during the war. They were risking their lives having me there at all. They had a staff of servants and gardeners, some of whom were Nazi sympathizers. I had to remain hidden from them. There were rewards for turning in Jews, and many poor servants wouldn't have thought twice about informing."

"It must have been awful." Jackie paused, and then added, "In a former lifetime I spent years in solitary myself. Amazing, isn't it, how you have to reinvent your own rules when everything falls away after a few months."

"I lost two toes to frostbite. The worst thing was the darkness. My eyes lost the capability of adjusting to light, and to this day sunlight hurts my eyes because my rod adaptation atrophied. Living in darkness for years caused my mind to wander so that there were times when I had no control of my thoughts. I finally began to count the corn in the well and to devise ways to divide it up. I utilized statistical equations and checked their accuracy by counting the corn kernels by hand to see if these equations made any sense. I realized I had to keep my mind busy nearly all of my waking hours or else it became harder and harder to remember who I was or in what way I was different from the other farm creatures."

Jackie was now on the edge of his seat with his elbows resting on his knees. He had found someone who had spent as much time as he had in solitary. He began speaking in an animated voice that I had rarely heard from him. "I know *exactly* what you mean. When I was in solitary I did the same thing. I looked at every rule society had come up with and I tried to find reasons for why they needed it. Not being an educated man, I came up with some strange stuff, but I *think* it kept me sane."

Dr. Von Enchanhauer leaned forward, clearly empathizing with Jackie, and looking directly into his eyes he continued, with the pressure of speech of the Ancient Mariner. "All of my activities involved higher learning, so I could reassure myself that I was in fact Conrad Von Enchanhauer, a man who was a tutor who was holed up in Sofia's barn, who had a life before he became demeaned in this appalling way. But I could no longer convince myself that I was an innocent man. The little voice inside of me became louder and he incessantly whispered, 'If you are "the chosen people," why are you treated like cattle and given table scraps, and why do you steal corn from the animals?' I gave up talking to the sly Cassius, the inner voice who drawled anti-Semitic epithets. I resolved to occupy my mind with analytical tasks in order to block out what had become for me 'the human condition.'"

I snapped to—incredulous. "Wait a minute. Are *you* the same Von E. as the Von E. regression formula in multivariate statistics?"

"Yes, I am one and the same," the doctor answered.

"Amazing! That was how you discovered it—during the war in a well. Unbelievable. *Wait*—they always use corn kernels and husks of corn in the example. *I'm blown away!*" I said, flopping back in my chair.

Dr. Von Enchanhauer touched my shoulder in appreciation for my knowing and appreciating his theory, and continued, "We have digressed from my hand injury. On a cold, sunny Sunday, when I thought all of the servants were at Mass, I crept out of my hole to stroll for five minutes in the barnyard to ease my back, which had gone into spasm. Obviously it was too risky, because I was seen and reported by an informer. The following day the Nazis arrived on the estate and immediately entered the barn. They walked directly over to the well, which was crudely covered by boards hastily nailed together.

"The Gestapo lifted the well cover and threw in a lit torch, hoping that if there was a Jew down there, he would be smoked out. I grabbed the torch and ground it out with my hand before it had a chance to hit the tinder of dry corn husks and flare up. I smashed it against the well with my arm until you could smell burning flesh. I never let out a peep or they would have come down the sixty-five feet to the dark bottom for me. Finally they threw water down to prevent a fire and my arm began to smoke. They assumed they had been misinformed or else the Jew had escaped. They attributed the smell of the flesh to the rats that are always found in grain elevators."

As he looked down at his arm, he said, "It looks particularly bad because the skin liquefied, ran and needed medical attention. Sofia, of course, couldn't risk coming to the barn for days because, although she didn't know who the informer was, she knew that he was watching her every move. I, in turn, could not come up for months. The skin began to heal, but as you know, burns are very painful when they are healing. So this happened in October of 1942, and I didn't heal until eight months later, and then never successfully."

I turned to Mrs. Von Enchanhauer and said, "This must have been agonizing for you at the top of the well or silo or whatever it was, knowing that it was not water putting the fire out but the flesh of the man you loved."

She nodded as though it had been yesterday. Her voice never faltered as she said, "We had to offer the soldiers some schnapps and ask them to dine with us. I knew there was a collaborator in the house, but we didn't know who, and so I didn't dare go out for a long time. Eventually my father figured out it was the son of the charwoman who was selling information. It was an excruciated time."

"Excruciating, dear."

God, what a pedant. Why correct your wife's English when she is expressing such pain?

"Would you mind terribly letting us see your arm?" I asked, as Jackie gave me a look indicating he couldn't believe I was so callous.

"Certainly. Dear, you may want to leave the room," he said gently.

Sofia nodded and said as she stood, "I'll order tea."

He took off his shirt very gingerly, displaying an arm that was white and whose skin was like dripping lava, which moulded land formations near his elbow with peninsulas of skin dripping down his arm to the wrist. The top, near the shoulder, looked as though someone had heated it, borrowed some skin and patched it up.

His chest had a cavernous look not uncommon among sedentary scholars, but his chest hair didn't look like the hair on his head. It was greyish blond and the hair on his head was dark and curly. Aware that some people have different hair colour and beard, I still found it odd.

"Thank you, Dr. Von Enchanhauer. I am sorry we had to ask you to do that. What doctor did you see for your arm?" I asked.

"No one, actually. By the time I did get to see a doctor, it had healed in this deformed way and there was nothing to be done. The skin was held so precariously on the bone that the specialists decided to leave it."

"Who were these experts?" I persisted.

"I'd have to look up their names. They were associates of Sofia's family."

"We'll be leaving now. I would appreciate it if you could give us the name of the doctor," Jackie said.

"I am sure he would be dead now. He was far older than I."

"They may still have the records," Jackie said, refusing to let him off the hook.

I decided to watch his face closely as I dropped the whole enchilada to see how he'd react. He didn't have the defences of Anna or else he was a great fake. "I am sorry to be the bearer of bad tidings, especially after hearing what you've already been through. But we have heard some sad news." His wife was just entering the doorway. She slipped in and sat down near the door. Von E. leaned his head against the back of his wing chair and closed his eyes the way children do when they're terrified on a roller coaster but can't get off.

"Anders Konzak has been murdered," I said.

Von E.'s eyes opened wide and he paled, which made him an even more unimaginable hue. His hands began to shake. He mumbled, apparently in Yiddish, *"Genug is genug."* He did not go over to his wife but sank further in the chair, put his elbows on his knees, let his head drop in his hands and sobbed the most piteously sad sounds. He tried to stop; he began to rub his face and his whole head like a mother giving a child comfort. He hadn't yet buttoned his shirt and his chest was heaving. He began mumbling, "He didn't know, he simply didn't know."

"Know what?" I asked.

His wife stepped in. "Dear, I believe you should lean back and breathe deeply. You've had a shock." She was trying to shut him up and I again wanted to loosen his tongue, especially at this moment when he hadn't had a chance to raise his defences.

"He didn't know what his effect was on people. He was just searching for truth, like the rest of us. He was a total innocent, like a young puppy, too exuberant to know that the slipper he chewed had any meaning to anyone. It's all my fault. I should never have allowed him to have that job. It was his downfall. What was I thinking? Oh God, a whole life and now this. When will it end? Have I not had enough?" He looked at Jackie and pleaded, "When will it end?"

Jackie leapt to his feet and crossed the room, laying a hand on his trembling back. Von E. sobbed, "When *wet shoyn kimen a sof cy deym alemen?*" He stood and collapsed his emaciated body into Jackie's ham-sized arms. Von E. began bucking his head into Jackie's anvil chest, howling, demanding an answer of Jackie, "When *wet shoyn kimen a sof cy deym alemen?*"

Jackie had no idea what he had said, yet he held him tightly and responded, "I know. Sometimes solitary is easier." Tears ran down tributaries in the elderly wrinkled face as Jackie rocked back and forth with him.

Unable to deal with this emotional turbulence, I walked into the hall with Mrs. Von Enchanhauer in tow. Never losing her stoicism, she said, "Once you have lived through a war, nothing is the same." As an afterthought she inquired, "Who killed Professor Konzak?"

"We have no idea. He has been found dead in his apartment."

"I was not attached to him, but he was like a son to the doctor."

"Doesn't he have his own sons?"

"They never shared any interest in his Freudian pursuits. They are sailing enthusiasts, run factories. They really don't understand him." She walked over to the case that was full of sailing trophies and said, "They resented his keeping the archives alive as a major preoccupation. He had trouble getting close to them. They were like my side of the family."

"Did you love your husband?" I asked.

"Please do not use the past tense, Miss Fitzgerald. My English is good enough to know that is inappropriate."

"I was under the impression that when you loved a husband, you comforted him in his pain, but hey, that's only an impression. I mean, I killed my husband when he complained, so I guess I'm no authority on wifely ministrations," I admitted.

"What can you say to a man who has made a fool of himself over a silly American boy and undermined his life's work? It's best to let him filter through it and I will deal with the dregs. There is too much of a maelstrom at the moment."

"Why did you hide him for four years?"

"I believed he was a good man and a talented one, and I still do," she said evenly.

"People don't marry men they describe as *good*. They may hide them, but they don't marry them."

"All social mores do not represent those of the Americans," she said with quiet authority. "People like you and Anders Konzak think the world is simple and it's not. I envy you your simplicity and I loathe your naïveté." She walked slowly upstairs.

20

PAIRED IN SOLITUDE

—

The element of sexuality was astonishingly undeveloped in her.
— FREUD AND BREUER, *Studies on Hysteria,*
"Case of Anna O."

AS JACKIE AND I walked to the car, I could feel waves of rage rolling toward me. I said nothing as he slammed the gears. After about a half-hour of swearing at other drivers he finally spat out, "Gee, Kate, I hope you had a chance to see *all* of the antique dishes."

"I think I managed," I said, wondering why it was that when women leave it to men to comfort someone they are cold bitches, yet if men leave it to women they are "handling it their own way."

He began driving dangerously fast and yelled, "What the hell did you tell him about Konzak's murder for and then walk out like the WASP ice princess?"

"How come you can't be called the Wop or the Kraut or the ex-con, but you can call me the WASP ice princess whenever your soppy little heart desires? I'm sick of taking the WASP rap." When he didn't say anything, I spat out, "Got it?"

"You've never lived in solitary. The guy deserves something other than your disdain or indifference."

"How many detectives does it take to comfort a suspect? And please remember, he is a *suspect*. The great, tragic doctor is the one who got his wife off the topic of Bozo, you may recall, if your memory can do more than slur advantaged groups."

"For your goddamn information, you're more a suspect than he is. Pretty soon you'll have armed guards outside your door. They won't be there just to keep the bad guys out, they'll keep the bad girls in. Or have you ever been told that before?" Jackie asked, stepping on the accelerator. "Ever heard 'Recidivism rate, thy name is Kate'?"

I looked at him aghast. Was this thing going to get pinned on me?

Knowing he'd rocked me, he pushed his advantage. "We have been bullshitting around here for light-years while your great brain steams ahead. Where has it got us?" As we headed up Brompton Road, Jackie yanked the steering wheel and said, "I'd better take off my Kate-coloured glasses. Why the fuck did you tell him about Konzak's murder?"

"I wanted to see if he would say anything in time of trauma. It's a rudimentary technique understood by most interrogators, except for those who don't know Jack-shit. More neural pathways open up to store trauma, and often the response is too much for the defence mechanisms and you get far more information in those few seconds following the trauma. You were comforting him. I let you do what you were doing well. You're overreacting, and it's not going to be helpful to the case."

As the car fax machine grunted out a message, Jackie said, "You know, in certain situations upper-class girls are always the same. I remember being the bad boy who went to a rich good girl's house once when I was out of the can for the blink of an eye when I was a teenager. She really liked me. I used a toothpick at dinner just like I did at that pub. No one told me not to use it or to stop. They just looked at me the same way that you did when I cleaned my teeth. No one said a fucking word. There are all of these rules that are unwritten, and really you and Mrs. Von Frigidaire know them and we are the poor Jew and working-class stiff who can slobber over each other while you discuss the china." His voice suddenly thundered, "What kind of *bullshit* is that?"

I had nothing to refute, so I just picked up the fax that had spewed out between the bucket seats and read it aloud. "'Re: medical records of Conrad Von Enchanhauer. In 1963 Von Enchanhauer had a stomach X-ray, barium swallow for a suspected ulcer. At that time he had his appendix.'" I fought my facial expression to keep the I-told-you-so muscles from contracting.

We drove in silence until we sighted the archives where, thankfully, I was getting dropped off. The windshield wipers snapped at the rain as we pulled into Anna Freud's circular drive. I had about four or five days' more work to do in the archives while I *thought* Jackie was going to follow up on Von E. and scour Europe for The Wizard. I waited for him to issue future plans. I didn't want to be the haughty WASP brat who was bossy as well.

He didn't say anything. Instead he drummed his fingers annoyingly on the steering wheel, so finally I said, "Look, I know there are class differences. You don't like my lack of emotion in what you perceive to be a crisis and I don't like your table manners. We still have to work together, and neither of these features are deal-breakers."

"Do you have a warm bone in your body?" he asked in what sounded like genuine puzzlement.

I touched his shoulder and said, "The whole thing is sad. But we have no idea what the truth is. I don't think he's the killer and he obviously had a special feeling for Konzak. But you know there are crimes of passion. You're the one who said that Von Enchanhauer was gay.

"I had assumed that Von E.'s attachment to Konzak was that he wanted to bask in Konzak's exuberant self-confidence. Konzak personified the carefree nature that Von E. had lost with the war. But that may have been too psychologized. I am famous for not seeing the nose on my face. Maybe it is as simple as Von E. was a homosexual in love with Konzak."

"That arm and the solitary really got to me. He's the only man I ever met who did as much solitary as me. I knew exactly where he was at when he said he had to keep telling himself he was actually a *Homo sapiens*," he said, resting his head on the steering wheel.

"You were so great at comforting him, I felt totally at ease leaving the room. Obviously there was some kind of bond I didn't want to interfere with."

He nodded, faced out of the driver's window and mumbled something conciliatory that I didn't hear.

As I opened the car door, I said, "Speaking of saying the truth when traumatized, what is this shit about me being the bad girl locked-in thing?"

"I'm just worried, that's all. I found out from someone I had done some work with a few years ago who now works with Interpol that Konzak has been reported missing. I'm sure by now they have found the body. Pretty soon they're going to figure out that you were the last to see him. You were seen in public at a restaurant—I wasn't. God knows what Gardonne has up his sleeve. It could be worse than what Von Enchanhauer had up his. I'm feeling pressured to get a jump on this thing and I hope you know how important speed is here."

"I'll try to do everything in the archives in a week—but that's pushing it." I opened the door and turned to him, hesitating, waiting for him to tell me where he was going and where we would meet up. I said, "So?" He just looked at me until I said, "I have no idea why you refuse to tell me your, or our, plans. For some reason you set up the tiresome dynamic where I am the nagging wife."

"You sure got tired of it. As I already said, I'm going to do some research on Von Enchanhauer and The Wizard in England and in Europe. You say you need seven days. I'll be back in one week and then I'll have booked us on a flight back to Toronto. Let's not forget, Gardonne may be trying to kill us, but he is still paying our per diem."

I headed up the sodden path overgrown with ferns. All the thick leaves were drooping from the continuous rain and their fronds were almost covering the crumbling brick pathway. I saw the slimy silver line left by a snail as it too had crawled toward the door of the archives. As I closely examined the silver pathways, I realized it must have been a slug because snails leave a broken road while slugs leave a continuous one. I only hope our culprit left the glittering trail of a slug and not of a snail.

I sorted through all of Freud's appointment books from the fifteen years in question. It took hours, and I was so filthy by the end I looked like a coal miner. Five minutes before I was going to give up, I saw a note in an appointment book that indicated "zero"—a small O was drawn. Historians must have assumed that Freud had an empty hour for lunch or for his research. However, the letters to his colleague Ferenczi said that he worked twelve *straight* hours seeing patients for all of that year. I noticed from the rest of his correspondence that he never exaggerated about work. It wasn't fashionable then as it is now to say, "I worked so hard I'm exhausted." Yet here was a spare hour. Then it hit me like a tsunami: Freud's O didn't mean a blank but was a code for a name—a patient—Anna O.

I couldn't believe it. I knew I'd hit pay dirt. I looked at the name below the O, knowing that would have been Freud's next patient. He or she would have seen Anna O. every day as she left Freud's office at one o'clock. I ran my finger down the list of patients looking for the next name — Stein, unfortunately a common name in pre-extermination Vienna. I could look through Freud's financial records and see if I could find a bill for a Stein. I tore through everything until I found the valise for that year, and discovered an invoice to a Herr Chaim Stein of 133 Strasbourg Place, Vienna.

As I was photographing the relevant documents, I heard an uneven clumping on the stairs. Christ, it was Elsa the limping housekeeper. She balanced outside the door and said, "Miss Freud has asked you to join her for toads in a hole."

God, I can see adopting the English language and even high tea — but the cuisine! It doesn't get any worse than toads in a hole. (Not to mention pigs in a blanket.) Opening the door, I said, "Certainly, I'd love to."

Elsa's face registered surprise and anxiety. Obviously Miss Freud having guests was out of the norm, and Elsa was extremely protective of the woman she perceived to be too fragile for company.

Miss Freud smiled as she stood at the table greeting me. "Good afternoon, Miss Fitzgerald. I hope I haven't been presumptuous in intruding on your time?"

"Not at all. I'm hungry and this means I can eat quickly and get back to work." As she dished out the food, I said, "Whenever I have toads in a hole, I am reminded of the stanza by Philip Larkin, who said:

For something sufficiently toad-like
Squats in me, too;
Its hunkers are heavy as hard luck,
And cold as snow . . .

That poem reminds me of a man named Bozo, who told me he
lived in Freud, as his id. Have you ever met him?"

"No, I don't think so. I do remember that Professor Konzak
mentioned him on several occasions, saying that he was paranoid but interesting. He gave quite a good paper on my father
which was well thought-out, but the basic point was paranoid."
I remained quiet to see if she'd go on, pulling the therapeutic
silence trick that Gardonne had used on me. The theory was
that the patient would fill in the silence if it got awkward
enough. It worked. "Paranoia is like any theory, it is only as good
as its inventor. Bozo is an inventive paranoid and his work is brilliant, but nonetheless unbalanced. He's an excellent researcher.
He has uncovered letters and memorabilia on my father in
places where we never thought they existed. He could be quite
useful as a detective but dangerous as a theorist."

"If his theory is based on his extensive research, how is it
paranoid?"

"Van Gogh was a brilliant artist, but it would be a mistake to
think his sunflowers were representative of the real sunflower.
They were, in a visual sense, *more* than the sunflowers, one
could say a paranoid view of the sunflowers because he read too
much into them. Now in this particular case I am at an advantage: I knew the real sunflower, and I can assure you Freud did
not resemble the brilliant, but unreal, portrayal of Bozo's."

"We are quite worried about the Machiavellian kingpins in the
New York Psychoanalytic. We wonder if some of them may have
hired someone who threatened and eventually killed Konzak."

"Really? How American."

I agreed, laughing.

"It's unfortunate that Americans with all their ingenuity have come to rely on Freud's reputation so heavily. After all, psychiatry is a growing science, or should be," Anna said.

"I don't think that psychoanalysis is really a *science* any more than evolutionary theory is a science." I continued after a sip of tea, "Isn't one of the prerequisites of a science that it can be proven and therefore *disproven*? If you try to disprove Freud, you are in *denial*. For example, if I say to my analyst that I don't have sexual fantasies of my father, then I'm told I've repressed them. How do you disprove a theory like that? Psychoanalysis has no 'falsifiability,' as Karl Popper calls it. How do you disprove evolutionary theory? What are you going to say: 'I was there three million years ago, and no, bird plumage isn't getting brighter?' However brilliant psychoanalysis and evolution are, I believe they are still theories and not sciences." Hoping I didn't sound pompous, I added, "That of course is only my opinion."

I had more meals with Anna as the days tumbled on, and we often finished the evening with a late night tea together. We were cut from the same bolt and could finish each other's sentences. I couldn't help imagining how I would have liked to have been Anna Freud's daughter. I wondered if mothers and daughters acted like this in real life, or did they, in fact, argue about who took the last tampon.

One evening as I was leaving her office, putting my teacup on a side table, I noticed a beautiful picture in a standing frame of a teenaged Anna Freud with her father. She looked like a demure, coltish fraülein in a Heidi dress with a smock and pinafore, and her father was looking adoringly at her, the two figures set against the flowering Alps. "This is a beautiful picture of you with your father. Whoever took it caught a moment of perfect happiness on your face, and on your father's. Look, even the faces of the flowers are nodding in the wind."

"Yes, it was my brother Ernst. He enjoyed photography."

"Were you mountain climbing? Your father is wearing a suit."

"Sort of. My father discovered when we were younger we would become bored hiking, so he made it interesting and invited us all to find various kinds of mushrooms. It was a contest to see who could find the biggest, the most yellow, one of each species in his mushroom book. We all became quite proficient at it. In the picture I have found the largest mushroom and I am terribly proud. You see, I'm holding it," she said, pointing to her hand in the snapshot. "As for the attire, my father always wore a suit."

"Oh, that's a mushroom. I thought you were holding a yellow flower." I noticed how young and sensuous Anna Freud looked in the picture. Now she had wrinkled skin, her hair was stripped of its shine and her bones had turned into osteoporotic pieces of meringue. What had happened to the beautiful, robust girl in the picture? It must be a living hell to have a young, nubile brain housed in a decaying frame.

As I was leaving the archives, I caught a glimpse of myself in the hallway mirror and of the pale eyes and colour-robbed hair of the woman who was stalking me, reminding me that I would be the next to shrivel. The tall blonde looks that men had found beguiling were fading, by what felt like time-lapse photography. Soon I too would be an eccentric who lived with her dusty volumes and with the faded memory of these days of working as consultant in a murder case, or, as Jackie termed it, "putting in your time on the Freudian dick beat." I could see myself someday eating tinned tuna, devilled ham and probably even Spam, seeing no one for weeks on end. Actually, the thought didn't frighten me as much as one might think; in fact it was beginning to sound rather appealing.

When I got back to my bed and breakfast, I had an aerogram from Jackie:

Dear annoying Anglophile:
I cannot bear another night in this class-obsessed puddle. Fortunately you've had your five days of heather and the moors. Apparently The Wizard is yet another who doesn't share your enthusiasm for the isle or else he's masquerading as a clerk at Marks & Spencer. God knows his teeth wouldn't give him away.

There appears to be some urgency to get back as the inquests are lining up. We will tie up a whole courthouse going from room to room with Konzak's, Bozo's and probably The Wizard's. (The autopsies must have lined the hallway—think of the refrigerator space!)

Seriously, take what you need if you aren't finished. We fly to Toronto tomorrow at 9:30 a.m. I'll pick you up at 7:00, so wear something low-cut.

A wild and crazy guy in my Hudson Bay jacket—Forget this London Fog shit,
     Deerslayer

21

GLITTER FADES

—

There is an intellectual function in us which demands unity, connection and intelligibility from any material, whether of perception or thought, that comes within its grasp; and if, as a result of special circumstances, it is unable to establish a true connection, it does not hesitate to fabricate a false one.

—FREUD

LET'S FACE IT: Toronto isn't New York or London. However, there is something reassuring about returning to those rows of solid brick homes. When that wolf licks at your door, you know you're as safe as the most obsessive of the Three Little Pigs.

You can slide into its polite conventions the way you slide into your lambswool slippers. Every Canadian has had a pair of those sometime in her life. Long ago they had little labels that said the hide had been made by "genuine Eskimos." (I never saw a lamb in the frozen tundra.) You could remain toasty in them as you padded around the wide-plank pine floors on gloomy Saturday mornings of endless winter in what you thought would be endless youth, before the era of "responsibility" and "personal growth" pressured you into believing in more than comfort.

As we rode downtown in the airport limo, Jackie shattered my contentment by griping, "What I hate about this place is that the squalor is all so new and attitudes are so old. This multiculturalism is a pile of crap. At least in the U.S. people know they're *supposed* to be Americans. On the Fourth of July, Americans don't get into their hokey native costumes. The woman across the hall from me gets done up in one of those Norwegian deals with the colourful aprons and ribbons to take folk dancing. Christ Almighty, I thought she worked for the International House of Pancakes."

As usual, he had a point. However, if I hadn't been too tired to argue, I would have pointed out that a testimonial to the Canadian national character was that someone like Konzak referred to the country as "a Gulag" and the people as "boring." All that meant was that Canadians never batted an eyelash at his theories. You don't have to be from Missouri to say "Show me."

As our limo nosed along in snarled traffic, Jackie said, "Well, while you were luxuriating on the gondolas of the Erie Canal, before you were gallantly rescued, for which you have remained ungrateful to date, I hit the Bozo circus tent and, let me tell you—there isn't enough going for three rings."

The mention of Bozo made me think of his communal home. I wondered if Shawna would hold anything against us. After all, when Jackie and I entered her world, she lost her two best friends and the place got trashed. Christ, I'd be furious if I were her. I got a sinking feeling at the thought of it. Nonetheless, I asked what he'd found out about her.

"Shawna is from a small Ontario town called Paris."

"Even that's delusional," I said.

"Her father worked for the city."

"Doing what?"

"You know, public works."

"What are those?"

"Like fixing potholes and clearing snow."

"Oh, 'public works' sounds philanthropic," I said.

"You're a *really* grounded person, Kate," Jackie said, looking at me as though I were from planet Remulac.

"What's her mother do?"

"She's an agoraphobic." Jackie added, "Hasn't been out of the house in seventeen years."

"Probably hasn't missed much," I said.

"Judging from your wardrobe, you may be fighting the same affliction," he said, glancing at my black cashmere sweater peppered with moth holes from college days.

"You're lucky hoodlum attire has remained so stable over the years," I said.

Jackie ignored me. "Mother weighs over two hundred pounds. When she was first married, she worked at Woolworth's in Notions. Now she has no notion of working at all." As he flipped open his tiny spiral notebook, he continued, "Own their own home, no debts, father likes his beer. She has a brother who, thanks to the father's union seniority, got a job with Public Works."

"How Ed Norton."

"High school graduate. Shawna's known at home as, get this, *Betty*. She never did too well in school, but did win a number of art contests in high school for modelling clay figures. They were mostly abstract but caught someone's eye in a Toronto art school. The winning prize went to her sculpture entitled *Curious George Is a Siamese Twin*." I raised my eyebrows in interest, but Jackie wasn't buying it. "All that means is there is someone in Toronto as flaky as she is and they found each other."

"Actually, there is something about her work I like. You have no idea how many compliments I've had on my donkeys. If they were marketed well, they could sell."

Not wanting to go there, Jackie moved on. "Now Bozo, he's another story altogether." As he thumbed through his copious notes, I noticed he had highlighted some in yellow. Jackie was really a contradiction. He didn't seem like the highlighting type. He'd told me he took a course in speed-reading and comprehension when he got out of jail, because he felt he'd lost so much learning time in solitary. He'd had more thinking time than most people, but less learning time. When he went to college he had to catch up, so whatever he read had to sink in the first time. He even read the newspaper with a highlighter.

"Bozo's father, a physicist at a power plant in Trois-Rivières, Quebec, died when Bozo was twenty years old. His mother is still alive, an alcoholic with a liver the size of a Bronx housing project. She became a boozer while Bozo's father was slowly, very slowly, dying of Huntington's chorea, a neurological disease which eventually paralyzes every muscle in your body."

"Oh yeah," I said, "it's an unusual disease, autosomal dominant."

"Sounds kinky."

"It has a fifty-percent chance of being inherited by the offspring. I think Woody Guthrie and his father had it."

"Bozo showed no signs of it, nor does his brother, who is nine years his senior. The brother seems as right as rain. I visited him and his schoolteacher wife. They're God-fearing hockey parents who put their children in enrichment classes. Bozo's brother said the mother is a hopeless alcoholic and wasn't able to give Bozo the care he needed. The brother said he was lucky to be so much older before the father went under with the illness. Described the father as a guy you could count on. The mother began taking a few nips to get her through dad's illness and by the end it was Bozo who did most of the chronic care. The brother spent the last decade of his father's life away at college doing a doctorate in electrical engineering and only went home for chaotic Christmases."

"So Bozo's most formative years were spent with a paralyzed father whom Bozo tried to communicate with and a drunken mother," I said.

"Apparently the father could hear but not speak. He could only move his eyelids. Bozo worked out a type of Morse code blinking system for the father to express himself. Bozo invented this elaborate language that he believed his father used to communicate with him. Some people have studied this code at MIT and say it's a brilliant system that far exceeds anything developed thus far for communicating with the paralyzed. However, when his father died, Bozo lost interest in pursuing it. Now get this: the brother agreed the code was brilliant, but he doesn't think his father blinked in any more than a random way. He thinks Bozo made up the relationship with his father."

I said, "I think most of us make up our relationships with our fathers."

Jackie nodded and said, "I remember driving to my father's big house when I was nineteen in my Buick Riviera. He'd made it as a real estate developer. I was then a big-time heroin dealer strung out on the stuff myself."

"Why did you go? Had he ever shown any interest in you all those years?"

"None. He left when I was two. He was poor when he left, which only made my mother, sister and me slightly poorer." Jackie hesitated. "I wanted to show him how well I'd done. It's comical when you think about it." He started laughing. "I actually thought that having a big heroin business and a glamorous high-class call-girl lady friend was doing well."

"What did he do?"

"Called the police the second he saw the car in the driveway. When I went to the door, he left the burglar chain on and only opened it a crack, just enough for me to see that he was actually genuinely terrified." Jackie put down his notebook and rubbed his chin where the humour had drained away. "I never saw him again." After a long silence he said, "I don't know what he thought I was going to do to him. I just wanted to show him my car. "

As we swung off the highway and headed downtown, I thought of what Anna Freud had said about my father and how he'd used his rationality as a cover for an inability to feel. The cloying scent of the two pine air fresheners hanging from the rear-view mirror of the limo was making me nauseated, so I rolled down the window as Jackie continued on about Bozo.

"He failed all kinds of courses in high school. I looked through his records and he only attended sporadically and wrote on some grade ten test in history, 'Further extrapolations on a yet more boring theme.' MIT took him because of his off-the-chart College Board scores and his code work, which they considered an exceptional independent study. Many of the professors I spoke to remembered him clearly and thought highly of him, especially in computers. Fifteen years ago, when computers were the size of rooms, he wrote a program which was a mock Freudian psychotherapy session as a joke and it was a runaway hit. They have pictures of students standing in lineups to use it."

"Oh yeah, Konzak mentioned that program when we were at dinner. It's been written up everywhere. I had no idea that Bozo wrote it. Wow." I said.

"Okay, little Miss Freudian Dick wannabe, are you ready for this? In his junior year MIT had to expel him. He became obsessed with the idea that Las Vegas hotels pumped more oxygen in the room at night to keep people awake and gambling. He wanted to expose this *crime*."

"In Mafia-run Las Vegas?"

"Yep," Jackie said.

"Why?"

"Who knows? He would only work on his Las Vegas project and he said no one would pay attention to him and, what's more, those who denied his truth were part of the plot. Apparently the professors weren't denying it. However, they questioned what it had to do with theoretical math at MIT. They ultimately had to expel him because he failed too many courses, and was finally labelled a public nuisance. Oddly enough, two years later the Environmental Protection Agency was checking Las Vegas hotels for asbestos dust from air ducts and that sick-building syndrome and they found that the owners *were* in fact pumping in the equivalent of heavy oxygen so people felt 'up.' Since they were on a high, they kept moving and gambling. When they went home, they had crashing headaches and slept for three days."

I remembered what Anna Freud had said about Bozo being brilliant but paranoid. She had said his theory on Freud was interesting, the facts were fascinating, but they didn't reflect Freud's actual behaviour. Bozo's brother said the same thing about his code; the theory was brilliant, but it didn't reflect the father's behaviour. In the case of the Las Vegas oxygen, it was an idea that seemed paranoid, inappropriate for his discipline as a science student, but turned out to be scientifically verifiable. I thought about what Anna Freud had said about Van Gogh's marvellous painting of the sunflowers. The artist was paranoid, the painting is brilliant, but it is not an accurate representation of sunflowers. I decided to ask, "Was Bozo ever hospitalized?"

"No."

"Medication?"

"No."

"Alcohol?"

"No. Drugs on every other Saturday night only, said he had work to do. No known sexual activity of any kind, heterosexual or homosexual. Ring a bell? Just a joke. Did teach the eyelid language to The Wizard in the event he was ever paralyzed," Jackie said as he flipped his notebook shut.

"Did The Wizard know why Bozo wanted to learn the language—that he had a fifty-percent chance of getting Huntington's chorea?"

"No idea," Jackie said.

"I'm convinced that Betty, alias Shawna, knows where The Wizard is holed up. I think we can get it from her if we trail her long enough," I volunteered.

"It shouldn't be that hard to follow her, given that she never goes out. Hey, maybe she has agoraphobia like her mother," Jackie said.

"She says she is going to the unemployment office, but she never gets further than the porch."

"Great, Dvorah blackmails an exhibitionist and we follow an agoraphobic."

"You know we were under the influence of drugs the night that they got killed," Jackie said.

"No shit, Shylock." I wasn't going to go there. For God's sake, it was humiliating enough just to think how I'd behaved on the dance floor, let alone speak of it.

"Take it easy," he said, regarding the ferocity of my tone. "Did it ever occur to you that The Wizard might have killed Konzak, then Bozo, and then split?"

"No, Jackie, I never thought that a guy who disappears after the crime without a trace could be guilty." Carsick, I leaned my head on the headrest and closed my eyes.

As the limo pulled into my condo and I had one foot out of the car, Jackie reiterated, "I will take care of Edgar and Hari, and you're dealing with Shawna. You and I will meet tomorrow night at your apartment after you've seen Shawna."

I stepped out of the limo and thought for the first time that Lake Ontario actually smelled like fresh air.

That evening as I turned into Bozo's sidewalk, I noticed a sign on the lawn in homemade printing which said,

ROOMS FOR RENT, GREAT VEGGIE HOME, CATS WELCOME

I knocked on the warped screen door. Finally Edgar appeared from what seemed to have been a deep sleep. "Hi, Edgar. It's Kate," I offered in a false cheeriness that made even me wince.

He didn't recognize me for a moment and then said, "Oh, yeah . . . Kate. Didn't you already get what you wanted?"

"I came to talk to Shawna about some earrings."

He turned and yelled in no particular direction, "Shawna, it's Kate, that woman from the publishing company or wherever. She *says* she wants to buy earrings."

"Send her in the kitchen," Shawna squealed.

I passed Bozo's bike still in the hallway. The house was in considerably more disarray than it had been when Bozo and Wizard lived there. Shawna looked a little less bright-eyed. She was surrounded by glitter and was stringing tiny cappuccino-makers on earring wires. "I'm calling these earrings 'Steamed.' Holt Renfrew is willing to try to sell one sample pair."

I actually liked them. "My donkeys from around the world caused quite a kick," I said, pointing to the *equus* idiots hanging from my ears. "They were much coveted in my apartment building, and several women wanted your card or phone number."

"Excellent," Shawna said without much enthusiasm. However, she did perk up enough to add, "I'm thinking of doing a zebra theme as well to promote racial harmony. You know, black and white living on the same body."

Realizing I'd run out of jewellery small talk—and besides, what do you say to someone who thinks zebras represent racial harmony?—I came to the point. "Shawna, I'm sorry about what happened to Bozo. I wanted to come over and say that in person. I also wanted to tell you that Anders Konzak, the director of the Freud academy, was killed." Shawna looked up from gluing on her plastic handles. "I know that you don't know him, but he was killed in the same way as Bozo. We believe that it was the same person who murdered both of them. The reason that I am coming to you today is because we are concerned that The Wizard is in danger."

"Who's *we*—got a mouse in your pocket? My father used to say that."

"The murderer wanted to kill The Wizard too, but something stopped him. We think he was scared away. Can you help us at all?"

"We know our phone is bugged. Once I was talking to my glitter supplier and two men broke in and ordered veal sandwiches from San Francesco's."

"Pretty clever underground operation," I said, wondering if Jackie had hired Abbott and Costello to run this tap.

"Let's talk about when Edgar goes to work at the Aboriginal Dental Clinic and Craft Store. Some guy follows him and even goes into the 7–Eleven if he buys gum," Shawna said.

"Honestly, those guys couldn't find their way out of a paper bag," I said.

"Really, so un-gumshoe," Shawna agreed. After looking out the smudged window for a long time, she said, "I don't know if I should say this or not, but Edgar is mad at you guys and said that as soon as you came on the scene, things started to go bad."

I nodded in agreement since, after all, it was true.

"I told Edgar that it was stupid to think a woman would kill Bozo. I mean, look at TV, or even history. Women don't kill — men do. Besides, I told him that when people come to take you out to dinner, they don't come back and kill you. Jeepers, it's not a fatten-you-up Hansel-and-Gretel thing we have happenin' here. I just don't know what really *is* happening," Shawna said, looking lost and frightened for the first time.

We sat in companionable silence at the table. She looked so tired and pale that my heart, or whatever is left of that shrivelled organ that I picture looking like a sun-dried tomato, went out to her as I said, "Life must be different for you since you lost Bozo and The Wizard?"

"Yeah, I'm lonely, and I sort of don't have any routines any more. Bozo ran a tight ship, you know: shop on Thursday, cleaning on Friday, that kind of thing. I don't like to go out a lot, and they used to, as Bozo said, 'interface with the world' while I kept the home brownie fires burning. Hari, Edgar and I are trying to hold it together."

After shaking my head in sympathy, I ventured, "I was down at the Ontario College of Art and I saw your sculpture *Curious George Is a Siamese Twin*. I really like your stuff."

"I did that many moons ago."

"It showed talent," I said. Oddly enough, I *did* believe her art had the same powerful mixture of irony and innocence as her personality. Shawna shrugged and looked down at her glue-glittered hands.

"Are you willing to help me with the investigation?"

"Are you going to do something about our weekend desserts?" she asked. Clearly, she thought Jackie and I were somehow involved with the police. She probably thought the publisher scam was just another cheap undercover number, like the bumbling idiots who followed Edgar or tapped the phone.

"No, we're only interested in solving this crime and stopping another murder from happening." I seized the moment. "I can be sure nothing happens about the drugs and your unemployment scam, but I need your help."

"I was going to help anyway," Shawna said, looking angry for the first time.

"Is there any way you can get The Wizard to call me?" I asked.

"I haven't seen him since the night of Bozo's murder. I want him to come home. Maybe he disappeared. After all, he *is* a Wizard—it's an occupational hazard." Shawna said this without a shred of irony. What I like about Shawna—and now that I think about it, her art has the same quality—is that she knows I think what she is saying is totally flaky, but she doesn't care, she still gives it her full shot.

I tried another approach. "What do you know about Bozo's relationship to Anders Konzak?"

"Not much. I know he sent him, Android Konzip or whoever, stuff in the mail sometimes. Letters, once in a while little boxes. I saw them on the vestibule table by the front door where he left things to be mailed."

"Did he talk about Konzak?"

"Sometimes at dinner The Wiz and Buzzie would continue a conversation they'd started earlier. I have the feeling that Buzzie Bear was mad at the Konzak guy, 'cause he said things like 'He won't get away with it' and stuff like that. Sometimes they laughed and said, 'He just doesn't get it.' They were, like, giving him hints, and then I think Konzak used something, some kind of idea, from Bozo, because Buzzie had smoke coming out of his ears about it."

"What was it about?"

"I don't know. Buzzie and The Wiz read something in the paper that Android said. Bozo and The Wiz were really hoppin' mad and said he was going to be sorry."

"Have you ever heard of Dr. Von Enchanhauer?" I asked.

"No."

"Do you remember who Bozo or The Wiz wrote to?"

"Tons of people. I used to give the letters to the mailman. I always looked because I like stamps. I was thinking of polyurethaning some and making them into earrings called 'Zip Code.'"

"Shawna, I'm going to make up a list of people and I want you to remember if Bozo or The Wiz wrote to them, okay?"

"No problem-o," she said while gluing.

"Great. Thanks. I'll drop it off as soon as I can." I stood up to leave and said, "Oh, by the way, did The Wizard and Bozo ever fight?"

"Not really. They had big kind of intellectual battles, but they were just discussions, at dinner mostly. You know, like, is Freud really bad? Bozo always said no, it was Android who was bad, and Wizard said it was the Wildinwoods or something."

"The *Wildinwoods*? What was that about?"

"I don't think that was the exact name, sometimes I have trouble with the specifics, but it was something like that. The Wizard used to write to them, the Wildinwoods guys, and to the Darwin foundation."

"Android" was obviously Anders, but who were the "Wildinwoods"? Sounded like a couple or a company. I filed it for later reference and forged ahead. "Even though you liked both The Wiz and Bozo very much, did you think they were a little strange?" Why I should be asking someone who glitters bananas about strange, I had no idea.

"They were strange but nice, and I loved them both." As she spoke, her eyes filled with tears.

"Did they ever seem paranoid to you?"

"Never. They both worked really hard all the time. They didn't want to be part of organizations because they just weren't the type. But hey, at least in my mind, that's no biggy," Shawna said, rubbing her glittered finger across her running nose, leaving some pink glitter on her left nostril.

"Did anyone in the house ever talk about their childhoods?" I asked.

"When Edgar gets drinking he can go on a bit. He's a Cree from Alberta. When he was five years old, the government sent him to residential school seven hundred miles away for eight years."

"That could enrage you."

"Not ideal for family life. He only talks about it when he's been drinking. Then he gets riled up and starts fights with the mailman and the knife sharpener and whoever happens by."

"What's he do?"

"Odd jobs. Well, not really *odd*, just seasonal. In the summer he does landscaping and snow in the winter. Now he's doing carpentry at the Native dental craft centre place."

"What about Hari?"

"He doesn't say much. He lived with some Pakistani relatives, but there was some trouble with the wife or something, so he moved out. Sometimes his relatives from Scarborough call and he yells at them in Indian and then hangs up and then he mutters under his breath in Uruguay or something for a few hours."

"What about Bozo?"

"He never said. He has an older brother who called him and invited him there, but he never went. Once his brother came here, but they didn't seem to know each other very well. I don't think his parents are alive."

"His mother is alive, but her brain is pickled in alcohol."

"That's not too alive."

"What about The Wizard?"

"I don't know much. He never mentioned anyone and I never got into the detective number. He knows a lot about china and porcelain. I imagine he is from some fancy family. You know, you can tell. For some reason I always felt I shouldn't ask him."

"What about you?"

"Oh, you know . . . Well, I guess you don't. Small Ontario town. Dad worked for the city. Mom stayed home. My brother lives on the same street. He married his high school sweetheart. Are you getting the drift?"

"When did you last see them?"

"My brother came down two years ago to see a Maple Leafs game with his wife and kids. They stopped in for a tea. I send presents home for Christmas. It's hard for me to get away, with the unemployment office keeping tabs on me, and my mom has poor circulation and doesn't get out much."

Like every seventeen years, I thought, but said, "Are they happy?"

"Happy? That's kind of heavy. I would have said Wizard, Bozo and I were happy and they were kind of marking time. But guess what?" She put down her tiny jar of paint, looking puzzled more than angry, and said, "They think *I* am weird and *they* are normal. You know, my dad has his house paid for, he goes to the Legion, and my mom has Dunkin' Donuts and her programs. I mean, they don't cry or wail from pain, but 'happy' is not a word that jumps to mind."

The stories matched Jackie's research. It didn't seem that Shawna had anything to hide. Except the whereabouts of The

Wizard. It was also strange that Jackie couldn't get any information on The Wizard. The man didn't seem to have a past.

"Shawna, I'm leaving now and I want you to tell The Wizard, if you see him, that he's in danger and he should call us if he ever gets in touch with you. I believe we could protect and help him."

Shawna continued covering her tiny cappuccino-maker earrings with grey modelling paint as she said, "Happy trails."

22

THE EVOLUTION OF MOTIVE

—

How odd that anyone should not see that all observation must
be for or against some view if it is to be of any service.
— DARWIN

I WALKED HOME from Shawna's. My doorman said, with a
microscopic tinge of disapproval that only Canadians can manage, "There's been a man here to see you."

"Well, who was he?" I asked, not feeling up to his little game.

"He looked Canadian."

The ruddy-faced, salt-and-pepper-haired security guard who
looks like he might have been a stand-in for Captain High Liner
looked blank as I said, "Next time, get the name and not the
nationality. It cuts down on the numbers."

I hadn't been in my apartment for five minutes when I heard
the buzzer. Pressing my intercom, I inquired, "Who is it?"

"Dr. Gardonne."

Christ.

"I just got back to Toronto and I have some . . ." He paused,
sounding genuinely upset. ". . . unfortunate news."

"Come up," I said, giving him a staccato blast with the intercom. What's he doing here violating my personal space? At least in jail no one could drop in.

"It's late," I said as I poked my head out of the door, hoping my face looked as bone-weary as I felt.

"I'm afraid I have some rather upsetting news, Kate." He gazed down at a loose thread on the oriental carpet as he sat on the couch with his hands limply falling between his legs. He ran his hand over the back of his neck and craned it as though it felt cramped. I'd seen him do this before when he was nervous or overworked. I knew he wanted me to ask him what was wrong, but I wasn't going there. He could inch out on his manipulative limb alone.

He leaned forward and said, "I went to Jack Lawton's highrise apartment complex today up in Don Mills and the balcony was surrounded with caution tape. There were police in the lobby and when I asked what was wrong, they said he'd *probably* committed suicide. The ambulance had left shortly before I arrived." He looked beseechingly into my eyes.

I hated Dr. Gardonne at that moment. I made my eyes glass over so he'd only see the reflection of his contrived self. I could tell my feelings were starting to snowball down a steep escarpment. I conjured up stoic images from my childhood. I imagined the black-and-white wooden duck decoy that diligently held my family's dining-room door open for forty years. Fighting back the tears with every fibre of my being, I visualized the stalwart tin soldier who stood at attention as he melted in the fire, moments after the ballerina had finally noticed him.

"Kate . . . Kate?" he persisted.

I had deadened my entire body out to the extremities and had donned a full-mind condom. I'd not allowed the slime of Dr. Gardonne to ooze in for nine years, and I wasn't going to start now when he hoped my defences were down.

"Kate?" he said, raising his voice.

"Yes?" I inquired.

"I realize this must be hard for you. I'm available to talk about it if you wish. That's why I came over at this hour. I wanted you to hear it from me."

"Do you bill OHIP for house calls? Feel free to include the travel time for downward mobility."

"Kate, I believed you deserved to be told in person."

"Well," I said, letting out a pent-up breath, "you told me."

"Don't you want any details?"

"No," I said, edging toward the door.

"I thought perhaps we could work together. I could take three weeks' vacation time and we could devote ourselves to talking about those missing tapes and . . ." He again gave me his trademark empathetic mugging.

"I'll be fine and would prefer to continue alone, thank you. I've almost wrapped it up anyway," I said, silently thanking my father for role-modelling the icicle that I had instantly become. Being able to throw psychical hailstones overhand can come in handy in emergencies when an absence of feeling is *de rigueur*. As I walked over and opened the apartment door, which I assumed was a hint even he would catch, I said, "I'll keep you abreast of any new information that emerges."

As he stood in the hallway, he said, "Kate," and this time his voice had a crisper, harder ring, "I'm not going to mince words. You are no longer my patient. You may maintain whatever demeanour suits you. But please remember, it was exactly this hauteur that turned the jury against you the first time."

The first time. Holy shit. I was so frightened I couldn't hear the rest of what he said. His droning voice whipped around my head like wind trapped in a mountain pass.

"Please remember that there are dead bodies piling up like sandbags for a flood. It was Jackie who could play artful dodger with the police, not you. I'm trying to help Kate Fitzgerald the convict, who was the last to see each victim alive."

"I know who the killer is. When the murderer can't resist the cheese, the spring will pop. Believe me, I'm using a bear trap to kill this mouse. Just one infinitesimal move and he's finished." With that, I closed the door.

I went out on my balcony and let the lake breeze blow on my face. My skin felt like wax. My knees weakened and my legs were shaking as I leaned against the wrought-iron railing. I considered jumping, but then dismissed the idea as ridiculous. I wasn't in *real pain*. It was just a return to duck-decoy numbness. I could live with that. I mean, really, what had I planned to do? Move to a cheap high-rise complex and live with an ex-heroin dealer who used toothpicks and had tattoos? How long would that last? For Christ's sake, I was married to another WASP, like myself, and I *killed* him. Add class differences and Jackie's temper and mine and I might become a mass murderer.

I knew what had happened. I was attracted to him physically, though even that was fairly incomprehensible. He wasn't my type, too big, too beefy, too rough-looking. For the first time in my life I understood why the word *chemistry* so perfectly describes physical attraction. Two elements combine to form a completely new compound. Hydrogen and oxygen combine to make water. What could be more innocuous than a drink of water? Add some heat or some pressure to the same elements and you get a bomb.

I could handle the attraction. After all—it happens. However, when Jackie became emotionally appealing, I cut him off. If he touched my hand while leading me across a street, I would psychologically amputate my arm at the elbow. After Jackie spoke to Dr. Gardonne on the Isle of Wight, I felt I could no longer trust him. He seemed relieved when he got that message.

The drug dance at the Bamboo was what all drug things are—just an aphrodisiac. I didn't want to get into some romantic crap about our whole bodies touching and turning each other inside out, even though it felt that way. I mean, Jesus, there are crack addicts all over the place who buy into that Don Juan soulmate crapola when all they are is high and horny. Pretty simple when you look at it that way.

Then why the hell do I have so many tears rolling down my face that my turtleneck is already wet?

I must have been standing out there for a long time, because the sun had gone from yellow to orange and had burned down into the lake. I leaned my elbows on the railing and looked down as cold Lake Ontario lapped at the breakwall, leaving its usual foamy chemical residue. God, life is short. I couldn't believe I'd missed the opportunity to just let something happen with Jackie. Someday I'll be Anna Freud's age and people will say what a boring life Kate Fitzgerald led. I actually wailed aloud, *"Jesus Christ, you idiot, why can't you seize a moment instead of pondering it into senility?"* A psychological replica of my father—many words, but few deeds.

I held tight to the railing, feeling vertigo. I couldn't bear to look through the wrought-iron slots at the dirty water swirling below. I couldn't afford to let go or I'd have to blow out all the freezer burn of a lifetime, right down to the coal-filled Christmas stocking I got from "Santa." Even my father said my grandmother was mean to have done that. He sure learned at the foot of the master. I felt like Jackie was the first man who really knew me and liked me anyway.

He had to ablate his emotions to prove he could cut it as well. Jackie, alone since nine in an adult jail. The first crime he

committed was running away from his mother, and he did it so
often she had him locked up as a "runaway" and eventually he
became a real criminal. I didn't run away. I bought into the
Kate-be-a-woman-unlike-all-others number and I actually
believed my father's parenting style would make me über-
normal. I was deluded into believing that *normal* and *rational*
were synonymous terms. How fucked-up is that? We were both
prisoners long before we hit jail. No wonder I felt so attached
to him.

I felt the vibration of the railing and realized I had been kicking the hell out of it with my foot. I knew I was getting way too
riled up. I had to yell at myself, *"Just stop!"* I told myself to read
out loud to block out any thoughts, the Shoppers Drug Mart
flyer, the *TV Guide*, anything. Get tired, go to bed and sleep it
off. I was really overreacting to this whole thing. It must have
been more the shock than the attachment.

God, was I a wannabe relationship-weenie or what? Like
those love junkies who read Harlequins or the women in prison
who deluded themselves into thinking their men would visit
them on the weekends that were not designated as conjugal.

I decided to stuff my head with Darwin until I had no space
left for fantasies. If intellectual endeavour had blotted out
prison, it should be able to blow out Jackie. Since a funeral was
out of the question, one of the ways to get through this whole
thing was to solve the case so I could in some way give it to
Jackie—a burnt offering. I could just picture that little smile
that he tried to hide—the one he used when he wanted to look
like a tough guy but was secretly pleased. I really liked that
smile.

While sorting out the documents and thick tomes, I was thankful I'd spent so many years plowing through all sixty volumes of

Darwin. All I really had to know was the Darwin–Freud overlap. That would be early Freud, when he was a biologist, and late Darwin, when he was interested in human emotion and instinct. Otherwise, the research would be like trying to find a needle in a haystack. Whenever Jackie came to mind, I'd cut him out and keep my mind running only in the Darwin groove.

I read away the night and most of the next day without answering my phone. I wasn't even tempted by its incessant, seductive, slant-eyed red wink, flirting to be answered. By the end I'd amassed the following on one of my bristol boards:

1. *Freud was a biologist for the first thirty-five years of his life. He worked on hermaphroditic eels as Darwin did. They both worked on bisexuality at the same time. Darwin, as a young biologist, had worked with the famous biologist named Ernst Brücke. Freud, in turn, had spent several years working in Brücke's famous lab.*

2. *One of Darwin's least popular books was* Descent of Man, *written in 1871. It was about the importance of sex. Darwin was a smart PR executive. He made his name on evolution and then, when he was mainstream, switched to the topic of sex. Victorian England couldn't say he was crazy since they were already prepared to use him as fertilizer in Westminster Abbey after he wrote* The Origin of Species.

   Freud, on the other hand, a slow learner when it came to knowing what the current Zeitgeist could handle, got into biology early and then switched into psychosexual theory before anyone had heard of him. In fact he already had a bad reputation for suggesting that cocaine wasn't addictive. He based this on the fact that he only used it to stay up late and work. God knows what he thought all those cocaine dens were for—a lot of hard work, I guess. Given that gaffe, I guess he thought he'd set it straight by telling the world about their unconscious desires for polymorphous perversity and their first lust for their mother. Believe it or not, he was surprised he didn't immediately garner a loyal following.

3. Darwin in one of his later books, The Expression of Human Emotions, *hypothesized that instinct was the tie between the biological and psychological; i.e., we have a biological instinct that becomes a psychological drive which must be met.*

4. Darwin posits two instincts, aggressive and sexual, Freud the same.

5. Darwin says everything on a body has its use and if you can't figure out what it's for, then the use is vestigial. All anatomical parts have a function, if not now, then in the past. Freud said the same of the mind: all psychological symptoms have a reason; if they are not apparent, then they are unconscious. For example, hysteria has a reason. Hysterical blindness is not random; the patient unconsciously doesn't want to see.

I read the correspondence between Darwin and Wallace throughout the day. It was amazing how cordial these men were to one another considering that they discovered the mechanism for evolution, natural selection, at the same time. Technically Darwin discovered it twenty years earlier but was still compulsively collecting hundreds of notebooks of examples when

Wallace appeared on his doorstep with a finished paper. Without a trace of rancour or jealousy in their correspondence, they agreed to share the discovery in a paper to the Linnean Society and also wrote to one another sharing all of their information. It gave the phrase "English gentleman" new meaning. Of course Darwin ultimately got all the credit. He was the one who was independently wealthy, having come from a rich, already famous family. Then he married his first cousin, the girl next door who happened to be from one of the wealthiest families in England. (As my mother used to say, "That never hurts.") Wallace, on the other hand, was a self-educated working-class man who made most of his discoveries "in the field." Unlike Darwin, he had to continue working to put food on the table. Darwin was able to pursue his scientific interests uninterrupted for the remainder of his life. Wallace remained hardy, travelled and collected specimens for most of his life while Darwin was an invalid, rarely going more than a few miles from home.

After about forty hours, I felt myself fading. My eyes were burning and I was beginning to see little bugs on the page. Dog-tired, I was afraid to go to sleep until I was beyond exhaustion. I didn't want to have any capacity left for thought or reflection. I peeled away my outer layer and flopped on the loveseat in my underwear.

I went through The Wizard's books looking for something light enough to be diverting. I came across *The Collection of Wedgwood China from 1882 to 1992*. As I began reading, I wondered why The Wizard had this book and others like it on the history of ceramics in England. Before falling asleep, I read that Emma Wedgwood was Charles Darwin's wife and the Darwins inherited the Wedgwood family fortune, which was considerable since Wedgwood china was the most famous in England for two centuries. In fact it dominated the world for over a century in worldwide sales of fine china. The Wedgwood family was one of the most influential in England. Not a bad neighbour, Chuck, I thought as I dropped off.

In that chasm between wake and sleep when one is literally falling out of consciousness, I had hypnagogic images of oily plates dropping from my hands. They hit the floor with a crash. I sat bolt upright. Wait a minute! *Wedgwood* was what Shawna was referring to as *Wildinwood* when she recalled the addresses that The Wizard had on his outgoing mail. I made a mental note to see Shawna tomorrow.

23

ARCTIC MELT

—

Among austere men intimacy involves shame
and is something precious.
—NIETZSCHE

WHEN I AM AWAKE, I can ward off my unconscious needs.
However, sleeping is more of a risky business. I had the following dream:

*I trudged along in the frozen tundra, feeling the Arctic air
freezer-burn my lungs. My throat cilia froze and I began to
wheeze. The leather of my briefcase was frozen and the
lock snapped off as I reached for my key. The door was
breathing on its hinges, like in a cartoon, and I loped in.*

*As I peeled off my Arctic gear, I glanced around at
empty junk food bags and cheap wine bottles that rolled
across the floor. I went into the living room, making my
way through the rays that streamed in the window from
the midnight sun showing the airborne dust particles that
were the size of kindergarten snowflakes.*

Some sort of fleshy shackle grabbed my foot. I glowered at the Gumby prostrate on the floor who had locked his bony, dry hands around my ankle. The man was so thin he looked like a survivor of some autoimmune disease. Something was eating his organs faster than his cells could divide and reproduce. His shirt billowed around his spindly neck. Even his hair couldn't keep up; he had lost patches and only little fuzzy down remained on the rest of his tiny, sweet-pea-head. His body was covered with sores that oozed and festered and dried like rust-coloured glue on his filthy shirt.

I lumbered over to the TV with the emaciated man as my ball and chain. As I turned the knobs, I was surprised to see myself on the educational channel. I was even more surprised to see myself reach out of the television with a gun and kill the male Gumby who was shackled to my leg.

As he was hit, his mouth formed a perfect donut and he appeared to be soundlessly screaming as I peered down the lip-lined hole in his face.

The man's body began to fall as though he'd been peeled off the ceiling. I waited for it to land, but it didn't. It was in free fall and I couldn't bear the suspended animation. I covered my ears and closed my eyes.

I half woke with a dry mouth, sweat pouring down under my black lace bra. My underpants were sticking to me. My hair was wet and clinging to my neck like leeches. I felt something crawling on my arm, so I hit it. Someone was shaking me. My hair was in my face. Shit, they killed Konzak, then Bozo, then Jackie, and now they were here for me. In some ways I was relieved. Life as usual had proven to be too much. I must have been confused, trapped like a fly between the storm windows, because when I looked up, I saw—Jackie.

I began shaking my head in an attempt to wake myself up. My heart was going so fast my arms began to tingle, and then they went numb. I couldn't get any moisture in my mouth and my tongue was swollen. I realized the only sound that was coming out was a hoarse whisper that croaked, "I've got to wake up."

"You *are* awake," he said, looking genuinely worried. He sat down next to me on the loveseat and rubbed my back as I lay on my stomach. He said, "Just take it easy and get your bearings. You're just sleep deprived."

"Gardonne was here and told me you were dead," I rasped.

"*Dead?* What an asshole."

"Then, after thinking that you were killed or committed suicide, I had the repeating nightmare, the one I've had for nine years, in which I kill my husband. Only this time it was so real."

"Sleep deprivation turns dreams into nightmares and makes them vivid. If you are sleep deprived enough, you can't tell if the nightmares are real or not. That's when the military start programming brainwashing. First they weaken and confuse your mind through sleep deprivation. I know some guys who were involved in it in prison. The armed forces test-drives this stuff on prisoners before they use it, as they say, 'in the field.'" As he rubbed my back, he must have felt my tremor. He said, "What was the dream? Want to talk about it?"

I mumbled the dream. He nodded, still rubbing my back and massaging my nape. "Is that dream what actually happened in real life?" he asked.

"Essentially, yes. Of course the real story was more complicated."

"Maybe you'd feel better if you dumped the real story out — but only if you want to. I can tell you one thing, it can't be worse than what I've done. I never went to prison for the worst stuff."

"I don't even know where to begin."

Trying to give me a jump-start, Jackie asked, "What was your husband like?"

I had to think for a minute. "A philosopher by training and inclination. However, he eventually switched into medicine, partly to please his parents and partly because there were no jobs in philosophy unless you wanted to be a corner pundit. He was bright—Anders Konzak would have said brilliant."

"Was it ever good?"

"We had all the trappings of being well matched, went to the same brother-sister private schools, cottages on the same lake, had common interests and even shared goals.

"I went off to England to study statistics and philosophy of science, and he went to Germany, learned the language and studied philosophy. After our European stints we came home and got married. He went to medical school and I did a Ph.D. in the philosophy of science in Toronto. We agreed on a life of reading and learning. We both wanted to experience as much of the world as we could."

"Not your typical vows," Jackie said, reaching into his pocket for a cigarette.

"When my husband finished medical school and I was still working on my thesis, he got an offer to go up near the Arctic Circle and be the doctor for Indians, the Dogrib band. It seemed to be a perfect beginning for us."

"You don't have to go to the Arctic to experience Natives. Grow up in the Canadian penal system and you'll be on top of them. When they didn't work out at residential school, the government called them unmanageable and threw them in jail with the rest of us unmanageables," Jackie said.

"We had no idea what culture shock was, or that we would need help. Of course I now see that if indigenous people go crazy when they come south, why wouldn't we go crazy when we went up north. You go past the treeline and there are no boundaries. Sometimes there aren't even shadows, nothing to anchor you. You become unhinged from the world. If you've got emotional boundary problems to begin with, your core is put on ice. We were literally frozen from the inside out.

"Our language failed us—something that we weren't used to. We could go to France and Germany and figure out the rules, but we had no language or translation to deal with the Arctic territoriality or lack of it. The Natives saw boundaries everywhere. The wind, the sun, the consistency of the snow told them all they needed to know, gave them their bearings. It's never the cold that gets the white man, it's the abyss. Looking back on it, we thought *we* knew things."

"You had no idea you had the Arctic street smarts of Mr. Magoo," Jackie said.

"Many of the patients my husband saw were addicts, gas- and glue-sniffing teenagers, alcoholic parents, fetal alcohol syndrome babies, refugees from residential school, or any combination of the above. The Arctic was harder for him than for me. He felt he was expected to cure all these woes since *he* was the doctor."

"Your husband wouldn't have been able to make a dent in that self-destruction."

"Of course he couldn't, and this brought out some sort of primordial guilt. I tried to tell him what was happening wasn't his fault, but he would wail, 'Then whose fault is it?'"

"Sounds like he had a whopper of an ego on pretty shaky stilts."

"I was not in daily contact with the locals, nor did I ever expect to change their lives. I went to the tiny library trailer and worked on my thesis. He began to withdraw. I kept on with my research and figured he'd get better. He would see people for five minutes or an hour, depending on his mood. He spent his time trying to do counselling, and wound up ignoring physical symptoms."

"Did you ever confront him?"

"In the beginning, but he'd just become furious and say I was trying to control his life and make him into the person he'd been before we went north. He said, and he was right, he was no longer that same guy."

"Did he know he was falling apart or did he think he was growing? Sometimes you have to fall apart in order to grow. You have to rip down one system and there is that awful lacuna before the new one is built. I remember it well. I was barely clinging to the wreckage when I made the switch from lifer to college student."

"He vacillated. However, when it came down to it, he refused to help himself."

"Why didn't you get help?"

"He *was* the help."

"Scary."

"He began staying in bed all day and letting the clinic go, sending anything that was an emergency case south by air. The helicopter pilot asked me how long he'd been an alcoholic. I hadn't realized until that moment that he'd become one. We'd stopped talking. Finally the nurse had to ask Indian Affairs to replace him, which was a relief to me. He began crying for long periods of time and would accuse me of hating him. I told him he needed help, but he refused to get it. The nurse left and they advertised for a new doctor, but no one would come, obviously knowing more than we did. Sometimes Natives came to the door in the night asking for medical help and he often just stared at them blankly and slowly closed the door."

"Didn't any of them complain?"

"No, they were used to neglect. Sometimes there would be a

flurry of activity in the night. My husband would get up and frantically write letters. I had no idea what they were about. They were addressed to Indian Affairs, the RCMP, and to his and my family. I began to function on automatic pilot and ignore everything except my work. I figured I'd wait till the summer and leave him there and return home, even if it violated our contracts. My parents wrote asking if *I* was feeling stressed, questioning me in a detailed way. I had no idea why. I never told anyone except the nurse about him. She died of ovarian cancer in Sudbury in the spring of that year. "

"Why didn't you return to Toronto?"

"He wouldn't come home and I didn't feel I could abandon him the way he was. Ignoring all evidence to the contrary, I kept saying things like he was the class valedictorian and would eventually return to his former state of logical grace."

"Did it ever register that you were frozen in the tundra with a madman?"

"Of course, but I was taught not to make a fuss about things. The only thing worse than murder in a WASP Canadian home is complaining," I said.

"How did you get through each day?"

"I wanted to get my thesis done and get out of the marriage. I realized I had never loved him in the way I read about love. I had respect for him and we seemed to want the same things from life. I began to realize that he was having a total breakdown, which I later learned was psychotic depression, but I turned it all off till I could get out. I thought it was my responsibility to stay. I thought quitting was the worst thing a person could do in life."

"I guess you just didn't get out in time."

"One night he came to me and said he was going to kill himself because I didn't love him. This had already happened about once a week, and I was worn down, and I finally said,

'Do whatever you want, and you're right, I don't love you.' He handed me a gun and said, 'I'm going to kill us both if you don't kill me now. I'm begging you to kill me.'

"I looked at his emaciated body covered in scabs, which were the result of constant picking at his own skin until tendons were exposed. His teeth were covered in white muck and he smelled. There was nowhere to take him for help because *he* was the doctor and the nearest hospital was twenty-four hours away by helicopter. He started to run toward me and we began fighting. It was like fighting with a cardboard Halloween skeleton. At one point I'd had enough. I held the gun to his head and shot him. He died instantly."

"Why wasn't it a botched suicide, or self-defence, or a mercy killing?"

"I didn't cry. That was my second mistake. I walked to the clinic and called the airport. Rodney, the helicopter pilot, came and took him away and said to me, 'It's a shame what happened to him.' I said, 'I'm sick of him': that was my third mistake. My fourth was not having slept with Rodney when he had made a pass at me four months earlier, and when I said I preferred a snowshoe to him. He was the star witness."

"Were you framed?"

"No, not exactly. My husband's paranoid delusion was that I had stopped loving him *and* that I was trying to kill him. The former was true and the latter was not. He couldn't see himself as unlovable, so I became the enemy. He couldn't just say, 'Hey, the extinction process that is going on up here can't be stopped by doctors and I can't hack it.'"

"Paranoids need enemies," Jackie offered.

"It was better than weakness. Maybe the whole thing was some kind of chemical imbalance that spiralled into psychotic depression. Who knows? His father had a *Hush . . . Hush, Sweet*

Charlotte–type sister who only got a day pass from the bin on Christmas. She eventually killed herself one Christmas Eve."

"What about witnesses?"

"The nurse in Sudbury was dead. Rodney, the pilot, saw me at my worst and had his own axe to grind."

"Didn't the letters he'd been writing sound insane?"

"The tone didn't sound insane at all. He was an intelligent man who could still sound very logical and persuasive. He believed in what he was saying and he eloquently explained his perceived situation to others. Of course the premise was completely insane. As it turned out, they were deranged pleas for help, sent to various authorities and to our parents, saying that I had been trying to kill him and I had forbidden him to help the Natives or to leave the house or I would shoot him. The majority of the letters were to Indian Affairs in Ottawa. They were found unopened in someone's in-basket. His parents had minimized what he had written but did lodge a complaint with the RCMP in the Northwest Territories. The Mounties said he or I probably had a touch of 'cabin fever' and as soon as the spring broke, everything would most likely settle down."

"Did you know about the letters?" he asked, butting out his cigarette.

"Not about the content."

"Didn't the RCMP or his parents call you?"

"The RCMP has more to worry about in the Northwest Territories than a doctor's marital squabble."

So far I'd told the story in a kind of somnambulic state. I was, however, beginning to wake up. I sat up and grabbed a cigarette from Jackie's pack and lit it, which was strange since I hadn't smoked since I was married. I put my feet on the coffee table and leaned my shoulder against his on the loveseat for support.

"What about your folks?" he asked.

I felt more humiliation relating the part about my parents than I did about the murder. The more the shock of seeing Jackie alive wore off, the more I wondered why I'd begun talking about this whole mess. I tried to wrap it up. "Presumably my parents believed my husband. Anyway, their official version was they didn't want to 'interfere.'"

"You didn't want to complain and they didn't want to interfere. I guess those are good traits for building a frontier, but they suck on an individual basis," Jackie said.

I nodded, rubbing my neck and twisting it from side to side. "I'm sick of talking about this. Anyway, I was brought to trial. The helicopter pilot and William Drybones, an Indian elder who was at the clinic hoping to see a doctor for his pancreatitis, heard me saying 'I'm sick of him.' My fingerprints were on the gun, and he was shot, so said the forensic pathologist, in a way he couldn't have done it himself. My husband had written entreating letters to all concerned about my deranged state and they'd ignored his written pleas. I was convicted. My husband's father was a prominent man who raised a big stink, called in a few favours."

"Yeah, I looked him up in *The Globe*. They referred to him as 'Andrew Stoddart, one of Canada's most revered Supreme Court Justices, who was crushed by the murder of his brilliant son, Dr. John Stoddart.'"

Nodding, I continued, "My parents 'remained neutral,' to use their phrase. All of the agencies had basically screwed up. They didn't want to face the music—someone had to pay the piper. Better *me* than them."

"Didn't your parents offer to help pay for a good lawyer?"

"No. My father, forever judicious, said he wasn't there and had no idea who did what. Obviously my father was terribly embarrassed about his career in the legal reform area."

"Did you try to convince them of your innocence?"

"Once. My father basically said in his well-honed monotone that passes for sensible among his cohorts that my husband had warned him and he was now sorry he'd ignored him. He pointed out he'd given me a private school education and I was now on my own. He said he'd seen me grow up with, and I quote what he said in court, 'a marked degree of obstinacy.'"

"You've never mentioned your mother."

"She only spoke to me once to say, 'Don't you know how hard this is on your father?'"

Jackie blew smoke to the ceiling. He said, "No one expects to be framed, and if by some fluke he is, no one expects their parents to be so . . . neutral."

"I wasn't exactly 'framed.' There was a fraction of a second where I twisted the gun to point it at his head when we were fighting. They say I pulled the trigger. Although it's all a fog, I presume I did. Anyway, the bullet went into his brain and not mine. So I guess that's known as murder."

Jackie said, "That would do it." He thought for a few minutes, shook his head and added, "I guess you were doing what you were told or what people asked you to do. I mean, isn't that what getting a Ph.D. is about?"

"Everyone with a Ph.D. isn't a killer. In fact I don't remember what went through my mind when I killed him. I mean, it sounds as though I can explain the whole thing, but really I am only describing the circumstances which led up to the murder. I could have wrestled him to the ground, or hit him on the head with the butt end of the gun, run away, or told him to go ahead and kill himself. I mean, there were other rational choices. Each second of your life is a decision tree that leads to millions of options. I chose to kill him and I have no idea why. I mean, look at all the women around who are beaten to a pulp every day who have far fewer resources than me. They don't always kill someone when in a tight spot."

"I've seen you in action. Your need for control and your belief that everything is your job is formidable. I have no idea what your ol' man did, but whatever it was sure put you in a straitjacket. I don't know how long someone can stay in that getup before they crack. Most other people would have been taught that it wasn't their job to take responsibility for the ravings of a depressive psychotic. They would have detached, believed they had the right to cry uncle—ask for help or admit the situation was too much. For you that is never an option. For you weakness, or whatever you call it, is a taboo. I'm no shrink, so I have no idea why."

"At least my parents were consistent. Maybe I misportrayed them. They made it clear in the beginning of my life that they had certain expectations. When I was a child, everyone in my family had to bring a newspaper article to dinner every night and discuss it."

"What if you said something your father disagreed with?"

"You could 'debate,' as he called it, but it had to be on logical grounds. I was always head girl and best athlete and a prefect, but at some point I said fuck it, and fuck them. So they said it back to me when they had the chance."

"Funny, my parents said the same thing to me. They just said it earlier, so they saved me jumping through the flaming hoops you had to go through. My father bailed before I could talk, and my mother didn't wait much longer."

Suddenly I felt cold, so I curled my legs underneath me. As I lit one cigarette from another, I began to think of what Darwin said about bonding. Offspring will do whatever is necessary in order to get nurtured. Maybe Jackie and Anna Freud are right. I didn't feel I had the right to ask for help. My father wouldn't have approved.

Who knows? There are people who have far worse parents than mine. Maybe Jackie and I were just two misfits who were now justifying our screwed-up lives.

"It's amazing what people survive. I would have been sick of your husband. I think the problem is you didn't have the right female response after the fact," he said.

I nodded. I was talked out.

"How many people know all this?" he asked, turning his head to look directly at me.

"Gardonne knows the skeleton, but none of the flesh around it."

"Speaking of flesh, you're covered in goosebumps."

"I woke up in a cold sweat and now I'm sitting in clammy underwear at dawn," I said by way of explanation.

"I never pictured you in black lace."

"I got it from Konzak's drawer."

He stood up and crossed the room. I thought he might be leaving and, much to my dismay, I felt panic as though he might be lost or killed. "Where are you going?" I demanded.

"To your room to get you a sweatshirt. You're shaking like a leaf from the cold."

When he came back into the room with that sexy sway-backed walk, he threw me my red hooded sweatshirt. I knew I didn't want the sweatshirt. What I really sought was his body for warmth. I hesitated before pulling it on and looked into his eyes. The look screamed, *I don't want to live another cautious moment. I'm slipping . . . Shit. I'm a detective who's been on my own case too long.*

Jackie read it all in a second, let out a long breath and said, "Kate, it was easy to feel something for me when I was dead. You know, the road not taken and all that. There was no real risk to your feelings." Jackie flopped down in a chair opposite me. He put his head in his hands for a minute and ran his fingers through his curly angel hair. "But I'm alive and I'll be here tomorrow, when the old Kate makes a comeback."

He was talking to me like I didn't know what I was doing. For Christ's sake, I knew I wasn't myself. I was taking a break from myself, but it felt great. My defences were down and I was acting on my feelings. However, it did begin to descend like a dirty fog that he had a point. The last time I did what my feelings told me to do, I killed my husband.

As I pulled my sweatshirt over my bra, and my frontal lobe began to kick into gear, I thought of how I, like Anna Freud, will eventually sit in front of my old-age home on the lock-top brick in a white plastic lawn chair and relive yet another moment of caution.

As I stood to get my jeans, I thought of how much I wished I could drop the safety net of rationality and do the circus act cold turkey—just once. It would hurt for sure, but never having done it hurts more in the long run. Instead of a big pop of the balloon, it's a small leak until it's deflated, dull and misshapen and ultimately gets swept up for the next show. I think I'd rather go out with a bang.

He looked relieved when I put on my sweatshirt. Flaring up, I said, "I know I'm not acting like myself. I'm not completely oblivious, you know. I'm aware that with your death and now untimely resurrection, I have had a trauma. I am also aware that people have personality changes when they are in the throes of a trauma. I just want to say one thing. You have a fantasy that once people have sex, the dynamic of sexual politics ruins all hopes of a rational relationship. Well, I have news for you, Casanova: it's intimacy of any kind that makes that happen. *Emotional* closeness does the same thing." As I yanked on my jeans, I continued, "So wipe that smug look off your face. You *think* you've made it unscathed in this relationship? Once you get close emotionally, the damage is already done. Sex is just a physical instant replay. You think we're still climbing up the ladder, you don't know we're sliding down the other side." I sat down to put on my cowboy boots.

"Maybe for you. Freud made the mistake of universalizing his feelings. I wouldn't suggest following suit." He walked over to the balcony, opened the French doors and stood outside, flicked his cigarette towards the lake and continued, "I think I told you about my father's girlfriend who sucked my dick in the bathtub when I was four. What I didn't tell you is she also held my hand and took me for my first ice cream, snuggled with me in bed and read me my first storybook, all on the same day. You know what? It was all so good I didn't know what part was the sex.

"That night my mother never picked me up and my father still wasn't home, so the woman let me sleep in their bed and snuggle up to her. When my father got back, he found me in his spot and told me to sleep on the couch. I said no way and he literally kicked me out of his bed. I was amazed that he thought she was *his* girlfriend. I adored her and assumed the feeling was mutual. Remember, no one had ever been *nice* to me before. I didn't know what *niceness* was or how to interpret it—where it belonged on the chain of emotional connection. I went to the kitchen drawer, got a butter knife, and threatened my father with it. His girlfriend laughed." He looked out at the morning commuter ferry from the island as it parted the icy waters of Lake Ontario and he repeated, "*She laughed*. My old man got up, called a cab in the middle of the night and sent me back to my mother's. Soon after that I began my next maturational stage, reform school."

He turned, looked at me with eyes that screamed years of solitary confinement and warned, "Don't go there with the closeness and the sex thing. I can beat the sex thing to death looking for the closeness. Believe me, you don't want to be there for that."

"I think you find the closeness thing as scary as I do," I said.

"The window for learning closeness was only open a crack by the time I hit solitary. By the time I got out, it was nailed shut."

"I believe you put yourself in solitary so you wouldn't have to deal with closeness again."

He nodded, paused and then said, "Solitary felt better than anything I ever had that was supposed to be closeness. In solitary the walls never laugh at you."

Suddenly his mood switched from sad to angry and he picked up a cracked flowerpot from the windowsill and threw it over the balcony as though it were a lit bomb. He warned in a voice that sounded as though it was from the belly of a beast, "Don't mess with the sex slash closeness thing." He turned and his eyes had a caged look, the kind that could jump and strangle you when you turned to set down your tray in the prison cafeteria. He threw me my new Blue Jays baseball cap, saying, "You don't know what you're getting into and I really don't want to go there."

He stayed on the balcony with his arms folded in front of him, watching the lake with its scurrying boats trying to dock in fierce winds. Finally, after about a half-hour, he returned and popped his head into the kitchen where I was having a cup of tea and said in his normal gruff voice, "You know, if I was going to commit suicide, I would have done it in the first week of working with you. Why wait months? To top off your other charms, you're grouchy and hungry. You need a meal. I'll wait for you in the lobby."

24

THE NAME GAME

—

Biographical truth is not to be had, and even if it
were it couldn't be used. Truth is unobtainable;
humanity does not deserve it.

—FREUD

JACKIE AND I sat across from each other on our Swiss gingham benches in Mövenpick Restaurant. Looking around at the relentless cheeriness of the decor, I asked, "Christ, who decorated this place, Heidi on amphetamines?"

"This menu is bigger than the blue-print of a bank," he said, hoisting it in the air. "Life was easy when all you could order was the blue plate special."

When I glanced up from my menu, I caught him smiling. I gave him the what-are-you-so-happy-about look, but my scowl didn't seem to dampen his spirits.

"Listen, thanks for caring about me when I was dead."

"Easier than when you are alive." Hoping to get off the topic of my erstwhile horrendous display of sentiment, I said, "What the hell is wrong with that twisted pretzel Gardonne?"

"I don't think he's as dumb as you think he is, Katy."

Katy? What's that about?

"I hope not, or he'd have to have a compass to find his way to work," I said.

"Speaking of work, you'd better check your answering machine."

When I went to a pay phone to call in for my messages, I heard the following in the unmistakable drone of complacency: "Kate, this is Dr. Gardonne. I am terribly sorry that I inadvertently passed on some misinformation, but if you had kept me more informed, it wouldn't have happened. As you may already realize, Jackie is still amongst us. I had gone to his apartment and noticed his balcony was cordoned off by yellow caution tape. The building was surrounded by police cars and when I saw a resident from the building, he said there had been a suicide off a balcony. Kate, I am terribly sorry for any pain this may have caused you, although you were remarkably stoical even for Kate Fitzgerald. I hope—" The tape cut off.

God, too bad I didn't have him on my answering system for ten years. He would only have had one minute to baffle my brain. I went in and got Jackie to listen to the tape. After he hung up I asked, "You don't *believe* him, do you?"

"No," Jackie said slowly, obviously not convinced. "What's he want? The more I know him, the more I'm coming to your view that he is pitting us against each other. He has tried to make me see you as dangerous and paranoid, and then he tried to tell you I'm dead."

"He enjoys mind games for their own sake. I've seen him thrive on them for years."

"I don't buy it. Maybe he does that in therapy. Remember, he's still getting paid for every session he had with you. No one in prison gets better, but this is the real world. He is spending real money for us to work together, yet he is trying to undermine the relationship."

"Money is nothing to him, he has buckets of it. Besides, it's the psychiatric association's money, not his," I reminded him.

"He had to know that eventually I'd find the rumour of my own death exaggerated."

"Of course. What he was doing was using shock treatment. He wanted to create a scorching, traumatic moment when my defences were lowered and he could smoke out my real feelings. That's exactly the technique I used on Dr. Von Enchanhauer when I sprang Konzak's death on him."

"It didn't work."

"Yeah, well, I've had nine years to steel my defences against him. You're new."

"The problem is there *is* a half-truth in what he says," Jackie said.

"What? You're half dead? Tell me something I don't know."

"I mean my balcony *was* cordoned off by caution tape. The railing was loose. When I was throwing a cigarette off, I felt it give, so I told the super and he got out the caution tape and said the welder would be there in less than a week. There was a suicide on the other side of the building. A guy jumped off the sixteenth floor. I was out when it happened. However, there was a note on the elevator about trauma counselling for all those people who saw the skydive."

"There is always a grain of truth in what he says—that's the problem. Gardonne is really good at what he does. He can keep you off-kilter for years. I know I said he wasn't intelligent, but he's wily and a master at manipulating any situation to his advantage. He's made a living at taking advantage of tragic situations since he was a kid. I don't buy for a nanosecond that he thought it was you splattered on the pavement." After thinking for a minute, I realized something else. "He's afraid we found out about the island caper from Dvorah Little. He didn't count on us getting together, since we both have solid reputations as loners. He is narcissistic enough to think if I wasn't interested in him, then I wouldn't be interested in anyone. By the way, I'm not bringing up the sex-slash-closeness thing, I'm just looking at the *situation*, for want of a better term, from Gardonne's point of view."

"You've a unique way of not bringing things up."

"Gardonne already has power over me with the parole. You, however, scare him. He is trying to get dirt on you. He wanted to tell me you were dead, hoping that in my distress my guard would fall and I'd spill my guts. Then he could blackmail you for being involved with a co-worker and, what's worse, a suspect. After all, it's not as though he didn't learn blackmail at his mother's knee."

Jackie leaned back and touched the cigarettes in his chest pocket, obviously longing for one as he said, "You're out of touch. I don't work for the government. He couldn't blackmail me. I don't give a shit who he sings to. Who's going to fire me—God?"

"If he thought he could prove we had a relationship, he could tie you into the murder rap he might be planning to pin on me. Then even God couldn't help you."

"I'm going on record as saying that I believe he's in love with you—couldn't let you go when your prison term was up and kept you involved with him through the investigation. He can't bear the fact that we have some kind of involvement. He sniffed it out in England, you know, on the Isle of Wight."

"Why would you think he was interested in me?" I asked, having no idea why Jackie so misunderstood Gardonne's MO. He was silent for a full minute and looked away. I said, "Hello? Hello? Earth to Jackie!"

Obviously trapped by what he'd said and not wanting to respond, he replied in a low voice, "He would be a fool to see you every week for nine years and engage with your mind and sit across a desk from you and not be in love with you."

I felt a warmth travel up my trunk, but his earlier warning and my own nature made me ignore it. I said as rationally as I could manage, "Love is not his system of barter. Power and a desperate longing to be part of the Mercedes and tooth-implant class is what makes him tick." Fortunately the waitress appeared. "Could I have a bowl of muesli, please?"

"Right away, and those earrings are fabulous," the waitress said as she leaned over to examine my bacon-and-egg ears. "Perfect for the all-day breakfast."

"Thanks, they're concept earrings and were handmade."

"Concept earrings, great idea!" She hoisted the menus and trotted off.

As I sipped my coffee, I focused only on what had to be done and made lists as I talked. "The key to this case lies in three things, which I believe I know. Bozo was right, the whole puzzle is—*The Name Game*. I want to go to Shawna's and see if she can remember the names of any people whom Bozo and The Wizard sent letters to. The three crucial names are Chaim Stein, the Wedgwood family and the late, but not too late, Anna O. I believe that between Bozo and The Wiz they corresponded with all three, and therein lies the solution to the murder of Konzak and Bozo, and possibly The Wizard," I said, dipping into my muesli.

Looking into my bowl, he said, "Who the hell eats pink porridge, Barbie Bear?"

Ignoring him, I continued, "After we eat, I'll go to Shawna's."

"I bet she'll be in."

"Then I have to do a few last-minute scans in the archives in London before we wrap this up, so we'll need tickets to England."

I looked up at him as he sat with that insouciant grin, arms folded, legs splayed in the isle. "What's with you?"

"*She's back*" was all he said as he grabbed the bill and walked out.

As I pulled up at the curb in front of Shawna's house, I noticed that since I'd last been there the *For Rent* sign had the following addendum:

Jerks? I Don't Think So.

Shawna looked like she was aging by time-lapse photography; maybe that's what happens when a face loses its animation. As I looked across the sticky kitchen table at the childish creature opposite me laying out her tarot cards, her hair hung in strings and her Indian dress looked like she'd bought it at the Manhattan transfer. Hari ambled into the kitchen, opened a jar of dried nuts that looked fuzzy with age and somnambulated out. Shawna had lived in a supportive family as a jeweller "at liberty." Now she was no more than an unemployed agoraphobic holed up in a rooming house.

"I can tell how much you miss Bozo and The Wiz," I said. Shawna, never quite on top of the moment, eventually nodded. We sat in a companionable silence for a while.

"Want me to do your cards?" she asked with ashen enthusiasm.

"I'm not into it. By the way, I want to buy some more earrings. Give me more of the Donkeys from Different Lands series. They were a hit in my building. I never get in the elevator that someone doesn't comment on them." Actually, this was true, to my surprise and to Jackie's amazement. "I could sell a dozen for you."

She brightened. "That's the best thing I've heard in a while."

"Life isn't the same without the guys, is it," I said, genuinely feeling for her.

"No." She paused, running her hands through her dishevelled hair. "I have a little trouble getting out and they always did the outside stuff and never bothered me about it. I felt good when I went out with them, if I had a little munch first. We really cared for each other. I never questioned their stuff and they didn't question mine. I felt so lucky. My dad always wanted my mom to be something she wasn't, you know, like the Moose Lodge organizer of the Christmas party. Bozo and Wizzy never wanted me to be anything except what I felt like being. I would do anything for them and they would do the same for me . . . Anyway . . ." Her voice trailed off as she gave a final shuffle to her tarot cards. Shawna continued in the voice of a Victrola that needed rewinding, "Edgar said he wouldn't take my earrings to Holt's, that I should learn to do it myself and all that pull-yourself-up-by-the-bootstraps bilge. You know the 'straight talk' that just makes you feel exhausted before they've even finished." She sighed. "Maybe I do need a kick in the behind. Who knows?"

"Shawna, when I was here last, you said you gave the mailman the letters that your housemates piled up on the front hall table. You mentioned that you might remember who they were sent to if I brought in a list."

"Hit me up."

I handed her a pile of envelopes with one name written on each. I was hoping the names on the envelopes would jar her visual memory. I explained that as she went through the pile and looked at each name, I would say the names aloud, hoping to give her auditory memory a jog as well. God knows she needed some prodding after all the years of imbibing what she referred to as her "little munches."

"Dr. Willard Gardonne?"

"No," she said, shuffling to the next envelope.

"Dvorah Little?"

"Nope."

"Chaim Stein?"

"Yes."

"Shawna, do you remember anything about the address?"

"No."

"Let's push on, then," I said, trying to hide my growing enthusiasm. "Anna O.?"

"Yuppers. Bozo sent those. I don't remember the address, though . . . Wait, I think it was in care of someone, but I forget who."

I was over the moon but tried to act composed as she continued flipping the pile of envelopes.

"Anders Konzak? . . . Yup, lots, and a few packages."

"The Darwin Foundation?"

"Yeah, from The Wiz."

"The Wedgwood family?"

"Yeah, Emma. My mother has a pug named Emma. I remember now—it wasn't Wildinwood, it was Wedgwood. It's the name of the china. You know, like the stuff The Wiz collects."

"He doesn't seem the type to collect Wedgwood. But now I remember, when we had that Indian dinner here, you served dessert on The Wizard's blue Wedgwood plates."

"Yeah, he has more in the kitchen cupboard. He showed me some pieces that matched the originals in one of his books—real collector's items."

"I'll look later. What about the name Brücke?"

"Yeah, but I forget who wrote it. It had like two little mouse turds over the letter *u*."

"Yes, that's right. It's an umlaut. What about Dr. Von Enchanhauer?"

"No." She kept shuffling.

"Anna Freud?"

"No, but Bozo mentioned her to The Wiz. I think he liked her."

"Do you remember what he said?"

"No, but I'll think about it."

"Jackie Lawton?" I asked, giving her another envelope.

"No. Is that the same Jackie that worked with you?" Shawna asked. As I nodded, she continued, "He's hot, don't you think? Not in an in-your-face kind of way, more sort of . . . a Hud with edge."

"I thought Hud already had edge. But I know what you mean."

"Why would Bozo write to him?"

"I don't know. He is a detective and you never know exactly who those guys are working for."

"Tell me about it! They order Swiss Chalet on the tapped phone. Jackie also came here asking if Bozo had ever written to *you*. He probably wants some of those drugs we had at the Bamboo. Jeepers, I can't believe we gave drugs to a detective — maybe even a narc. That was so *El Stupide*. Anyway, when I said no, Jackie asked me not to mention that he had been here inquiring about you, but somehow I feel you're going to be the one who finds Bozo's killer. I want to help you for Bozo's sake. Besides, I don't trust those kinds of men, you know, the kind of guy who watches Monday night football. Even if a guy is as sexy as Jackie, I believe all non-external genitalia should stick together. I don't like to say 'sisterhood' 'cause it's beginning to sound clichéd. The bottom line is, women should tell each other everything. That's why I'm telling you what those detective guys are up to."

Shawna babbled on, not appearing to notice my sinking look, like a pigeon who just landed in the drying epoxy. I had an instant replay of the conversation I overheard Jackie having with

Gardonne on the Isle of Wight and the penny dropped in what had obviously become a rusty brain. I felt a wave of heat and my skin crawled with the goosebumps of humiliation.

Shawna, still oblivious to her impact, went on as though she were discussing the colour of her cappuccino earrings. I interrupted her, saying with far more equanimity than I felt, "Listen, Shawna, I don't want you to tell *anyone*, any detective, psychiatrist, the FBI, the CIA, the local police, Edgar, Hari or the RCMP, what we talked about. *And* get going on those earrings. By the way, remember, I can retail your earrings, and I doubt those guys will become enamoured with glitter bananas."

"Got it," Shawna said, giving me a thumbs-up.

—

PART IV

FATHERS AND DAUGHTERS

—

25

—

LOVE'S LOBOTOMY

—

Illusions commend themselves to us because they save us pain
and allow us to enjoy pleasure instead. We must therefore
accept it without complaint when they sometimes collide with
a bit of reality against which they are dashed to pieces.
— FREUD, *Thoughts on War and Death*

As I BUCKLED my seat belt in the plane for London, I said to
Jackie, "Well, when we next put our feet on the Canadian
Shield, I'll have this all solved."

"Are you planning on sharing any of your insights with me?"
Jackie asked.

I looked at him with only a fraction of the rage I felt, and said,
"You were obviously in solitary confinement the day they taught
teamwork."

"Kate, I don't know what you're talking about." His patient
tone sounded as if it had been stretched to its pathetic little
limit. "You've been a suspect from the beginning, or didn't you
realize that? We *did* discuss it at one point in Konzak's apartment. Maybe you conveniently forgot that conversation or you

were too upset by the murder scene to take in what was said." When I didn't respond, he said, "It happens."

I'd had enough betrayal to last a lifetime. My fury was rumbling and threatening to explode as I hissed into his ear, "You've been following me around trying to get something on me."

"Kate, you're a convicted murderer and you were the only person at the scene of both crimes. Of course you're a suspect."

"Do you think I killed them?" I asked.

"No. Do you have Alzheimer's as well as a bad temper?"

"I forget."

"We discussed this weeks ago. You have no motive for killing either of them."

"That is the *only* reason you think I didn't do it?"

"That's the reason I gave to Gardonne. Kate, there has been a murder here and Konzak is getting mouldy. He had powerful connections and rich parents. There'll be a murder investigation that will eventually focus on you, and I know you couldn't care less, but also on me."

"You know, my roommate in prison used to say, 'You lie down with dogs and you get up with fleas.' Now I know what she meant."

"Jesus. *Kate.*"

"Not even Shawna was as stupid as I was. I had to get the news from her about you nosing around at Bozo's place getting fingerprints or whatever you learned to do in your match-cover detective school course."

Jackie just shook his head and looked straight ahead at the stewardess who stood in the front of the plane accessorized in a yellow gas mask. My mind was sprinting. I felt like my psyche had reached its anaerobic threshold. Finally I just let it rip. "I *now* know why you were in solitary confinement. They don't put you in there for cutting in line. I thought I was above the manipulations of a psychopath. Both Gardonne and I underestimated you. Maybe the brutal truth is we both thought we were above being manipulated by you."

He looked up and I saw that the whites of his eyes were the yellowish colour of bile. I had wounded him. I knew his record was riddled with the word *psychopath* and how painfully that word must have been etched on his mind. I'd caught him by surprise and he was staggering. I knew he would steady himself and come back full force.

He spoke in that slow, deliberate way people do when they're delivering verbal bullets. "Since we're on the topic of manipulation, I'm beginning to understand why your husband framed you. He'd hoped the permafrost would make the black widow dormant. No such luck—she had too hard a shell and she was used to the cold. You made his life unbearable, but why should you get out unscathed? He knew no one would believe how cruel you were."

"Not cruel enough at nine to be labelled incorrigible." Disgusted by my own gullibility, I added, "And I *believed* your version."

"Did your father have your number early or what? The first time he saw the sadism you loosely call feelings, he said this child had better opt for rational thought. He didn't abandon you. He just wised up early," Jackie said, getting a cigarette out of his pack and tapping it on the armrest.

I was stung as I knew I'd stung him. The party had ended. The piñata hung by a frayed string. Sleep deprivation, paranoia and emotional battering had weakened it, but the fatal blow was some kind of inexplicable attraction. But the only goodies that spilled out of the piñata were betrayal, abandonment and the detritus of a life of disappointment. We'd both thrown betrayal at each other like gorillas throw excrement at the viewers at the zoo: take *that* and *that* for invading my privacy.

I looked straight ahead for the rest of the flight. Neither of us read or said a word. I had to admit relieved resignation. I knew Jackie well enough to realize we'd wiped away any shred of possibility of sexual or emotional intimacy. What an awful way to achieve the distance that we both needed. I sensed that beneath Jackie's gaping wounds he was also relieved. How else do the brakes work? They have to burn a little rubber.

We had to circle Heathrow for ages since it was raining cats and dogs. By the time we got our luggage it was after midnight and was still, as the English say, "spitting" by the time we got into London. The city sanitation workers had been on strike for weeks and the rain hit the dirty streets in oily rainbows. The homeless outside Victoria Station used black garbage bags to insulate themselves from the wind and dampness.

The next morning I drove the rental to Von Enchanhauer's Kensington Gardens condominium, with Jackie slumped in the passenger seat. I wasn't telling him what I'd figured out about the case. Until he deigned to talk to me, he would have to remain a passenger. I suspected the plan was to let me work through my little intellectual maze and then at the finish line he would turn me in. They, whoever *they* were, would have their murder all sewn up and then, with one last shake of the dice, I'd be right back in jail and never pass Go again.

We silently mounted Dr. Von Enchanhauer's stairs. The door was opened by Tefonia, the robotic maid. I stepped forward and, using the Avon lady style guide, said, "May I speak to Chaim Stein, please."

Tefonia didn't blink. She opened the door wider and led us to the sunroom, whose windows were wreathed in tangles of silver lace vines. The buds were patiently waiting for the sun to shine so they could sprout their airy clouds of white blossoms.

Tefonia marched in front of us and said in an autistic staccato blast, "Dr. Stein, there are two people seeing you." Both Dr. and Mrs. Von Enchanhauer looked up from their morning *Times* with a horrified jolt.

"To whom are you speaking, Tefonia?" Dr. Von Enchanhauer asked.

But she was gone. Both Jackie and I took seats across from the Steins.

Regaining some composure, the doctor turned to his wife. "Sofia, may I please have a private interview with the detectives."

On her way out she said, "Miss Fitzgerald and Mr. . . . Jackie, I shall have tea sent in."

"Thank you, my dear." He carefully folded his paper, smoothed it and looked at me. "Now, how may I help you?" he inquired.

"Mr. Stein, why did you do it?"

"First of all, I'm Dr. Von Enchanhauer, and I have no idea what you are talking about."

Glancing over at Jackie, I noticed he had that kind of face that lifers get, the kind that betrays no feeling whatsoever, the mask that works inside and out. The cover that even lie detectors can't get under. I could only imagine his discomfort. He *must* be wondering if the pressure was smothering my reason.

"Maybe you can tell us about the Chaim Stein who was Freud's patient. The young man who was racked by guilt and homosexual panic. He would now be exactly your age. Your file has been altered and some pages have been removed. I wonder why? It must have something to do with why Mr. Stein changed his identity and became Dr. Von Enchanhauer."

"Why would I do that?" Dr. Von Enchanhauer asked.

"You tell me. *I'm* Kate Fitzgerald and always have been."

"I've been married to the same woman all of my life and worked as a quiet psychoanalyst," he said while looking over at Jackie, searching his impassive face for support.

"I don't know why you've felt the need to have plastic surgery. That must have been a really macabre experience in those pre–Jane Fonda days. That's what happened to your arm. They took skin and cartilage from your arm to make a longer nose and to build up your chin. It was no accident that you had a so-called appendectomy at the same time that Dr. Rudolph Meyer was performing the only plastic surgery in the world in London at the Royal Vic. Your wife made the arrangements." I stood up, walked toward the door and said, "Wouldn't it be best if we called her in now?"

Dr. Von Enchanhauer held on to his newspaper as though it were some important private document. Then he let his muscles relax and *The Times* slid to the floor. "No, she's been through enough. How did you know?"

"The first hint was your hair. I've a keen eye for deformity. I can spot one at twenty-twenty. I'm from the most critical family in North America. My father was a judge and I learned to make judgments early in life. Your hairline looks like a Ken doll's. There are too many hairs in one follicle. The hair on your chest is golden blond and the hair on your head is dark and curly. It's possible that you dyed your hair, but you couldn't have given yourself *that* hairline."

Dr. Stein sat there looking at his trouser cuffs and picking tiny pieces of invisible lint from his knees. "Perhaps you could enlighten me as to what aspect of plastic surgery is against the law?" he asked.

"Either you've committed a crime or you did something reprehensible during the war. I assume it had to do with the war, since you allowed the surgeon to take a skin graft from your arm instead of your thigh, where skin is usually taken. The concentration camp number was on your right inner forearm, slightly up from your wrist. With that number we could have traced what camp you were in, and from there checked on your war crimes."

He stretched his head forward like a turtle coming out of its shell. His voice had the first note of hostility I'd ever heard from him. "I committed no war crimes. I have lived through hell" — now he was roaring — "and committed no war crimes." He leaned back as though he had become sick of repeating the same thing. I could tell that this was an old accusation by the way he flared up so quickly.

He looked over at Jackie, trying to elicit some help. When he saw that Jackie had checked out, he addressed me. "What happened to me during the war was unspeakable. I was tortured to the point of deformity and had to have my features restored."

"You deformed yourself. Why?"

"How dare you insinuate otherwise or even mention bringing my wife into a situation that has already been extraordinarily painful for her." He leaned forward in his chair and said with glacial formality, "I have thus far been co-operative with your jejune foray into the detective genre, Miss Fitzgerald, but I want to assure you that your impertinence has become repugnant to me."

"You don't have a corner on repugnance, Herr Stein." I got up and walked over to the fireplace and leaned on the mantel, letting him know I didn't have to take his superciliousness sitting down. The person with the facts is the one in charge; I'd learned that in my crib. So I proceeded. "I noticed there was a concentration camp number on the arm of your maid Tefonia. I wrote it down and traced it through the Holocaust Museum in Israel. You two were together, weren't you?"

"No, you are wrong, I'm afraid. You may have whatever fantasies you wish, but I am not prepared to be insulted any further by your paranoia. I know a little about your past as well, Miss Fitzgerald."

"Sorry, I'm not even going to nibble on that one. We learned this one a long time ago in America: the best defence is a good offence. Ask Vince Lombardi."

"You are most unpleasant. I warn you, this has nothing to do with Anders Konzak and it will only bring up pain for everyone concerned."

"Especially you," I pointed out.

"Believe it or not, I'm thinking of my wife and sons, and particularly of Anna Freud. She has had too many defections lately. She too fought the Gestapo. Why bring it all up again?" When I stood impassively, he tried another route. "There is the honour of others at stake here, and I can't betray them. I'm afraid I'll have to call the authorities in on this if you persist." He began to get out of his chair with an air of righteous indignation.

I walked over, leaned on the carved arms of his antique leather Gainsborough chair and looked into the pale eyes of Chaim Stein. "Listen, you lie to me again and I'll let the press in on this. So far I'm not interested. If this has nothing to do with Konzak, then why, when your wife mentioned Bozo, did you shut her up?"

"I felt that he was of no consequence at all. He was just a paranoid who was having delusions of grandeur. He had hoped that he would be chosen as the Freudian director and was outraged when Anders Konzak was appointed. This was a ludicrous fantasy on the part of this Bozo character, since I'd never even met the man."

"You corresponded with him. You think Bozo was hallucinating when he had lunch with you and Konzak at the Holiday Inn last year in Syracuse?"

"No. He wrote to me. Really, I must call the authorities."

Jackie spoke for the first time. "We *are* the authorities."

I added, "Oh wait, there is one more authority we can call on." I walked back toward the fireplace and then slowly turned, faced him and said, "It would be . . . let me see . . . Hendrik."

That was it; the dam broke. Chaim Stein leaned back in his chair and began to weep. He wailed like an abandoned baby. Jackie looked at me as though I should try to stop, or at least comfort, him. He sobbed and leaned over in his chair with his head in his hands. His crying was like a rhythmic spasm of an empty accordion. His wife stood in the doorway looking horrified, while the maid paced up and down in the hall, muttering and rubbing her apron with her palms.

When his grief showed no signs of abating, his wife asked him if he wanted to be alone. He nodded his assent. She drew the sliding parlour doors shut and I heard her gently urging Tefonia to return to her duties.

We sat waiting for him to compose himself. Finally he looked up and Jackie gave him a Kleenex from my backpack. Jackie patted him on the shoulder and Chaim Stein touched his hand. "I'm sorry this has to be so painful," Jackie said, leaving his arm around him.

Stein took a deep breath, looked at me and said in a defeated tone, "What must I tell you?" He put his head in his hands. "Excuse me, I don't feel well." Sweat began pouring down his face and he staggered toward the bathroom as fast as his quivering legs would carry him.

Jackie turned to me when we were alone and whispered, "Who the hell is Hendrik?" Hearing the footsteps of Dr. Von Enchanhauer's return, Jackie added, "Go easy on him. He's already broken. He'll spill his guts anyway, so there is no need to ride roughshod over him."

"Is that what the people said about you after you stole their life's savings?"

"Save the dominatrix number for Dr. Gardonne and the other candy-asses that get off on it."

Ignoring him, I said, "Not to get off the fascinating topic of us, but please make sure that Von E. gets a guard for the night. No phone calls coming in for twenty-four hours."

The doctor returned and was somewhat composed. He flopped down in his chair and said in a quivering voice "Is there any way we could talk about this another day?"

"I'm afraid not," I said, "but I will keep the questioning to a minimum." I inquired in a slightly softer voice, "How did you happen to be held at the Von Enchanhauers' home during the war?"

"I was Sofia's French tutor. She had no trouble with the language, but the literature was very different from German and she was somewhat adrift. We got along very well and felt the same way about most things in life. I believe that she began to love me as the months went by."

"You looked different then. In fact you looked like an Aryan dream. You had blond hair and a high forehead, and you could have passed as a model for a Nazi youth poster. Sofia fell in love with the Aryan youth who had only one tiny problem: he was Jewish."

"Who told you this?" he asked.

"Basically your wife did, the time she said your children looked like you, when I looked at that picture of them on the boat with Anna Freud at their sailing regatta. She lightened up for the first time and a sensual look crossed her face as she pointed out the father–son resemblance. It was the first time I saw how much she had loved you. Of course I was talking about the pre-operated you. That was Chaim Stein she loved, the one that was an extension of herself. You looked like brother and sister." He reluctantly nodded as I went on, "So she agreed to hide you during the war. Sofia's parents were not interested in saving any Jews, so after having it out with them, she hid you in a well or silo, as you described. However, after the first year an informer in the house turned you over to the Gestapo."

"I was taken to a small camp just outside of the Austrian border. I was treated as miserably as everyone else." Von Enchanhauer spoke with a deadly cadence.

"Until Hendrik," I pointed out.

Chaim looked down and his eyes welled with tears. "I have never had a strong sexual appetite, but Hendrik was the only other human that I have passionately loved. He was my first and last love. He was an Estonian who was brought in by the Nazis to run the camp. He was without malice."

"Except he exterminated people," I reminded him.

"These things are impossible to explain. He hated his job, but he didn't want to go to jail for desertion. He was no different from those Americans who napalmed villages in Vietnam. He had signed up because he was either going to starve in Russia or eat in Germany. We had a beautiful friendship. I taught him about literature and music and he taught me about nature and its sacredness." Von Enchanhauer was silent for a moment and serenity had replaced tragedy on his face. For the first time he looked almost handsome. "Eros has its own master. He won't listen to who is on what side in a war. He knows when he has found his mate for life and never questions it. I felt that I was always a homosexual, but he was not, and felt that the only man he had ever loved was me. He was a simple man who said that he was not willing to let happiness run away. He knew we must always be together."

"Did this relationship have a physical side as well?" I asked.

"Yes, of course, when people love each other, there is a physical side to it. Ours began after the first six months or so," he replied.

"How did the other inmates of the camp feel about this 'relationship'?"

"I have no idea. The primary concern in the camp was not how people felt about one another. Staying alive was our only concern."

"Especially yours, Chaim." I took just one step toward his chair and said, "You lie to me one more time and the humiliating ordeal that Konzak dragged you through will feel like a romp in Hyde Park—only this time it will be your hide—stretched and nailed to the front page of *The Washington Post*."

He sat silently for a moment, closed his eyes, took a long breath and said, "They hated me and said I was a capo."

"A what?" Jackie asked.

"They are Jews who helped to run the camps. They often sold information about other Jews to the Nazis for favours. The term means 'one who turns on his own,'" Von Enchanhauer explained.

"How did you feel about that?" I asked.

"After the war, guilty, of course. However, at the time I was relieved. I knew that my agony was now lessened. Every night I was taken to Hendrik's room, where it was warm, clean and disease-free, and I had food. What they didn't understand was I would have left the warmth and the food to be with him. Love makes us all do strange things. The food ran low near the end of the war and we had nothing. Even the guards were hungry. The inmates, weakened by malnutrition, began dying of typhus. Finally everyone was dying, and there was no one around to do even the basic clearing away of the bodies. The soldiers were deserting, and there were only three staff left at the end of the war: one cruel guard, Hendrik and the commandant. There were five inmates including myself when we heard that the Americans were liberating us. We had no food, the staff had no bullets or supplies of any kind. The guard knew he was going to be in trouble because one woman said, 'I'll see you swing on a rope for this, and then when they take you down, I'll shave *your* head.' The other four prisoners were gypsy women. They were hard to kill. They were shrewd and tenacious, and the commandant, realizing the Germans were going to lose the war, wanted to get rid of them in case they were witnesses against him at some war tribunal."

"There's a man with foresight," Jackie said.

"Unfortunately, the commandant had no bullets and had run out of gas. They obviously weren't going to die of typhus even when injected with the virus. There was some anaesthetic left, since they'd performed their surgeries without it. They chloroformed the last four and performed lobotomies on them to render them harmless but keep them alive so they could say that they had done their best for them. They figured the Americans wouldn't know what lobotomies were in 1945."

"Who performed them?" I asked, knowing the answer.

Chaim began fumbling with his Kleenex and wringing it in his hands until it frayed. "The guard did the first one with a rabbit knife after the patient had a whiff of chlorotorm. He made me do the rest because he said I was a doctor. I originally had a Ph.D. in philosophy. Then I went back to university later to earn my M.D. In fact I had only had about eight months of medical school at the time. I was terrified and shook while doing it, and Hendrik had to take over for me." Stein glanced up from under sagging lids at that moment and said, looking at Jackie for some kind of pardon, "One does a lot to stay alive."

"Survival is an instinct," Jackie agreed, placing his meathook paw on top of Von E.'s wizened cabbage-leaf hand.

"When the Americans came, they were shocked, of course. The guard and the commandant conspired, saying that they had tried to save everyone, but Hendrik had withheld food at gunpoint and had only taken care of himself. The Americans put Hendrik in an armoured truck. As he rode away, I saw his eyes from behind the tiny barred window in the khaki vehicle. That was my last image of him." As Von Enchanhauer alias Stein spoke, tears streamed down his face, travelling in the wrinkled rivulets of his sagging jowls. "The Americans came into the barracks and one American said to another, 'Look at this guy sleeping through all the noise under a white blanket.' He yelled in his innocent Midwestern twang, 'Get up, buddy, the war's over. You're going home!' As he touched the blanket to shake him awake, the blanket scattered: it was layers of white maggots. The bones were perfectly cleaned of flesh.

"The Americans were vomiting and I remember one burly American soldier asked me, 'How did you let things get like this?' That line was engraved on my psyche."

"Why that line?" Jackie asked.

"Because it spoke of such arrogance and innocence at the same time. He had no idea what depths humans could sink to and still survive. He thought that somehow we, the Jews, had *let* this happen. He was blaming the victim because he had no idea what it was to be completely powerless. Nothing had ever happened to him. Not even his grandmother had died. How could he know?"

We all sat in silence for a moment and Von E. continued, "I wanted to kill myself, so I went into the barn where the lobotomized walked in a circle like oxen. I took a hot coal and lit some hay. I wanted us all to die, I guess for letting this happen to us. Tefonia, one of the lobotomized living dead, smelled my burning flesh and ran over and put out the fire. The next day I was thankful to her. There is no point in killing oneself the day the war is over. I had simply broken down at the end. I brought Tefonia with me, and she has worked here ever since. She is never a problem because she has no memory, unless it's prompted, and then what she says is by rote. You asked for Chaim Stein—that is a pathway she remembers. But she has no events around it. She knows me as Dr. Von Enchanhauer as well and sees no contradiction."

"Why the plastic surgery?" asked Jackie.

"There were people who were transferred out of our tiny camp early in 1943, and my reputation had spread. People needed to blame someone, anyone, in order to deflect blame from what *they* had done to stay alive. I had never turned anyone in or shared any secrets of any kind, nor had Hendrik asked me. We rarely talked of the war, but only of what we would do when the war was over. We were going to buy a farm near Strasbourg and walk at dawn and feel the breath of the morning upon the mountains." Von E. briefly smiled for the first time and I saw a shadow of the handsome man he must have been. "I returned to Sofia because I was still in hiding, now from my own people, and her father arranged my surgery in London. I had lost all my family, and no one ever recognized me. I had a hair transplant. I had autografts for the correction. At that time, flaps and relatively large free grafts were the methods employed in the English-speaking world."

"Where else were they doing it?" I asked.

"In 1939 a Japanese dermatologist, Shoji Okuda, in a report virtually unknown in the West, described the use of small full-thickness homografts of hair-bearing skin for the correction of alopecia of the scalp, eyebrow and moustache areas. The surgeon even built his own machinery to bore out grafts."

"Was there a big call for hair replacement in Japan in the 1940s? Was Frank Sinatra on tour or what?" I asked.

"Are you forgetting Hiroshima, Miss Fitzgerald? Dr. Okuda was a very busy man." We were silenced. "I then dyed my hair, curled it and changed my face. Tefonia never knew who her parents were after the lobotomy or that they even existed, so she followed me, and each day her life begins anew."

"Why did you choose to look so Semitic?" I asked.

"Miss Fitzgerald, Mr. Lawton, if you had spent your life passing as one thing, wouldn't you begin to dislike the person you were hiding?"

"Probably. But on another level we are all ashamed of the person we are hiding," Jackie offered.

"Well, when I had the chance to have the surgery, I asked to look Jewish so I would never go through this again. Having the outside match the inside was important to me. Had I looked more Jewish, I would have died long ago—which again would have been the outside matching the inside."

"Why did Sofia want to go on with the marriage?"

"She loved me and had waited for me. She thought she was committed in her love for me. We were married at her insistence, before I went to London. She said she had lost me once. We had a nearly chaste relationship, which was fine for both of us. I believe we have made a better than average marital adjustment in that we share mutual respect, which, judging by what I read, is quite rare. Of course, I should have told her everything, but please don't forget it was post-war Vienna and nearly everyone had something to hide."

"What happened after you returned?" I asked.

"She never loved me again, in the romantic sense, after the surgery. Sofia might deny that, but I feel, or believe, it to be true. Nor did I return the same man as the one who was torn away from her and sent to the camps. My heart was now a vestigial organ, and she knew it. When Hendrik left in that khaki-coloured truck, I watched my heart leave my body, never to return. All that was left was an atrophied chamber which I have totally given to Sofia, the boys and to my work. I wish I had more to give them, but I fear I am only blocking out time until my soul can be lifted off the respirator."

"How does Anders Konzak fit into this?" I pressed.

"I don't know exactly. I assume he's connected to my past in some unconscious way. Certainly it was irrational of me to choose him to follow me as the Freud director." Looking down at his hands and shaking his head in bewilderment, he continued, "It was such a betrayal to Freud. I have spent my life trying to help others to understand their sexual and aggressive instincts so they won't be subjected to the sublimation of them as I was in the death camps."

"What sublimation was going on with Hitler?" Jackie asked.

"Hitler mobilized the primitive aggressive instincts of others and re-channelled them as patriotism. Hitler was a—"

I interrupted, "Let's not get bogged down in politics. Go back to the analysis of Chaim Stein."

"I believe that I eventually made a good adjustment to my homosexual orientation, but I was analyzed again by Freud the year I got back from the war in 1945 so I could accept my previously unacceptable instincts. I wanted the world to understand Freud. Yet I did the most to undermine Freud by hiring the likes of Anders Konzak."

"Were you interested in Konzak sexually?" Jackie asked.

"No, not to my knowledge. He was, of course, handsome," Von E. acknowledged.

"Was he like Hendrik?" Jackie asked.

"No, not really. Hendrik looked like the typical Estonian with a sturdy, broad, strong face; he was a quiet outdoorsman. Anders had an amalgam of American brashness that has never known problems and has lived a life in which the melting pot has worked. Anders had no need to understand himself. He had a joy in life and was always willing to share it with others. Life with him was amusing. It had infinite possibility. He shared Freud's enthusiasm for psychoanalysis, which was so infectious that I felt I was rediscovering it. Things that I never noticed before—the gargoyles' expressions, the texture of the wood, the uniqueness of every door and transom—sprang into focus. There is something virginal about someone who has always lived a charmed existence. I realized that I had sacrificed my pleasure in the beauty of others. I surrounded myself with people who were also emotionally deadened, because I felt comfortable with them. When Anders pursued me, I tried to get away from him, but as he persisted I began to thaw a bit. It's hard to make comparisons. 'Is he like Hendrik?' The answer is no, not at all, but something in my unconscious equated the two. I was drawn to him, perhaps at some level hoping that since he had such copious quantities of enthusiasm for life, he could spare some for me."

Jackie asked, "It is my understanding that the majority of Nazis taken prisoner weren't killed after the war. Did you ever see or hear from Hendrik again?"

"No." Dr. Von Enchanhauer looked straight ahead past the two of us. "Sometimes I think I see him on the street and then, when I get closer, it turns out to be someone who often doesn't even resemble Hendrik."

The three of us were silent for what seemed like a long minute. Dr. Von Enchanhauer looked up, meeting my eyes for the first time, and said, "Lest you judge my behaviour, please be cognizant of the likelihood that under similar conditions anyone would do the same thing I did. The electric shock studies of Milgram showed that people in an American test group were willing to give electric shocks to subjects in an experiment simply because a man in a lab coat told them to do it. We are not as free as we would like to imagine."

Dr. Von Enchanhauer paced the room. It seemed as if he was verbalizing *for the first time* what had been haunting his mind daily for forty years. "We all wear a thin veneer of civilization. But Anders, like many others who have not faced the enemy from within or without, had no idea of his nihilistic side and its capabilities. People who are not as fortunate as Anders have been put to the test; that mirror has shown us our true reflection. We haven't sat in safe philosophy classes and discussed the *nature* of evil or bantered about its banality, but we have had evil enter our souls and pierce them with pitchforks."

Tears were streaming down his face. He went on looking down at the floor. "I have a recurring dream about a beautiful blond man who calls and beckons me from a distance. I am wearing a long white lab coat. I am running toward him, but I never get any closer. I trip over the lab coat, which is much too long, and I fall to the ground. As I land, my eye pops out. I stand up and try to replace it in the socket, but it has turned into a cat's eye marble. It is no longer a real eye. I try to look for the blond man, who has turned into Hendrik, with my good eye, but he has disappeared into the Bavarian forest, or else I can no longer see with only one good eye, I'm not sure which. I wake up feeling a terrible sensation of guilt combined with loss.

"I always wake from this dream drenched in perspiration. Strangely enough, I stopped having this dream when I met Anders."

I was beginning to understand his reaction to Konzak's death. He turned what was clearly an exhausted face to gaze out the window. He said, "One thing about living the life I have led is that tragedy has become my currency. I cannot expect anything else if I am to barter in life at all."

"Do you have any idea who may have killed Konzak?" Jackie asked.

"Probably I myself, because of the horse blinkers I chose to wear where he was concerned. I might as well have pulled the trigger. Hiring him to do this sensitive job was like hiring a termite to work in a carpentry shop. He had too much emotional largesse. Of course he had no idea of his impact on others, or for what stakes *they* were playing."

He leaned against his chair, looking pale. Seeing his wife at the door, he dutifully stood up, teetering but still managing to be polite. She said, "I don't want to be rude, but I need to point out that this interrogation has gone on for far too long. My husband has a bad heart and I see how ashen he looks. His breath is rattling. I believe he needs his rest."

Jackie nodded to me and I knew that, even though I was getting crucial details, I'd pushed as far as I dared.

As we neared the car, I reached for the driver's door.

Jackie said, "I'm driving."

"Why?"

"Because I said so."

"Gee, I wish I could have such nimble use of language," I said.

Jackie locked a hand on my shoulder, spinning me away from the door. Glaring at him, I walked around to the passenger side and threw the keys over the top of the car.

As we sped away, Jackie immediately got on the mobile to one of his underlings. "News on Enchanhauer—alias Chaim Stein.

Keep him under guard, full detail, tap the phone and follow him. I don't want him talking to anyone. Top priority."

As we rode along Kensington Road past Queen's Gate, Jackie finally said, "Good work. How'd you do it?"

"What part?" I asked, figuring two of us could play the brusque game.

"Chaim Stein, Hendrik, the whole number."

"I found Freud's book with the case notes. All I really had was the dream with the name Hendrik. Freud must have been saving it for another book on dreams that he proposed but was too sick to finish. The date was during the second analysis of Chaim Stein, and the age was right. Most of the other analysands were women at that time. I knew Chaim was hiding something when it was uncovered that his appendix wasn't missing, so I tapped into the hospital records in plastic surgery under Chaim Stein with the suspicion that his Ken hairstyle was too much. Finally, the white lab coat in the dream symbolized 'the doctor.' Then there were hints like denying Bozo, and I remembered that you said he must be gay because he didn't look at my behind. Finally, who would hire Tefonia as a maid if you didn't have to? I knew she was the personification of some guilt trip. I was going to ask for Chaim Stein, and if she said, 'Who?' I was going to forget it. No one with the bucks and the panache of the Von Enchanhauers would hire such a lobotomized creature. Anyway, that is only half of his story."

"Jesus, he really seemed to love that Hendrik guy. Do you think he's dead now?" Jackie asked.

I shrugged. "The head honchos got theirs at Nuremberg, but the little Colonel Klinks scattered like church mice on Sunday," I said.

"Those studies on authoritarian personality done by men in white coats in psychology labs were interesting. They suggest we would all have done the same thing."

"Yeah," I said, as disgustedly as I felt. "And oddly enough, they found that even the college freshman would behave just like Von Enchanhauer under simulated circumstances. I love social psychology studies. They're like wallpaper to a decorator. They can hide cracks or faults, and you can always find one that fits your needs."

As we approached Knightsbridge, Jackie tossed his head back and said, "You know, I really felt for the guy."

"Remember, you're only hearing *his* version of the story. He has learned over the years to be a chameleon. Von E. knows how to make himself look pathetic, not responsible for anything."

"So you think he's lying?"

"No." I hesitated for a moment. "I think the story is more complicated than that. He has chosen his version of the truth, which makes him the victim. It's rare to find a victim with so much power and money."

"Jesus, I wouldn't want to be on any of your lists," Jackie muttered, getting out his lighter.

"I was so hoping you'd sign my dance card."

"I'll drop you off at Anna Freud's archives to look up your final details—whatever they may be."

"You're the designated driver," I said.

26

EXCISED

—

> . . . Brücke carried more weight with me than
> anyone in my whole life.
> —FREUD, postscript to A *Question of Lay Analysis*

As Jackie pulled onto Anna Freud's circular drive on two wheels, I suggested he check out the Chaim Stein/Von E. transformation by going to the Royal Vic, the Holocaust Museum, the Jewish archives and various Jewish libraries.

He gripped the steering wheel as though it were Krazy Glued to his hands and was the only thing holding him back from pouncing. He hissed between stabbing breaths that made his chest rise and fall like a bellows, "Don't give me orders. I'm not part of your castrated, lobotomized crew, or your adoring public who's into jail chic. I know how to verify information."

"You're so good at hiding your attributes. No wonder you're a detective."

His voice rose as he snarled, "Are you willing to share any of your *theories* with me yet? We're supposedly working together and there is a murderer out there stalking us."

"No, I'm not."

"Why?" he asked, sounding genuinely puzzled.

"The truth, since that is the theme of the day, is that first, if I'm wrong, I don't want to be criticized, and second, I don't trust you. You may use this against me. Maybe you're on the other side. Maybe you're waiting for me to solve this and then, if I get too close to figuring it out, you can bounce me back in the Bastille, or something more expedient and less bouncy."

"Kate, we don't have the time for you to luxuriate in paranoia." He flopped his head onto the steering wheel.

"I know what I've said is extreme, probably too extreme. But I *know* there is more than you're telling me. I'm the one at risk. Let's see . . . who is going to take the heat? A murderer on a Temporary Absence or a detective who has been out for armed robbery for fifteen years? It wouldn't be the first time a woman got screwed."

"You're letting some emotional shit between us that never went anywhere interfere with our work."

"Well, I'm sorry if I am behaving unprofessionally. I guess I'm just the bad seed, the girl even a father couldn't love." Mimicking Jackie's deadpan voice, I said, "The aging, skinny ex-con who . . ." Before finishing that remark, I opened the car door and began getting out of the passenger seat.

He leapt across the seat, grabbed my arm with incredible strength and pulled me back into the car. I cracked my head on the corner of the door just above my left eyeball socket and it began to bleed. I saw little red squiggly lines in front of my eyes that resembled amoebas under a microscope. Then kaleidoscope colours sprinkled over the dashboard, which looked as though it were breathing. I could hardly hear what he was saying. I pulled my arm away and staggered out of the car. I'd heard enough "truth" for one day.

A long minute after the doorbell rang, the housekeeper, Elsa, greeted me with her usual taciturn eloquence. "Don't bleed on the rug."

"It's not like anyone would notice." Why the hell was I bothering to defend myself to a character out of a Mel Brooks movie? As I trudged upstairs, I tried to unravel when things started to go off the rails in my relationship with Jackie. My mind felt like a spastic colon, so I gave up on it, deciding to sort out this Konzak thing first. After all, I had the rest of my life to deal with my trail of relationship destruction. Christ, it was already dark outside, I had a headache and I had hours of work ahead of me.

I'd solved the first part of the puzzle and now I was working on the second, the Darwin connection. The only link between Darwin and Freud was Professor Ernst Brücke.

Brücke had an extraordinarily long career, over sixty-five years as a professor of physiology in the University of Vienna. Charles Darwin worked on hermaphroditic eels with Brücke when both were young men and Brücke was a docent studying in England. Darwin, in turn, visited Brücke's lab in Vienna. They were professional contemporaries, both interested in hermaphroditic physiology. Needless to say, hermaphroditic eel physiology was not a burgeoning field and the two men respected one another, exchanging correspondence for over thirty years.

When I went through Freud's university transcripts, I found that he had taken a course entitled Biology and Darwinism in 1873 during his first year of medicine. Obviously Freud never forgot what he learned in the course, or its teacher, because in his medical studies and in his post-doctorate training the professor who appeared most often was Ernst Brücke. By this time Brücke and Darwin were old men, while Freud was a young post-doc. There were copies of several papers on the physiology of eels that Brücke and Freud gave together, in the late 1870s. Brücke, probably the first to recognize Freud's genius, tried hard, to no avail, to get him a professorship at the university.

Clearly Brücke was the historical link between Darwin and Freud, and I had to find the Freud–Brücke correspondence. Finally, after two hours of searching, there it was, in an accordion file tied with a white ribbon. I couldn't tell if the correspondence was complete or if it had been tampered with. All the other correspondences had gaps with the note *Personal information* or *Extracted—of no relevance*. This was the only correspondence with no such note. I'd be willing to bet that some of the crucial letters were missing, however. As I read and translated the letters around the dates that were relevant, one line jumped out at me.

March 22, 1880

Dear Professor Brücke:

I, too, am sorry that the anti-Semitism of the time has prevented further University appointments. I know that you did your best to secure a professor's position for me and even agreed to share your already cramped lab space.

By way of a professional farewell, hopefully not a personal one, these have been the happiest years of my life and I have never admired a man more than I admire you. Your gift has more than compensated for the lack of a university appointment. I shall always use it wisely. I would be honoured, with your kind permission, to name my first male child Ernst, after you.

Sincerely,
Sigmund Freud

What was the gift? Konzak and all those who had gone before him assumed it was money; Freud was known for borrowing money in hard times. But why would Freud say "always," referring to money? Money would not be there *always*.

It was in Brücke's lab that Freud switched from being a physiologist to being a psychologist. What happened? What was the gift? I paced up and down the room wondering what is something you will always use wisely that is not money? Something you appreciate so much you name your first son after the donor?

Jews almost always named children after deceased relatives. Very rarely would you name a child after someone still alive, a non-Jew or a non-relative, particularly in Europe in the 1880s. Freud was not a religious man, but he was a Jew and made strong efforts to follow Jewish customs.

A while back I'd asked Jackie to do some research, which was complicated and even I would have had trouble. While dialing his number, I decided that this case was heating up too much to even consider one more loathsome personal detail about Jackie. If he was framing me, I'd find out soon enough. I had to shelve my fears. Who knows, maybe it *was* paranoia. Now that the case was cooking and I needed more hands to stir the pot, if we didn't work as a team, some lids would blow off. He answered on the first ring.

"Jackie, I need that info. Meet me in the dining room at the Savoy in two hours. I can't talk here. This is urgent." As I hung up, I felt the presence of someone behind me. I wheeled around to find Anna Freud standing in the doorway wearing an ancient Irish tweed suit reeking of mothballs, thick spun-cotton stockings and Wallabees.

"Elsa said your head was bleeding."

As I reached my hand up to my forehead, I felt something crusty. I was surprised when I saw blood smeared on my fingers. "Oh, I guess I've been thinking too much, blew a gasket!

Actually, I hit my head on the car door. I didn't realize it was such a gash. I guess my baseball cap acted as a tourniquet."

"I believe it needs cleaning. It may even need stitches. Although not a medical doctor, I have run an orphanage during wartime and I have bandaged more children's skulls than I care to remember."

Anna took me downstairs, holding my hand as though I were a little girl who had fallen off her swing set, and led me into the kitchen, where she dabbed the cut with a damp towel. "Elsa said you had an altercation outside with Mr. Lawton."

I nodded, realizing how tawdry fisticuffs in the front yard sounded. However, I didn't feel I could say "Oh, it's not like that," because no one thinks they're tawdry until they are.

As she ministered tenderly to my split skull, she said in a barely audible voice, "Beware of chameleons bearing investigations."

"At least in a war you know your enemies. You can really get bushwhacked in relationships," I said.

"Life is not always easy, is it?"

"I'm waiting for it to lighten up." I winced as Anna dabbed antiseptic on a wound that was obviously deeper than I thought.

"I have always found relationships to be like a cyclotron: ingredients go in at a reasonable rate, but they speed up and get out of control. That's why I like analysis so much. It gives one the time to slow down the whirling and sort out each feeling and follow it to its source."

"You're right, there's never time to get off. Centrifugal force just keeps you clinging. You can't figure it out because you're too busy just holding on."

"Actually, it slows down when you get older. The motor needs oil. But the sad irony is that when you finally start to understand, you've made most of your mistakes. You can't be eighteen again and do it over."

"Yeah, but you know what you *would* have done."

"Exactly."

"That's a nightmare," I muttered.

She smiled slightly as she snipped the gauze and said, "That's called wisdom."

"That's called too little too late," I said, looking at my humpty-dumpty skull in the blush-on mirror I'd pulled from my backpack.

"Who doesn't have regrets?" asked Anna as she dabbed. "Kate, I see so much of me in you. I, like you, once thought people who lived ordinary lives weren't really contemplating their existence or making the most of their lives. Now that I am older I see that they, the garden-variety *Homo sapiens*, who I once believed to be pedestrian herd members, are as introspective as anyone else. The difference is they saw what they wanted, went straight for it, thus making their choices early. They didn't suffer the ambivalence we—I hope you don't think it is presumptuous for me to say *we*— have suffered. Ambivalence comes from too many choices, from the feelings of omnipotence, of being exposed to too much too early. Delusions of grandeur make us feel we need to rise above others. We deny a lot of ourselves to do it. We are not above human instinct. Ideologies evolve and become extinct at a far greater rate than human instinct. Natural selection does not care about ideology, but only about survival and reproduction."

Elsa poked her head in the door and muttered that tea was ready. As we sipped our consoling cups, we discussed Freud's theory of penis envy and its manifestations in the nineteenth and twentieth centuries. Getting up to leave, I held Anna's hand momentarily, thanking her for the nursing care, and she promised to minister to my cracked cranium again in the morning.

When I walked into the Savoy dining room, Jackie said, "Where'd you get that shiner? Met a Jungian in a dark alley?"

Ignoring what was clearly not an apology, I forged on with the details I needed. "So?" I pressed.

"So we hit pay dirt. The Wedgwood Foundation did have a request for the letters from Josiah Wedgwood III to Charles Darwin in the year in question. The request was documented just three months ago. The man who asked to see the letters signed the register as Jemmy Button."

I laughed out loud. "Obviously a pseudonym, because the real Jemmy was a black Native whom Captain Fitzroy brought back to England on one of his many voyages. He was from Tierra del Fuego and never was accepted by the English as anything but a savage. Eventually Jemmy was returned aboard the *Beagle* on Darwin's famous voyage back to his native land, where they laughed at his civilized ways."

"Interesting," Jackie said, writing *marginalized man* in his little notebook.

"So we're looking for an uncivilized Darwinian with a sense of humour," I said.

"Waste your grey matter no longer. The Foundation librarian remembered that he had 'dubious oral hygiene.' In fact, she said that his general hygiene left something to be desired. He admired some of the porcelain samples in the cases and bought a creamer from the outlet store. She remembers this being odd because his shoes had duct tape holding them together, yet he was extremely knowledgeable about collectors' items of Wedgwood china. She also remembered that he had an American accent."

"Wow. It doesn't take a magician to know it was The Wizard," I said, unable to hide my glee at this discovery.

"Unless there is another fire-eating magician with bad teeth and lighter-fluid breath who is interested in Darwin and Wedgwood china," Jackie deadpanned.

"Or," I said, becoming more expansive, "who knows? Maybe interest in Wedgwood china and Darwinian theory and a compulsive need to wrap duct tape on one's shoes are all correlated on a recessive gene." Jackie almost smiled, so I continued. "Well it would be interesting if The Wizard had identical twins—one raised by The Wizard and one raised apart, adopted by a normal Midwestern Shriner. I'd wager you'd eventually find both twins on the same day at the Darwin archives drinking tea out of Wedgwood china and discussing how hard it is to find good duct tape for running shoes these days."

Jackie shook his head as though I was insane, but I could tell we were back on collegial footing. Leaning across the table, he said, "Listen carefully—here comes the kicker. I asked the librarian if I could see the letter The Wiz had copied, and she was shocked to discover it had been carefully extracted with an exacto knife from its leather binding. There's a record of each time they're brought out of storage, and the librarian is required to stay with the person who requests the material for the entire viewing time. That's how she remembered The Wizard so well; she watched him while he read. No one has signed out that volume since The Wizard. She is sure that page was there when The Wizard left, because she watched him like a hawk."

"Was she afraid he might disappear?"

"She was sure the thief must have looked at something else and then surreptitiously gone into the storage area and ripped out the letter in question."

"Did you copy the letter before it and after it?"

"Sure did, Katydid," he said, producing the photocopied sheets.

Scanning the letters, I could see that one was about the raising of roses and how to water them. "Listen to this English pedantry," I said, reading aloud. "'My Dear Charles: I am sorry to hear that your health is so poor. It is best to sit in the sun for at least one hour a day. In terms of roses, I recommend several fertilizers . . .' It goes on for two pages about fertilizers. Who says the English talk about the weather when they can talk about fertilizers?

"I want that *letter*. Christ," I said, pounding my fist on the Savoy's burled mahogany carved table. Between sips of Newcastle, I said, "Where did The Wizard hide his copy of that letter, and who stole the original one from the leather binding in the library?"

We ate silently and Jackie read the history of the Beefeater on the menu until I had a Eureka-style moment. "Jackie Jack fruit, you know what?"

"Not exactly."

I thought I had it but didn't want to say so quite yet, so I asked with my preternatural caution, "Do two things on a long shot. One, take pictures of all the suspects to the clerk at the Wedgwood Foundation and see if they recognize anyone as having been there in the last few months. Two, I want someone to go to Shawna's house to find that Wedgwood creamer The Wizard bought and look inside it for a folded document. If it's not there, then see if it's in any other piece of Wedgwood china in that house . . . Still no word on The Wizard's whereabouts?"

"Nothing. He seems to have no past. He changed his name, but the name he changed *from* was a pseudonym," Jackie offered.

"If they find it, get it to my room. Oh, by the way, be sure to show pictures of Elsa, Teutonic torturer from the Freud Mausoleum, and Tefonia, the bright light of the Stein house of mirrors. Their interest in china can't be coincidental. Remember, there are no accidents in Vienna."

"What do you think the letter says?" Jackie asked.

"I *know* what the letter says, but I want the evidence. See if you can get me an article summarizing Darwin's chronic illnesses, or send me an abstract. I feel I'm running out of time."

"Why?"

"I feel the murderer is going to strike again. I don't know why, but I feel I'm being stalked."

"I feel it too, the death rattle. We're closing in and he knows it." Jackie added, "Oh, by the way, you'd better tell me all you know about this case, because you're the one who probably knows who committed the murder."

I pushed back my chair to leave.

"Kate, your bullheadedness, or whatever it is that's going on in your fucked-up, overworked brain, has not made you the sharpest tool in the shed of late. I'm going to try and rub your nose in the big picture, which you are refusing to see. I have no desire to call you crazy or paranoid or whatever it is that you've been labelled. I have, however, noted the supreme irony of your telling me that teamwork is not *my* forte." His voice rose with each line of his soliloquy, and I could see him telling himself to calm down as he was starting to gather stares from the Savoy Grill glitterati who I'm sure already found him, as they would say in England, NOCD (Not our class, dear). "First of all, two men are dead and now *you* know what they knew. Secondly, the killer doesn't know that you're keeping secrets; he thinks Gardonne and I know what you know. Finally, and most importantly from my point of view, one bomb to the car or to the Savoy and we're *all* fucking history."

In desperate need of a nap, I felt a whirring in my head as I slid out of my chair and left the dining room without looking back.

27

TWO SLIPPERY EELS

—

And pleased on Wedgwood ray you partial smile
A new Etruria decks Britannia's isle,
Charmed by your touch, the kneaded clay refines,
The biscuit hardens, the enamel shines
The bold Cameo speaks, the soft Intaglio thinks.
—ERASMUS DARWIN, "The Economy of Vegetation"

I'D HAD A SHOWER and was taking a nap when I was awakened by Jackie, standing next to my bed. "I've been knocking for ten minutes."

"So I'm not the Princess and the Pea. It's the middle of the night. What do you want?"

"The telegrams have come through. They did some good work quickly."

I was wearing black underpants and a tank top. He tossed me my jeans as I stumbled out of bed and ran my fingers through my hair. As I pulled on my cowboy boots and reached for my Donkeys From Different Lands earrings with Mohawk haircuts and safety pins through their tiny brown noses, I said, "So lay it on me, brother."

"Be in the grill in ten minutes for a late dinner. It's open all night. Once you're paying these prices, you can bloody well wear what you want—so just hurry.

I stumbled into the grill with a sleep crease on my left cheek, wearing my moth-eaten black uniform.

When I flopped into my chair, instead of saying hello, Jackie said, "You were right, Einstein, on two out of three counts. First of all, no one from the Wedgwood Foundation recognized any of the suspects, and we ran the Von Enchanhauers through as is and in costume. Nothing."

"I take it that wasn't the Einstein part. Next . . ."

"Bingo!" He leaned toward me and whispered, "Next . . . the letters from Brücke are available and his great-granddaughter is in a cloistered convent in Arlington, Virginia. Yes, she did receive her great-grandfather's collection of letters and some were indeed from Freud to her grandfather, and yes, she does remember one that talked about a gift. And yes, it was around March of 1880. In fact, it was on January 31, 1880. She didn't photocopy them because she didn't feel that was ethical. After all, why would someone pay so much for the originals? She sold them to a man whose teeth had seen better days for —are you ready for this deal?—for 800,000 big ones. The Wizard paid with a Viennese international money order—"

"Where did The Wizard get that kind of money?" I interrupted.

"Obviously not from professional wizardry," Jackie said. "Four months ago he opened a bank account in Montreal and deposited a cheque from Steinway Imports—this is a holding company for the acquisitions wing of the Freud estate. The cheque was initialled by Dr. Von Enchanhauer, alias Chaim Stein."

We looked at each other, said "All right!" and hit each other's palm the way ghetto youth do when they seal a drug deal. "Wait, there's more magic on The Wizard," Jackie said.

"A-mazing," I said.

A waiter scurried over to quiet us down by taking our order. Glancing down at the menu of hackneyed literary allusions, I said, "I'll have the David Copperfield Arrives at Yarmouth and a Coke."

"Make that a double Yarmouth."

When the waiter asked Jackie how he wanted his potatoes, he said, "Surprise me." Getting the hint, the waiter left.

Jackie looked around, then leaned over the table and, speaking softly, said, "I sent a man over to the Bozo-hyphen-Wizard household and oddly enough Shawna was home. She found the Wedgwood creamer, which was next to a bizarre Russian samovar, and guess what was rolled up like a Dead Sea scroll. Ta-dah!" he said, unrolling a photocopy of the missing letter from Josiah Wedgwood to his son-in-law Charles Darwin, written on heavy crested Wedgwood stationery. "I don't know what the hell this means," he said, handing it to me.

31 January, 1880

My dearest Charles:
I have been handed two extremely unpleasant tasks that are listed in order of their repugnance: The first is the hasty preparation I must make in order to avail myself of what my dear wife and your esteemed sister, Caroline, refers to as, "Christ's revelation of eternal Life." The second and most painful, Charles, is the censure that I must deliver as executor of the Wedgwood estate. I give you my utmost assurance that this admonishment is in no way related to my feelings for you as a brother-in-law, a

school chum and first rate grouser. However, a lifelong
friendship doth not an executor make. So here dear fellow,
I must don the mantle of family responsibility. I wear the
yoke that attempts to balance the Darwins' and the
Wedgwoods' financial needs. Please be cognizant that I
am not addressing our families' personal needs but those
of future generations. With that inadequate preamble,
allow me to quickly expel my fiscal responsibilities as this
yoke is exceedingly onerous even for, as our Oxford
educated cousins are fond of saying, "the likes of a
Cambridge man."

It has been brought to my attention that you plan to
publish some vagaries about the polymorphous sexuality of
creatures. The family lore is (and I am sure, dear relative,
it is only said by a prattler or a flibbertigibbet) that you
planned to publish on these topics in regard to the Homo
sapiens. Our family has weathered the storm of Evolution,
and your affiliation with my sister-in-law, Emma
Wedgwood, is most fortunate in the domestic arena, but
while I regret having to bring up indelicacies to a relative
by marriage, and a neighbour by proximity and, most
importantly, a friend by inclination, it has for a certain
epoch, been injurious to the sale of our pottery.

Now that we have all weathered the ecclesiastical storm
raised by your evolutionary theory and with a burial plot
assured in Westminster Abbey, I would find it irresponsible
if you were to publish these odious ideas of wanton
Zoonomia. We have been obliged to bear your grandfather's puerile poetry and his two illegitimate children; we
were willing to call that the excess of another century. One
of the most illustrious traits of your forefather, Erasmus,
was his industrious nature and, despite his portliness, his

strong constitution and his unwavering ability to acquire pecuniary means. He was manifestly wanton in certain regards, but he was able to provide for his voracious appetites. However, when one is less stalwart in constitution, one must defer to those who assist in supplying the daily exigencies for those who pursue higher learning in the field of naturalism.

I mean this to be far less censorious than it might read. We need to protect the Wedgwood wares for the future Darwins and Wedgwoods. Perhaps it has been too many generations of our families commingling with first cousins, but with each, we have a weakening of personal energy. When I reflect upon what our grandfathers Josiah the first and Erasmus Darwin accomplished, I feel enervated at the thought. You, my dear Charles, have the genius of your grandfather Erasmus Darwin, but not his energy or the tenacity to procure a fortune for generations to come. With my grandfather, Josiah the first, gone, no living Wedgwood has the genius, the energy, the tenacity, the originality or the inclination to make a living for themselves to say nothing of future generations. It is my unpleasant duty to inform you that it is the Wedgwood reputation that will keep our future progeny afloat on the great Trent and Severn Canal. I realize that you are no "poor preacher," nor am I presently impecunious, but our families' futures are both, my good Charles, dependent upon the good name of Wedgwood.

There has, fortunately, been a turning of the tide and you are at the present moment revered for your efforts. The sales of our pottery have risen correspondingly, and again burgeoned to their previous levels. Charles, I implore you to remember that porcelain is only the

*linguistic countenance placed on the clay of the earth. It
is only worth its name and the reputation of its maker,
no matter how skilful the potter's or the artisan's hand.
I therefore must protest your inauspicious and untimely
drawing of the Wedgwood family through the mire along
with prurient theories that are, if I may take the liberty
of saying so, the contrivances of an idle mind. It is no
wonder you suffer from dropsy if these theories are
entertained in even a minute part of your waking life.*

*Thank you for attending to a man who has only the
interests of the family name at heart, and the Wedgwood
Foundation for centuries to come.*

You remain my revered brother-in-law,
With kindest regards,
Josiah Wedgwood III

I carefully folded the letter and looked up.

"So what's the bottom line?" Jackie asked.

"Chuck, I like you as a person—I mean, we grew up together.
But you publish this kiddie porn and you are screwing with the
family fortune. We may be flush now, but who is going to set up
the children's trust funds? No one in either family has an ounce
of business sense. We are all living off the Wedgwood name and
we need that factory to keep dishing out the Wedgwood plates.
Otherwise, we are up the industrial creek.

"We have a business that can be ruined by your reputation,
Chuck. Sure, Erasmus could be as randy as he wanted—he was
making millions. No one is putting up with that bullshit from
you, Mr. Microbe Chaser, especially since you're doing it partially on the Wedgwood dime."

Jackie handed me another document. After unrolling it I
continued, "Now we find the second letter, dated two weeks

later. This one's from Charles Darwin to Professor Brücke. Well,
Chuck, that was a quick crisis."

February 15, 1880

Dear Dr. Brücke:

*I am writing to you in utmost confidence and I know I
can rely on your discretion. It is with great fondness that
I remember the laboratory work we did together when we
were both young and eager men. Now that we are both in
the twilight of our time, certainly I more than you, I want
to again rely on your generosity. I have written* The Origin
of Species *since our last meeting and* Descent of Man
and The Expression of Emotions in Man and Animals.
*Despite the mostly undeserving accolades that I have had
the privilege to receive, there was no time more pleasant to
me than the time we researched the hermaphroditic eels in
your laboratory.*

*It was most kind and fortuitous when you remembered
to write to this aging gentleman to tell me of your young,
eager student, Sigmund Freud. I am amazed that he found
the Reissner cells of the eel that we searched for for so long.
The receipt of your letter makes me perilously close to
believing in divine inspiration. I have made several
discoveries, or should I say more humbly and accurately,
I have certain stray ideas which I believe could be part of a
theory of the human psyche. Were I a young man, I would
pursue them and attempt to muster the same volume of
evidence that I was able to procure for my theory of
evolution. I am told by my dear wife that I would still be
amassing evidence if it had not been for the simultaneous
discovery of evolution by my esteemed colleague Alfred
Wallace. My obsessive, or overly zealous, nature had not*

allowed me to publish until I had amassed every fact. The
Origin of Species *was, to the amazement of many, going
to be only an abstract of the book to come. I had amassed
over 300 notebooks with information on each idea suggested in the work. My dear wife said that Wallace was
sent to us from above to save the world from my unending
tedium. There is something of truth in this for I was
shocked to find that the slim published volume was
thought to be more than ample by the general populace.
What I felt was an almost cavalier expression of the theory
on my part, I was assured by my correspondents was
burgeoning with example. I was at that point forced to rely
on the grounded sense of my good wife.*

*I digress as always, and wish to return to the name of
the gifted Viennese docent, Herr Sigmund Freud. This is
a fortunate man, indeed, who has the joy of intellectual
freedom while mine has been pillaged by fame. He is not
fettered by six children, nor dependent upon the good
auspices provided by an indubitably generous, always
stalwart, brother-in-law. My relative is quite right in
pointing out to me that the Wedgwoods were the cornerstones of the industrial revolution and that the family
had one of the first successful factories in England by
1759. He is quite within his rights when he says that it is
the Wedgwoods who have paved the way for the leisure
time of the Darwins, as this is the second generation of
the families to commingle. I am afraid I lack the sense of
expediency for business and therefore must count on the
benevolence and good offices of those who have given me
time beyond my measure to work unfettered in my
gardens and on my travels. I shall not resent handing
over my newest theories to your Sigmund Freud to*

develop, if he deems them of any merit. From what you have said in your letter, he would be an ideal candidate. At the risk of crowing, I do want to let Herr Freud know that he may accept any acclamation that arises from the ideas. Now the sword of Damacles! He must also be the sole bearer of any ungovernable norotiety that could result. By giving the ideas to him I must dissociate myself.

I am often plagued by Thomas Carlyle's description of my elder brother Erasmus as "patiently idle," yet he distinguished him from this writer, his younger brother, by calling him "the honest Darwin." I prefer not to view this as an issue of honesty but one of disposition. Of my delicate health you are undoubtedly aware, since I have been unable to travel to scientific congresses for over twenty years. Both my brother Erasmus and I suffer from a certain undefined melancholia and dyspepsia for which there seems no cure. Thus we are doomed to ill health and to limited irruptions of energy.

I have endured one cataclysmic event, the evolutionary theory and the event of Darwinism and the battle with the creationists, while I was trained, ironically, as a preacher. I had to bear the sociological support of Spencer and the astonishing political affiliation of Karl Marx and the rage of the utilitarians and the derisive comments of the common man.

I feel, therefore, I must hand over the mantle to someone younger and of a stronger constitution, who bears the exigencies of life with more resilience and who has the pugilist's need for intellectual battle. I am confident that with these gifts he will prove to be the real conquistador of the mind. Please explain to Herr Freud that this is my only

*communication with him and it will be through your
offices as intermediary.*

    I remain your loyal laboratory cohort,
        Charles Darwin . . .

Encl.: abstract of theory of the mind.

*P.S. Please note that I am able to offer my salutations but
for a limited time in my earthly paradise. I am presently
writing about the action of worms, which I am sure will be
my last work. I am impressed by the worm's discernment
and will not be the least troubled to be down among them
soon. I am without strength to relate the entirety of my
theory, nor can I footnote and attribute justly to others
their contributions, but I ask the reader to bear with me in
this mere sketch.*

    *Finally, it is not without amusement that I note that it
was my dear friend Wallace who forced my hand the first
time; and now it is another Englishman, death himself,
who forces another abstract from me . . . Sketch
enclosed/notebooks to follow.*

ABSTRACT OF THE THEORY OF MIND

In my book The Descent of Man, *I have stated that the
theory of sexual selection is more prominent than my
theory of natural selection. This means that the major
mechanism for evolution is through the sexual instinct.
The survival instinct is also present, but, for example, in
deer and other mammals there is often a fight to the death
in a battle for a mate. This places the sexual instinct above
all others.*

The human psyche has developed in order to reproduce, and to take sexual pleasure. The song of the bird is a mating call which arouses the male or female into sexual action. The dance of the strutting species as they prance before the females is culturally replicated by the dance of the ballet and the modern ball. These are mating rituals which have been labelled as "culture." Culture, in terms of sexual selection, is an arousal mechanism that replicates the mating rituals of other mammals. The strutting of the turkey and the fanning of the feathers is no more than the stroll in the park on Sunday where we all preen.

Adaptation is one method of evolution, but it is far slower and more random than the sexual or reproductive instinct. The reproductive instinct produces many lives in a generation while a mutation is only one. Those who do not have the urge to reproduce will eventually not do so and those individuals will not carry on the genetic line and it will die out. Those that have the strongest sexual instinct will survive to reproduce even more with the same instinct.

The problem is that humans have evolved such large brains that they have to be very immature at birth in order for their heads to emerge from the birth canal. The child is, therefore, dependent on the parent, or the mother in most cases, for at least 16 years, which is a record length of time among mammals. This is four to six years after the child is of reproductive age. Some mechanism must prevent males from mating with their mothers and fathers with their daughters, as often happens among other mammals, and even frequently among Homo sapiens in Tierra del Fuego. There is too much jealousy between the father and son and marital disruption among the husband and wife when the son takes the mother, i.e., the power of Oedipus. Fate

*decrees Oedipus must be blinded as a result of his deed.
The Gods represent the father.*

*In order to accommodate our extensive grey matter we
must withhold our sexuality until we leave home and
"spread our seed" as in the maple tree, and not fertilize
those seeds too close to home. What happens to the child's
sexuality? It must be suppressed or repressed. Because we
have evolved to be genetically burdened with the sexual
instinct, it lies under the surface even in a repressive
culture which demands its denial. In a civilized society
sexual instinct cannot display itself in obvious venues such
as through smelling for estrus as in dogs, or by force as I
have seen among the natives of Tierra del Fuego; instead it
must bore its way under our civilized veneer and appear in
such insidious forms as humour, dreams and slips of the
tongue. Everything that does not contribute to our tie or
bond to our parents must be repressed because we, as
children, are undefended and need them to protect us.*

*We are all born with atrophied sexual organs of the
opposite sex; this is something we have both seen in
dissections from arachnids to mammals. What is the
female clitoris but an atrophied penis and what are male
breasts if not atrophied mammary glands. All humans are
attracted to their own sex at one point and then they
decide on their orientation, which is almost always,
because of the pressures of evolution, the one which will
produce progeny.*

*How to keep a civilization flourishing without inner
turmoil which would destroy it, yet acquiesce with the
sexual instinct, is the most important question and our
greatest challenge. I believe we have met it admirably,
albeit not flawlessly. We as a civilization have made rules*

*that keep our sexuality curbed. There are the incest rules
and the rules against child sexuality. Children are told
that the expression of sexuality is forbidden and that there
is moral retribution for feeling sexuality. Religion stresses
this function. This is Civilization, and these, my dear
Freud, are its discontents. We have plugged the hole in the
dyke, but it is necessary for a certain amount of leakage,
i.e., some kind of pressure valve, or the whole wall crumbles
from the pressure. Let out the sexual instinct enough to
prevent the overflow, but do not open the floodgates. Let it
leak out through dreams; designate mating rituals as
"culture." Invent ballet and drama, and live with fantasies.
Balance the need for civilization and the evolutionary
needs for sexual instinct to display itself.*

*All of civilization is a ruse for camouflaging the sexual
instinct, and those of us who realize it and attempt to
disseminate the information will be labelled as iniquitous
and ostracized as a Mephistopheles. I have found this to
be true after only the most mollifying of allusions to such
thought in my work.*

*The mentally ill are those unfortunates who suffer from
an organic malaise or who have repressed too much, and
the sexual need comes out in a symptom or as it is in those
who are lascivious and have not guarded their sexual
instinct in any way. We need defence mechanisms to
camouflage our sexual instinct, but not an overabundance
of them, or we become neurasthenic.*

*I have worked out these defence mechanisms and have
august examples—at the risk of braggadocio, I would say
proof— in 2,000 pages of notebooks to buttress this data. I
have studied various civilizations and it is apparent to me
that the degree of civilization is directly proportional to the*

repression of sexuality. Intellectual work is itself a sublimation for sexuality. The freer a society is sexually, the less it
will invent and the more it will be reduced to sloth.

Instinct that is closeted is similar to the new invention of
hydroelectric power. It needs to be harnessed in order to
provide energy for the society. The loftier the civilization,
the greater its energy must be harnessed. It is like a gas:
put it under pressure and it will do its work for you.

In summary, I may, as my industrious brother-in-law is
fond of saying, be suffering from too much leisure time,
and my data may be correlational and not causal, but I
feel I must share a lifetime's work, which for various
convoluted reasons, one being my constitution and the
other being time constraints, I have been unable to pursue.

If I may presume even further on your patience, and I
hope that I do not sound like a blowfish, I would suggest
that the study of the ontogeny and phylogeny of the
human psyche would be successful under the auspices of
several singularly atypical methodologies. One would be
to study the mentally ill as Charcot has done and see
what happens when the veneer of civilization has been
scraped away by mental decay, as in Bedlam. May I
suggest that there are no random actions; all of the
incoherent vagaries that patients make point to some
phylogenetic state; these unconscious mutterings as
Schopenhauer terms them, or mind mysteries as I am most
comfortable terming them—all of these rantings must be
listened to and decoded. I leave the ultimate science of
decoding the human mind to you.

Second, I would suggest investigating the sane who are
having trouble retaining their sexual rules. For example,
blindness might be caused by a female who could not

repress her sexual feelings for her relative and she did not let herself see it. I saw a form of mesmerism in South America which placed people temporarily in an uncivilized state. I understand it is also being experimented with presently in France.

Lastly, I would be hyper-vigilant with the compos mentis, *or "normal," people and carefully study their inner mind or their fantasies. These sexual feelings would emerge through slips of the tongue, dreams, symptoms and fantasies.*

If you could find a brave soul who is representative and in vigorous mental health but could allow his mind to regress to his pre-civilized state, you would find several keys.

There are rules for behaviour as there are rules for the flora and fauna, and it is our responsibility to find them and to categorize them. It takes an unusual Homo sapiens *to study those of his own species, because it is not like dissecting the eel for its bisexual nature and its hermaphroditic Reissner cells, but would be recognizing our own sexual feeling toward those around us, for onanism and for the ultimate polymorphously perverse individuals we are. Who can subject himself to such difficult scrutiny? . . . Dr. Brücke suggests the conqueror of the mind is Sigmund Freud.*

My best wishes as I hand over a difficult mantle.
      Charles Darwin

"Jesus Christ, no wonder Freud got so far so quickly." I was amazed to see the seeds of the sexual instinct, bisexuality, sublimation, latency, repression, defence mechanisms, even the Oedipus complex, to say nothing of handing him the methodology on a silver platter: study dreams, slips of the tongue, all symptoms have meaning, free association. My mouth was dry. I'd failed to salivate while reading, causing my voice to crack when I attempted to speak. Finally I looked up into Jackie's expectant eyes. "Darwin outlined the cornerstones of the theory of psycho-analysis for Freud and even gave the rudiments of the practice. Brücke, the physiology professor they both shared in different eras, was the go-between. What an *incredible* connection!" We stared at each other as I reeled, aware this was more than a grain of sand in the development of intellectual history.

"Is Freud a phony?" Jackie asked.

"I don't think so, but he hasn't exactly been forthcoming about where many of his ideas came from—but then, he couldn't be, Darwin made that clear. It's a complicated issue and I would have to spend some time sorting out the letters and the intellectual influence of Darwin on Freud in the light of this. I can't do it now because there's a murderer breathing down our necks."

"Kate, what would you do if you were the murderer?" Jackie inquired.

"I would make sure I got these letters," I said, waving the documents, "which the murderer looked for in Bozo's and then The Wizard's room."

"I think he got what he wanted in Bozo's room and was caught in the act in The Wizard's. The Wizard was smart enough to hide his stuff elsewhere—in the creamer in the kitchen," Jackie said.

"Then I would go for the notebooks and the other information that Darwin discusses—the notebooks of evidence or examples. I'd be willing to bet that they're missing." After I thought for a minute I added, "Darwin was really sick as he wrote this abstract and he died two years later, so they may not have been sent."

"Kate, go to the Freud archives and look for those notebooks and I'll find out from the Wedgwood Foundation or the Darwin archives if they have them."

"I may have to go myself, it may be spread in other notebooks." I was feeling jubilant as I announced, "We must have this closed by this time tomorrow."

"If I were Josiah Wedgwood, I would have destroyed them the second Chuckles went to the great biology lab in the sky. Josiah predeceased Darwin. He went down with the worms about a month after he wrote the letter. And by the way," Jackie asked, "why the hell didn't Freud destroy the letter from Darwin?"

"He did. Brücke had the original. Either Brücke or Darwin had sent Freud a copy."

"This *is* a fax of an original," Jackie said. The detective I put on it says if you hold it up to the light you can see the watermarks and you'll see it's dated in the 1800s. Brücke is not stupid enough to give away an original letter from a famous man he admired."

I nodded.

"So who's the murderer?" asked Jackie.

Putting down my fork after eating what tasted like something David Copperfield's coach ran over at Yarmouth, I said, "I'm out of here. It's late and we need to be up early. I'll call you when I'm up and we can go together and check two last things at the archives. Be at the continental breakfast at eight o'clock tomorrow and I'll tell you right at this very table who did it." I left the restaurant to the triumphant beat of an imagined John Philip Sousa march.

As I rocketed toward the clouds in the Savoy elevator with its magnificent bevelled glass top, I began dropping the pieces into the puzzle. Jackie knew next to nothing about Freud, and

Gardonne was a fake. Maybe Jackie was hired to follow me to see if I could smoke out Gardonne's real identity. Maybe the whole Freud plot was a red herring. Now that I've found out about Gardonne, maybe Jackie has been hired to kill me. Could he kill someone? A little querulous voice that lived inside me that carried the inside track hissed—*yes*.

As I got closer to the starless sky it suddenly hit me afresh that Gardonne and Jackie had discussed me as a suspect and clearly had dissed me in ways only two men can when discussing a woman's "unique proclivities." I'd be damned if I was going to share my revelations. After all, it was my work that led me to the murderer. They're the ones who trailed behind with their detective magnifying glasses chained to their dicks. When they wanted to leave me out of the loop, they felt no compunction about it. They probably had a motion-detecting camera watching me in my room, and I bet they saw more than my Freudian slip.

After I floated to my floor the glass door opened, and before I walked down the hall I'd said to myself, Call me paranoid, call me a poor team player, but don't call me gullible. I'd get up at four a.m. and be at Anna Freud's to bask in my own glory before either of them could roll over and say, "The early bird catches the worm"—in this case, the glow-worm.

28

—

BONDING HURTS

—

O father! O father! Now, now keep your hold
The Erl-king has seized me—his grasp is so cold.
—GOETHE

AFTER I RANG the doorbell at Anna Freud's, the blistered shellacked door finally creaked slightly and a startled Elsa craned her neck around the door frame and squawked, "You. Who else would have the gall to ring twice before the cock crows?"

Four-thirty *was* a tad early. As I sheepishly opened my mouth to apologize, she snarled, as much as one can snarl without her teeth in, "These deaths are on your shoulders. You Americans reap the spoils and mow down those who are no longer necessary to them."

I really didn't have the time for her venom, although as I edged past her and stomped up the stairs, it didn't escape me that I'd alienated nearly everyone around me. *Quelle surprise.*

The storage area for the archives was in a garret lined with old trunks that had dust-coated spiderwebs knitting them together. When I brushed one off to sit down, it was eerie to see the swastikas stamped on the turtleback lid. It seemed as though the trunk itself was humping its back, trying to shed its ominous past. When I looked around the room at the other trunks, one piled upon the other, I saw that I was surrounded by totem poles of swastikas. Little did the Nazis know what they were letting out of the country. They made a big mistake with Einstein and Freud; one of them to end the war and the other to analyze their destruction.

After I'd worked for a few hours, I heard plodding footsteps. As the door began to squeak open, I smelled mothballs. A peaked Anna Freud appeared, saying, "Hello, Miss Fitzgerald, how is your head?"

"Outside's mending. Inside's same dark gaping wound it's always been. How're you?"

She staggered on the landing. I pulled up a trunk piled high with extra portfolios for her to sit on. "I'm a bit dizzy. As I walked up the stairs, I reached for the banister. I sometimes feel weak when I'm standing."

"Don't worry, have a seat. I feel dizzy when I try to have an emotional life and breathe at the same time."

She smiled, saying, "Ah, an affliction I'm familiar with. You now have all the prerequisites of an analyst."

We laughed, easily knowing that we shared enough of a bond to understand each other's humour. "How is the case proceeding?" Anna inquired

"Very well. I hope to wrap it up today."

"Then you know who the murderer is?"

"Oh yes. I've known for a long time. It's just that I like nice neat packages, you know, all my ducks in a row. I can't abide an appealed case. I hate that court-order-and-remand routine. I'll keep truckin' until I get a simple written confession."

"I'm often struck by our similarity, Miss Fitzgerald. I too dislike a patient to resist or argue. I prefer to set the trap so he or she is fully ensnared, for if you only catch a foot, people are like mice—they may gnaw off the appendage and limp away. I will wait until they make the Freudian slip and then tell them to listen to themselves."

We sat in quiet contentment, the two Cordelias of the dusty attic, realizing that we were in the presence of the writings of one of the greatest minds of the twentieth century, and that we were surrounded by the various stages of his intellectual development. I felt the kindred spirit fill the room. Together Anna and I basked in our shared understanding of the value of these old, uncatalogued documents, tucked in marbleized accordion folders and tied with decaying black ribbons.

"It seems to take longer when you work towards certainty," I said. "I'm sure Dr. Gardonne is impatient with me, but in the end it saves time. That's the problem with emotions: they're so untidy, always with loose ends. It's hard to close things up."

"But that's the beauty of emotions. Art is so dependent on emotions for its raw material *because* they exist in infinite varieties."

"I disagree," I countered. "They're pretty much the same. That's what the classics are for. *King Lear* is about all of us as daughters. It is only human narcissism that makes us believe that emotions come in every flavour."

As we sat, I heard the tinkling of a bell. "Oh, that's for me," Anna said. "I told Elsa to call me if there was a long distance. I am expecting to hear from my American publisher."

"Let me help you down the stairs," I offered.

"No, I'm fine. It's only low blood pressure. I feel it when I lift my arms." As she began to rise, she said, "Please join me for tea in an hour."

"I'm filthy from the dust."

"Then I'll bring it up here." As she stood, she glanced back at the convex swastika she'd been sitting on and brushed the grime from her skirt.

By the time Anna returned an hour later, I'd turned the whole room upside down looking for those notebooks. As Miss Freud looked askance at the room, she said, "You're obviously looking for something specific. Does the murderer know that he has been psychologically surrounded?"

"I believe so," I said, putting things back in the boxes.

"I have admired your diligence, and your cautious strategy. I have come to be very fond of you. I wish that you had been my . . ." She hesitated, seeming to search for a particular word, finally saying, ". . . patient. I feel that I could have helped you in ways which would have made your life more bearable." She laughed and said, "I think I'm slowly picking up your American penchant for exaggeration. Perhaps the word 'bearable' has a flair for melodrama."

"I guess we've both had unbearable lives. That must be part of our bond," I agreed.

"In what ways unbearable?"

"We've both been used by our fathers to advance their intellectual endeavour, and we're both angry about it while feeling too dependent on their approval to do anything about it. Have you ever read 'Fra Lippo Lippi,' a poem by Robert Browning?"

"No, I'm afraid I haven't."

"Our unwilling devotion is perfectly exemplified in the poem. The errant friar is fettered by chains that he no longer believes in. He commits sins against a Catholic Church he feels is corrupt, but he still feels guilty about the 'sins' as the Church defines them." I stopped sorting through notebooks and quoted from the poem:

"Those great rings serve more purposes than just
To plant a flag in, or tie up a horse!
And yet the old schooling sticks, the old grave eyes
Are peeping o'er my shoulder as I work.

I'll mail the whole poem to you."

Anna looked concerned and said, "I fear that your transference to me is causing you to identify too much with me. This is a boundary issue. My feelings are not yours."

"Aren't they? We have both murdered people," I said nonchalantly while tying a ribbon on an accordion file with hands that had become black with dirt.

Anna Freud poured the tea and handed one to me. Declining the Wedgwood cup, I continued quietly but deliberately, "No thanks, I'm not a fan of poisonous mushroom tea, although I'm sure it beats Sanka." Calmed by the facts at hand, I continued packing the documents that I'd examined and had piled everywhere. The boxes were so old and decrepit, they crumbled to the touch. "I wondered how a woman of your advanced age killed the likes of Konzak and Bozo, but I see that you gave them this mushroom tea first, which caused hallucinations and then convulsions and finally death within a few minutes. Then you simply had to cut their throats. It was clever using the *Amanita phalloides* mushroom—interesting name under the circumstances—commonly known as the death cap. It is hard to detect from other mushrooms in that it has sweet white flesh with a slight yellowish tone. Its one distinguishing feature is its unpleasant sweet smell, which can be boiled away," I said, holding up the teacup. "Very few people would know that it is hard to detect in the blood, and that when it's mixed with saliva it changes its chemical properties. But of course the Freud children all became experts on mushrooms as children, when their father set them in competition with one another in the Alps to find the best, the brightest, the largest, the most sensuous and the most poisonous mushroom. I know what it means to go the limit—or over the limit—to try and please daddy."

"The question, of course, is *why?*" Anna Freud asked in her detached psychoanalytic-session monotone while she sipped her Earl Grey. "I have withstood a lot. Why would I do such a thing now?"

"How about the combination of rage, fear, love, shame and mostly loyalty?" I said with my back to her while placing a mouldy notebook on an upper shelf.

When I turned around, Anna was looking steely, as was the gun she was holding at waist height. "A woman of my advanced age can still pull a trigger. I could always say I came in, saw the disorder and thought there was a burglary in here and shot, not having any idea it was you. After all, I can say you had never used this room before. Elsa will be loyal."

"Of course she will," I agreed. "She has been in the past. Even during your postpartum depression."

"I regret to inform you that I have never given birth to a child."

"Tell Anna O. that—you know, that woman who lives within you. The girl who was analyzed by her father and who had to tell him all of her sexual fantasies. The same girl who transferred all those fantasies onto him until they culminated in birth, a phantom birth, the result of her fantasized sexual relationship with her father."

"You're committing the sin of presentism. My father had no idea what effect the analysis would have on me," Anna said.

"Rubbish. Another analyst, Ferenczi, a man you knew well, wrote to Freud asking if he should analyze his child and Freud responded, 'I advise against it,' cleverly omitting that he was at that time analyzing his own daughter. If he didn't know it was harmful, then why did he deny it to his best friend?" I asked.

"Maybe he felt Ferenczi's child could not handle it?"

"And *you* could? . . . You met in his office for an hour a day for years, and you divulged your sexual fantasies and your childhood love for your father, which became libidinized during the analysis. He was getting so much good material for his theory and unconsciously for his ego that it never occurred to him to stop you."

"I stopped him," she said.

"You sure did. Your analysis came to an abrupt conclusion on September 22, 1893, when he entered the room for his usual session and found his daughter screaming like a woman in full labour, panting that she was giving birth to his child. You were six centimetres dilated, had prolactin in your urine, and you were lactating."

"My stomach was heaving and I gripped his arm in terror," she said, clearly reliving her labour. "He looked at me the way an old dog looks when he has had an accident on the rug."

"He peeled off your fingers one by one and ran out of the room, abandoning you to the culmination of your libidinal needs. The question, of course, was who he was going to get to help him, since he was implicated in the deed. He couldn't get his wife, Martha, to assist you in the throes of childbirth, for she had made it clear long before that she wanted her children to have nothing to do with psychoanalysis. She knew that her husband was not above using his children for his own mental masturbation. She managed to keep her other five children away from him, but you were the last born, a mistake, and Martha had burned out."

"I was the psychoanalytic guinea pig," she said with her first hint of anger.

"In an experiment that blew up on the couch. Freud faced a dilemma. He couldn't leave you alone in your labour, which you and I know was a labour of love. Yet he had to run for the family doctor, Joseph Breuer. So he tore into the adjoining waiting room and grabbed the next young patient, who was passively anticipating his analytic hour—Chaim Stein. Freud asked Stein to help you in your moment of need and to make sure you didn't bleed to death. Mr. Stein was a teenager who was seeing Freud for homosexual panic. Really Freud had no choice. You and Chaim Stein both bonded to your imaginary baby. Chaim Stein, alias Dr. Von Enchanhauer, held your hand during your delivery, and by the time Freud had returned with Dr. Breuer, the birth was complete. Chaim had cut the cord of the seduction theory."

"We both spent our lives burying that theory," she said, dismantling a cobweb hung on the dormer beside her.

"It's no wonder you had a postpartum depression. You lost your baby to reality and the father abandoned you at the same moment—to say nothing of the whole psychoanalytic experience over five years. What did *that* do to you?"

She leaned forward on her trunk. Her gun drooped, aimed to the floor. "I was libidinally lobotomized. All of my sexual feelings were funnelled toward my father. My transference was to the man who had also received my preadolescent sexuality. My entire libido had to be repressed because I could not detach it from my father. I was in a permanent stage of latency. The impulses were connected in my mind to the incest taboo, and I never allowed them to surface."

"Until Anders Konzak."

"Yes, until Anders Konzak." She exhaled and leaned against the stucco wall that held nearly a half-century of Freudian dust in every crevice. "I was successful in blocking out the affections of all men. Believe it or not, I was once attractive to men, but I was scrupulous in my avoidance of them as though they were a different species. My one love affair had ended disastrously. Most men in the Freudian circle were timid followers. They never pushed beyond my first or second rejection."

"Your father was careful not to have leaders in his presence."

"Anders was different. He wanted the post of director of the academy. He was using me and I knew that, but he was flirtatious and courted me. I knew what he was doing as he brought me gifts of beautiful lace blouses and things I would never have bought. He made me laugh and he sloughed off all of my derision and rejection of him as a snake sloughs off its skin. At first I was frightened because my defence of spurning while my libido was dormant was not working. He couldn't even hear my repudiation. He knew it for the defence that it in fact was." Anna was ignoring the gun completely and seemed fully engaged in explanation. "I had never had a courtship before. Although I knew it was for ulterior motives, I almost didn't care. You see, we were using each other. I was using him because I wanted to have a real, human, romantic relationship before I died, and he was definitely going to be my last chance. The one thing that brought me back to my senses was the consummation of the courtship—the sexual act."

"Why?"

"I found it to be overrated. It was not as assuaging to the ego as courtship. It was merely a physical romp—two pieces of sandpaper rubbing until there's no more texture," she said, rubbing her two index fingers together in demonstration.

"I'd rather have sex than a courtship," I said. "At least you know what is supposed to come next."

She ignored me, continuing on with what must have been a lifetime of pent-up feelings. "During the brief time that I was engaged in a relationship of sexual intimacy with Professor Konzak, I began to realize he was indeed a danger to psychoanalysis. Journalists from *The Washington Post* began skulking around and questioning me about the archives and the Fliess letters. Anders' version of the seduction theory appeared in print."

"Why did that upset you so much? He had no proof."

"I know that *now*." She began pacing as she spoke. "I couldn't believe that I had let Dr. Von Enchanhauer and my own libidinized desires allow such an ill-advised choice. Surely Dr. Von Enchanhauer's choosing Anders as the Freud director was motivated at some level by his anger at my father. My own anger at my father reluctantly ratified the choice. I am not blaming Dr. Von Enchanhauer. I should have been more vigilant." Her words were flooding out as though a dam had been broken.

"On a conscious level I saw Anders as a self-indulgent egoist who wanted attention more than admiration or the search for truth," Anna said as our eyes locked for the first time. "Miss Fitzgerald, you must understand, I believe in psychoanalysis. I know if everyone followed its principles there would never be a Hitler in power. People would understand their instincts and they would not have sexual and aggressive aberrations which result in rape and war, because people would find the appropriate routes for these impulses and they would not act on them. Anders was threatening to put an end to all that. Psychoanalysis is one of the only hopes for civilization. I had no intention of letting Anders Konsak give the world the weapon it wanted—to deny the unconscious by denying its messenger. What is one life compared to this untold damage?"

"This is a very inspiring message, but it doesn't explain the death of Bozo or the missing Wizard."

"I know nothing about either of them." She began spinning the combination locks on various trunks, testing her memory.

"Both you and Dr. Von Enchanhauer have your roles down pat. His is the victim who can't take one more tragedy. Except he is a millionaire who has one of the most coveted jobs on the planet. You are struggling to save humanity from its own destructive forces. The only fly in your ointment is you had to murder two, maybe three men to protect the world from its murderous impulses. Yet you both ignore some rather crucial facts that mar your performances. Let's try this version on for size and see if it fits the data more appropriately. It's my observation that all heroic acts have a self-protective core. Let's face it," I said, stepping between her and the trunk she was fiddling with, forcing her to face me, "all of civilization can be summed up in one line—*We all have something to hide.*" I couldn't help but wonder if she had any idea that she was no different from all the other ideologues who killed others for what they termed "the greater good." I mean, even Charles Manson had an ideology if you're willing to count "helter skelter."

"Proceed, by all means, and I would certainly never disagree with your preamble," Anna said as she sat on a steamer trunk. The gun, although still in her hand, lay on her lap like a steel grey napkin at high tea.

"You and Dr. Von Enchanhauer had a lot to hide, as did your father before you. Why did Freud, a man with such a lively mind, surround himself with such lacklustre men as Ernest Jones and the other lackeys of the Freudian circle? None of them ever made a contribution to psychoanalytic theory, other than to expand on Freud's material in some pedantic way. Some of the women, like Lou Andreas-Salomé and Marie Bonaparte, had something to say, but Freud nullified them by analyzing them. They were emotionally beaten into submission through

transference. Feisty intellectuals were transmogrified into adoring daughters who could see no wrong in their beloved
all-knowing daddy.

"You desperately needed a director for the Freud academy.
Dr. Von Enchanhauer was getting too old and tired. You both
needed someone loyal, like Von Enchanhauer, or you needed
someone with limited insight who would only catalogue things
and never get to the bottom of the Anna O. mystery, because
that would be bad for both of you.

"You found the perfect specimen, Anders Konzak. Read his
Russian criticism: he never found or made one original comment. He only juxtaposed academic jargon, went to conferences
in sunny cities with gourmet restaurants, and wore a corduroy
jacket with patch pockets to classes. His rich, indulgent father
got him into an Ivy League school and then an average guy with
spectacular looks and charm was unleashed on the world. You
and Dr. Von Enchanhauer and I know that Anders Konzak was
totally benign. He would never have come up with the seduction theory versus the real world if it hadn't been for Bozo's
intervention. Bozo was one clown whose antics you didn't count
on. He gave the information to Konzak in exchange for an introduction to Von Enchanhauer. He then promised to get more
information for Konzak if he introduced him around to the
Freudian pool. Konzak was embarrassed by Bozo's presence, but
knew he himself didn't have the intellectual weight to make a
splash. Konzak's espousal of Bozo's revision of the seduction
theory put him smack dab in the middle of the global village,
where he could bask in attention. Konzak wasn't going to bite
the IQ that fed his grey cells, so he agreed to introduce Bozo to
Von Enchanhauer at a convention in Syracuse.

"Konzak pulled a low trick on Bozo, though. When he took
Bozo out to lunch with Von Enchanhauer, Konzak passed off

the revised seduction theory as his *own* original idea and implied that Bozo was willing to do some menial detective work for them. He suggested to Von Enchanhauer that they hire Bozo as a research assistant. Basically it was a gofer position where he would have been a glorified photocopier. Bozo was insulted, but he did get the meeting he wanted. He paid back Konzak in kind by refusing to give him the second part of his theory." I took a breath and looked up at Anna O. for confirmation.

"Part two was that I was Anna O.," she said as she finally managed to open one of the trunk locks.

"Right, so we had Konzak's paper on Freud's seduction theory, which was brilliant and put Konzak on the intellectual highway. The only problem was he needed Bozo to do the driving. The ideas in the paper were all Bozo's, and Konzak had promised his clamouring public a second part of what he humbly referred to as his 'revelations.' Konzak now needed his second instalment from Bozo.

"*Why* had Freud said little girls have fantasies of seducing their fathers instead of acknowledging the obvious incest that was the father's idea? Bozo refused to tell Konzak any more because he had been betrayed by him. Konzak stalled for time. He said that the reasons would be out soon, when the correspondence was published in the thus far unpublished letters."

"He began to panic as the publication deadline approached," Anna volunteered in agreement.

"That's when Bozo began playing with him as a cat plays with a mouse. He sent him taunting hints in the mail as to why Freud had posited the seduction theory. He mailed him one-line clues, and once he sent him a little plastic key ring with a record which had *The Name Game* as the title. Just when you were relaxing in post-coital disappointment with Konzak, he popped *The Name Game* key chain on you. You began to sweat and knew it was a matter of time before Bozo spilled the Anna O. goods."

I began to sing in a haunting whisper, *"Anna, Anna bo-banna, bo-na-na, fanna fo-fan-na. Fee fi mo-man-na, Anna."* This came to me in a dream. There was Annette Funicello—another Anna, dancing with a young man. I didn't recognize the man for a few days, but then I remembered a picture from my childhood home that was perched on the mantel in my father's study. It was of my father as a college boy on the Princeton rowing team. That smiling, self-confident, almost cocky man was the one dancing with Annette. I woke up and eventually put it together. My unconscious got it before my conscious. There was your namesake, Anna, dancing with a father. Granted, it was *my* father, but in my unconscious mind I had identified with you.

"It all fit together for me. I figured out something that Konzak had not. You are Anna O. and you were never Dr. Breuer's patient. You were locked up with your father every day telling him your innermost thoughts, which, if they are like anyone else's on earth, are probably sexual. He inserted your thoughts and unconscious revelations, metamorphosed into *his* theories, into other patients' case histories. When one figures out the chronology, many of the incidents were from your case history. It is possible, and this is only a speculation, that there were no other patients. All the female cases were aspects of your psyche and all of the male cases were aspects of your father's—a family business."

I'd been pacing, concentrating on my explanation. I stopped for the first time and looked into Anna Freud's eyes. The faded woman before me looked blank, as though her mind was rusty and had seized up. She clearly hadn't heard a word I'd said for the last few minutes. After she'd opened the trunk lock, she never looked inside. The combination lock just hung, swinging on the catch.

I forged ahead as everything slid into place. I loved it when my mind was swinging from idea to idea like an acrobat. The spirit of Bozo was swinging gracefully from bar to bar toward me and catching me in mid-air.

"Now we come to the question of why Dr. Von Enchanhauer, né Stein, was loyal to both you and your father for his entire life. Freud alluded only once to the fact that he would always be discreet and he assumed Chaim would be the same. Freud's polite understatement spelled out the following: 'Hy, my loyal patient, I know all about your homosexual Hendrik-Shmendrik concentration camp past. I will destroy your files and will tell only my daughter the truth about you, for safekeeping. But remember, Chaim, my boychik, you ever blow my daughter's cover, now or after I'm gone, and you'll have all of Buchenwald down your altered hairline.' You agreed later to keep each other's identities secret. You both had reason to hide your true identity—thus Bozo's taunt, 'the name game.'

"Chaim Stein became Dr. Von Enchanhauer and you remained Anna Freud and the birth was attributed to the hysteria of Bertha Pappenheim, a patient of Breuer's who, according to the Swiss hospital, the Burghölzi, was housed in its wards during the time indicated. Dr. Breuer was pleased to go along with the action plan and claim Anna O. as his own if Freud would write *all* of *Studies on Hysteria* and give him co-authorship."

"How did you know about Chaim Stein?" Anna asked in amazement.

"When I read the hourly datebook for 1893, I figured that 'O' didn't mean a free hour but the patient Anna O. The next name was Stein. I read his history and tried out the name Hendrik on him."

"So the credit belongs to you?"

"Bozo's hints helped me enormously, particularly when he said that Freud was playing with the reader," I said.

"My father and Bozo had more in common than meets the eye."

"Exactly. Your father really tempted fate by calling your analysis the case of *Anna O.* He even used *your* name! He was taunting the psychoanalytic community with this red flag, but he had stacked the deck with boring, prosaic, unimaginative scholars, except for one—Carl Jung. When Jung figured out a few things, Freud got rid of him . . . mind you, not without fainting first."

"How did Bozo, of all people, figure it out?"

"He was outside the system, with only an intellectual interest in it. He wasn't a psychoanalyst making money from the theory, nor was he a disgruntled devotee trying to disprove it. He was fascinated by the development of science. He asked himself the right question: if there was incest all around, perpetrated by the father, then *why* did Freud postulate it in the other direction? Bozo was on to the fact that Freud substituted his own experience for his patients' experience, and Anna was the only daughter he had in analysis."

"No one is completely objective. However, he did indeed ask the right questions."

"Freud believed that he had found a *universal* phenomenon. Girls seduce their fathers and then fantasize sexual experiences with them. Needless to say, this was not happening all over the world. All over the world girls were, in reality, being seduced by their fathers. Freud didn't seem to appreciate that all other fathers were not analyzing their daughters. Far from being a universal phenomenon, he was the only one doing it. What happens when a father and daughter get together and she free-associates her sexual ideas for years? Well, guess what—she becomes libidinally attached to her father and culminates her fantasies in a pseudocyesis."

"One father who did it, and one daughter who survived it . . . barely." Tears streamed down her face and a small, pitiable moan escaped, which resembled the agonized sob a mother would make over the grave of her newborn.

"*Exactement* . . . so, Miss Freud, Konzak was perfect for you. He had no idea of your involvement. The problem was that Bozo was getting closer, and the circle's shrinking circumference was making you nervous. The other problem for Konzak was that, true to his boastful little heart, he led you to believe that *he* had figured out the seduction theory himself."

Trying to contain her pain, she began pacing around the room. She busied herself wiping cobwebs off trunks. She opened one marked *Family photos*. She pulled out a sepia photo of rows of empty cribs. The picture was labelled *The Jackson Nursery, 1937.* "Why, I haven't seen this orphanage picture in years." As she stood back, gazing at the propped-up picture, she casually asked, "Why do you think *I* killed him?" As she shuffled through pictures, she stopped at one of herself and her sister Sophie. Both little girls wore twin party dresses and held twin dolls.

"Several reasons. He was going to expose you and the Anna O. debacle and he was going to turn on Freud. You couldn't have that, even though you hated Freud for stealing your sexuality and offering it up to science—"

Anna's eyes narrowed and she sprang to life. The limp arm holding the gun was again raised as she interrupted, "After the pregnancy I was sexually deadened. I was too close to losing my sanity to risk a sexual feeling of any kind. As the years went by, I mellowed and eventually became less enraged at my father. I—"

Now it was my turn to interrupt. "Less enraged? I don't think so. He stole the one thing you wanted—children. You founded those orphanages to help children who had no parents. They were like you. Your mother, Martha, was turned into a rival, and your father was your analyst and fantasy lover. You were an orphan. That's why you related to other orphans. You started child analysis so you could repeat that time with your father, only now you were daddy and the child was you. You had the chance to do it right. *You* wouldn't let libidinous behaviour run wild. *You* had the compulsion to repeat your analysis in a pure form."

Tears again spilled from her rheumy eyes. I knew I'd hit the emotional bull's-eye. I suspected this was the first time she'd cried in years. She hadn't written the best papers on defence mechanisms for nothing. Those rock-hard defences protected her all her life from mourning the loss of that empty womb, that child that was aborted to reality.

A new voice bathed in pathos emerged from her. "He stole children from me. All I ever wanted was a baby. I spent all of my life with children. He had a sex life and a family, but he took mine. I was a dried-up spinster when I was in my twenties. He publicly lamented my single status when he knew how much I loved children. A whole orphanage couldn't fill that phantom womb and that feeling of isolation." She turned her head to the side as though she was visualizing something she couldn't bear to look at, and continued, "Miss Fitzgerald, do you remember the boy in the bubble?"

"You mean the boy who was born with no immunities and has to live in a plastic germ-free tent in Texas? Everyone in prison followed that, because he was in solitary and he'd never committed a crime."

"I couldn't bear to see his little hand try to touch his parent through the plastic bubble. I felt only *I* knew the agony he was suffering. I was asexual, and condemned to live in that bubble and yet love and adore the man who put me there. Of course there was rage. That's why it was easy to slit Anders' throat. The rage had been aroused again. I also had to stop him from letting everything come out. Yes, I hated the man who stole my libido. Don't you hate the man who robbed you of the feelings you so desperately need?"

A vision of my smiling father on the sailboat in his white skipper hat telling me, his first mate, to let out the sail flashed before me as I said cautiously, "Yes. But I love him too, or I wouldn't have bought into it." As I heard that statement said aloud, echoing in the cavernous attic, I realized how true it was and how much energy I had spent denying it. I too kept repeating my relationship with my father: first my father, then my husband, then Freud. Christ, what a lineup. It was all so unnecessary. Only little girls think they have a perfect father. Growing up is realizing he isn't perfect and he doesn't need to be. He hasn't betrayed me; he's only human. Christ Almighty, why had I devoted so much to sanctifying him and then hating him for not being my fantasy of him? What a colossal waste of time and energy.

Finally I came out of myself enough to glance over at Anna Freud. While she was still ignoring her gun, I decided to push on. I knew she wouldn't act until she'd heard everything I had to say. She loved tidy bundles of facts too much for that.

"Let's move on to Bozo and The Wizard. After killing Konzak, you realized Bozo was behind it all, because he continued to send hints to Konzak at the academy. When you opened the mail of the recently deceased Konzak, you found out that Bozo and The Wizard knew the real Anna O. was you. They even sent some mail to Anna O. at this very address," I said, relying on Shawna's memory of Bozo's addressed envelopes.

"That was pure cheek, or as my father would have said, real chutzpah," Anna said, looking at a 1920s picture of herself and her father having a tête-à-tête at an outdoor café in The Hague.

"You realized that you had to kill Bozo, so you sailed with the Von Enchanhauer boys from Cowes, on the Isle of Wight, to Newfoundland in record time. After all, they'd sailed around the world several times in a huge ocean-going vessel that had every bell and whistle. That way you had no customs to deal with. You flew American Airlines to Toronto under the name Bertha Pappenheim. You're a lot like your father in the tempting-fate department. You could have used any name, but you chose one that gave a small hint to the initiated. You, like your father before you, had an unconscious need to be caught, or else delusions of grandeur in assuming no one was quite as clever as you. You were only in Toronto for a few hours before you took the plane back to Newfoundland and sailed back to Britain.

"While you were there, you also planned to kill The Wizard, but he wasn't in his room. You tried to find his documents, but you couldn't because when you reached up to his top shelf you got dizzy, due to your low blood pressure, and knocked over a shelf that you'd grabbed to steady yourself. It fell and made a crashing noise. What you didn't know was that the Darwin letter wasn't in the room."

"Where was it?" she asked.

"Hidden in a Wedgwood vase in the kitchen. You fled, and then you worried because Dr. Von Enchanhauer had received a grant application from The Wizard explaining he needed money to go to Brücke's great-granddaughter's in Virginia to purchase letters about Freud that would shed some light on his possible intellectual debt to Darwin. The Wizard had previously sent Konzak the 'survival of the fittest' slogan that let you know that The Wiz, like Bozo, was willing to go public with Freud's unacknowledged debt. Dr. Von Enchanhauer realized that the Darwin–Brücke–Freud caper was over. You both agreed that the situation was dire. Dr. Von Enchanhauer held the purse

CATHERINE GILDINER

strings of the archives and decided to pay off the impoverished Wizard. Von E. was shocked when The Wizard paid the $800,000 to the Carmelite convent for the letters. Dr. Von Enchanhauer meant the large sum as a bribe. The Wizard realized that you two were trying to shut him up permanently, so he ran for his life. Whether or not you found him, I have no idea."

"I didn't."

"Dr. Von Enchanhauer showed you the letters. You went to the Darwin and Wedgwood archives to cut out the material, but you were too late. The Wizard had beaten you there, found the letters which would accompany the Brücke correspondence and photocopied them. Your only hope now was to cut the letters out of the correspondence and permanently destroy them, kill The Wizard, and find his Xeroxed copies and destroy them too. While you were at it, you could get his copy of the Brücke–Darwin–Freud correspondence.

"It was clever having Elsa go to the Darwin archives in drag for you. She wouldn't need much of a costume. You forgot you couldn't camouflage her club-footed gait and that German-Cockney accent. I should have known she would be good with an exacto-knife. You should work as a detective," I said, quite pleased with my own detective skills.

"And you should be an analyst."

"I guess they're not that different. The detective traces the conscious, the psychoanalyst the unconscious trail. Unfortunately, the most significant difference is in the pay scale," I said.

"When did you first know?" Anna asked, absorbed by her intellectual curiosity.

"My first hint was the smell of mothballs. I was in Konzak's room right after the murder. There was a smell of mothballs in the room and in the hall near the back stairwell. I didn't recognize the smell at first because it was so faint, but I kept replaying the tape I'd made in my mind of the dinner I'd had with Konzak, and when he said the clothes you wore smelled of mothballs, the penny dropped. From there I figured Von Enchanhauer was in on it too."

"Actually, he wasn't. I think he suspected, but he learned a long time ago never to ask unnecessary questions. He felt his libidinal, or whatever it was, attachment to Anders would be the opening of a Pandora's box," Anna said.

"The night you murdered Konzak, in the time between your little poison-tea party and slitting his throat, while I was thundering across Vienna in hiking boots, you went through his diaries and found that he actually knew very little. He pathetically believed his *big* revelation was that Freud had analyzed Bertha Pappenheim and called her Anna O."

Anna agreed. "He had put together a few tawdry details incorrectly and had never deciphered the hints that Bozo and The Wizard had sent." She was still calmly standing up family photos carefully on the trunk as though it were a mantelpiece.

"Only moments after you murdered Konzak, you realized the people who really needed to be silenced were Bozo and The Wizard. You were reeling from this shock when you had another surprise. Konzak neglected to mention that I was on my way to his room at 1:30 a.m. You heard my footsteps, hid behind the door and waited for me to enter. When I was disoriented from seeing the carnage, you turned off the light and ran out the emergency exit, which you had previously propped open. You were right, as usual—I slipped and you got away. You knew you had to make haste and kill The Wizard and Bozo. It was no trouble finding them because they, like lambs to the slaughter, had always put their return addresses on their correspondence." I looked again at her eyes and asked, "The question is why? You're old. Why now?"

"I have given my life to this movement. Certainly I didn't want the humiliation of owning the Anna O. identity and the phantom pregnancy, and I couldn't bear the idea that Freud was a dissimulator and was writing for those who would someday unravel his lies. Don't forget, at that time there was no other way to achieve his goal. He didn't have the luxury of another century. All great inventors take risks—it's part of the process. He didn't know what would happen to me in the analysis. How could he have known if it had never been done before? I live with the belief that if he had known of the libidinal attachment and its effects upon me, he would never have done it. We don't know what we do to other people, do we?" she asked. Then, staring at a picture of herself holding her father's hand as they were leaving Vienna on a train in 1938, she quoted Lear, "'Upon such sacrifices, my Cordelia, The Gods themselves throw incense.'"

I didn't want to get derailed by the havoc we as humans wreak upon each other. Having fully sorted out the Anna O. conundrum, I pushed ahead on the Darwin issue. "What about the Darwin letter? Really, Darwin had covered much of what Freud supposedly discovered."

"Yes." She looked away and her eyes welled up. "I couldn't bear to think that I had given up everything for an imposter, for a man who had received his ideas from Darwin and passed them off as his own. I really loved him and I couldn't stand for him to suffer that humiliation, even posthumously. No matter the cost, I was going to protect him." As she began to be consumed by her own diatribe, I tried to think of various alternatives for getting out of the room. "He fought these battles alone and bore the scorn. He was exiled from his homeland because he was a Jew." Her chest was expanding and contracting like an accordion. The rage which was forced out altered her voice into a range of unfamiliar shrillness. "Darwin suffered none of this, *ever*. He did not deserve the credit. He didn't even have to earn a living, while my father had to support a large family and parents and my mother's relatives. You see, Miss Fitzgerald, bonding is not all positive or negative, but it is fierce," she said as she roughly gathered up the pictures and opened the trunk with one hand. The other hand was reserved for her gun, which she soothed at her chest.

"Miss Freud, don't you see that none of this was necessary? Your father extrapolated one letter into twenty-three volumes — to say nothing of the fact that he probably had already discovered many of his own ideas by the time he received it. He succeeded in putting a theory based on repressed sexuality on the map in the Victorian era. Also he developed a *method* for accessing the unconscious. That still takes a genius. The Anna O. cataclysm was indeed another matter, but the public could have forgiven him just as you and I are willing to do."

"I don't forgive him, I love him," she said, laying the pictures in the trunk and slamming the lid shut. Suddenly my mind made a gestalt switch. As Anna Freud unhooked her psychological chain mail and stepped out of her defences, a murderer emerged, with the narrow flattening of the eyes and the schizoid removal of feeling that I could almost see drip off the end of her gun.

I was dealing with the world's authority on denial. She cocked her gun and said, "It is too bad it had to be you. In my conscious mind I thought Anders might tell you what I mistakenly thought he knew about Anna O."

"How did you know I was having dinner with him that night?"

"I met him in the afternoon immediately after you'd had lunch with him. I had escorted some patrons from England to Vienna to see Freud's home. Professor Konzak, as was his habit when he met someone who appealed to him, rhapsodized at length about your lunch together. He spoke of your brilliance and your physical attributes. My fears were piqued when he mentioned that early Freud was your special academic interest. When he said that he had to break a dinner engagement for that evening that Dr. Von Enchanhauer and I had been invited to as well, I assumed, knowing him in his courtly mode, that he was cancelling dinner with us to have dinner with you.

"The truth, or should I say the unconscious reality which is always a more universal truth, which just occurred to me, is that I was afraid Anders would love you. That was another reason that I killed him that night. My most pressing terror was what if he had sex with you and made fun of me, of my dried-up body and my awkward fornication skills?"

"Isn't that a little far-fetched?" I couldn't help but say.

"No, it isn't. You see, I have the tape that Anders made of his tryst with Dvorah Little. One of their lewd topics was laughing at certain aspects of my mating ritual. I couldn't bear a repeat of that humiliation. I had been shamed once before in my own home. I had to live with my brothers and sisters knowing about my post-partum depression. I couldn't bear the knowing smiles of pity for an elderly spinster who was used by her father and then, in his theory, blamed for it. The little girl as seductress. You know, he made me read that paper to the Berlin congress when he was ill. I felt everyone in the room knew that little girl was me."

I smelled the metal of the gun as my eyes darted around the room searching for any nook or cranny that would save me from a bullet. I desperately wished that Jackie would appear.

Christ, I'd done it again! I'd focused on the ideas, done what I was supposed to do, but had never actually thought of the reality or taken seriously the obvious: if Anna Freud was going to kill anyone in her path to protect her father, she would also kill me. Why the hell had that not hit me? Again I'd been defeated by the tawdry details of the world that most people get as easily as falling off a log. I thought frantically, and the best I could come up with was to try to flip her to another level of consciousness by digging for the responsible citizen who must be wedged in that frontal lobe somewhere. "Despite not having a love life, which I'm convinced is overrated anyway, did you ever think that you did more for humanity than most other people?"

"Frankly, I don't care. No one has ever loved me. When I die, many will mourn for the requisite fifteen minutes, but no one will truly be touched by my passing."

Well, that didn't work. Clearly she was way beyond the stage where I could appeal to her superego. She was still mired in child-hood shame. I'd opened the Pandora's memory box and now I was facing the killer who snaked out. Anna was cocking her gun and aiming it at my heart. I hoped she'd have as hard a time finding it as I'd had. I thought of rushing her, but at this close range the bullet would travel faster than I could drop to the ground.

It's amazing what can rush through your mind in a second. I was terrified, but to be truthful, I was also relieved. It would be over and I'd not have to try so hard to get nowhere. I had no one to blame but myself. What fantasy was I engaging in when I was convinced that bringing in Anna was a piece of Sacher-Torte? I was picturing arresting Anna Freud, the leading intellectual, not the murderer who stood before me.

I remembered what Anna had said about omnipotence and how in some ways I felt like an inferior person but in others I felt as if I were special. It was at this moment that I realized that I thought only *other* people actually died. My feelings of being above everyone were clearly a grandiose fantasy, started by my father and perpetuated by delusion—one that I had paid for on layaway for the last nine years, and was now about to pay for in full with my life.

A lot of emotional debris clears away when you're looking down the barrel of a gun. I realized why I'd shot my husband: I believed I was above the law. I'm going to be killed by my own narcissism. I believed as long as I was behaving as I *thought* I should, the world would understand, since I was somehow allowed to be different. I thought if what I did was *rational* and I could explain it, I would be excused or forgiven or even told I did the right thing. What Anna said about my father's inability to feel and passing that off as a virtue was true, as was Jackie's comment that I thought I had no right to ask for help. I believed I had to act. I did what I *thought* my father would admire.

I shook my head at this realization and said, "Anna, let's raise a cup to our fathers." I held up a teacup, of the non-poisonous variety, and said, "To the men who devoted enormous amounts of time to us—alone in a room for years—you being psychoanalyzed and me being rationalized." I shook my head and snickered at the absurdity of it.

She reached over and picked up the cup with the poisonous mushroom concoction, tapped my Wedgwood Earl Grey cup and made the following toast: "Lou Andreas-Salomé once showed me a letter my father wrote her in 1935 where he quoted Goethe in relationship to me, saying, 'We all depend on creatures we ourselves have made.'" She put the cup to her lips and said, "Miss Fitzgerald, my point wasn't to kill anyone, it was to save my father," and without hesitating drank her hemlock in two big gulps.

She said in quite a normal tone of voice, "I have less than seventy seconds left, so I'm afraid I'll have to demand the floor. Please be so kind as to do me and my father one favour. Do not let the world know that I have committed these assassinations. You see, that would only reflect poorly on my father as a parent and ultimately cast a shadow on psychoanalysis. For the same reason, please do not divulge the Anna O. identity or the Darwin contribution. If that is not possible, then I certainly understand. I feel I may leave my guard post knowing you will do your best.

"Now, if you don't mind helping me to the floor, as I expect to soon be suffering from tonic and then clonic movements."

As I assisted her to the dusty floor and made a pillow for her from my sweatshirt, she began to seizure. I saw she was trying to say something, so I leaned over as she stammered, "My father used to say, '*Es soll eimem nicht zulommen, was man aushaltern Kann.*' Sorry, my *Mizinikil*, why am I speaking in Yiddish to you?" Her voice was a dry rasp. It sounded as though some internal demon was twisting her trachea, as she managed to whisper, "It means 'What one is able to bear is seldom what one must bear.'" Her violently quaking body had slowed to a slight tremble. Her last breath was a long exhalation.

CLEAN STREETS

—

We think by feeling. What is there to know?
I hear my being dance from ear to ear.
I wake to sleep, and take my waking slow.
—THEODORE ROETHKE, "The Waking"

THE AIRPORT LIMO, entangled in a traffic jam, nosed down the wide expanse of Toronto's University Avenue. The purple spring tulips on the island divide were defiantly holding their heads up even though they were about to be replaced by the summer impatiens. As I looked out the tinted window, it hit me that I'd missed a whole season.

Switching my eyes to the rear-view mirror, which held the carefully etched message, *Objects in mirror may be closer than they appear*, I gazed upon Jackie. He looked remarkably sullen, especially since I'd managed to solve the case. I wondered if he was waiting for an apology for skipping out on our last breakfast at the Savoy. He'd hardly said a word since I'd called him from Anna Freud's to say she was dead.

Attempting to jolly him out of his mood, as that seems to be the role of women worldwide, particularly after they've kept the ship afloat, I said, "Well, we're back home alive and we solved all of the problems. Konzak can no longer slander Freud, we know where Konzak got his information, we found the murderer and learned a bit about Freudian history to boot—all, I might add, for a thousand dollars a day plus expenses."

"Yup," he grunted, looking out the opposite window.

As we drove past the hospitals with rows of wheelchaired patients plunked in the sunshine, I realized I would be leaving him in less than a mile and I didn't see any reason to make it a rancorous departure. I tried to think of a subtle way to make some rapprochement, but neither subtlety nor rapprochement were ever my fortes. Instead, I blurted out, "Look, obviously you're angry about something. Why don't you just spill it out instead of moping around like a taciturn teenager?"

He pulled out a cigarette and flipped open a silver lighter that was engraved with the words, *Love forever, Crystal.* He took a deep breath, let it out slowly and said, "It's hardly worth the energy. You are who you are. I am who I am."

"Humour me," I said.

He rolled down his window a few inches and blew smoke out. Having taken the same anger management course, I could feel him gathering all of his resources to remain calm using self-talk and rehearsing what he wanted to say in his head before he spoke. He began speaking evenly and slowly. "I work with you for an entire season in four countries through two, maybe three, murders and then in the home stretch, when there is a murderous dragon breathing fire down our necks, so close she is singeing our collars, what do you do?" He turned and looked at me. "You become paranoid—not just suspicious, but you flame out in full-blown paranoia that almost cripples the operation." Throwing his hands in the air, he said, "Who ever heard of working a case with someone who won't tell you what they know?"

Before I had a chance to respond, he continued, "As I sat having my third cup of coffee in the Savoy dining room, I realized you were a no-show. You know something, in all the years I've been on this earth, I thought everything bad that could happen had already happened to me. I realized as I sat at the Savoy with all the German and Saudi tourists, eating my soggy English muffin, that I'd never been stood up before—"

"It's not exactly Auschwitz," I interrupted.

"Just a minute, I'm speaking. You asked and I'm answering," he snapped. "It was then, at breakfast, that I had to acknowledge to myself that we have a murderer shaking the death rattle. However, in your clouded vision *I* had become the enemy. Your paranoia had compromised the job to the point that we were both in jeopardy.

"Finally, after I'd gone back to my room, I got a sheepish call from you, telling me Anna was dead, Elsa was sobbing and you *suddenly* needed me. So I had to go to Maresfield Gardens and four countries and mop up. And then you demand that the press doesn't know the murderer is Anna Freud. I manage to do it all, and you never once apologize or say thank you." Then he shouted, "That's why I'm pissed off!"

The cab driver looked in his mirror at Jackie and said, "Man, that would piss *anyone* off."

"Who asked you, Mr. Nosy Parker?" I said to the cab driver. Then I turned to Jackie and said, "Look, I am not averse to saying I'm sorry, but first hear where I'm coming from."

"If you're not so averse, then why don't you just say it?"

"I *had* to be careful. I was the last person seen with two, maybe three men who were killed and I was a convicted murderer out on TA, not even a real parole. I had to watch my back. Gardonne was a lying psychopath who would think nothing of getting rid of me in jail or otherwise if he thought I found out he was involved in the island caper. If he wouldn't have killed me, he would have forced me into silence. And for your information, my dour detective, silence is achieved in many ways. First he revokes my parole, then he 'Form 40s' me, saying I'm a danger to him or others. Then I'm his to do with whatever he thinks is, quote, 'best for society.' That entails so many electric shock treatments that I have no idea of my own name let alone his. If he ever found out I knew the Onondaga saga, he'd fry my brains so all I'd have left would be random speech—known as 'word salad.'"

Jackie took a breath to say something, but I steamrolled ahead. "Just let me finish. You admitted to me that I was a suspect. You told Gardonne I was a suspect, you snuck around dusting brain prints at Shawna's house after the Bozo's murder. She told me out of 'sisterly solidarity.'"

"Sisterly solidarity my ass. She told you because I wouldn't dance with her."

Now I was raising my voice. "Listen, I have spent a lifetime thinking I could depend on people and it was always a big mistake. Thank God I never believed in Gardonne when I was in the pen or he'd have had me a drivelling idiot in a designer straitjacket."

"You were in the pen?" the cab driver asked.

I leaned over and yelled into the front seat, "Butt out!" I tried to calm myself as I continued, "He spent nine years trying to tell me he had my needs at heart. I know you for six weeks and Gardonne is your employer and you call me *paranoid*. I call it *fucking careful*. Sure I erred on the side of caution. And in your case I was wrong. But life teaches people lessons and I learned mine."

"There are always new lessons to learn. They call it personal growth," he said.

I could see the lake with its whitecaps, so I knew we were only minutes from my apartment. I really wanted things to end differently, but as usual I had no idea how to make it happen.

As we pulled onto the road that snaked along the lake, Jackie said, "You did a great job on the paperwork tracing Anna Freud. I honestly didn't think it was her. You are bloody lucky that she opted for plan A, the suicide, and left a confession. Obviously she had entertained a plan B, which was shooting you and saying she thought you were a robber. Did you know her revolver was loaded?"

"I think she would have let me drink the poison tea if I hadn't stopped her, but even she knew it had gone too far. I also think she believed I would do my best to shelter Freud." I looked over at Jackie and half smiled. "You also did amazing work, and quickly. How the hell did you get the authorities to bury it in London, Vienna, the U.S. and Canada?"

"It was surprisingly easy. In England, Anna was their hope for a Nobel Prize. They were happy to say she'd died of natural causes. God knows she was old enough." As I nodded, he continued, "She began child analysis and has a far bigger name in her own right than I'd ever realized. The Freud home and museum is a big London tourist attraction. I mean, you can't have a royal wedding every year. Something has to keep the tourists flocking. Also, Anna Freud had solid friends in important places. The Brits really appreciated what she did with the war orphans. She had also taught an amazing number of child therapists and had all kinds of support among the young graduates. According to my notes, no one had one bad word to say about her." He flipped his notebook closed and said, "So what was the point of a media circus? No one would have been helped."

"What about Vienna?"

"The Viennese were begging *me* not to tell the media," Jackie said. "Vienna is run on tourism. Tourists flock to feel the intellectual ferment of the past and visit all the homes of the intellectual and musical greats. No one there wanted anyone in the Freud family besmirched.

"The Canadians agreed to keep the Bozo murder quiet once they knew she'd killed herself. Most people who lived near Bozo were not the type to co-operate with the police. Sadly, the death of Bozo never even made the *Parkdale Flyer*. The local police had assumed it was a drug deal gone bad with The Wizard getting out of town."

"None of you, Gardonne nor anyone else ever found The Wizard?" I asked.

"Never did," Jackie said, shaking his head. He flipped through his notebook. "The U.S. was another story. Vienna and England leaned on them, and in the interests of international diplomacy, they agreed to keep it quiet. Konzak was an only child and both of his parents are dead. No one asked a thing. Cause of death was listed as robbery. Oh, out of interest, guess how many people came to Konzak's funeral?" Jackie asked.

"I have no idea."

"Three."

"I bet Anna Freud had thousands at hers."

"Speaking of Anna, why do you really think she decided on the tea party instead of the warm gun?" Jackie asked.

I thought about it for a moment and said, "She only planned to kill Konzak and then she realized it was Bozo and The Wizard who had the real information, so she then had to kill them. She realized it just couldn't go on. Maybe I'm flattering myself, but I think she trusted me. She finally came to believe that if she killed herself, the information would die with her and I would do my best to keep a lid on it. My being loyal to her meant being loyal to her father."

"Just out of curiosity, if it weren't for Anna, would you blow the whistle on Papa Sig?" Jackie asked.

"First I'd read everything and attempt to sort out what was true and what wasn't. I honestly think Freud pulled the psychological wool over the eyes of his readers who believed the pathology was from other patients. Much of the material came from him and from his daughter Anna." I turned my head, looking at Jackie full on as I asked him, "What would you do if you believed you were on to something, like a really important theory, but you didn't want to hang your or your daughter's unconscious out to dry?"

"Camouflage the origins but just get the theory out, before I died," Jackie said.

I nodded, saying, "I can forgive him for what at best we'd call a Machiavellian presentation or, at worst, deceitfulness. Remember, Freud called himself a 'conquistador.' He was a survivor. He presented a theory that must have been pure anathema to most Victorians. Yet he and the theory survived and made it into the twentieth century. He survived the Nazis and got out as late as 1938. He survived mouth cancer for years, as did the talking cure. He wrote and amended his theory right up until his last day."

"Not many would call Freud the flim-flam man," Jackie said.

"I've followed his work since he was dissecting hermaphroditic eels in Brücke's lab when he was still a student. I believe he was an *intellectually* honest man. He never soft-soaped that theory for what must have been a hostile audience. I knew Konzak misunderstood Freud *personally* when he thought that Freud would have sacrificed his seduction theory because of personal gain. He would not have given up what he thought was the truth just for a few referrals. He was way too tough for that. I'm not saying Freud's theory was always right. My God, Freud himself amended it many times, saying he'd originally been wrong, but he never postulated any theoretical matter for personal gain. To me intellectual truth is more important than how it is presented."

Jackie nodded. Although he didn't say so, I wondered if he thought I was covering for Freud as Anna Freud had done. I said, "Maybe you think that is an excuse or I'm making false distinctions. Maybe I'm doing for Freud what I did for my father and husband. Who knows?"

"Do you think Freud was fair to Anna?" Jackie asked.

"Parenting is not easy—that's why I'm not one. In some ways I think he named her 'The Case of Anna O.' because that's what Freud gave Anna—nothing—one fat zero. No one wants to be a guinea pig rather than a daughter. However, Freud didn't fully know what would happen. The analysis did indeed arrest her development and she did almost have a breakdown. But who knows what would have happened otherwise? On the other hand, she has lived a life that is far more unique and productive than many others."

I saw my condo in the distance. Although traffic was only inching along since a Blue Jays game had just let out at Exhibition Stadium, I knew I had to ask the following question and was appalled that I'd left it so late. "What about Gardonne?" Although I kept my tone casual, Jackie knew Gardonne's power over me was still an albatross. He could dump me back in the calaboose before I could say "habeas corpus."

Jackie immediately wiped the smile off his face. "I thought about that. Gardonne knew the wood-chopping Boy Scouts champ from the bowels of Onondaga wasn't going to cut it, so he felled Young Ned Mapple in one clear cut by changing his name and basically his identity. However, he is a genuine doctor, in that he graduated from a medical school, albeit a fly-by-night one. He only passed the Canadian boards on his third try—but he did qualify. In this world anyone can call themselves any name they want. Being an upper-middle-class phony isn't against the law, it's just pathetic." Jackie took one last, long drag on his cigarette, threw it out the window and said, "We've really got nothing on him."

"Well, I never said he was stupid."

"What he did with the island caper was misuse of a patient's information and that could cost him his medical licence, but most likely he'd just get a slap on the wrist. Konzak and the patient he got the information from are dead. Dvorah Little is still around to testify on the blackmail, but she'd be on the hook for that—not Gardonne." Jackie opened his window to let out the smoke and let in the reek of Lake Ontario's pollution. He then said as an afterthought, "You know, you're right, he's smooth."

As we pulled into the front U of my condo, I spotted Gardonne's midnight-black Jaguar XK in the visitors' parking lot. Jackie and I exchanged glances, knowing that the next five minutes were fairly pivotal to the rest of my life.

"What's he doing here?" I asked.

"I called him from Düsseldorf airport telling him we had a wrap-up. I also told him our flight number and that I wanted my money ASAP." When I looked disgusted with him for telling him our flight number, he said, "Sorry I'm so working class I actually wanted to get paid." He looked up at my building. "Strange as it may seem to you, I wasn't given a luxury condo for breathing."

As we were about to enter the lobby, I said to Jackie, "I know him better than you, let me handle this."

"The last time I let you handle things—"

I interrupted, "The job got done."

As we crossed the marble foyer, there stood Gardonne in his natty black wool slacks and charcoal cashmere turtleneck. He headed our way and gestured for us to have a seat in the cavernous room that overlooked Lake Ontario. Typical of him to offer me a seat in my own lobby. At least he wasn't obtuse enough to think I'd invite him up to my apartment.

He greeted us cordially, shaking hands and smiling. Jackie said, "Well, things got a bit hairy there for a while, but we landed on our feet."

Gardonne was holding two pay envelopes, obviously waiting for Jackie's and my summaries. I rifled through my backpack and gave him the lengthy report on the Freud–Anna O.–Darwin–Konzak–Bozo–Wizard connection. Jackie had labelled his file *The Seduction and Evolution of a Murder Caper*. Jackie also handed him a shorter document outlining all the expenses and said, "There are no loose ends." Apparently Jackie didn't consider the still-wandering Wizard a loose end. I guess we tallied things differently. That must be why he's in charge of expenses.

Gardonne lifted one eyebrow, letting Jackie know he wanted some elaboration. Jackie obliged as only men can oblige, with a one-liner that passed for a full explanation. "Konzak was permanently silenced; the psychological association got what they wanted; Freud's name is still sacrosanct; and London and Vienna still have tourist attractions."

Gardonne slid the antique white Crane envelopes across the glass coffee table and said, "Well, you've both done an exceptional job." Gardonne looked at me and smiled, that same smile I'd received from Helen Mapple, and continued, "I can only hope that the parole board will be willing to value your good work as much as I have. Unfortunately, they are less well versed in Freudian theory than in parole violation. Let's rely on their generosity of spirit and forgiveness, even for such egregious offences as break and enter and unlawful border crossing."

How the hell did he know I'd been in his room in the Isle of Wight and crossed the U.S. border alone? Although I remained deadpan, he knew he'd stung me. He was itching to throw away the key. I'd suspected he'd do this, but I assumed it had taken Jackie by surprise.

I buoyed myself up and pressed ahead, realizing it was now or never. "Jackie, it sounds as though I may not see the shoreline again for a long time, so I suggest we go over to the island today."

"I hate the food there," Jackie complained. "It's too expensive. Let's go somewhere with real punch, like the glove capital of the U.S."

"Come on, you haven't been to the island in ages! Helen of Troy concessions took over all the snack bars a while back. Although it's criminally expensive and bland, it's predictable." I glanced at Gardonne, who was waiting for the valet parking.

"I'm not going anywhere with a face like that," said Jackie, grimacing at my black eye, which was now yellowing on the edges. He continued, this time drawing Gardonne into our conversation and using the tone men employ when they want to subtly complain to one another about political correctness, especially regarding women, "Christ, I'll be labelled a wife batterer in seconds flat. Right?"

Before Gardonne had a chance to respond, I said, "So I'm no Helen of Troy, but then, who is?" I looked directly at Gardonne.

"Didn't she only cause trouble?" Jackie asked.

"Well, at least she used Trojans," I said, and Jackie chuckled. "Let's go to the island. It's a gorgeous spring day and here comes the ferry," I said, looking out the window at the dock. "By the way, I'd love to go back to upstate New York in the fall when the leaves are changing and it's dappled with Mapples."

The valet entered the lobby and held out the keys to Dr. Gardonne, who turned to me and said evenly, "Kate, you have been a far better detective than I could ever have imagined."

"Thanks," I said, knowing I'd snared him.

He paused for what seemed forever and then said, "There is no real reason for you to come to the parole hearing. God knows you've travelled enough. My report will suffice. Why don't I just courier you your pardon."

"Tomorrow, by registered mail," I said, looking straight at him. With Jackie at my side I had a witness.

He hesitated, knowing it would not be easy to do in a day. As he walked toward the door, he capitulated. "Tomorrow."

At that point one of Onondaga's finest stepped into the revolving door to revolve out the only slightly scathed Dr. Gardonne — a man I never had to see again.

I collapsed onto the ottoman and gave a long whistle to let out pent-up anxiety. Jackie came over and slapped my hand and we dissolved into hysterics. Finally, as he dried his eyes, he said, "The Helen of Troy number was priceless. Did you see him stop in his tracks?" As Jackie collapsed into a chair, looking more pensive, he said, "Isn't it interesting that, among men, no matter what your cover, your Achilles heel is always your mother?" As he lit a cigarette, he thought for a moment and added, "You know, that's as true in a prison block when you call a guy a motherfucker as it is on the leather psychoanalytic couch."

The doorman came over and told Jackie there was no smoking. Jackie ambled toward the door, dragging quickly as he motioned the doorman to get him a cab.

As I walked him to the entrance, I asked, "What about Gardonne continuing to practise psychiatry?"

"What about it?" Jackie asked, as though I was being petty.

"Why should he be allowed to continue? He's abused client privilege."

"*Come on*," Jackie said, "no one gets any help in prison anyway. The most you can hope for is not to get completely fucked mentally or physically. Gardonne's benign compared to some of the shrinks I ran into."

"He was smart enough to know how stupid he really was. Is that self-knowledge? He went into a field where he was totally unaccountable. After all, if prisoners complain about authorities, they are just being antisocial."

"That's what you said about Freud's lack of accountability. If you complain, you're in denial," Jackie said.

I had to laugh, saying, "Everyone is seducing somebody. I mean, the psychoanalyst seduces the patient into believing that he is some sort of hallowed human being, the good parent."

"Everyone has their little scam. You start unravelling them all and you've got a house of cards."

The doorman came in and waved his white glove at Jackie, letting him know his taxi meter was running. I was relieved I hadn't had time to think about how I'd say goodbye. I hated that emotional bilge. I walked him out to the cab. There was nothing left to do but lean into the window that had a tiny sign in the right-hand corner that said *Bulletproof glass*, shake hands and jump back as the cabbie slammed into drive.

I watched the cab round the circular drive. When it started out toward the street, Jackie looked out the back window and waved. I thought of when Von Enchanhauer saw Hendrik's face out the window of the armoured car for the last time.

As spring turned into summer, I looked out the window at the lake and enviously watched blue-suited rowers, who wore matching caps with crossed oars on the front, glide by in single sculls and some chug by in teams of four and eight.

I had to perpetually remind myself that I didn't *have* to be on the inside looking out. I'd missed a decade of dawns and I could make up for lost time. In an aberrant moment when I actually exercised my free will, I decided to join the rowing club, which was right near my condo. I took Jackie's advice to heart about not being a team player and began rowing in a single scull at five-thirty in the morning. I liked having my own boat and fighting the elements and experiencing the changes in temperature. Sometimes it was choppy and chilly while it was still dark. After all those years of forced sanitized air, I loved how it warmed up as the sun rose. As I peeled clothing layers away, I could feel heat entering my bones.

It was at these times that I actually contemplated writing a book about Freud's intellectual influences, a sort of history of the unconscious. I think I'd pretty well given up identifying with him or needing him to be the perfect "dad." I don't know if that means I've finally grown up or taken a shaky step toward normalcy. Probably neither. I thought of how W. H. Auden wrote a beautiful eulogy to Freud, never needing him to be perfect. In fact he said "often he was be wrong and at times absurd," only he did make us see "how rich life had been and how silly."

I had a little ritual of getting a coffee at a dock workers' greasy spoon along the water at seven-thirty in the morning after my row. It was sandwiched between garbage warehouses and decaying docks where huge rusty steamers were permanently marooned. The geese, ducks, gulls and other birds squawked at one another greedily while circling the garbage barges. I kicked the fossilized goose crap off a plastic chair and sat outside, listening to the waves slapping the hulls covered in crusty barnacles.

I glanced at the menu, which offered a Promethean breakfast of liver and onions—obviously the dock workers' special. I had a particular affinity for Prometheus. Only the Greeks could come up with a punishment of tying someone to a rock to have his liver eaten every day by a vulture. I too gnawed at myself on a daily basis by remembering anew the humiliations of the last month. Not trusting Jackie and suspecting he had joined with Gardonne was so idiotic—paranoid even.

Anna Freud was right. The most humiliating parts are the bits of intimacy. Every day I imagined the shame of dancing with him and licking his body, thinking he was dead and sobbing, offering more than collegiality. I must be the only woman alive that a sex addict refused to sleep with. I swore I wouldn't think of him ever again, but then the vulture would show up the next day to dine upon my regenerated liver and, chained to my shameful memories, I'd go over it all again.

As if it wasn't bad enough to relive these memories, I had the equivalent of post-traumatic stress disorder. I often thought I saw him out of the corner of my eye. Whenever I took a second look, I realized it wasn't him. Once I thought I saw him pass and pulled an *Exorcist*-type swivel-headed turn, until I realized the man was short and Asian.

The strange thing was I had no idea why I was letting someone who was so spectacularly inappropriate creep into my psyche. What was a man who had tiny teeth, used a toothpick and wore Stanley Kowalski undershirts doing in my brain anyway? What a pathetic waste of file space.

A Clydesdale leg suddenly flew over the back of the chair opposite me, making the white plastic quiver. Even the most pugnacious geese scattered. "Hey," Jackie said as he plopped down opposite me and blew on his coffee.

"Hey," I said, breaking into a goofy grin. I figured if he could find me in this labyrinth of docks and freighters, and locate this dive with its corrugated tin roof and one outside table on a dead-end garbage truck run, he hadn't just happened by.

"You look pretty good out there. Improved a lot since you started."

"Spying?"

"That's what they pay me for."

I looked at him closely. He'd had a new haircut and was wearing a sort of Eddie Bauer black sweater and chinos. Not his regular mean streets ensemble. He looked like Pat Boone with edge. "Who cut your hair—Stevie Wonder?" I asked.

"Yeah, I got it done in Motown." Leaning away from the wind to light a cigarette, he said, "I notice you're at liberty since our last caper, or should I say, one and only caper."

"So?" I said, having got that line from him.

"So, you looking for a job?"

"Who's asking?"

"I got a big case. Involves several countries. The employer is the National Institute of Health in Bethesda, Maryland. Need someone who knows a bit about science."

"Well, you got the wrong person because I know a lot about science." Jackie gave me that so-nothing's-changed nod. "Thanks, but I like to row my own boat."

During the silence that followed, another line from Auden's eulogy of Freud popped into my mind. It was something about being "able to approach the Future as a friend *without a wardrobe of excuses.*" I looked up and met his eyes and asked, "Just one case?"

"Yup."

"Per diem or contract?"

"Per diem."

"Plus expenses?" I asked.

"Yes, but it ain't going to be the Savoy or the Sacher Hotel."

Jackie smiled, but only with his eyes, and we shook hands on it. He went in to get another coffee. I yelled after him, "Remember what I want in mine?"

I looked out over the lake. The sun was coming out. The garbage trucks had finished their run and I had to lift my feet for the yellow street-cleaning truck to spray and sweep. Yesterday's dirt swirled down the sewer. The sun finally cooperated in heating my sandalled feet, and I didn't have to hold the coffee mug any more for warmth.

ACKNOWLEDGMENTS

There are so many people to thank that I'll have to proceed chronologically. My interest in Freud was early and spontaneous—if Freud was in the air then I enjoyed examining the spores. However my interest in Darwin, while later, was sparked more than a quarter of a century ago by my thesis adviser Professor Ray Fancher and I want to thank him for sharing his enthusiasm and knowledge with me.

I want to thank my friends Anne Koven and Linda Kahn who unstintingly encouraged me to become a creative writer after twenty-five years as a clinical psychologist. I would also like to thank my husband, Michael Gildiner, who never wavered in supporting me through the years this process has taken. It must have been his example that our sons David and Sam followed, for whenever I flagged they were there for me. I'd also like to thank my son Jamey for reading the manuscript and offering recommendations.

My stalwart friends, Michael Laing, Abby Pope and Helen Mclean, read not one or two but three drafts—when it was twice as long. They helped me to cut the book in half before it ever graced a publisher's desk. You have them to thank for anything resembling brevity.

The best editor anyone could ever hope for is Diane Martin at Knopf Canada. She entered the mind of each character and caught their false notes. She could also smell a rat on the theoretical level. Whenever I was the slightest bit unclear in my thinking she drove an editorial Mack truck through the writing and helped me to clarify it. I would also like to thank my copy editor, John Sweet, whose Dickensian name suits him, though Hawkeye would also be appropriate.

Special thanks to my father-in-law, Chaim Gildiner, for help with the Yiddish, the Toronto Police for letting me trail along in a murder investigation and Dr. Hugh McLean for advice on the history of surgery.

Every reasonable effort has been made to contact the copyright holders; in the event of an inadvertent omission or error, please notify the publisher.

All titles authored by Sigmund Freud are part of a series that has been translated by James Strachey for Hogarth Press, London:

Freud, Sigmund. *Analysis Terminable and Interminable.* 1937. *The Standard Edition of the Complete Psychological Works of Sigmund Freud.* Volume 23. *Moses and Monotheism, An Outline of Psychoanalysis, Analysis Terminable and Interminable,* and other works. Translated by James Strachey. London: Hogarth Press, 1968.

Chapter 1
Quotation from *One of the Difficulties of Psychoanalysis* by Sigmund Freud, first published in 1917.

Chapter 2
Quotation from *Psychical Treatment* by Sigmund Freud, first published in 1905.

Chapter 3
Quotation from *A Tale of Two Cities* by Charles Dickens, first published in 1859. Reprinted by Signet Classics: New York, 1963.

Chapter 4
Quotation from Karl Kraus's *Die Fackel,* 1911. Reprinted in Thomas Szasz's *AntiFreud: Karl Kraus's Criticism of Psychoanalysis and Psychiatry.* Syracuse: Syracuse University Press, 1976.

Chapter 5
Quotation from Elbert Hubbard in *An American Bible* by Alice Hubbard,

first published in 1946. Reprinted in Leonard Roy Frank's *Quotationary*. New York: The Roycrofters, 1911.

Chapter 6
Quotation from Dennis Potter first recorded on the BBC. Reprinted in *Dennis Potter: The Authorized Biography* first published by Faber and Faber in 1998 and in *The Passion of Dennis Potter, International Collected Essays*. New York: Palgrave Macmillan, 2000. Reprinted by permission.

Chapter 7
Quotation from *Civilization and Its Discontents* by Sigmund Freud, first published in 1930.

Chapter 8
Quotation from "To the Rev. F. D. Maurice" by Lord Alfred Tennyson as it appeared in *The Complete Poetical Works of Tennyson*. Edited by W. J. Rolfe, 1898. Boston: Houghton Mifflin.
 Quotation from "On the Sea" by John Keats, first published in 1818. Reprinted in *The Complete Poems of John Keats*. New York: Modern Library, 1994.

Chapter 9
Quotation from *A Difficulty in the Path of Psychoanalysis* by Sigmund Freud, first published in 1917.

Chapter 10
Quotation from a letter from Sigmund Freud to Max Eitingon dated November 11, 1921. Published in *Anna Freud: A Biography* by Elisabeth Young-Bruehl. New York: W. W. Norton and Company, 1988.

Chapter 11
Quotation from Book IV of *Paradise Lost* by John Milton, first published in 1667. Reprinted by Signet Classics: New York, 1968.

Chapter 12
Quotation from *Emile* by Jean Jacques Rousseau, first published in 1762. Reprinted in a translation by Barbara Foxley, 1911.

Chapter 13
Albert Einstein's words quoted by Michael Frayn in an interview in *The Paris Review* by Shusha Guppy, 2003.

Chapter 14
Quotation from *The Critic as Artist: Part 2* by Oscar Wilde, first published in 1891. Reprinted in *The Complete Works of Oscar Wilde*. Glasgow: HarperCollins, 1994.

Chapter 15
Quotation from *Phèdre* by Jean Racine, first published in 1677. Reprinted in *Phèdre*, translated by Ted Hughes. New York: Farrar, Straus and Giroux, 2000. Reprinted by permission.

Lyrics from "The Name Game" by Lincoln Chase and Shirley Elliston copyright © 1965 by EMI Music Publishing. All rights reserved. Used by permission.

Chapter 16
Quotation from *The Moment and Other Essays* by Virginia Woolf. London: The Hogarth Press, 1947.

Chapter 17
Quotation from *Middlemarch* by George Eliot, first published in 1871. Reprinted by Penguin Classics: New York, 2003.

Chapter 18
Quotation from *Studies on Hysteria*, "Case of Anna O." by Josef Brewer and Sigmund Freud, first published in 1895.

Chapter 19
Quotation from *Against Interpretation* by Susan Sontag. Published by Picador: New York, 1961. Reprinted by permission.

Chapter 20
Quotation from *Studies on Hysteria*, "Case of Anna O." by Josef Brewer and Sigmund Freud, first published in 1895.

Quotation from "Toads" in *The Less Deceived* by Philip Larkin, first published in 1954. Reprinted by Marvel Press: Plymouth, 1977. Reprinted by permission.

Chapter 21
Quotation on dream analysis from *Totem and Taboo* by Sigmund Freud, first published in 1913.

Chapter 22
Quotation from *Charles Darwin in In Darwin and His Critics: The Reception of Darwin's Theory of Evolution by the Scientific Community*, first published by the University of Chicago Press: Chicago, 1983.

Chapter 23
Quotation from *Beyond Good and Evil* by Friedrich Nietzche, first published in 1886.

Chapter 24
Quotation from Sigmund Freud in a letter to Arnold Zweig, dated May 31, 1936, first published by S. Fischer Verlag in 1968. Reprinted by Harcourt Brace. Copyright © 1970 Sigmund Freud Copyrights Ltd., reproduced by permission of Paterson Marsh Ltd., London.

Chapter 25
Quotation from *Thoughts on War and Death* by Sigmund Freud, first published in 1927.

Chapter 26
Quotation from the postscript to *A Question of Lay Analysis* by Sigmund Freud, first published in 1927.

Chapter 27
Quotation from *The Economy of Vegetation* by Erasmus Darwin, first published in 1791.

Chapter 28
Quotation from *The Erl-King* by Johann Wolfgang Von Goethe. Printed in *The Oxford Book of Verse in English Translation*, edited by Charles Tomlinson. Oxford University Press: Oxford, 1980.
　　Lyrics from "The Name Game" by Lincoln Chase and Shirley Elliston copyright © 1965 by EMI Music Publishing. All rights reserved. Used by permission.

Chapter 29
Quotation from "The Waking" by Theodore Roethke, first published in 1953. Reprinted in *The Collected Poems of Theodore Roethke* by Doubleday & Company, Inc.: New York, 1966.
　　Quotation from the poem "In Memory of Sigmund Freud" From *Another Time* by W. H. Auden, published by Random House. Copyright © 1940 W. H. Auden, renewed by The Estate of W. H. Auden. Used by permission of Curtis Brown, Ltd.